BEN

A novel. And a true story.

Robyn S. Brown

eLectio Publishing
Little Elm, TX

BEN
By Robyn S. Brown

Copyright 2017 by Robyn S. Brown. All rights reserved.
Cover Design by eLectio Publishing.

ISBN-13: 978-1-63213-430-1
Published by eLectio Publishing, LLC
Little Elm, Texas
http://www.eLectioPublishing.com

5 4 3 2 1 eLP 21 20 19 18 17

The eLectio Publishing creative team is comprised of: Kaitlyn Campbell, Emily Certain, Lori Draft, Court Dudek, Jim Eccles, Sheldon James, and Christine LePorte.

Publisher's Note
The publisher does not have any control over and does not assume any responsibility for author or third-party websites or their content.

This is a work of fiction. Names, characters, places, and incidents either are the products of the author's imagination or are used fictitiously. Any resemblance to actual events or persons, living or dead, is entirely coincidental.

To Jacob and Joshua,
with much love.

ACKNOWLEDGMENTS

As much as I would love to take credit for the authorship *Ben*, I must give credit where credit is due. I give all glory to God for the concept of *Ben* and to the Holy Spirit for the words that fill the pages of this book. I was merely the vessel.

I am so grateful to those who contributed to make *Ben* possible in one way or another:

To Dan – for dutifully reading the chapters I left on the counter each night and for being the very first to know the story of *Ben*. For believing in me, sometimes more than I believed in myself.

To Mom and Dad – for your constant encouragement and support.

To Mom, Tom, and Kim -for being my "Guinea pigs"- for reading, editing, and offering your input as the story took shape.

To Aunt Pat – for immersing yourself in *Ben* in record time and being my collaborator when submitting proposals.

To Julie – for sharing your expertise about the publishing world, for answering my million-and-one questions (and not blocking my email address!), and for and keeping me from going down the wrong path more than once.

To Dee – for your constant prayers at just the right times (and even setting your alarm to remember!)

To Pastor Mark – for planting the seed of faith in my life and for helping it take root. I am eternally grateful.

To Christopher Dixon & everyone at eLectio Publishing – for taking a chance on a rookie author and for recognizing that there was a story to be told.

CONTENTS

Part I—Benji

Part II—Benjamin

Part III—Ben

This is a story about a boy named Benji,
a man named Benjamin, and a dear friend
named Ben. Hopefully you've already figured out
the obvious — they are all one and the same. After
knowing Ben for what seems like a lifetime, I
am blessed to share his story with you
in the hopes that you might come to
know him too. And who knows?
Maybe you already do know Ben.
There's only one way to find out . . .

~ Kate

Part I
Benji

"Let the little children come to me,
and do not hinder them,
for the kingdom of God belongs
to such as these."
Mark 10:14

CHAPTER 1
STARRY SKIES AND FIREFLIES

"He determines the number of stars
and calls them each by name."
Psalm 147:4

Have you ever had a friend you go so far back with that you can't even remember actually meeting them in the first place? A friend who it seems has always been a part of your life, from Day One? Well, for Katie, that friend was Benji. She had been told more than once that her mother first introduced them right around her ninth birthday when she was finishing up the third grade. Katie was an only child, not intentionally but by an unfortunate turn of events when her father unexpectedly passed away when she was only a toddler. Katie's mother knew that her inquisitive daughter, who might never have a sibling to play with (or even to fight with on occasion for that matter), would need the benefit of a friend who could teach her social skills and provide her with companionship beyond what a mother could give. Benji, who lived right down the street and always seemed to be around, fit the bill perfectly.

At first, Katie would obligingly get together with Benji only because her mother had arranged a "play date" rather than because of Katie's own initiative or desire. Katie, who was well adapted to her life of independence, seemed just as content to amuse herself with things like coloring books, bike rides through the neighborhood, or playing make-believe with the barrage of stuffed animals tucked into every nook and cranny of her small bedroom. But that all changed one spring afternoon when Benji stopped by her house unexpectedly. After knocking on the front door several times and getting no response, Benji turned to leave when the door opened and Katie's small face peered through from the inside. Dried tears streaked her cheeks, her eyes red and puffy. Before Benji could ask what was wrong, Katie tried to catch her breath.

"It's . . . my . . . kitten," Katie spluttered in between short gasps.

"What kitten?" Benji asked.

"My . . . mama . . . got me a new kitten," she panted, drawing in a deep breath and attempting to compose herself as best as she could. "One of Mama's friends has a cat who just had a litter of kittens, and Mama brought home the orange one for me. *But she ran away!!*" With that last sentence all of Katie's composure evaporated, and once again she was reduced to sniffles and tears that were quickly on their way to becoming totally uncontrollable.

"I only had her for two days," she sobbed. "And . . . I . . . didn't . . . even . . . get . . . to . . . name . . . her!"

"Well, it's only a little kitten," Benji responded compassionately, doing his best to sound optimistic about the predicament. "She couldn't have gotten *that* far. Have you looked for her?"

"Yes." Katie sniffled. "Mama and I looked *everywhere*. She's just . . . GONE!"

"Don't worry, Katie, you'll find her. I promise."

Benji left Katie standing on her front porch in a combination of shock and utter grief, a nine-year-old's heart broken to pieces over a tiny little fur ball that she had only known existed for two short days. But Katie's grief didn't last long at all. Not even a half hour had passed when another knock came at the door, and this time when she opened it she couldn't believe what she saw. Standing on the front step was Benji. And nestled safely in his arms looking no worse for the wear was the tiny orange tabby, purring contently.

"Benji!" Katie exclaimed, hugging him so tightly that for a moment it appeared as though she might suffocate the creature. "Where did you find her?" she asked, as Benji carefully transferred possession of the lost treasure back to its rightful owner.

"Oh, she was hiding under the shed behind that old vacant house down the street," Benji replied casually.

Katie's nose immediately crinkled like it always did when she was perplexed by something. "But she couldn't have been, Mama and I just looked there right before you came."

"Well," Benji offered, "maybe she was wandering around and just crawled under the shed a few minutes ago. I don't know. But all that matters is she's safe, right?"

"Right," Katie agreed, exhaling loudly. Her overwhelming joy at the return of her new family member overtook any wonderment at how Benji managed to find the kitten in the *exact* same spot where she and her mother had just searched. Trying her best to wipe the dirt streaks from her rosy cheeks where the tears had formed meandering tracks down her face, Katie redirected her focus toward the prize in her arms. "And *you*, little girl," Katie scolded, "you sure are a lot of trouble, aren't you? Running away and making me worry like that. You better never do that again!" she sternly informed the kitten as she softly petted it.

"Trouble!" Katie exclaimed.

"What?" asked Benji.

"Trouble! I'll name her Trouble!"

"Yep, that definitely seems to fit her," Benji agreed as they both laughed. Once Katie had sufficiently calmed herself, the two of them gently rocked on her front porch swing, taking turns showering Trouble with lots of love. The kitten basked in the attention in a rumbling purr that was entirely disproportionate to her little body of two pounds. And that afternoon Katie came to see Benji in a whole new light. He wasn't just *"Benji, the boy from down the street who I sometimes hang out with."* That day, he became *"Benji, my friend who would do anything for me."* Even though she didn't realize it herself, in some ways Katie felt as though Benji had truly proven himself a worthy friend that day. And in her book, it was something she would never forget.

With the end of the school year only a few short weeks away, Katie and Benji became inseparable. In many ways, though, they were quite the odd couple. Katie was stunning. She had aqua blue eyes and long dirty-blonde hair with flaxen and gold streaks that most grown women would pay a small fortune to try to replicate at a salon. But Katie's beautiful locks weren't the product of any expensive chemicals; rather, they were a gift from God. Regardless of her outward beauty, what made her most attractive was the fact that Katie didn't even know how beautiful she was. A tomboy at heart, she detested glitter or sequins of any kind, and she preferred a ponytail or pigtails to fancy bows, which she only wore in her hair on special occasions when she didn't have a choice. And because she had been blessed with her father's genes for height, she stood about three inches taller than all of the other students in her class, Benji included.

For as striking as Katie was, Benji was just as plain. He had wavy chestnut hair which was usually a little longer than it should have been and always a tad bit unkempt. The bridge of his nose and cheeks were splattered with just a few light brown freckles, as if someone had taken a paint brush and flicked it perfectly across his face. He was a bit lanky, not very tall, and really rather ordinary by any stretch of the imagination. You could always expect Benji to be wearing an old pair of jeans with grass stains on the knees and a faded T-shirt, except on "church Sundays" when his mother insisted he wear the one pair of khakis he owned that were about two inches too short. Although he was mostly unremarkable in appearance, Benji's eyes told a much different story. Light brown with microscopic flecks of amber dancing throughout, his eyes could captivate anyone in a heartbeat. When Benji looked at Katie, his gaze was so piercing that she became mesmerized, as if no one else in the world were as important to him as she was at that very moment. Eyes that made Katie feel, in a good way, like he wasn't looking *at* her but rather looking *through* her into her very soul.

Of course, neither one of them cared one bit about outward appearances, for better or worse. All they cared about was one another and spending as much time together as they possibly could. Fortunately for them, summertime would give them every opportunity. So the extraordinary girl and the ordinary boy became the closest of friends.

One of the really great things about being a kid is exactly that—being a kid. In a world where adults are perpetually going a mile a minute—running here and there, doing this and that, scheduling appointment on top of appointment, making to-do lists and then crossing items off of those to-do lists, existing *in* the world but not actually a part *of* the world, and rarely accomplishing anything of substance—children have the gift of slowing down to appreciate the grandeur of life all around them. To stop and smell the roses, so to speak. To notice the little things. And let's be honest, when it comes right down to it, the beauty of life is usually all about the small details which most adults either seem too busy to notice or too ambivalent to care. That's why we have children; to remind us of the things long forgotten and long overlooked, and Katie and Benji were certainly no exception.

Summer made its grand entrance a few weeks after the last day of school with balmy temperatures and days that were blissfully never-ending. The two companions had jointly decided that this would be their summer to explore. Not that they lived in some jungle or undeveloped wasteland, mind you. No, they lived in nicely manicured middle-class suburbia with a few surrounding farms and the city less than an hour away. For all intents and purposes it was like practically every other neighborhood, but when you are nine years old and have never been much farther on your own than the end of your street, the outskirts of the neighborhood might as well be another planet. And, of course, when it comes to exploring, two are always better than one, so Benji's willingness to take part made Katie all the more enthusiastic.

Their summer objective was to scout out the uncharted territory beyond the confines of Magnolia Lane, and their first official adventure began the Monday after the Fourth of July when all of the adults settled back into their familiar work routines. Katie's grandmother, whom Katie affectionately referred to as Grans, came over to watch her for the day while her mother worked at the local library. Grans had always doted on Katie, and Katie for her part felt a very special bond with the elderly woman since it was her paternal grandmother and the only real connection Katie ever had to her father. Katie loved it when Grans would tell her stories about how much she looked like and even acted like her father. She beamed with pride, and regardless of whether or not Grans' stories were completely true, they gave Katie the gift of claiming her own special memories of her father, even if they weren't memories they had actually made together.

Shortly after breakfast, Benji arrived at Katie's house, backpack in hand and ready to go. "Good morning, Benji," Katie's grandmother welcomed him warmly, "and what have you got there?" she asked, referencing the small blue knapsack slung over his shoulder.

"Hi, Mrs. Kirby. This is just some stuff we might need for exploring," Benji proudly announced.

"I see," Katie's grandmother replied, "and what are the essentials for exploring these days?"

"Um, there's bug spray, an extra pair of socks, paper and a pencil, a couple of Band-Aids, two Tootsie Rolls, and a bag of Goldfish crackers."

"Well, it looks like you certainly have thought of everything, haven't you? But just in case the Goldfish and Tootsie Rolls don't tide you over, I've made you some lunch as well." Katie's grandmother produced two paper bags with their names scrawled on the front. "I've packed you each a tuna sandwich, an apple, and a juice box. And you might even find a few chocolate chip cookies I baked last night."

"Thanks, Grans." Katie stood on her tippy toes to kiss her grandmother on the cheek.

"Thanks, Mrs. Kirby," echoed Benji.

Katie's grandmother escorted them to the front door. "Now remember, you two, don't go too far and make sure you are home no later than three o'clock. Do you have your watch, Katie?"

"Sure do," she replied as she held out her wrist for her grandmother to see the shiny black Timex her mother had given her two Christmases ago after she had proudly learned how to tell time.

"Have fun, be careful!"

Katie and Benji hadn't even descended the driveway when Trouble decided it was only proper that she should be able to join their adventure as well, so the little kitten followed only a few paces behind. Katie caught a glimpse of their tagalong. She discreetly peered over her shoulder a few times, careful not to make eye contact with her four-legged friend but only to see if Trouble would continue her pursuit. Sure enough, by the time they passed Katie's neighbors Trouble was still there, determined to be right in the middle of the action.

"Oh no you don't," Katie said as they doubled back and she picked up the kitten. "You can't come this time. You stay home and be good."

Katie safely deposited Trouble on her front porch step before skipping to meet up with Benji. But, once again, they didn't make it very far before they realized Trouble was only a short distance behind.

Katie sighed in frustration and swept the creamsicle-striped kitten into her arms while she headed toward her house. "I guess you're going to have to stay inside today," she relented.

"Hang on," Benji said, "let me try." Benji took Trouble, who by this point looked quite pleased with herself at being the center of attention, and set her gently on the grass next to the cherry tree in Katie's front yard. "Now you stay here," Benji informed the kitten. Oddly enough, as Benji left to rejoin Katie, Trouble didn't move a muscle. She just stared longingly with a pitiful look of disappointment that only a tiny kitten could flawlessly execute.

"How do you do that?" Katie asked in disbelief. "Mama said she's never seen a cat obey anyone before, except you. How do you always get her to listen to you like that?"

"Search me." Benji shrugged. "I guess I just have a way with animals. So where do you want to go today anyway?" he asked, changing the subject.

"I was thinking we could see what's on the other side of those woods down the end of our lane. What do you think?"

"Works for me," Benji replied, content to let Katie be the primary navigator in their endeavors.

In the bright summer sun the two friends chatted as they courageously departed the official confines of Magnolia Lane and entered the vast unknown, which in their case happened to be a small patch of woods adjacent to the homes across the street. They carefully avoided any briars or possible poison ivy, and they soon became completely immersed by the nature enveloping them—the birds chirping overhead, the occasional scurrying of disapproving squirrels as their territory was so rudely invaded, and the sunlight sparkling through gaps in the trees. Not long after they entered the woods, they came upon a stream that meandered through the undergrowth. After determining that it was too wide to cross at that particular point (and because they also weren't sure how deep it was, as their mothers had taught them never to enter water if you didn't know its depth), they walked a little farther until they came upon a large oak tree that had fallen across the stream, moss covering its trunk and its mass of tangled roots exposed along the far side. They easily crossed the natural bridge and continued along their journey until they could glimpse daylight peering through the trees just ahead.

Before long Katie and Benji had successfully traversed the woods, and they found themselves gazing out upon an enormous field. Katie was in awe. It extended as far as the eye could see in every direction, a thick blanket of emerald green grass without the slightest imperfection. In the center of the field stood the single most enormous weeping willow tree she had ever seen, a majestic presence so incredible that it was as if this tree kept guard over the field. Towering at least fifty feet tall, its graceful branches drooped so low they brushed the grass beneath. And with only a hint of a breeze, the delicate leaves swished back and forth creating their own soft melody.

Katie in all of her short life had never seen something so beautiful or so perfect. "Wowwww," was all she could manage in a whisper.

"Wow is right," Benji agreed.

The two friends didn't hesitate running through the field as fast as their legs would carry them until they reached the monstrous tree. Up close it was even more beautiful than it had been at a distance. They strained their necks to try to see the top of the willow, but it seemed to continue upward until it met heaven itself. They parted the branches and disappeared from sight inside of the massive tree. "It's like we're in a giant mushroom!" Katie exclaimed with glee. Its roots were so thick that they wove in and out of the ground, creating an entanglement of natural stepping stones and even a shallow bench. Katie promptly perched herself on the exposed root, patted the spot next to her so that Benji would join her, and they both took in their surroundings.

"This is the most beautiful tree I have ever seen," Katie said about their newfound treasure. "It's like we're in our own little world where we can see out through the branches but we're perfectly protected in here. This is so cool."

"It sure is," Benji answered.

"You know what, Benji? From now on this will be *our* willow tree. We won't tell anyone else about it, and this will be *our* spot."

"That sounds good to me."

"You promise?" Katie asked.

"I promise."

They sat in silence for what seemed to be hours even though it was likely only a few minutes when Benji decided that all of this exploring had made him quite hungry. They unpacked the bags that Grans had so lovingly prepared and gobbled down every last bit of the contents (chocolate chip cookies first, of course). After their stomachs were satisfied and they were completely relaxed in their new hideaway, they propped their backs up against the trunk of the tree and gazed up at cloudless cerulean sky that peeked through the branches overhead.

"Benji, do you believe in God?" The question came totally out of the blue, just the way children have a knack for asking the most unexpected of questions during the most seemingly random of moments. Katie waited for Benji's response, never once making eye contact with her friend but instead focusing on a ladybug crawling along the edge of her extended index finger.

"Well, yeah, of course I do," Benji answered without hesitation. "Why? Do you?"

"Oh, definitely," she replied as the ladybug continued its journey along her outstretched palm. "But Susie McCurdle says there's no such thing as God."

"Really? Why does she think that?"

"Well, first she says that if God were real, we should be able to see him. And then she says that if God really existed then he wouldn't let bad things happen to people."

Benji remained silent for a moment as if taking it all in. "What do *you* think?" he inquired of Katie.

"I think it's silly to say we have to see God for him to be real. I mean, after all, there are plenty of things we can't actually see but we know are out there. Plus, I think it kinda gives us something to look forward to."

"What do you mean?"

"Well, ya know how when your birthday is coming up, and you know you're going to get some wonderful present that's just for you but you don't know what it is?"

"Yes," Benji replied, trying to follow Katie's logic.

"Well, I think it's like that with being able to see God. I think God doesn't want us to see him now because someday when we go to heaven we finally will get to see him, and it will be like unwrapping the best birthday present we could ever imagine."

"Oh, I get it," Benji replied, "like it's going to be some great surprise."

"Yes, exactly," Katie said in agreement. "Plus, I feel like God wants us to trust him and love him regardless of what he looks like, so maybe God feels like it shouldn't be that important to us if we see him. We just need to know in our hearts that he's there." Katie had explained it all so matter-of-factly that it never even once crossed her nine-year-old mind what a deep question they had been pondering, a question that some of the greatest theologians have wrestled with for thousands of years.

At that point, the little ladybug had decided it was time to travel elsewhere, and with only a hint of a whir it lifted off of Katie's hand and disappeared among the gently swaying branches of the willow.

"So, then what about the other thing Susie said?" Benji continued. "That God would never let bad things happen to people."

"I'm not sure," Katie admitted. "I mean, I can see what she's talking about. I don't understand why my daddy had to die. But just because it happened that doesn't mean God isn't real or he didn't love my daddy. What do you think?" Katie shifted the focus to Benji in the hopes that maybe he could fill in the gaps that she could not.

Benji remained silent for a few seconds, tracing a small circle in the dirt with a twig. "Well, I think it's kind of something like this. God loves all of us because we're his children, right?"

"Right," Katie affirmed.

"And because God loves us so much he would never want anything bad to happen to us, either on purpose or by accident, right?

Another nod of affirmation.

"But God also knows that we have to go out and live our lives, and sometimes that might mean getting hurt. So God gives us that freedom to live in a world that might make something bad happen, but God is always there for us so that if something bad *does* happen he will help us get through it."

"I don't get it," Katie responded, crinkled nose and all.

Benji paused for a moment.

"Okay, then think of it this way. Your mom loves you a whole lot, right?"

"Yep." Katie smiled. "Mama tells me she loves me more than anything in the world, *even* more than I love her."

"Okay, and of course your mom would never want anything bad to happen to you."

"Of course."

"So in some ways, your mom would probably want to keep you in this little bubble all the time so she can always watch over you and make sure nothing bad ever happens. But if she did that, she would also know that you would never really be happy or free because you wouldn't get to go out and live your life."

Katie tilted her head slightly and brought her focus to Benji's warm, penetrating eyes.

Benji continued. "Just like today. Your mom knew we were going exploring, and she wanted you to go because she knew it was something that would make you happy. But she also knew there was a chance that something bad could happen. Like you could get stung by a bee, or you could be bitten by a spider, or you could trip over a branch and break your leg. Your mom didn't want you to get hurt or get sick, but she knew that she can't always keep you locked up somewhere because you have to be able to do the things you want. If she always kept you in that bubble, then it wouldn't really be your own life at all, it would be more like your mom living your life for you. You might be safe from anything bad, but you would never actually be free. So, your mom let you go exploring today because it was what you wanted to do, and because she loves you she wants you to be happy. But if you were to get hurt in any way, she would be there to make you feel better."

"I think I get it," Katie interjected, finishing the logic that Benji had started. "So what you're saying is that God doesn't let bad things happen to us on purpose. But he loves us and wants us to be free, so he lets us go out into the world even though we don't always know what will happen and even though we could get hurt. But if something does go wrong he is always there to help us."

"Yeah, that's how I think about it."

"Well, I think you're right. Besides, what does Susie McCurdle know anyway?" Katie scoffed. "So how did you manage to get so smart?" she joked as she nudged him hard enough that he almost lost his balance on the makeshift bench.

"I don't know." He shrugged. "My father taught me a lot."

"Well, your father must be a very smart man."

"Yep, he sure is." Benji smiled.

That afternoon Katie arrived back home with time to spare. She didn't waste a second exuberantly sharing with Grans the details about her adventures with Benji.

That perfect July day was only the beginning. Katie and Benji spent the rest of the summer making the most of every opportunity to enjoy the many miracles God had showered upon them in their little corner of the world. Their explorations may never have taken them too far from Magnolia Lane. Yet, with every new adventure they entered a world of timeless, worriless beauty where they had no agenda other than to live in the moment and appreciate the precious gifts of creation. They sucked honey out of the delicate petals of the honeysuckle vines intertwined along the back fence. They rubbed "butter" on each other's chins, making them powdery yellow from the buttercups dotting the entrance to their community. They searched endlessly for a lucky four-leaf clover in a field where the bunny rabbits ate heartily each morning at dawn. They caught and released countless peepers in the nearby pond who sang their nightly melody for the neighborhood to enjoy. They fed peanuts to the chipmunks who scurried among the maze of holes they had tunneled underground. They followed the jack-hammering of a woodpecker through the woods until they spotted the red-headed creature overhead, perched alongside a hollowed out tree. They spied a tiny wren as she constructed a magnificent nest, laid two eggs, hatched them, and tirelessly fed the hatchlings until they were old enough to journey into the great world. They even watched for hours from inside Katie's bedroom window as a spider spun silk with the utmost precision and created a perfectly symmetrical web that sparkled in the sunlight. The list was endless. Katie and Benji considered each small act of nature a true miracle they had been privileged enough to witness. And of course, the two friends visited their willow tree on countless occasions as well; sometimes doing nothing more than taking refuge under its umbrella of pencil-thin branches for a few fleeting moments, and other times spending hours there while engaging in some of the most profound discussions about life, much like they did that very first day. Regardless of what they did together that summer, Katie and Benji had neither a care in the world nor any particular purpose except to be fully present in each single moment.

———————————

The harsh reality of "all good things must come to an end" hit Katie like a ton of bricks when the steamy days of August hurriedly passed and the new school year loomed just around the corner. Katie had always loved school, so textbooks and homework didn't faze her in the least, but the thought of being cooped up indoors and not being able to visit their willow whenever the mood struck them was almost too much for Katie to bear. The last Saturday in August arrived and Katie knew she had to do something special to send the summer off in style, a grand finale of sorts. So, with permission from her mother and a deliberately ambiguous invitation to Benji to come over that Saturday evening at dinnertime, Katie was ready to put her plan into action.

Benji arrived promptly at six o'clock to find Katie looking more beautiful than ever. Her cornflower blouse splattered with white polka dots highlighted her bronzed skin, and from countless hours in the sunshine her pigtailed hair had become a light buttery blonde. Benji had arrived in his usual frayed shorts, half tucked in T-shirt, and fire-engine-red Little League baseball cap. Katie didn't even give Benji the opportunity to say hello when she grabbed him firmly by the wrist and proceeded to march him down the front porch steps toward the backyard.

"Where are we going?" Benji asked.

"You'll see." She smiled slyly, leading her willing captive forward.

As they unlatched the gate of Katie's picket fence and entered her backyard, Benji encountered the most inviting picnic he had ever seen. Between two dogwood trees was spread a patchwork quilt of pastels, on it an oversized white wicker basket which was surrounded by two neatly laid place settings. In the center of the blanket rested a fragrant bouquet of wildflowers bundled together with a bright yellow ribbon. Katie hadn't overlooked any detail, right down to the lemonade she hand squeezed, the PB&J sandwiches she fixed, and the chocolate cupcakes covered with heaps of rainbow sprinkles she had baked with her mother earlier that day. More than anything else, Katie had wanted this last summer day to be perfect, and she couldn't think of anyone she would rather share it with than Benji.

After enjoying a leisurely dinner, they packed up the remnants of their glorious picnic except the quilt, and they watched as the sky transformed itself first from blue to pale pink, then to fuchsia, and finally to a swirl of purple and orange. As if the approaching dusk were a signal to Katie that it was time to unveil yet another surprise, she ordered Benji to close his eyes as she disappeared momentarily into the garage. Quickly running back to where she had left him sitting, she inquired, "Are your eyes still closed?"

"Yep," Benji assured her.

"You promise?"

"I promise."

"Okay, you can open them now." And when Benji opened his eyes, he was surrounded by hundreds of clear twinkle lights that Katie had strung from the branches of the dogwood trees, carefully wrapped around each branch, illuminating the magenta sky.

"Ta-da!" Katie sang.

"That is so cool!" Benji smiled.

"I know, right?"

And as only God could deliver, at that very moment Katie and Benji were unexpectedly joined by more glowing lights around them. First a brief burst of light here, then another there; some right next to them, and others further off in the yard. Before they could completely focus on any single one it extinguished itself, but then two or three more popped up elsewhere. The bursts came more frequently and multiplied until soon the entire yard was blanketed with dozens upon dozens of yellow-green flashes from the fireflies who were only too happy to be a part of their summer send-off.

"This is even better than a fireworks display!" exclaimed Benji as he took in the brilliance all around him.

"It's like they knew we were going to be here tonight!" Katie beamed.

Katie and Benji spent a good while running through the cool grass in their bare feet, catching the little insects in their cupped hands and laughing as the light pulsated through the cracks in their fingers. At one point a firefly even landed on the tip of Katie's nose. She giggled and looked crossed-eyed as she said hello to her new companion. "I think he likes you," laughed Benji.

Eventually the fireflies began to depart, so Katie and Benji bid them thanks and settled onto the quilt as the heat of the day transposed into the crispness of nighttime. Realizing that their day was all but done, they lay on their backs next to one another gazing up at the millions of stars twinkling overhead in the endless black sky.

"Benji, how do you think God made the stars?"

"Well," he began slowly in a tone wise beyond his years, "I think that God said the names of each of the stars, and when he did the warmth of his breath created them."

"Yeah, I think so too," Katie agreed, as if she had known the answer all along. "That sure is a lot of stars to name though."

"Yep, sure is."

"Do you think God named any of the stars 'Katie'?"

"Oh, definitely," Benji replied without hesitation. "You see that bluish star over there right in the middle of those four smaller stars?"

Benji stretched his arm out over his head and extended his index finger toward a small cluster of stars off on its own.

"Yes, I see it."

"Well, that star in the middle, that's the Katie star."

"It is?"

"Sure it is," Benji replied.

"Cool," Katie said, her voice filled with awe. "I'll bet there's a Benji star too," she continued, thoroughly enjoying their little game.

"Yeah, mayb—" started Benji until he was quickly interrupted.

"There! Right there!" Katie pointed abruptly as if the star had been magically revealed to her. "That's the Benji star."

"*That* one? You mean that really big one right above us?"

"Yep, that's the one," Katie replied, completely convinced of herself.

"That's the North Star, silly."

"What's the North Star?"

"It's the star that is always fixed in the sky in one spot, like it never moves. It stays there all the time. In the old days sailors and travelers would use the North Star as their guide. They always knew that if they followed that star they would be pointed in the right direction."

"Well, that is your star, Benji, I just know it is. Yours is the North Star." Benji smiled to himself and made no effort to reply.

They sat in silence for quite a while after that, gazing contentedly into the brilliant light show that God had created just for them on that particular night. Although they easily could have lain upon the quilt until morning as they both resisted the reality that their final summer day had slipped into a memory, their droopy eyes betrayed them. They both fought back yawns, and Katie's mother called from inside that it was well past their bedtimes and Benji's mom was expecting him.

Katie, draped in the quilt, walked Benji home along with her mother. Then she began her nightly ritual to prepare for bed. After washing up, changing into her pajamas, and ensuring that the proper stuffed animals lay on her pillow, Katie climbed into bed. She patted Trouble, who slept soundly curled up in a ball at the foot of her bed, on the head. Trouble, who had retired hours ago when Katie and Benji were still playing with fireflies, opened one eye ever so slightly at Katie's touch, sighed, and immediately continued her peaceful slumber. Katie said her prayers, and as her mother kissed her goodnight she turned off the lamp to reveal the soft glow of a nightlight in the corner of her room. Her mother, as always, proceeded to close the blinds when Katie sprang up in bed and protested.

"No, Mama, don't close the blinds."

"Why not, sweetie?"

"Because I want to be able to see the Katie Star."

"The what?" her mother lovingly responded.

"The Katie Star. It's the star that Benji said God named after me."

"Oh, I see." Katie's mother readjusted the blinds so that Katie could see outside and sat next to her daughter on the edge of the bed. "Benji is a very special friend, isn't he?"

"Yes, Mama." Katie settled back onto her pillow, yawning and eyes half closed. "He's my very best friend."

"Well, I'm glad for you, sweetie." Her mother leaned over and brushed a strand of hair from Katie's forehead. "Everyone needs a best friend, and you couldn't have picked a better one. Good night, sweetheart, I love you." Katie's mother kissed her daughter goodnight and quietly pulled the bedroom door closed except for a small crack. Katie nestled snugly under her covers, tuckered out from the busyness of the day.

"Goodnight, Mama, love you too," Katie whispered, barely audible as she drifted off into her own special dream world.

Though that Saturday in late August might have marked the end to an unforgettable summer, little did Katie know that her journey with Benji, a freckle-faced ordinary boy, was only just beginning.

This is their story.

CHAPTER 2
INSIDE OUT

"The Lord does not look at the things man looks at.
Man looks at the outward appearance,
but the Lord looks at the heart."
1 Samuel 16:7

Getting most children to go to church on Sunday mornings is like pulling teeth. Some try to fib their way out of it—*"I have a stomachache."* Some try to bargain their way out of it—*"I promise if you let me sleep in I'll go next week."* Some try to reason their way out of it—*"If we go I won't have time to finish my book report."* And others literally go kicking and screaming as they are dragged out of bed and plopped into the minivan regardless of their tantrums. But then, every once in a while, you will find that unique little soul who actually *wants* to go to church. A rare breed, few and far between. Katie Kirby was just such a breed. She never gave her mother a hard time when practically every Sunday she had to put aside her tomboy clothes, dress like a young lady, and head to St. Paul the Apostle Church for their traditional morning service. St. Paul's was a small parish on the outskirts of town. It had been built at the turn of the century, and it claimed all of the country charm you would hope for in the white A-frame structure that sat perched atop a hill with brilliant stained-glass windows and oversized ruby red doors welcoming its guests. The adjacent cemetery dotted with gravestones dating back well over a century made the perfect hide-and-seek grounds to occupy the children while they waited for their parents after a Sunday morning service.

Now if you asked Katie *why* she liked church so much, she would immediately share with you what a great person Pastor Haddock was, how much she loved her Sunday school class, and how she learned all the important Bible stories. And to Katie's credit, she wasn't lying. Those things were certainly all *part* of the reason why

Katie liked going to church. However, there was more to it than that. What Katie didn't share but instead kept as her own little secret was that she loved going to St. Paul's because you just never knew what might happen in God's house on any given Sunday. Not *every* Sunday, mind you. But often enough. Usually when the church was packed to the brim (much to Pastor Haddock's chagrin), something would go haywire. Who ever said that God doesn't have a sense of humor?

Like the time when Mr. Finkle fell asleep in the middle of the service one Sunday. Well, first let's backtrack a little bit. Mr. Finkle *always* fell asleep in church. Pushing eighty, he had never made it through an entire service without his head bobbing from dozing off or that unexpected snort when his head drooped a little too low and he abruptly caught himself. One particular Sunday Mr. Finkle was a little under the weather from a head cold, so he was a bit stuffier than usual; and because he was taking cold medicine, he was also a bit sleepier than usual. Unfortunately for Mr. Finkle, the combination of the two created a perfect storm. By the time Pastor Haddock was midway through his sermon, Mr. Finkle's head was bobbing away, snoring just loudly enough that it was beginning to draw the attention of people sitting in close proximity. Katie typically sat two pews behind the Finkles so she had a bird's-eye view of the disturbance, and she was finding the whole thing quite entertaining. Mrs. Finkle, however, not so much. Sitting next to her slumbering husband, she nudged him gently as she habitually did when his snoring increased. But the cold medicine must've kicked in by that point because Mr. Finkle didn't move a muscle. Mrs. Finkle nudged him twice more as Pastor Haddock concluded his message, the offering was taken, and the congregation prepared for prayer. Nothing. With each nudge, not only did Mr. Finkle fail to awaken, but the guttural rumbling only grew louder from deep within his throat, a phlegmy snore that sounded like a cross between a distressed walrus and a Mack truck.

Pastor Haddock tried as best he could to proceed with the prayer as if nothing were amiss, but the snoring had started to create an echo in the sanctuary, and the people around him were either giggling under their breaths or sighing in protest. That was precisely when Mrs. Finkle, who was visibly mortified by this point, had had enough. Right in the middle of the Lord's Prayer she elbowed her husband so hard in the ribs that he instantaneously snapped out of his trance in utter bewilderment, arms flailing about and completely losing his balance. Before the congregation could finish the prayer with an "Amen," Mr. Finkle went flying into the aisle where he landed with a loud *THUD*. Mrs. Finkle turned her attention to her husband, who was awkwardly sprawled out in the center aisle, with a *"Boy are you gonna be in trouble when we get home"* glare. It took a few seconds for Mr. Finkle to collect himself, all while trying to appear as dignified as possible. Moments later he reentered the pew next to his fuming wife, completely clueless as to the disturbance he had caused. And of course, in the receiving line after the service when Mr. Finkle warmly greeted Pastor Haddock, he acted like not a thing out of the ordinary had happened. Of course he did.

Or there was the time when Mr. Callahan's pants split wide open during communion. The service that morning had been going along quite uneventfully until it came time for the Lord's Supper. At Pastor Haddock's direction, the congregants stoically proceeded single file up the center aisle until they reached the altar railing and knelt to receive the elements of bread and wine. Charlie Callahan, a recent widower who was a stubby yet portly man, waddled over to the railing. The second his knee hit the cushion you couldn't help but cringe at the sound of fabric ripping apart. The seam of his pants had split straight down the middle, revealing his paisley boxer shorts underneath. Now, one would imagine that Mr. Callahan, having heard the tearing of the fabric and feeling a sudden breeze on his posterior, would've discreetly stood and returned to his pew. That would have likely been the rational thing to do. But expecting the rational in church and having it actually happen are often two totally different things. No, Mr. Callahan continued to kneel, patiently waiting for the elements, seemingly not bothered in the least by the fact that his undergarments were on display for the entire congregation.

To make matters worse, and as if this unfortunate mishap weren't bad enough during one of the holiest times in any church service, Miss Teasley happened to be kneeling adjacent to him. Miss Teasley, God bless her dear soul, was a never-married schoolteacher who would offer assistance to anyone at any time. If there had been a church yearbook with a superlative for "*most likely to help a friend in need*," Miss Teasley would have won it. She was always willing to lend a helping hand for anything, and during the service that day Miss Teasley quite literally lived up to her reputation. Seeing that her brother in Christ was faced with a rather embarrassing predicament, it was Miss Teasley to the rescue! She very nonchalantly placed the palm of her hand directly over the open seam in Mr. Callahan's pants, sufficiently obscuring his boxers while he partook of the holy sacrament. The two of them acted like they were the only ones in the entire church, but all the while the rest of the congregation sat in stunned silence at witnessing Miss Teasley's hand resting precariously on Mr. Callahan's derriere. And the Murphy family, who were seated in the front pew, swore up and down afterward that as Miss Teasley stood to return to her pew, she gave Mr. Callahan the gentlest of pats before removing her hand.

It then became quite the topic of conversation at St. Paul's for some time afterward. And as often happens, the story was embellished the more it was retold—even to the point where Miss Teasley, the little Jezebel she was, threw Mr. Callahan down to the ground and declared her love for him right in the middle of the service. Miss Teasley, ignoring the rumors, went about her business like nothing had ever happened, and Mr. Callahan invested in some properly fitting pants. Yes, these were some of the moments at St. Paul the Apostle Church that led Katie to look forward to Sunday mornings, and the fact that her best friend was typically sitting right next to her through all of the action only made it that much more enjoyable.

Each November at St. Paul's was designated "Fall-Free-For-All" month for the music ministry. The choir took a much needed break to prepare for the demanding Advent season just ahead, so the music at the traditional service was, how should we say, "up for grabs." It was literally a free-for-all where anyone could volunteer to showcase their God-given gifts. Most people sang, some played a musical instrument, and one young man even rapped once (that didn't go over too well with most of the elderly members). The majority of the time the free-for-all was absolutely beautiful—Wendy Fox, a professional harpist, humbly strummed the delicate strings to "Amazing Grace," or Zachary Wilmer, a self-taught pianist and prodigy at only sixteen, tickled the ivories with a medley of hymns that had everyone's toes tapping. Nevertheless, this *was* St. Paul's we were talking about, so things didn't always go quite as planned.

Katie and Benji were regulars at the traditional service, so much so that they were given permission by their parents to sit together in their own pew so long as they didn't become disruptive. And on this particular Sunday after they took their seats and glanced at the bulletin, Katie abruptly exclaimed, "Oh my!"

"What?" Benji asked.

"Mrs. Pinkner is singing today."

"Oh my is right," Benji agreed. "This oughta be interesting."

Elouise Pinkner was a diminutive woman who had a larger-than-life presence wherever she went. Standing not even five feet tall, she was so commanding that most of the men in the congregation were deathly afraid of her. A single glance in their direction would send them cowering the other way. She wasn't particularly warm and fuzzy either, and with her spiked hair and perfect posture she more closely resembled a drill sergeant than the retired kindergarten teacher that she was (you could almost picture the petrified little five-year-olds standing at attention in her classroom). And Elouise Pinkner had such an enormous voice for such a small body that it could drown out anything else in a room. Today she was going to grace the congregation with her rendition of the timeless hymn, "How Great Thou Art." Katie and Benji immediately knew they would be in for an experience. And an experience it was.

As the churchgoers filtered into the sanctuary and greeted one another prior to the service, Katie and Benji casually dangled their feet from the pew while observing the growing crowd. Always one of the first to enter on Sunday mornings was Isaiah Washington. A middle-aged African-American gentleman, at six-foot-five he stood a good head and shoulders above anyone else in the congregation. Isaiah was unquestionably one of the most faithful men Katie and Benji had ever encountered. Not "faithful" as in loyal (although he was certainly that too) but "faith-full" as in full of faith. Isaiah never missed a Sunday. He was always dressed to the nines in a dark, three-piece suit, even on the hottest of summer days. He walked with a cane, had the slightest hint of gray hair along his temples, and he habitually wore bifocals off the tip of his nose as he glanced down upon everyone in a distinguished but not condescending way. And let me tell you, when Isaiah worshipped the Lord, he *worshipped* the Lord. He sat in the same pew week after week, and as soon as the opening announcements had concluded, he was fully and completely immersed by the Spirit. He knew every single word of every last hymn, and as he closed his eyes and sang with his hand raised to the heavens, you could just tell he was in the presence of his Almighty. Indeed, Isaiah seemed to have a connection with God that most people only dreamed they might achieve one day. Despite the fact that Isaiah was a man of few words (or perhaps because of it), he was well liked and affectionately called "Brother Washington" by men and women, young and old alike. In fact, he was the only Brother in the entire church.

"You see him?" Benji pointed as the organist began to play the opening melody.

"You mean Brother Washington?" Katie asked.

"Yes. Did you know that he goes each Wednesday evening to the local shelter, prepares meals, and even takes some of the homeless people back to his house for a few nights?"

"No, I didn't." Katie was enthralled. "How did you know that?"

"I just heard it from someone."

"Okay, then what about her?" Katie pointed to a middle-aged woman chatting with a friend not far from where Brother Washington was quietly contemplating. "I heard she makes clothes for the poor children in our school."

"Oh, she does, but not because she wants to help them."

"Really, then why does she do it?"

"She only does it because every year the local paper writes a huge article about her, and she wants to win the 'Citizen of the Year' award."

"Really? She looks nice enough to me."

"Oh, she is nice," Benji explained, "but she just likes the attention."

Katie was beginning to warm up to the little game that they had created. "Well, then what about *him*?" Katie pointed to a teenager who usually slumped in the pew next to his family, trying to be as inconspicuous as possible.

"That's Tony," Benji offered. "He wants to be a youth minister one day."

"What makes you think that? He never says a word in church."

"Oh, but he loves the Lord and he goes home and writes down notes from Pastor Haddock's sermons so he can research everything."

"I like this." Katie smiled.

"Like what?" Benji whispered, as the opening hymn began and everyone stood.

"This game."

"What game?"

"This game of making stuff up about people. It's fun."

"Who said I was making stuff up? Oh, and you see her?" Benji pointed to the woman in five-inch heels and a tailored navy suit with her auburn hair in a low ponytail.

"You mean Mrs. McCarthy?"

"Yep."

"Isn't she involved in like every project at the church?"

"Yes, she is, but she doesn't really believe in God."

"Okay, Benji," Katie said, rolling her eyes. "Now you're really losing it."

"No, I'm serious," answered Benji. "She comes each week because her husband is a Christian, but she doesn't really think that God exists and she's afraid to tell him."

"So then she just comes to church each week and pretends?"

"Pretty much," Benji replied sadly.

"That doesn't make any sense. Why would people come to church to be with God if they don't even believe in God?"

"Search me. But sometimes they do."

"How do you know all this, Benji?"

"I don't know, I just do."

"Oh, Benji," Katie giggled as they realized they ought to discontinue their discussion for the time being lest they get separated. As the service continued, both of them were their usual well-behaved selves until their previous discussion got the best of Katie.

"Okay, so what about Pastor Haddock?" Katie whispered as he took the pulpit in his flowing black vestments to deliver the morning message.

"What about him?" Benji whispered back.

"If you're so smart, what do you know about *him*?"

"Well," Benji began, "he likes being pastor and he definitely loves God, but sometimes he thinks he's not good enough."

"Not good enough for what?" Katie said under her breath.

"Not good enough to be a pastor."

"How do you mean?"

"He thinks about the mistakes he's made in his life, and he feels like he's no better than anyone else, so sometimes it's hard for him to have people look up to him."

"When did he tell you this?" Katie asked.

"He didn't, I just know. He wants to be a good pastor, but he also wants everyone to realize that he's human, just like they are. He feels like sometimes people expect him to be perfect."

"You sure do seem to know a lot about people!" Katie teased Benji, but this time a little too loudly because not even a second later, they felt a stinging swat on the tops of their heads. Neither one of them needed to turn around to see who had delivered the warning, because sitting directly behind them each week in *her* pew was Mrs. Peabody—or "Mrs. *Busy*body," as all of the children and most of the adults referred to her. Mrs. Peabody was a plump woman who always arrived at church in some hideous floral dress with a matching bonnet so large that if you sat directly behind her you would have absolutely no hope of seeing any part of the service. And Mrs. Peabody knew everything about everybody—not just in the church, but in the entire town. She wouldn't hesitate to remind you that her family had been members of St. Paul's for at least five hundred years, and, according to her, she had every right to know what went on in *her* hometown. She wasn't particularly fond of children either, so it was no small wonder that she never had any of her own. And nothing, absolutely *nothing*, got past Mrs. Peabody. When she heard some hot new gossip, you could be sure the rest of the world would find out in no short order. She didn't need Facebook or Twitter or any other type of social media either (she thought Facebook was a textbook with your picture on the front and Twitter was something a bird does). Nope, Mrs. Peabody just used good old-fashioned word of mouth, and her little tidbits of juicy gossip spread like wildfire.

Glancing at their mothers to see if they had witnessed Mrs. Peabody's reprimand, Katie and Benji dutifully settled into their pews to focus on what was left of Pastor Haddock's sermon. Afraid to utter another word, Katie grabbed the pencil from its holder on the pew and scribbled something on her bulletin. She shoved it onto Benji's lap.

"What about Mrs. Peabody?" it read.

Benji looked at her, perplexed.

"What do you know about *her*?" she mouthed.

And Benji leaned over, put his lips near Katie's ear, and replied, "You don't even want to know," as his eyes grew wide and he shook his head in dismay.

Katie chuckled to herself as Pastor Haddock said his last "Hallelujah" and the collection plate was distributed. Katie drifted off as the offertory music played, thinking about their conversation. She didn't really take Benji seriously at what he was saying about those people, because after all, how could a fourth grader know all this? Obviously Benji was making it up, a good way to the pass the time during the service. She enjoyed his make-believe stories about the parishioners, and there was no point in arguing with him about it. But then again, the odd part was that Benji seemed to have this uncanny ability to see people for who they truly were. To look beyond the façade that most adults so often put on for the rest of the world, and to see the person on the inside. Yes, there was definitely something unique about how Benji related to the world around him, which was probably why Katie had grown to love him so much.

Before Katie could let her thoughts get the best of her, Mrs. Pinkner dramatically rose from the front pew and ascended the altar stairs to the chancel area where she haughtily positioned herself in front of the microphone. Mabel Adams, the church's longtime accompanist, shifted from the organ over to the piano, ready for Mrs. Pinkner's cue to begin. With a nod and a clearing of her throat, Mrs. Pinkner broke into the first words of the hymn. *"Oh Lord, my God, When I in awesome wonder . . ."* she began, her soprano voice warbling confidently.

Her shining moment of glory continued without interruption right up until the chorus of the hymn. As soon as she sang the notes for *"How great Thou art,"* her pitch became so high that a very unfortunate thing happened. Mr. Dennison, who was hearing impaired, attended church every once in a while but always with his faithful service dog, a Golden Retriever named Nugget. And Nugget, upon hearing a sound well beyond anything Nugget knew was normal, began to howl. And howl, and howl, and howl! Mr. Dennison, sensing his dog's alarm, tried to comfort Nugget, but by that point it was too late. A chain of events had been set in motion and, like dominos toppling over, one thing led to another. Nugget continued to howl away. Mrs. Pinkner, well aware of the disturbance but determined to finish her masterpiece, sang louder, trying to mask the dog's baying. As Mrs. Pinkner sang louder, Mabel Adams pounded the piano keys all the harder. As Mabel pounded harder, Missy Foster's nine-month-old infant Abigail started crying, completely discombobulated at having been awakened from the peaceful nap in her portable carrier that sat on the pew alongside her mother. As Abigail cried, several of the younger children in the congregation put their hands over their ears and begged their parents to make it all stop. As the younger children protested to their parents, the teenagers began laughing uncontrollably. And as the teenagers laughed, the adults fidgeted nervously, wishing that *someone* would have the decency to put an end to the nightmare. The entire congregation was in a complete uproar and poor Pastor Haddock sat by helplessly, not knowing quite what to do and quietly praying the Lord might take him home at that very moment, a pastor's version of having the ground swallow you whole. Through it all, good ol' Mrs. Pinkner never missed a note, and she sang every last syllable of the four-stanza hymn. When she concluded, she took a bow and returned to her pew as if everything had gone exactly as planned. Katie and Benji, once they had stopped giggling long enough to compose themselves, looked at one another as if they weren't surprised in the least by the debacle that Mrs. Pinkner had bestowed upon the church.

In spite of the fact that all Pastor Haddock wanted to do after the service was slink quietly away to the confines of his parsonage, he dutifully greeted each congregant and shook his head awkwardly at the many remarks about what an "interesting" service it had been. Mr. Dennison, who was probably the only person at church that day more humiliated than Pastor Haddock, profusely asked for the pastor's forgiveness and explained that in all the years he'd had Nugget, not once had the faithful canine ever howled.

"I just don't know what got into her today," he repeatedly apologized.

"No worries," assured Pastor Haddock, "Nugget is welcome any time." He enunciated slowly so that Mr. Dennison could be sure to read his lips. And although Nugget was always welcome, Pastor Haddock was keen to rethink the whole idea of "Fall-Free-For-All" Novembers after that particular Sunday.

Before Pastor Haddock could greet another churchgoer in the receiving line, four-year-old Billy Watkins came tearing out of the sanctuary, barreling through the crowd. He ran right up to the pastor, practically tripping himself along the way, and wrapped his small arms around him in a huge bear hug that only reached up to Pastor Haddock's waist.

"Well, hello, Billy," the pastor chuckled.

"That was the best day at church EVER!!!!!" erupted the young boy. "Can we do that again next week?"

Pastor Haddock chuckled nervously as he extricated the overly enthusiastic boy from his pants.

"Oh, I don't know about that, Billy," he replied. "I think we've had quite enough excitement for a while, don't you?"

The remainder of the congregants filed out of the sanctuary, most of them making light of the catastrophe to help cheer Pastor Haddock, although a few took an unnecessary jab or two at him for having lost control of "his" church service. While most of them made a beeline for the exit so they could go about their Sunday chores, a good few lingered in the oversized narthex, enjoying fellowship time where coffee and a few light snacks were set out on a table.

Katie and Benji milled around a bit, helping themselves to some orange juice and a handful of pretzels. Because their mothers had a few things to see to in the kitchen, the two children were directed to remain in the fellowship area until their mothers returned for them.

Perfectly content to keep company with one another, they settled in on the velvet loveseat in the corner of the room.

"Benji, why do you think adults do that?"

"Do what?" Although Benji had moved on from their earlier conversation, Katie obviously hadn't.

"Why do you think they pretend to be someone they're not? Or why do you think they hide who they really are?"

"I don't know," Benji answered honestly. "Maybe they are so worried about other people liking them that they think they have to be someone different than who they are. Or maybe they think they'll even like themselves better."

"But shouldn't it only matter if God likes them?" Katie astutely observed.

"It should," Benji sighed.

Munching on the pretzels while more than a few crumbs landed on Benji's worn khakis, they curiously watched about half a dozen men standing nearby, gathered in a circle and sipping black coffee while deep in discussion. At first neither Katie nor Benji paid one bit of attention to the conversation. Soon, however, they couldn't help but overhear bits and pieces, so then they became curious as to what was so important. After only a few moments, Katie had deduced that the men were searching for a new chairman of their church's philanthropy committee since the current one had stepped down due to health issues.

"I think Ed's your man," one of the group commented. "After all, he's got years of experience, and he's the best local accountant we have in the area."

"I'm not so sure about Ed," another challenged. "I think it should be Chuck Lancaster. Chuck's always got his hand in something, and he is so visible in the community that everyone would know him immediately. He could really help draw a crowd."

"No, I still think Ed's the right choice," countered the first man.

"Not to complicate things," a third spoke up, refilling his Styrofoam coffee cup at the dispenser, "but what about Bill Harris?"

"Bill? Why Bill?" two others who hadn't yet spoken replied simultaneously.

"Bill's reputation around here is that he's a man with a plan. Bill will definitely be the one people will expect to fill the position."

The dialogue continued until each of the men had chimed in his respective two cents. That is, all except for Brother Washington, who stood silently and pondered the direction of the conversation. Without warning, Benji rose from his seat next to Katie and joined the group, although it took a few moments for him to be noticed by the men since he stood a good foot shorter than the rest and had to work his way into the tight circle.

"Excuse me, sirs," Benji said politely. "I wasn't trying to eavesdrop, but I heard some of what you were talking about. Did you say you were looking for a new chairman of your philanthropy group?"

"Yes, why?" one man replied, eyeing Benji suspiciously while wondering why in a million years this young boy thought he could be a part of their adult conversation.

"Well, what about Mr. Scott?" Benji quietly offered.

"Mr. Scott?" the same man shot back sarcastically. "Do you mean *Wayne* Scott?"

"Yessir."

Two other men chuckled, and the first once again took the lead. "Why, he's not even thirty years old yet. A baby I'll tell you. And besides, what experience does he have?"

"Not only experience," added another, "but what visibility does he have? Who in our church even knows him?"

"Besides," said a third, "he's only a handyman. Not much prestige in *that*," he chuckled.

Several of the other men joined in heckling Benji's seemingly ludicrous suggestion, but not Brother Washington. He just stood silently, towering over the rest of the group and peering down curiously at Benji from his bifocals.

At this point most children would probably become at best uncomfortable or at worst visibly upset, but not Benji. As Katie sat perched on the loveseat, she watched her friend stand his ground and proceed to take the cluster of men completely off guard.

"Maybe he's not well known," Benji began, "and maybe he doesn't have a fancy job, but he's a good Christian who loves God, and he has helped my family with projects around the house many times. He would be a really good man for the job. And after all, what about David?"

"David???" several of the men echoed one another. "Who on earth is David?"

"You know," Benji said confidently, "David from the Bible."

One of the men broke into the conversation and firmly clasped his hand on Benji's shoulder, ushering him out of the circle toward his little playmate. "Now this is getting ridiculous. Young man, I think you need to go ba—"

But before Benji could be escorted away, Brother Washington finally broke his silence. "Wait just a minute," his baritone voice bellowed as he motioned for Benji to return. "Let the boy speak."

Benji made the briefest eye contact with Brother Washington in gratitude and then continued. "Well, remember in the Bible when Saul was king of Israel and he wasn't doing a good job because he had stopped following the Lord and instead started doing what he wanted to do?"

"Mmm-hmm," one of the men mumbled.

"Well, God told Samuel to go to Bethlehem to anoint the next king, one of Jesse's sons. God said he would show Samuel who the next king was supposed to be."

Before Benji could continue one of the men rudely interjected. "Why are we listening to him? He's only a kid, and he's making stuff up." Obviously not at all well versed in the Bible, several of the men gave him a sideways glance, and Brother Washington held up the palm of his hand, bringing immediate silence to everyone. "Continue," Brother Washington told Benji.

"Well, when Samuel arrived in Bethlehem each of Jesse's sons came forward. And each time, Samuel thought, 'This must be the next king.' But each time God told him no. Then Samuel asked Jesse if he had any more sons. Jesse answered that he still had his youngest son, David, but he was out in the field because he was a shepherd. As soon as David came in from the fields, God told Samuel that he was supposed to anoint David as the next king. So you see," Benji continued, having succeeded in finally captivating the men's attention, "David didn't look like anything special. He was the youngest son and only a teenager, but God knew what was inside David's heart and that he was supposed to be the greatest king of Israel. It didn't matter what David looked like on the outside, it was what was on the inside that mattered to God. And I know Mr. Scott, and Mr. Scott has a heart for God even if he isn't very old and he doesn't have a fancy job. That's all."

Benji didn't wait for a response. Having spoken his piece, he left the fraternity of bewildered men and rejoined Katie on the loveseat, but not before he caught some of the hushed comments among the men.

"How does he know all this?" one said incredulously.

"And he acts like *he* is teaching *us* the Bible!" another offered indignantly.

"I don't know how he knows so much, but I heard his father taught it all to him," offered another.

"Who is his father, anyway? Have you ever met him?"

"No, I've never met him, have you?"

"Sure haven't. I'm not even sure which one his father is."

After a few moments the men lost interest in Benji and redirected their conversation to more important things, like the division rivalry football game scheduled for later that evening. Brother Washington, however, discreetly extricated himself from the group and approached Benji. Looming above the two children, he peered down at the young boy for a few moments in complete silence. Oddly enough, Benji seemed comfortable and met Brother Washington's gaze with ease. Neither of them blinked an eye. After what seemed like hours to Katie, Brother Washington finally spoke.

"I know who you are," he informed Benji.

"I know you do," Benji acknowledged.

And then it was quite apparent that Brother Washington was very carefully considering his next words. Looking straight at Benji more lovingly than Katie had ever seen one person look at another, Brother Washington gave the slightest nod of his head.

"Thank you."

It was all he said to Benji, but for some reason those two simple words carried the weight of burdens more profound than Katie could even begin to understand, and they carried a gratitude beyond what any finite language could express.

Benji made no reply, but his eyes glimmered at Brother Washington in a mysterious connection of understanding between the two. With that, Brother Washington turned and left.

"Benji, what was he thanking you for?" Katie inquired.

"Nothing much," Benji responded. "Just a few things I helped him out with one time."

"Oh. Well, you must've been a pretty big help, 'cause he seemed awful grateful."

"It was no big deal."

"I think it was to Brother Washington," Katie disagreed, as their mothers collected them from the loveseat and they left the few Sunday morning stragglers behind to head home. "I think whatever you did really meant a lot to him."

Benji smiled. Indeed it had.

CHAPTER 3
A DIFFERENT SCHOOL OF THOUGHT

"For God did not give us a spirit of timidity,
but a spirit of power, of love, and of self-discipline.
So do not be ashamed to testify about our Lord . . ."
2 Timothy 1:7-8

Katie and Benji had attended Franklin Elementary School since kindergarten. The lone public primary school in Bakersville, it was situated adjacent to the community park where it split the small town into four equal geographical quadrants of north, south, east, and west. The north and south were the residential subdivisions, the west was comprised of local farms, and the east boasted the commercial district. The school was populated by a conglomeration of children from different backgrounds and means. Franklin prided itself on instilling in its students a sense of self-worth and an education second to none in the entire region. To its credit, the teachers and staff at Franklin did go above and beyond in many respects. They created outreach programs to feed the needy families in the area. They initiated a "ban bullies" notification system where students could anonymously seek assistance if they felt targeted or discriminated against for any reason. They even began a mentoring system where the older students would serve as "big brothers" or "big sisters" to guide the younger students through the highs and lows of elementary school life. The parents of Franklin children praised the school to the hilt. By all outward appearances, it excelled at everything.

Nonetheless, as advanced as it was, there was something a little *off* about Franklin Elementary. Not "off" in a break-the-law kind of way. No, not that at all. Just off as in a caving-to-the-pressures-of-modern-society kind of way. For as much as Franklin Elementary wanted to stand apart from all the other schools, it also wanted to be exactly *like* the rest in one very obvious way. Bluntly put, in more recent years Franklin Elementary School strove to become religiously sterile.

At first neither the parents nor the students took notice. But very subtly, the changes manifested themselves in more obvious ways. For example, when the students in science class studied human existence and development, all references to creation of man and woman by God were removed from the lesson plans. So too was the discussion from history class about how the founding fathers of America strove to build a country with God as their foundation. At Halloween students were sent home with a letter explaining to parents that during their school's upcoming parade they were expressly prohibited from wearing costumes of angels, devils, any participants in the nativity scene, or anything that might be perceived as religious in nature. When late December arrived and the schoolchildren were about to be dismissed for a week-long holiday, they celebrated with a "winter wonderland" party rather than the Christmas party they had enjoyed in years past. No longer could the children exchange gifts or put up a tree with twinkling lights. That might send the wrong message.

The children, for the most part, were confused as to why so many of their long-standing traditions were being taken away from them. Parents grew concerned, but typically they were either too busy or too cowardly to speak out. Through it all Franklin Elementary School rested firmly on its laurels that it was better to go with the flow and keep out of trouble than to take a position and risk controversy. Like the house constructed of flimsy straw felled by the Big Bad Wolf, Franklin crumbled under the same kind of peer pressure that it always taught its students to fight against.

The proverbial straw that broke that camel's back came one bitter cold February morning, when it seemed as though no matter how many layers of clothing you added, you just couldn't keep warm. Katie had arrived at school that Monday, peeling off her marshmallowy down coat, wool scarf, and mittens. She then commenced her morning ritual of retrieving notebook and pencils from her backpack, securing her lunch bag in her locker, and situating herself at her desk and copying down the morning geography drills. Benji, who sat two rows over from Katie, was already hard at work. Just as Katie had matched a dozen or so states with their capitals, Principal Wexley's voice reverberated over the PA system for the morning announcements. The principal shared with children the quote of the day and some additional important reminders before she closed with the exciting news that snow was predicted for the afternoon which might result in an early dismissal. The mere thought of getting out of school early prompted an immediate cheer from all of the elementary school students and an immediate dread from all of the teachers, knowing full well that it would be a monumental challenge keeping them focused for the rest of the day. What on earth was Principal Wexley thinking?

Once the announcements concluded and Mrs. Wexley signed off, Mr. Collins requested his fourth grade class to rise while they directed their attention to the American flag mounted in the corner of the classroom. *"I pledge allegiance, to the flag . . ."* the class recited in perfect unison. During the Pledge, Katie happened to glance over at Emma Rodgers, another student who was standing next to her. Emma, a small girl for a fourth grader and unusually shy, kept mostly to herself except at recess when she would habitually seek out the same two girls for either a game of hopscotch or cards. As they reached the conclusion of the Pledge, Katie couldn't help but notice something very odd. In the last line of the Pledge, Emma said every word except "under God," during which she was glaringly silent. Katie and Emma briefly made eye contact, but Emma quickly looked down to the floor, hoping to avoid any further interaction. Katie had meant to ask Emma about it, but she soon became preoccupied by Mr. Collins's history lesson so Emma's curious silence left her mind as quickly as it had entered. Katie never gave it a second thought.

That is, until it happened again the next day. Same morning routine, same announcements, same Pledge, and same pregnant silence by Emma when it came time to say "under God." This time Katie wasn't about to let it slip her mind. Midway through the day their class's recess period began, but because it was too cold outside they were relegated to indoor activities in the gym.

Benji always loved playing dodgeball with the other fourth graders, and he was typically one of the last students to be tagged "out." But before he could join in a game, Katie pulled him aside.

"Benji, did you notice anything weird about Emma Rodgers?"

"No. Why, was I supposed to?"

"Well, this morning when we were saying the Pledge, Emma didn't say the whole thing."

"Maybe she forgot some of the words," Benji offered.

"No, it wasn't like that. She definitely knows all the words. Right at the end where we say *'one nation, under God, indivisible,'* she said everything but the 'under God' part. It was like she didn't say those two words on purpose."

"Are you sure?" Benji questioned Katie.

"Yes, I'm positive. And if you don't believe me, watch her tomorrow morning. I'll bet you anything she does it again."

Katie was absolutely right. The next morning Emma sat quietly through the announcements, dutifully rose to recite the Pledge, and said every last word by heart. Except, *under God*. But this time, Katie wasn't the only one watching. Benji was too. As soon as Emma omitted those two words, Katie's wide eyes darted directly to Benji. *"See, I told you so!"* her look said.

For the rest of the morning Katie couldn't focus on her studies. All she wanted to do was talk to Benji, but she couldn't find any opportunities to get him alone. Finally, at lunchtime she had her chance. She rushed to grab her lunch bag and practically pulled Benji out of the line in the cafeteria, ushering him to the nearest table with empty seats.

"*Now* do you see what I'm talking about?" she asked, far too worked up to even begin thinking about enjoying the ham and cheese sandwich with pickles that her mother had packed her.

"Yes, I did see it actually."

"What do you think it's all about?"

"I really don't know," Benji answered honestly. "I've never noticed her do it before."

"No, me neither," Katie agreed. "Well, we are just going to have to get to the bottom of this."

"Okay, detective," Benji chuckled as he gulped down his applesauce and chased it with a carton of chocolate milk. "Let me know what you find out."

Lunchtime was over in a short half hour, and due to yet another report of impending snow, once again indoor recess followed. Katie wasted no time scoping out Emma from the multitude of fourth graders who occupied the gym, all restless from being cooped up indoors and eager to burn off some excess energy. As Emma sat with Janie Millbright on the mats in the far corner of the gym and played a game of Go Fish, Katie seized her opportunity.

"Hi, Emma," Katie offered warmly.

"Uh, hi," Emma replied, barely audible.

Katie got right to the point. "Hey, I noticed that for the last couple of days when we say the Pledge of Allegiance, you haven't said the whole thing."

"Really?" Emma averted her eyes and fidgeted, clearly uncomfortable with the direction of the conversation.

"Yeah, but not the whole Pledge. Only the words 'under God.' You never say them anymore, and I was just wondering how come?"

Emma sat stone silent, clearly contemplating her best course of action—whether she should flee for the girls' bathroom, outright lie, or just fess up and tell the truth. Since Emma was neither a sissy nor a liar, the latter won out.

"Umm," she hesitated. "My daddy won't let me."

"Why not?" Katie asked, thoroughly confused.

"He says there's no such thing as God, so I shouldn't say something if I don't believe it."

"Well, *do* you believe it? Do you think God is real?"

"I think so," but then she quickly backtracked, "I don't know. I'm not really sure. Maybe," she finally admitted. "I guess I think there is, but my daddy's super smart, and he's says there's not, so I don't know what to think."

Emma nervously looked at Janie, and Katie quickly realized that she had probably pushed the conversation too far. Not wanting to embarrass Emma, she backed off and returned to where Benji was involved in a heated game of dodgeball. The brief conversation may have been over, but Emma's actions (or, more properly, her *in*actions) during the Pledge still lingered in Katie's thoughts.

Like a skipping record player, that night Katie kept replaying in her mind what Emma had said to her during recess. Did Emma really believe what her father had told her? How could she? And how could she refuse to say the words of something that they had all been reciting since before they were old enough to read? Although Katie tossed and turned most of the night, preoccupied by something that shouldn't have caused her a second thought, the next morning she awoke determined not to let it bother her. After all, she rationalized, each person was entitled to her own opinion. As long as Emma wasn't bothering anyone else, she could say (or not say) whatever she wanted. And Katie had *almost* convinced herself of that until she arrived at school on Wednesday morning only to find that Emma's political statement (or rather, silence) had spread throughout the entire school! As it turned out, apparently Janie Millbright wasn't very good at keeping a private conversation, well, private. Janie had shared Emma's confession with some of her friends, who in turn informed Mr. Collins, who then told Principal Wexley. By the time all of the children filtered into their classrooms, it was the hot topic at Franklin Elementary.

But it wasn't until Thursday when everything abruptly changed. At first nothing appeared out of the ordinary. Mrs. Wexley's familiar voice came over the morning announcements as cheerful and informative as ever. She shared about the upcoming Friday evening band concert and pleaded with all of the students to dress properly during the winter months due to the dangers of hypothermia. She then signed off with her rousing, "Go Get'em Gophers," a tribute to their school mascot Gus the Gopher. But when the intercom went silent, other music began to play in classrooms. All of the students immediately recognized the tune.

"All right, class," Mr. Collins announced. "Please everyone rise. We're going to start something new. Instead of reciting the Pledge each morning, we will all stand at attention to the flag and listen quietly as the melody of the Star Spangled Banner is played." Mr. Collins then put his right hand over his heart, pounding it slightly to make an impression. Some of the students followed suit, more because they didn't quite know what to do than because they wanted to, and others just stared at the teacher quite puzzled by this turn of events. But not Katie. She immediately realized what was going on. Glancing past Emma, who to no one's surprise was staring at the floor tiles again, she made eye contact with Benji. And she knew, without them having to exchange a word, that Benji disapproved of this new "routine" as much as she did.

During the next several days Katie made it her number one priority to find out what the sudden change of course was all about. As each day passed and the Pledge was replaced by the national anthem, Katie managed to dig a little deeper and uncover what was *really* going on. It didn't take her long to fill in the gaps that had been missing. You see, one thing almost all elementary school children love to do is *talk*. Now let's be frank; just because they tell you something doesn't necessarily mean what they are saying is true, but many times it will give you an overall picture of the truth. With broad brush strokes, that is. Furthermore, there is no better place to pump grade-schoolers for information than on the school bus, the epicenter of social activity for the children where teachers can't oversee them, parents can't overhear them, and bus drivers can't give their undivided attention to them lest they drive off the road and cause an accident. Ah yes, the bus was a breeding ground for inappropriate remarks, mysteriously missing school supplies, and, most importantly, gaining the inside scoop. It's quite amazing what one can learn during a ten-minute bus ride from school to home! Katie and Benji worked those bus rides to their advantage.

By the time afternoon Bus #313 had pulled onto Magnolia Lane midway through the following week, Katie and Benji had fitted all the puzzle pieces into place. Mr. Rodgers, Emma's father, was some powerful county politician who knew all the "high-up" people and was directly involved with the local school board. Mr. Rodgers apparently had a great deal of influence, and he wasn't afraid to use it. Emma's parents had been separated for almost a year, and unfortunately for Emma, they didn't get along very well at all. Mrs. Rodgers had full custody of Emma, and Mr. Rodgers, in a bid to regain custody of his daughter, took issue with every last parental decision Emma's mother made. And it just so happened that the one thing Mr. Rodgers objected to most was Mrs. Rodgers's recent involvement in one of the local churches. Although Emma quite enjoyed being a part of the church, Mr. Rodgers couldn't stomach the thought that his soon-to-be-ex-wife was actually raising their daughter in a more loving, wholesome environment than he could provide with all of his clout.

One day when he had Emma for a weekend visitation, Mr. Rodgers informed her that he did not believe in God. He coaxed Emma that because Emma was such a "bright" girl and "smarter than that" to believe in imaginary things, she shouldn't believe in God either. He told Emma while he was practically in tears that the school was wrong for *making* her say the Pledge if she didn't believe in God, that she shouldn't let any school system force her to do anything, and that he would protect her no matter what. Emma, who of course wanted to bring attention to herself about as much as a mouse wants to attract the attention of a cat, pleaded with her father not to say anything to the school about it. After a lot of begging, tears, and Emma's solemn promise that she would not say the words *"under God"* in the Pledge, he relented and let the whole thing go.

Well, at least until the entire school found out about it. Then for Mr. Rodgers there was no turning back.

The same evening that it spread like wildfire through the school, Mr. Rodgers made a few phone calls to all the right people. By the crack of dawn the next day, a handwritten note rested atop Mrs. Wexley's desk explaining that Mr. Rodgers was going to personally sue her, the school, *and* the county board of education if her pupils did not stop reciting the Pledge of Allegiance immediately. And for good measure he even added to his veiled threat that he would have her served with a Cease and Desist Order if she dared defy him. As a result, that morning the Pledge of Allegiance went mute in Franklin Elementary School.

In the days to come Mrs. Wexley was flooded with complaints from almost every other parent in the school. Emma's mother was even mortified that her daughter had become a helpless pawn caught in the crossfire of a nasty divorce and something much bigger than whether she should recite two simple words each morning. Even she called the school to express her regret over her husband's irrationalism and begged Mrs. Wexley to reverse her stance. Despite the protests, Mrs. Wexley was afraid to stand up to Mr. Rodgers's threats. It appeared as though he had won the battle.

Given the commotion throughout the week, Mr. Collins accomplished very little of substance in his classroom, and the children were grateful to look forward to a long weekend ahead. Happy to be away from the controversy, Katie cheered up considerably when she remembered that Friday was "girls' night." Twice a month Grans would join Katie and her mother for dinner and then some quality bonding afterward, whether that meant watching a movie, playing a game, or just sitting on the front porch devouring some of Grans's homemade apple pie (which was, according to Katie, the best in the whole world). Unfortunately for Katie, however, this girls' night carried with it the tension from the past few weeks at Franklin Elementary School.

"'Dear Parents and Guardians.'" Katie's mother read aloud the letter that Katie had brought home from Mrs. Wexley. "'We would like to inform everyone of a recent change to our morning structure at Franklin Elementary School. In order to be respectful of everyone's wishes and to be sensitive to their religious beliefs or lack thereof,'" her mother continued, rolling her eyes at Grans, "'we have decided to replace the recitation of the Pledge of Allegiance with the playing of the Star Spangled Banner. We hope you will explain the reasoning behind our decision to your children and support our wonderful school in fostering religious tolerance and acceptance of all kinds. We thank you in advance for your support on this matter. Sincerely, Martha Wexley, BS, MA.'" The letter made no mention of Mr. Rodgers or his bitter tirade, but it didn't have to. Every single parent at Franklin Elementary, including Katie's mom, knew what this was really all about and could read between the lines.

"This is ridiculous!" Katie's mother hissed, shoving the letter on the kitchen table and pushing it away as if it carried some contagious disease.

"What, Mama?" Katie wondered.

"I'm sorry, sweetie." Katie's mother shook her head, disappointed at her outburst. "It's just such a shame to me that one man who is being nothing more than a big bully has been able to change one of the most fundamental traditions of your school. And think of poor little Emma," she added, "she probably just wants this all to go away."

Grans sipped her hot lemon tea as they all sat around the cozy kitchen table. "It was all very different back in my day."

"What do you mean?" inquired Katie.

"Well, today they do everything they can to take God *out* of the schools. But not when I was a young girl. No sirree. We wanted God *in* our schools. Not only did we recite the Pledge each morning, but we also said the Lord's Prayer. I can picture it just like it was yesterday—all twenty or so of us. Sitting quietly at our desks, hands folded, heads bowed. It was beautiful."

"And look at the schools now," Katie's mother interjected. "Why, pretty soon you will probably get kicked out of school if another classmate sneezes and you say 'God bless you!' I tell you, it's just not right."

Grans continued nursing her tea. "I'll never forget the one time when I was in second grade, Miss Nash's class. It was right after lunchtime. We were all sitting at our desks working on math problems when we got word that there had been a horrible accident."

"What was it?" asked Katie.

"Well, the high school down the road had been dismissed early that day. And one of the buses full of teenagers stalled over some railroad tracks. The bus driver tried everything, but no matter what he did the bus wouldn't start. That was when they all heard the whistle from the train blowing. The bus driver quickly began to usher the children out either end of the bus, but not all of them made it out safely before the train struck. As word filtered around our little school, all of the teachers stopped whatever lessons they were teaching, they had us all join hands, and they led us in prayer for what seemed like hours. If teachers did that today," Grans sadly admitted, "they would likely be dismissed."

"So were all of the kids okay?"

"No, Katie, I'm afraid not." Grans shook her head. "One of my best friends lost her older brother on that bus. Indeed, it was a very sad day. But you know what?" she continued, hoping to end on a positive note. "We all got through it. We had each other, and we had the Lord."

"That's exactly what I'm talking about," Katie's mother continued. "These kids today need to know that God is with them all the time, everywhere. Not just in a church on Sunday mornings." Taking a deep breath and a cue from Grans, Katie's mother rose from the table to retrieve her bubbling lasagna from the oven, along with some hot garlic bread with extra butter. "Well, you want to know something else? We are not going to let one silly man ruin our girls' night, are we? So let's say we enjoy a nice dinner and forget about this whole mess."

"Deal," contributed Grans.

"Deal!" echoed Katie.

Following Katie's traditional "Grace," the three women enjoyed a hearty dinner and spent the rest of the evening playing Scrabble before Grans bid them farewell and returned to the senior citizens' community where she had a quaint apartment only a few miles down the road. Although the discussion never returned to Mr. Rodgers or his ultimatum, Katie couldn't get it off of her mind. And that evening after her mother tucked her into bed, her wheels were spinning. All she needed was Benji on board. It might have to wait until morning, but Katie had a plan.

Katie woke bright and early the next morning as the golden sun filtered through her blinds. Her first order of business: track down her friend. She gobbled her breakfast of waffles as fast as she could, said goodbye to her mother with a kiss on the cheek as she swallowed her last gulp of orange juice, and rode her bike over to Benji's house. Almost a year had passed since that fateful day when Benji had rescued Trouble from certain doom, and during that time the pair had grown closer than ever. They spent practically all of their free time together, and Katie felt an ease around Benji that she had never experienced before. Their conversations came naturally to both of them, and no matter what Katie shared of her heart, Benji never once judged or thought less of her. Funny, for having spent so many years as the independent only child, Katie had formed such a bond with Benji that she couldn't imagine her life without him. He had almost become an extension of her. She was grateful not only for the friendship they shared but for Benji's keen ability to sense just what she needed. Benji always seemed to know the right thing to say or do, and oftentimes he didn't even need words. For Katie, it was enough simply to have Benji sitting next to her. His presence in her life made it complete. Even in times when Benji wasn't physically with her, Katie could still feel him guiding her.

Katie pedaled furiously down Magnolia Lane in her pale blue coat and striped hat, the neighborhood quiet on that winter Saturday morning from the late risers in the community stealing a few extra hours of sleep. Fortunately the bitter cold had capitulated to a much warmer weekend, and the frost-covered grass sparkled like millions of tiny diamonds in the morning sunlight. Benji's mother greeted her at the door, and when Benji appeared a few moments later it was obvious that he, like most of the rest of the community, had still been asleep. Katie wasn't fazed in the least.

"Come on," she demanded as Benji rubbed a sleeper from the corner of his eye and tried to focus on this energy ball at his door.

"Come on where?" he asked.

"Come on, we're going to our willow tree. We have *got* to talk."

"But it's so early, and it's cold out," Benji protested.

"Oh, don't be such a baby." Katie was in no mood for arguments. "It's not *that* early and it's *much* warmer than it's been all week. Just get a coat on and let's go!" A perfect salesperson, Katie was.

"All right," Benji slowly acquiesced. "Gimme a second."

Katie waited impatiently for the five minutes it took Benji to pull a pair of jeans over his pajama pants, grab a coat, and meet her around the side of the garage with his bike.

"So, are you going to tell me what this is all about?" Benji mounted his bike and tried to catch up with his friend who was already clear down the driveway.

"You already know," Katie turned and shouted over her shoulder, all without breaking stride.

Benji realized it would be futile to try to extract any more information out of his friend, so they abandoned their bikes along the edge of the woods and trekked the remainder of the way to the willow tree in silence, their steamy breaths briefly leaving puffs of smoke in their wake. By the time they reached the giant tree, Benji was pooped and clearly out of breath. He plopped down on the upturned roots to rest as he fingered the leafless branches that felt like delicate strands of uncooked spaghetti that could snap at the slightest touch.

"So," he puffed as his heartbeat finally returned to its normal rhythm, "is this about Emma Rodgers?"

"No," Katie answered matter-of-factly.

Benji was shocked. "It's not?"

"No, it's not. It's about something much more important than Emma Rodgers."

"Okay, you've got me. So then what's this all about?"

"It's about standing up for what's right. And it's about not letting someone, no matter how smart they are or how old they are, tell everyone else what they have to do. And most of all, it's about being fair to God."

The fire in her eyes and the passion in her voice boiled over.

"So," Katie continued without letting Benji get a word in edgewise, "I have an idea. That is, if you're up for it."

"Let's hear it."

It was simple enough. Yet it sent a clear message to Mr. Rodgers, Mrs. Wexley, and the entire school just how Katie and Benji felt about this new turn of events. The two friends conspired under the willow tree for over an hour until their gloved fingers were frozen and their cheeks were as red as cherries regardless of the break in temperature. When they started to lose the feeling in their toes, they decided it would be wise to head for the warmth of Katie's house, where Trouble was likely curled up in front of the fireplace, and beg some hot chocolate from Katie's mother. Their plan was complete, and they were more than ready to put it into action.

Monday, February 27th. Day One. Arrival at school. Check. Morning announcements. Check. Stand at attention to the flag. Check. Listen quietly while the anthem is played. No check. Instead, Katie and Benji took a much different approach—they jointly recited the Pledge of Allegiance. Every last word of it. And just loudly enough to be heard over the anthem so that each fourth grader in the class glanced their way. When the students reassumed their seats, Katie couldn't help but notice the faintest of smiles flicker across Mr. Collins's face. The rest of the day passed without incident.

Tuesday, February 28th. Day Two. Same game plan. Same execution. Different result. This time when Katie and Benji recited the Pledge, a handful of other students joined them. This time an emphasis was unmistakably placed on the *"under God"* portion of the Pledge. This time a few of the students who hadn't joined in giggled quietly under their breaths. And this time, Mr. Collins didn't smile.

"Katie and Benji, may I see you both for a moment?" The request came as soon as all of the students had settled into their grammar exercises. Mr. Collins motioned for the two to join him at his desk, and they immediately obeyed.

"I noticed you both have decided to recite the Pledge of Allegiance each morning."

"Yes, Mr. Collins," they replied in unison.

"You are aware of our new school policy, are you not?"

"Yes, Mr. Collins."

"Then would you mind sharing with me why you have chosen to recite the Pledge even though it's against our policy?"

Katie took the lead without even glancing Benji's way to see whether he had planned on replying. "Because it's not fair, that's why."

"What's not fair?" Mr. Collins asked.

"It's not fair that we aren't allowed to say the Pledge anymore all because Mr. Rodgers says he doesn't believe in God, and because he doesn't then Emma shouldn't, and because Emma shouldn't then we all get punished and can't say it." The words came spilling out so quickly that Mr. Collins could barely follow.

"And, well, I *do* believe in God," Katie said defiantly. "And I *do* I think I should be able to say the Pledge whenever I want, and I don't think Mr. Rodgers or anyone else should tell me I can't."

"Benji?" Mr. Collins shifted his attention to Benji, who still stood mute.

"Yeah, everything that Katie said," he piggybacked.

"All right, you two." By the expression on his face it was obvious that Mr. Collins was clearly sympathetic and even likely in agreement with Katie and Benji's plight. "I understand your point, and I actually think it happens to be a very good point. But what you need to realize is that we have certain rules at this school. And as a teacher here, I have a responsibility to follow the rules and to make sure that my students follow the rules as well. So, I will have to give you each a warning. I'll let it go this time, but if it happens again there will likely be consequences. Do you understand?"

"Yes, sir," they echoed one another.

"I hope you know that I consider you both very bright students, and I would hate to see you get into trouble."

Katie and Benji returned to their seats without so much as a word between them. Even in silence, they knew that their plan was working.

Wednesday, March 1st. Day Three. More defiance. More support. More consequence. As everyone in Mr. Collins's class stood and the anthem played, so many children joined Katie and Benji in the Pledge that their small voices managed to drown out the music. The words grew louder, and the looks of defiance from the children grew more resolute. Yet Katie and Benji, not seeking the attention but knowing they had to stand their ground, fixated on the flag with expressionless faces as if they were oblivious to the rebellion they had instigated. Fully anticipating that they would be called forward to chat with Mr. Collins again, Katie and Benji began their journey to the front of the classroom even before their teacher had summoned them. Other students peeked up from their history books, anxious to see what fate might await the two rebels.

"Katie, Benji," Mr. Collins sighed, "we had this discussion yesterday about saying the Pledge. And I shared with you both that if you continued to defy school policy, that unfortunately there would be consequences."

"Yessir," they agreed.

"And I'm very sorry to say, but this afternoon I am going to have to make phone calls home to each of your parents and explain what has been going on." Mr. Collins looked at the children hoping to get some reaction, but there was none. "Is there anything you would like to tell me before I do this?"

"No, Mr. Collins," Katie replied. Benji shook his head to confirm that he had nothing to share either.

"Very well, then please return to your seats."

That afternoon when Katie arrived home she was surprised to find her mother acting completely normal, like nothing at all had happened. She greeted Katie with a kiss as she always did, inquired about her day at school, and fixed Katie an after-school snack of sliced apples and peanut butter while Katie tackled her math homework. Dinner was just as uneventful, and as Katie cleared the table and began her evening chores of loading the dishwasher and feeding Trouble, she wondered if Mr. Collins had forgotten to call.

But that evening when Mrs. Kirby tucked her daughter into bed, the topic was finally broached. Katie's mother pulled the covers snug under her chin, then added an extra blanket since the temperatures were due to dip below freezing. "Mr. Collins called me this afternoon," her mother began.

"Oh," Katie replied, not so much as a question but more in resignation.

"And he explained to me what's been going on the last few days with you and Benji."

"Yes, Mama." Katie averted her eyes from her mother and began playing with the yellow bow on her stuffed bear which lay protectively next to her. "Am I in trouble?" she finally mustered the courage to ask.

"Katie, I want you to know something."

Oh boy, here it comes, Katie thought.

"I want you to know that I'm very proud of you."

"You are?" Katie asked incredulously.

"Yes, sweetie, I am. I am proud of you because you stood up for something you believe in. And I want you to know that I will support you completely if you decide you want to keep saying the Pledge."

"*Really?*" Katie could hardly believe what she was hearing.

"Really." Her mother smiled as she brushed her hand across Katie's cheek. "Now I want you to know that normally you need to follow the rules in school. But I think this is one exception when I have to say I think the school is in the wrong. And I believe that you and Benji have shown your dedication to God in a beautiful way."

Katie's thoughts were jarred at the mention of her friend's name. "What about Benji? Do you know if he got into trouble?"

"I had a conversation with his mother today, and I can assure you that Benji's mom feels exactly the same way I do. And just so you know, Mr. Collins thinks the world of both of you. He really didn't want to have to call me, but he had no choice. He shared with me that you have both been very respectful to him."

"Oh, I know," Katie responded. "Mr. Collins is a really nice teacher, and I know he's not trying to get us into trouble."

"All right then, my dear." Her mother smiled and gave both Trouble and Katie one last pat on the head. "It's time for you to get some rest. Goodnight, sweetie, sleep tight. And stand your ground, my love."

"I will, Mama, thank you. I love you so much." And with that, it was lights out.

Thursday, March 2nd. Day Four. A voice of solidarity. A journey down the hall. A conversation. Whether it was because of the fast approaching weekend or predictions of a major snowstorm in the forecast, the students in Mr. Collins's fourth grade class were more rambunctious than usual, which translated into their being unified for a cause. Lucky for Katie and Benji, that cause just happened to be the Pledge of Allegiance. This time when the Star Spangled Banner began, the *entire* class recited the Pledge. Loudly. Triumphantly. Even forcefully. The entire class, *including* Emma Rodgers. Mr. Collins knew it would happen eventually, and he also knew that the matter was out of his hands. Very regretfully he informed Katie and Benji that they would have to make a trip to Mrs. Wexley's office to discuss their actions further. Rather than being intimidated, the two friends were invigorated with a renewed sense of purpose after having received blessings from home and the solidarity of their classmates. They weren't the least bit afraid of Mrs. Wexley, and they were ready for whatever she was going to dish out.

The pair walked quietly down the corridor until they entered the main office. Miss Shaw, the office secretary, didn't need to inquire why they had come. "You can have a seat over there," she said as she gestured at two burgundy chairs next to the oak door with a "Principal's Office" sign affixed above the frame. Perhaps Katie should've felt trepidation, perhaps she should have been nervous, but she was none of those things. For one, she had her very best friend by her side. And for another, she knew that what she was doing was right.

A few moments later Mrs. Wexley summoned them into her office where they were joined by Ms. Bell, the school guidance counselor. Legend had it that Mrs. Wexley had been the principal at Franklin Elementary School for almost sixty years, and if you asked Katie she looked every bit of it. Seated behind her mahogany desk with numerous diplomas and certificates prominently displayed on the wall, she had pulled a chair up for Ms. Bell so that the two school administrators were facing Katie and Benji. Clearly, this was going to be an inquisition.

The first part of the conversation wasn't much of a conversation at all. It was more of a lecture in which Mrs. Wexley informed the children how, as students of this stellar elementary school that has received numerous awards for character and integrity, they were obligated to follow school policy. She then continued by explaining how they had not only disrupted Mr. Collins's class, but they had become a nuisance and a menace to other students. Ms. Bell, who couldn't have been more than twenty-two years old and fresh out of college, nodded her head in vigorous agreement to everything that Mrs. Wexley said without contributing a single original thought of her own. Katie and Benji became somewhat bored at being talked *at* for so long. That is, until Mrs. Wexley struck a nerve.

"Furthermore," she chastised the children, "if the two of you are so keen to talk about God, then you can go to church for that. School is not the place."

"Excuse me, Mrs. Wexley." Benji was the first of the two to dare speak.

"Yes, young man?"

"Do you mind if I ask you something?"

"And what might that be?" she challenged him.

"Do you go to church?"

"Well, of *course* I do," she answered as if Benji had posed an absolutely ludicrous question to which the answer was obvious.

"Didn't you learn in church that God is a part of our lives no matter where we are?"

"Well, yes," Mrs. Wexley hesitantly admitted, betraying the slightest hint that she was becoming flustered.

"Doesn't the Bible say that the Lord our God will be with us wherever we go?" Benji continued.

"Uh," Mrs. Wexley stumbled over her words.

"And doesn't Jesus promise us that he will be with us, even to the end of the age?"

"I am well aware of what the Bible says," Mrs. Wexley retorted, attempting to sound convincing although failing miserably at it. "But young man, you are blatantly disobeying school rules, and it will not be tolerated as long as I am principal here!" Mrs. Wexley cleared her throat, regrouped, and continued to fire ammunition at Benji. "Now *I* want you to tell *me* something, young man. Does God teach us to disobey those in authority?"

"Well, actually, Mrs. Wexley, God's own Son disobeyed the authorities."

Katie, who by this point was thoroughly enjoying herself, sat silently and stared at the barrage of folders messily spread out on the principal's desk. She had seen Benji in action more than once when discussing the Word of God, and she knew without a doubt that Benji could hold his own against anyone. Any kid, adult, or even principal for that matter.

"Oh, he did, did he?"

"Yes, he did. There were many times when Jesus disobeyed rules because he wanted to do what was right out of love. And he knew they were rules put in place by people who didn't care about really knowing God deep down inside. You see," Benji explained almost as if he were the one talking to a child, not vice versa, "Jesus knew that above all else he had to obey the rules of his Father in heaven, and any other rules made by man were secondary to that."

Mrs. Wexley had become flummoxed, although it wasn't entirely clear whether it was because she didn't know if Benji's comments were accurate or because she had been outwitted by a ten-year-old. In a desperate attempt to preserve her dignity, she punted the conversation over to Ms. Bell in the hopes that the rookie guidance counselor could pull a Hail Mary and save the day.

"So, Ms. Bell, what are your thoughts on the matter?"

Ms. Bell shifted uncomfortably in her seat, noticeably clueless of how to respond. Rather than entering into a theological discussion that was clearly above her head, she decided to take the safe route and stick to whatever those four years of college had taught her. Katie, for all intents and purposes, might as well have been invisible. The focus was one hundred percent on Benji.

"Benji, tell me," Ms. Bell timidly began, "has everything been all right at home recently?"

"Yes, Ms. Bell." Benji looked completely bewildered by the question.

"So you haven't been experiencing any problems?"

"No."

"Any trouble with your parents?"

"No."

"With your siblings?"

"No."

"In school?"

"No."

After a series of predictable questions by Ms. Bell followed by a series of "no's" from Benji, she finally reached the last of the tools in her box. Looking helplessly over at Mrs. Wexley, this time it was she who needed rescuing.

Although Mrs. Wexley would never admit it to herself let alone to anyone else, she subconsciously realized that her ship was sinking fast. She rose from her desk and motioned for the children to exit. "Well, I think we are done with this conversation." She announced it abruptly as if she had just achieved some glorious victory. Katie and Benji, however, remained seated, perplexed as to what the meeting had accomplished.

"Excuse me, Principal Wexley," Katie finally interjected. "So does this mean we will be allowed to say the Pledge of Allegiance?"

"What it means, young lady, is that if I hear one more word that you are disrupting Mr. Collins's class in any manner, you will have me to answer to. But what I am not privy to personally shall not be my concern any longer."

"But what does that—"

Before Katie could finish her question (which, by the way, would have been another inquiry as to what exactly Mrs. Wexley's ambiguous statement meant), Benji grabbed her by the arm and pulled her out of the office into the crowded hallway of children preparing for their afternoon art classes. And as soon as Katie saw the ear-to-ear grin plastered across Benji's face, she no longer needed clarification. Katie knew that two educated women, who between them boasted years of higher education, lots of fancy degrees, and countless awards of achievement, were no match for a ten-year-old boy.

Friday, June 9th. Day Seventy-One. Wrapping up. Looking ahead. Taking a break. The last day of school had finally arrived. Winter had lingered well into March, but it finally gave way to blooming daffodils, cherry blossoms, and the return of the robins. And just as quickly as spring came, it went. Summertime was officially here. An outdoor picnic and field day were about to commence, but not before Mrs. Wexley wished everyone a healthy and happy summer during the morning announcements. After she signed off with a cheer, each class at Franklin Elementary School dutifully listened to the Star Spangled Banner as they stared blankly at the flag. That is, each class except one. Mr. Collins's fourth grade class hadn't played the Star Spangled Banner in months. Instead, they recited the Pledge of Allegiance, in glorious harmony, with their hands proudly resting on their hearts. And they said every last word.

Mr. Rodgers may have won the battle, but Katie and Benji had won the war.

CHAPTER 4
IS THERE A DOCTOR IN THE HOUSE?

"Jesus answered, 'It is not the healthy
who need a doctor, but the sick.'"
Luke 5:31

"PAGING DOCTOR MARKS, PAGING DOCTOR MARKS, PLEASE REPORT TO RADIOLOGY. DR. MARKS, TO RADIOLOGY." The invisible voice came over the loudspeaker as Katie and her mother passed the time in the waiting room, Katie reading *The Last Battle*, C.S. Lewis's final installment in *The Chronicles of Narnia* series, and her mother flipping through a months-old *Southern Living* magazine that had been discarded on a nearby coffee table. Katie was relieved the day had finally arrived, although she couldn't wait to have it behind her.

Fifth grade had practically flown by in the blink of an eye, fortunately for Katie. Mr. Collins had been replaced with Mrs. Russo, a stern teacher who was very good at imparting wisdom but not so good at developing genuine relationships with her students. And a unified fourth grade class had turned into an overcrowded fifth grade class with what seemed like every ten-year-old in all of Bakersville except the one she cared about most. Benji. This was the first year in all of their schooling that, by the *un*-luck of the draw, they had been relegated to separate classrooms. Katie tried to hide it as best she could, but she was downright miserable without her best friend. The weekdays seemed never-ending, and she counted down until the weekends when the two could steal away some time together.

But it wasn't just Benji's absence from her class that made the fifth grade particularly difficult for Katie. She had also been sick quite a bit. Always a healthy child who more than once had a perfect attendance record at the end of a school year, Katie had been plagued by tonsillitis at least half a dozen times since school started in early

September. In fact, she had missed more days of school in this one year than she had in all of her other elementary school years combined. Of course her teachers were more than understanding about it. Katie was an exemplary student who had never earned below an A in any class. But the makeup work and after-school tutoring sessions had taken their toll on her. It seemed as though Katie's mother was making doctors' appointments every other week, and no matter what medicines they prescribed, the relief was only temporary at best. It was a vicious cycle. Katie would bounce back to her usual chipper self only to be knocked down again by another bout of the sickness. And each time the tonsillitis came back, it did so with a vengeance. Katie lost much of her appetite or any energy tucked away in reserve. Even on the weekends when she didn't have extra homework to catch up on, her enthusiasm had been so dulled that she rarely wanted to head outdoors to play. Oh, she spent just as much time with Benji as she could. She had come to love her freckled-faced friend so much that nothing would stop her from seeking his company. However, anymore their time together consisted of lying on the couch watching movies or playing Monopoly. Benji never once complained, but it was obvious that Katie was not the same spunky girl she had been the year before.

After what seemed like their hundredth trip to the pediatrician's office when Katie's mother was at wits' end, Dr. Myers finally suggested what everyone knew needed to happen.

"I think Katie should have her tonsils out."

Dr. Myers spent close to an hour explaining to Katie and her mother what the procedure entailed, how it was likely the best (and perhaps only) option to rid Katie of her chronic tonsillitis, and what the recovery process would be like. As soon as the informational session was over, Katie looked at her mother pleadingly, willing to do anything for some relief. Katie's mother didn't have to spend much time considering her options because all she wanted was her vivacious daughter back. A tonsillectomy it was.

Fast forward several weeks later through three appointments with an ENT specialist, multiple calls to insurance companies, and a parent-teacher conference with Mrs. Russo, all the loose ends had been tied up and Katie's surgery date had been scheduled. Usually a pediatric tonsillectomy was considered outpatient surgery, but Katie's ENT had detected a hint of a heart murmur in Katie. He advised Katie's mother that the best course of action would be to keep her overnight in the hospital to be on the safe side. Of course, when Katie learned that she would be having a sleepover at the hospital, she quite predictably became concerned that Trouble would be all by her lonesome. That is, until Grans promised to spend the night at Katie's house so that the two-year-old feline would have plenty of company.

By mid-April, Katie was all set. At 6:30 a.m. the Monday after Easter, Katie curled up in the waiting room chair at University Hospital, still half asleep, waiting to be called back for surgery.

About fifteen minutes later her turn had arrived.

"Kathryn Kirby?" The petite woman was dressed head-to-toe in blue surgical scrubs with a shower-cap-type thing on her head that puffed up on the sides so that only the tiniest hint of auburn hair poked through. She had the same shower-cap type things on her feet as well, and she clutched a clipboard to her waist. Katie thought the woman reminded her of a Smurf, and she couldn't help but smile.

"I'm Katie," she replied as she hopped up from her chair and her mother replaced the magazine on the coffee table.

"Hi, Katie, I'm Nurse Holly. I am going to spend the morning with you as Dr. Henderson removes your tonsils. If you need anything at all, you can ask me."

Holly was very warm and friendly, making small talk while ensuring that Katie was prepped for surgery and ready to go. She led Katie through a maze of corridors to a room with a bed and lots of beeping machines along the wall. Katie was asked a series of routine questions, dressed in a hospital gown with cartoon cats and dogs on it and the same shower-cap things that Holly wore, and her vitals were taken and recorded.

"Okay, Katie, it looks like you're all set. I'm going to let Dr. Henderson know you're ready and he will be back shortly to talk to you."

"Thanks." Katie smiled back. Holly pulled the privacy curtain, and Katie dangled her feet off the side of the hospital bed while her mother sat in the chair next to her.

Dr. Henderson arrived in no short order and rehearsed every last detail of the surgery and recovery. He was followed shortly thereafter by the anesthesiologist, whose bedside manner made both Katie and her mother feel at ease. Katie lay down on the hospital gurney while her mother held her hand, and they wheeled her around a corner into a very chilly room with glaringly bright lights. Holly was already waiting for her in the OR. She bent over to ask Katie if she was all right, and Katie gave a thumbs-up and a smile. Holly and another attendant then gently lifted Katie onto the surgical bed. The anesthesiologist placed a mask over her small face and reminded her to take several deep breaths as they had discussed. Within only moments everything became fuzzy. Katie's eyes drooped, and the hand that her mother lovingly held flopped limply to the bed. Katie was out.

Precisely at one o'clock that afternoon, Katie began to emerge from her deep slumber. She blinked her eyes, trying to focus on her surroundings while also attempting to wake her mind and recall exactly where she was.

"It's okay, sweetie, you're in the hospital. You just had your tonsils out. Everything went fine. Dr. Henderson said you did beautifully. You're a real trouper." Dr. Henderson had warned Katie's mother that Katie would likely awaken confused and disoriented, and she didn't want her daughter to panic.

"Mom." Katie tried to talk but the words wouldn't come out. Her throat burned.

"Shhhh," Katie's mother interrupted, her finger pressed against her lips. "Don't try to talk. Just rest. The nurse is going to bring you some ice cream in a little bit. That will help soothe your throat. But for now just stay quiet. Okay, sweetie?" Dr. Henderson arrived for his afternoon rounds and examined Katie.

"Good news," he informed mother and daughter. "Everything looks great. Your incisions are healing nicely, and you will be all set to go home first thing tomorrow morning."

"Thank you so much, Doctor," Katie's mother said gratefully.

"Happy to be able to help," he offered. "I'll stop by in the morning to review discharge instructions with you and a few minor restrictions for the next week."

"Restrictions?" Katie mouthed.

"Don't worry, Katie, it's nothing major. You'll have to eat soft foods for the next several days, but I have a printout for your mom showing what you can or can't eat. And look on the bright side—you can have *all* the ice cream you want!" Katie liked the thought of that.

"No rough play, no P.E. for a week, and after that you should be good as new. And best of all, no more tonsillitis."

"Yay!" Katie whispered. While Dr. Henderson shared a few final instructions with Katie's mother, Katie's head began to nod and once again she drifted off.

The next time she awoke several hours later the effects of the anesthesia had worn off. Katie was alert and feeling much more like her old self. When she did a quick scan of the room she practically jumped out of her bed with joy.

"Benji!" she croaked like a frog. "You're here!"

"Your mom brought me." Benji smiled at his friend. "I'm glad you're okay."

Katie's mother joined in the conversation. "Grans came up for a few hours to watch over you while I ran home to take care of some things, and I just happened to find this young man on our front porch step. He was wondering how you were doing. So I spoke with his mother to see if he could come visit for a while, and voila!"

Katie was thrilled beyond words. Her throat still hurt terribly, and her arm was stiff from the IV running through her veins, but she didn't care about any of that. All she cared about was seeing her friend.

"Oh, and by the way," Katie's mom began, "Grans wanted me to tell you that Trouble is doing just fine. When she arrived at our house this afternoon, she found Trouble sunning herself in the windowsill. Trouble said to tell you that she misses you, and she can't wait for you to come home tomorrow." Katie was relieved to hear that her next-best friend was safe and happy. In the two years since Trouble had joined their family, she had grown into a gorgeous tabby. Sleek and as soft as mink, Trouble's beautiful coat of rust and melon-colored stripes formed a bull's-eye pattern on her flank. Her four paws and a bib under her chin were pure white, and Katie loved how her green eyes glowed in the dark. Trouble had also learned to live up to her name very well, getting herself into some of the darndest places like the neighbor's shed, the heating vent, and the top shelf of the linen closet curled up on stored away winter blankets. She even hitched a joyride to the neighboring town one day when she hopped into the back of a delivery man's truck without his knowing. Fortunately, the man heard her meowing in the back of the truck and kindly delivered the delicate package home.

Katie's mother began to unpack a cooler filled with sustenance. "Grans brought you some chicken broth when you feel up to it. It has cooled off quite a bit, and Dr. Henderson said it would be fine to sip when you're hungry."

Although her mother chastised her not to talk too much, Katie felt compelled to fill her friend in on the morning's events. She described for Benji every last detail, including feeling very "warm and fuzzy" until everything went blank. And for as much as Katie's mother wanted her to keep quiet, she was overjoyed at finally having her daughter back. Happy and healthy.

The dinner hour quickly approached. Katie was propped up in bed by several fluffy pillows underneath, her trusted teddy bear next to her. She had a voracious appetite and she heartily ate every last drop of the smoothie, pudding, and Grans's chicken broth that had been set out for her. Meanwhile, her mother and Benji finished some turkey sandwiches that Grans had packed for them.

"Mrs. Kirby, would it be all right if I went and got a drink? Benji asked after finishing the last of his bottled water.

"Sure, Benji." She rummaged through her purse and pulled out a dollar bill and some spare change. "I think I saw a soda machine down the hall near the nurses' station."

"Great, thanks." Benji took the money and left.

After they finished eating Katie became engrossed in her *Narnia* book, intently devouring Lewis's fantasy masterpiece. Her mother, exhausted from the events of the day, leaned back in the recliner that she would use as her makeshift bed later that night and closed her eyes for what she expected to be a few seconds at most. But before she knew it, the exhaustion washed over her like a rolling wave on the seashore, and she was fast asleep.

BANG! Katie's hospital door flung wide open, striking the door jamb violently. "Does *this* young man belong to you?" Katie's mother was jarred from her sleep and bolted upright in the recliner, trying to process what had just happened, who this woman was, and why she had hold of Benji by the ear as he stood stiffly next to her.

"Excuse me?" she asked.

"I said, does this young man belong to you?"

"Uh, yes," Katie's mother answered. "He is here with us. Is there some problem?"

The woman finally released her grip on Benji. She was tall and slender, with fire-engine-red hair pulled back so severely in a bun that it looked as though she wouldn't be able to wrinkle her forehead even if she tried. Her skin, so pale, was almost translucent. The heavily applied blush on her cheeks, caked on aqua-blue eye shadow, and blood-red lipstick only made her that much more alarming, in a clown-like horror story way. She wore green scrubs with frogs sitting on lily pads. Apparently this woman was a pediatric nurse. *Interesting*, Katie's mother thought.

"Well, let me tell you something," she barked, not giving Katie's mother the opportunity to get a word in edgewise. "This young man was just caught in the psychiatric ward talking to some of the *patients*." The way the nurse said "patients" it was immediately evident that she had a certain disdain for them.

"He was?" Katie's mother asked, surprised.

"Yes, he was. And when the head nurse questioned him about who he was and what, exactly, he was doing there, he told her that he was praying with the patients." The nurse rolled her eyes in complete disbelief. "Now I *know*," the nurse continued defiantly, "that he was not praying with them."

"Benji." Katie's mother tried to get Benji's version of events, but it was no use. Nursezilla kept right on going, this time staring directly at Benji, her beady eyes aflame with self-righteousness.

"And besides all that, young man, how did you even get into the psych ward? Which by the way," she added, glancing sideways at Katie's mother, "is clear across the other end of the hospital from the pediatric ward."

Katie propped herself up further in bed, curious as to what Benji would reply.

"I just knocked on the door, and it opened."

"You knocked? You *KNOCKED*?" Her question, really more of a statement, dripped with sarcasm. "Young man, there is no way on this earth that you *knocked* on the door and it opened. First of all, that door is kept locked at all times. Furthermore, no one can gain access to that ward without a badge, and not even all of the hospital staff have clearance. The door doesn't just *open* when you knock!"

"Well, it did for me. I knocked on the door, and it opened." For Benji the answer was quite simple.

"Look, Nurse"—Katie's mother strained to read the woman's nametag—"*Joy*." She involuntarily coughed when she finally managed to read the bold letters of the nurse's last name printed on the tag, choking on the irony of it all. "Nurse Joy. I'm sure there is some explanation for all of this."

"Yes, I'll say there's an explanation. The explanation is that this hoodlum was trespassing on restricted hospital grounds." Nursezilla was so immersed in her tirade against Benji that she never once took notice of poor Katie, who *should have* been resting quietly.

"Okay, so let's *assume* that you knocked and the door magically opened as you said. Then tell me this. What, exactly, were you doing there?"

"I was visiting some of the patients."

"Visiting?"

"Yes, visiting."

"And did you *know* any of these patients?"

"Not really," Benji answered honestly.

"Then why were you visiting them?"

"Because I thought maybe they needed the company." Benji's answers to Nurse Joy's many questions were straightforward enough, but it was obvious that Nurse Joy wasn't buying any of it.

"They don't *need* visitors. Young man, in that ward there are drugs addicts, drunk drivers, and people who have been sent here because they are a threat to themselves or to others. What they need is a lot of time alone to think about what they've done!"

Katie's mother was taken aback by the utter lack of compassion in Nurse Joy's tone, especially for someone who was a pediatric nurse.

"But that's why they need visitors more than anyone else," Benji offered. "And that's why I wanted to pray with them."

"Well, I *NEVER*," Nurse Joy spat.

Katie's mom had just about enough of Nursezilla. "Nurse Joy," she began, "I want to thank you for returning Benji safely. And I also want to thank you for your concern, but my daughter had her tonsils out this morning and she is trying to rest, so I will kindly ask you to leave now." The annoyance was obvious in her mother's voice, but she had decided to take the high road rather than stoop to the nurse's level. Katie's mom rose from her recliner and motioned toward the opened door, ready to usher Nursezilla out.

Looking completely indignant, Nurse Joy turned to leave but not before getting the last word. "Ma'am," she directed her remarks to Katie's mother, "I expect you to take personal responsibility for this here child. And if I hear one more peep that he has been somewhere else in this hospital that he was not supposed to be, I will personally make sure that he is banned from the premises." And with that, the Wicked Witch of the Children's Wing rode off on her broom.

"Well," Katie's mother said to the two children with a sigh, "she was just lovely, wasn't she? A real bundle of *joy!*" Before very long they all broke down in laughter, Katie straining not to laugh too hard for fear she might rupture the incisions in her throat.

Although Katie's mother was quite curious about Benji's wanderings through University Hospital, and especially how he managed to get himself into a locked ward, she decided that it wasn't the proper time to pursue the issue so she let the matter drop.

"Well, you two, after all that excitement I could use a little bit of fresh air. Benji, can I trust you with watching over Katie for a few minutes while I step outside?"

"Sure, Mrs. Kirby."

"And will you promise me that you aren't going to take any more excursions while I'm gone?"

"Yes, Mrs. Kirby." Benji smiled.

"All right then. Benji, if you need a nurse for any reason, the station is down the hall to the left, although I would recommend trying to find someone other than Nurse Joy. And Katie also has a call button on the remote next to her bed." Her mother motioned at the device tucked next to Katie's arm that was free of the IV drip.

"I'll take good care of her, I promise."

Once Katie and Benji were alone in her hospital room, Katie immediately inquired about Benji's time visiting the psychiatric ward. There was no need to rehash the preliminary details that

Nurse Joy had divulged. You see, Benji never lied about anything. So if he said he knocked and the door opened, it did. And if he said he wanted to keep the patients company and pray with them, he did. Katie just wasn't quite sure *why*.

"Hey, Benji." Katie's voice was slowly returning to normal, but it still felt as though she were swallowing fire and had gravel in her throat. "Why did you want to go in and see those people if you didn't know any of them?"

"I don't know, I just felt like they needed the company. Maybe someone to talk to."

"You don't think they needed to be alone like the nurse said?"

"No, not at all. Actually I think that's probably what put them in the hospital in the first place."

Katie's nose crinkled. "What do you mean?"

"Well, I think most of the people in there have felt very alone for a long time. Like the people who are supposed to love them and be there for them were against them."

"Yes, but like Nurse Joy said, they have done some bad things."

"That's true about some of them," Benji agreed. "But none of us is perfect, right? We *all* make mistakes. And maybe if they knew that they really *weren't* alone and that someone cared about them, they wouldn't need to do bad things anymore."

Katie considered Benji's words thoughtfully. "So what did you pray about with them?"

"I don't know." Benji shrugged. "All kinds of things. That they would get better. That they would be happy again. That they would be strong enough to stop doing things they shouldn't do. That they would admit they made mistakes but also that they would forgive themselves for those mistakes. Stuff like that."

"Did they say anything to you?"

"Some of them did."

"What did they say?"

"They just said, 'I'm sorry.'"

"And what did you say back to them?" Katie wondered.

"I said, 'It's okay.'"

The two friends sat in silence for a while, tired from the long day but thankful to be together. With the constant humming of the hospital instruments in the background, Katie slowly lost any little bit of energy she had left.

"Hey, Benji," she said as she pulled the blankets close and curled up next to her teddy bear.

"Yeah?"

"I'm glad you're always here for me."

Benji smiled.

"I hope I never feel like those people down the hall."

"What do you mean?"

"All alone. Like no one is there for me and no one cares about me. That must be a terrible way to live. And, well, ever since I can remember you've always been there for me." Katie yawned, fighting to stay awake but losing the battle.

"Benji, will you promise me something?"

"Sure, anything."

"Promise me you will never leave me, no matter what?"

Benji's piercing eyes looked directly at Katie. "I promise you Katie. I will never leave you, and I will always be here for you. No matter what."

Katie smiled, satisfied that her friend would keep his word. "Will you lay next to me?" She shifted over on the narrow bed, leaving a sliver of space just wide enough for Benji to scoot in next to her. And before he could maneuver over the bedrail, Katie was fast asleep.

Only minutes later Katie's mother returned to her hospital room. A warm smile spread across her face at the sight she beheld. Curled up on the bed slept two precious children of God. Benji was huddled in a semi-fetal position on top of the blankets, looking a bit squished with his head half off the pillow and his feet dangling over the side of the bed. Katie lay snugly under the covers, her golden blonde hair draped angelically around her face and spilling onto her shoulders. She clutched her teddy bear with one hand. Katie's other hand was firmly grasped in Benji's.

As Benji snuggled close to Katie and they both drifted off, the young man at the opposite end of the hospital in Room 217 retrieved his cell phone from the tray next to him. His hands trembled from a combination of the detox his body was enduring and the medications coursing through his system. He hit Speed Dial #3. He waited.

"Hello?" the voice on the other end of the line answered.

"Mom, it's me."

"Jeremy?" the woman quietly asked.

"Yeah."

"Why are you . . . ? Are you still in the . . . ?" Each time his mother tried to form a sentence, the words slipped away.

"Mom, I'm sorry." It was all he could muster as he tried to contain the dam of emotions that were desperately trying to break through. Tears rolled freely down his cheeks.

"Oh, Jeremy." The woman sighed deeply, a sigh that carried the weight of the world.

"I want to change, Mom, I don't want to do this anymore."

"Jeremy, I *want* to believe you, but you've said this so many times before." She paused briefly. "And nothing ever changes."

"I know," he admitted, swallowing as the tears flowed harder. "I know, you're right. But this time it's different."

The doubt surfaced in his aching mother's voice. "What makes it different? We have been down this road with you. How is it different?"

"It just is this time, I know it." Jeremy tried to clear his head so he could adequately convey the conviction that stirred deep within his soul. "I know this is gonna sound crazy, but I met this kid today.

He came into my room, and the second he touched my hand I felt different. Like I didn't want to keep living like this and I wanted to change. Like I wanted to turn my life around."

"Kid? What kid?" She began to doubt her son's lucidity. After all, she had seen the lowest of lows from her addict son in the past, and that often meant hearing things from him that were simply too fantastical to be true by any stretch of the imagination.

"I don't know. I don't even know his name. But I promise you I'm not making this up, and I'm not hallucinating. He was here."

"How did he even get into your room?"

"I have no clue." Jeremy laughed through his tears at the absurdity of it all. "I know this sounds crazy. Believe me, *I* even think it's crazy, but I swear to you it happened. He came into my room for a few minutes and he prayed with me. And the whole time he prayed I just knew that I was better. Mom, that kid healed me."

Countless times in the past she had heard him say many of the same things about wanting to change. But this time she heard something in her son's voice that she had never heard before. She heard redemption. This time, she knew he truly meant it.

"I believe you, Jer. I believe you."

Those three simple words of affirmation were all Jeremy needed to hear. He was finally released of his bondage. The dam had burst. Jeremy was free.

"We'll beat this together," his mother assured him before they ended the call.

Jeremy took a deep, cleansing breath. He placed the phone back on the tray and put his hands behind his head while he stared at the ceiling tiles. A beautiful smile spread across his face as a few lingering tears meandered down his cheeks. It felt good to smile. It was something he hadn't done for as long as he could remember. The rainbow after the storm. And all because of some mysterious kid.

Only one question occupied Jeremy's thoughts for the rest of the night—*Who was that kid?* And only one answer came. *My savior.*

CHAPTER 5
WEEPING WILLOW

"He will wipe every tear from their eyes."
Revelation 21:4

"I'm never going to see her again."

It was the first thing she said to him when he saw her. Of course he knew right where she would be. On the overcast August afternoon, the humidity penetrating the air, his heart raced as he found her huddled against the trunk of their willow. Her knees pulled up to her chest and arms cradling her legs, she rocked back and forth and shivered even though it was pushing ninety degrees outside. Katie looked Benji dead in the eye. Without the slightest hint of emotion, she said it again.

"I'm never going to see her again." She didn't cry. She didn't even flinch. It was like she was a million miles away. She was numb.

"That's not true, Katie. You are going to see her again."

"Oh yeah, how do you know?"

"I just do."

"And what makes you so sure?"

"Because God promises us. And God always keeps his promises."

Katie searched Benji's eyes for some understanding, but at least for the time being she couldn't find what she was looking for.

"I'm sorry about your Grans." Benji knelt down and rested his hand on her shoulder. Katie gave no reply. She only continued rocking, staring off in the distance.

Her day had started out like every other carefree summer day. After breakfast with her mother and routine chores around the house, she had spent the afternoon with Benji and some of the neighborhood children running through sprinklers and crunching on popsicles. When she headed indoors for dinner, she knew as soon as she saw her mother's face that something was terribly wrong. Before her mother could say a word, the sinking feeling in Katie's stomach told her that it wasn't going to be good. And it wasn't.

The same morning that Katie and her mother enjoyed blueberry pancakes and sausage, Hilda Emory, Grans's longtime sewing companion, arrived at Grans's apartment to pick her up for their usual Thursday morning breakfast at the local coffee shop. But when Hilda knocked, no one answered. Hilda knocked again. Still no answer. Knowing that Grans was never late and never missed a breakfast date, Hilda became concerned and called 911. Two county police officers arrived within minutes. They recorded all of the pertinent information from Hilda and then summoned the owner of the apartment complex for the master key. They entered Grans's apartment, and they found her. She was lying peacefully in her bed, having died in her sleep overnight. On the adjacent nightstand was the glass of water she always brought to bed with her and her well-worn Bible earmarked to the Twenty-Third Psalm. Her slippers were positioned at the foot of the bed so she could dangle her feet over the edge and easily slip them on the next morning. Her blinds were pulled, and her bedside clock was still beeping from the 7:30 a.m. alarm set to rouse her for her breakfast with Hilda. Everything in her apartment was just as she had left it the night before. Not a thing out of place, and no sign whatsoever it had ever crossed Grans's mind that that particular night would be her last. In fact, a few hours later when the officers had managed to contact Katie's mother and she arrived at the apartment, she even found a fresh-baked apple pie still sitting on the stove to cool from the night before.

Now most of us would probably consider ourselves lucky to leave this world in such a peaceful and uneventful way. No suffering, no gut-wrenching goodbyes, no rushing to complete "bucket lists" of things left undone, no hurriedly making amends with loved ones over things left unsaid, and no fear of the unknown journey ahead. None of that. Just here in this world one day, and then the next day, eternity. Lucky indeed. And from Grans's perspective, she probably did feel lucky. But from the perspective of an eleven-year-old girl who had just seen her grandmother full of life only two days before, and who was *supposed* to see her grandmother again in two short days, it was more than she could comprehend. Katie was never given the chance to say goodbye or to tell her grandmother how much she loved her. She never had the opportunity to prepare for what was coming. She also ached from having not only lost her grandmother that day, but also in a way having lost her father all over again too. Grans was the only tangible connection Katie had ever known to a father who was taken from her when she was far too young. So Katie mourned for the loss of the bridge that Grans had so lovingly been between herself and a man she never knew.

To make matters worse, the first day of the sixth grade was right around the corner. Katie had been anxious enough about the pressures of middle school. Now she would be forced to begin a new chapter in her life while trying to wrap her head around this unfathomable loss. It was all more than she could handle.

Benji knew how much his friend was hurting. She had never once been to *their* willow tree by herself since the day they had first discovered it. It had been over two years, and it was always their special time together. But this time, Katie found solace in being alone.

"What do you think it's like?"

"What do I think what's like?" Benji replied, caught off guard by her question.

"Heaven."

"I think it's everything that God promises us it will be."

"Yeah, but what do you think it's *like*?" Benji could tell that Katie was in no mood for feel-good answers that only scratched the surface. At that very moment, she needed her friend to be brutally honest with her. And she needed her friend to go deep.

Benji took a deep breath and considered his words carefully. "I think heaven is a place more wonderful than we could ever imagine. A place where no one gets sick or gets hurt, where no one is ever sad and where there is nothing but love. People won't have to worry about getting old or dying because once they're in heaven they will be alive forever, even though they will be alive in a different way than they are on this earth. And I think that once we're in heaven God will be with us in a way that he isn't with us in this lifetime. Kind of like the way that God walked with Adam and Eve in the Garden. I think when we get to heaven God will be with us like that. So we can actually see him and hear him, maybe even touch him."

Katie looked deep into Benji's mesmerizing eyes, silently beckoning him to continue.

"I think heaven is going to be like the most beautiful place on earth times a million. With colors like rubies and diamonds and emeralds that sparkle brighter than anything we have ever seen. It will have crystal clear rivers running through it with a light so brilliant that it will make the sun look dull by comparison. And that light will be God, who will make everything so beautiful because it will all be in God's presence. I think it's one of those things that we won't ever be able to really understand until we experience it."

"So you think Grans has seen all of that?"

"Yes, I do."

"What about her? What do you think she's like? Do you think she's still old and has wrinkles? Or do you think she's young again?"

"I think that when we get to heaven we will be the same person on the inside as we were on earth, but we won't exactly be the same on the outside."

Katie crinkled her nose. Benji knew more explanation was needed.

"I think it's kind of like this. When we're born, we come into this world and have a body while we are on earth. That body is ours the whole time we're here, even though it changes in different ways as we get older. Then when we die I think God gives us a new body, a heavenly body. Same spirit inside of us, but not a body for earth but instead a body for heaven. God gives us something brand new that won't get old or broken down like our bodies do now. It's almost like during our lives on earth we are only this seed, and when we go to heaven the seed dies and becomes something so much better."

"I'm still not sure I understand," Katie confessed.

"Okay, then try thinking of it this way. Take this willow tree," Benji offered, glancing upward at the massive tree which enveloped them. "At one time this huge tree was only a seed, right?"

"Yes, probably a long time ago."

"And if I asked you right now to dig up the seed from this tree, could you?"

"Of course not," Katie quickly replied. "The seed doesn't exist anymore."

"Exactly. The seed doesn't exist. You can't dig it up and find it, because it's not there anymore. Instead it has become this beautiful tree. And think of this too. If you had the seed from this willow tree in your hand, it probably wouldn't be any bigger than an inchworm and it wouldn't look like anything special. But when that seed died and the tree sprouted, look at what it became. Think about how this one tree is so perfect and it gives shade, it's a home for birds and other creatures, and it is so much more amazing than the little seed it started out as. All that seed needed was the chance to grow into what God meant for it to be."

"So you're saying that Grans is a seed?"

"Kind of." Benji half smiled. "I'm saying that when Grans was here on earth her body was still only that seed. She was only a small part of what God meant for her to be. But when she died, that seed died with her and she grew into the beautiful creature that God intended her to be all along, just like our willow. No wrinkles or even any certain age, just a body that will always be perfect and will never get old and die."

"So if Grans looks different than she did when she was here, how will I know her when I get to heaven one day? Will I even be able to recognize her?" Katie had stopped rocking and had settled back against the tree, a calmness beginning to come over her.

"Because of what I said before. On the outside our bodies might look totally different when we are in heaven, but on the inside we will be the same. We will have the same love in heaven that we do when we're on earth. I think it's all about love."

"And why is love so important when it comes to heaven?"

"Well, for one thing the Bible tells us that love never fails. And never means never—not just in this lifetime but forever. We can always count on love to be a part of who we are. So I think that we will love the same way in heaven that we do on earth. That same love will bring you and Grans together even if you don't look exactly the same. Plus, Jesus said that one of the most important things we can do is to love one another. I don't think Jesus would've said that if he only wanted love to be something temporary in this lifetime when he knew that we would be in heaven forever. I think Jesus meant for us to love each other forever."

"So because Grans loved my dad so much," Katie continued, "when she died she got to be with him again."

"Exactly. That love reunited them with each other. It doesn't matter what they look like in heaven. They will know each other by their love. That's also why in heaven there won't be any more sadness or tears."

"What do you mean?"

"Well, I know you don't remember when your dad died because you were really little. But I'm sure your Grans was sad."

"Yeah, I know she was. Even sometimes now when she would talk about Dad she would start to cry a little bit."

"But you see, when Grans got to heaven and was with your dad again, there was no reason for her to ever be sad. She would never have that pain of having her son die, because she got to be with him again and this time it would be forever."

"Yes, but don't you think my dad was a little sad in heaven before Grans got there?"

"No, I don't think that at all."

"Why not? I mean if he still loved her he must've missed her while he was in heaven and she was still here on earth."

"I don't see it that way. For one thing, heaven is such a perfect place that I feel like we will be completely content just to be there. But besides that, I don't think heaven has time like we do."

"Huh?" Katie responded.

"I think that here on earth what seems like a really long time to us, like months or even years, doesn't feel like a long time in heaven. Actually, it might not even feel like any time at all has passed."

Katie sighed. "I'm confused again."

Benji thought for a minute about how he could better explain himself, and then it clicked. "Okay." Benji redirected his conversation along a path that he knew his friend would understand perfectly. "Remember when you read *The Lion, the Witch and the Wardrobe*?"

"Sure, that's my favorite book ever."

"And remember when Lucy was playing hide and seek with her brothers and sister and got into Narnia for the first time through the wardrobe? She spent hours there, having tea with Mr. Tumnus the faun and walking around in the woods. Right?"

"Right."

"But then what happened when she left Narnia by going back through the wardrobe into the spare room and she found her brothers and sister again?"

"Ohhhh," Katie replied, finally catching on. "She told them she was back and they shouldn't be worried. She figured they would have been looking for her because she had been gone for such a long time."

"Right, but what did *they* say?"

"They thought she was being silly, because she had only been gone for a few seconds. And the wise professor told Susan and Peter later on that Narnian time was probably different from time in our world so that Lucy wasn't making it up at all."

"So do you see what I mean?" Benji asked.

"Yes, like time in heaven isn't the same as time here. And what seems like forever here could only be a few seconds in heaven, if that."

"I think it's a very good possibility. A thousand years to us could be like a day to God. So your dad didn't have to miss Grans because in heaven it wasn't a long time at all."

Katie sponged off of her friend's ponderings. Without even realizing it, she had stopped shivering. Katie intently examined Benji, and for the briefest of moments she saw someone much different than a straggly soon-to-be-sixth grader with dirty jeans and wavy hair that had curled into ringlets from the humidity. She saw someone wise beyond his years, an old soul but even still different. She continued to stare at him as if expecting that something would reveal itself to her. Something just within her grasp yet miles away. Like those times when you're trying to think of someone's name. It's right there on the tip of your tongue but no matter how hard you focus, it still eludes you. Whatever it was, it eluded Katie. Even so, this mysterious feeling about her friend left her with a sense of unexplainable peace.

"Sometimes I don't understand you," Katie finally shared.

"What part didn't you understand?" Benji asked, prepared to revisit their conversation.

"No, not what we talked about. I understand everything you said about *that*. Sometimes though… sometimes I don't understand *you*."

"There's not much to understand." Benji smiled half-heartedly.

"You just know so much. And whenever you tell me something, I know it's true. I can't explain how I know, but I do. Like when you told me I would see Grans again one day. As soon as you said it, I knew deep down you were right. I *will* see her again one day."

As Katie continued to stare at Benji in wonder, the condensation permeated the air to the point that the gray sky could contain it no longer. Light raindrops sporadically pattered the willow, collecting on the delicate leaves until they fell to the ground like teardrops. One here, another there.

"Benji?" Katie looked over to her friend, tears welling in her blue eyes.

"Yes?"

"I know I will see her again one day, but it still hurts."

"I know it does," Benji assured her as he pulled her close to him.

"I miss her so much."

"I know you do. I know you do."

Finally, like a dormant volcano that had been awakened from a deep sleep, Katie permitted her tears to flow freely. Deep, gut-wrenching sobs erupted from her very soul. Benji hugged his friend, and he cried with her. As they huddled together under the shelter of their tree, the few droplets grew into a steady rain that carpeted the entire field. And for a brief time, Katie found comfort in knowing that creation wept with her.

Early the next morning Katie shuffled into the kitchen to find her mother sitting at the table, coffee cup in one hand and scribbling something on a pad of paper with the other.

"What's that?" Katie asked.

"Oh, it's nothing." But before her mother could put it away, Katie peered over her shoulder.

"Are you writing Grans's obituary?"

"I'm trying to," her mother sighed, "but I don't seem to be getting very far."

Katie read the few words recorded on the paper and made a sour face. "That's boring."

"Thanks a lot," her mother answered a little sarcastically.

"I'm sorry, Mama, but it is. That doesn't sound like Grans at all, it just sounds like some old woman."

"Well, sweetie, do you think you could do a better job?"

"Actually I do. We need to make it something that Grans would love. Something that will tell everyone just how special she is to us."

Katie's mother could hardly disagree with her daughter's sound logic. "You know what? You are absolutely right. Who said we have to write the same old boring things that everyone else does? I tell you what. Why don't you help me, and we can write it together."

Katie immediately scooched a kitchen chair next to her mother, smiling. "So where do we start?"

For the next few hours the mother and daughter sat side by side at the kitchen table and pored over Grans' obituary. Katie was cozy in her blue terry cloth bathrobe and slippers, her golden hair flowing down her back in a messy but striking way. As she sipped a glass of milk, her mother nursed her morning coffee. Through their efforts they went through quite a few drafts of the obituary, balled up several sheets of paper and tossed them to the floor for later disposal in the trash can, and crossed out or added to the tribute countless times. In the midst of it all, they both cried and laughed as they shared stories of the beloved woman who had touched their lives in so many different ways.

"There," Katie finally said.

Holding up the finished product, Katie's mother read aloud the fruits of their endeavors:

> On August 20th, Kay Doris (née Ellison) Kirby arrived in heaven to angels rejoicing and trumpets sounding. After she met the Lord himself she was reunited with her loving husband, Herman, and her devoted son, Michael. What a celebration it was!
>
> Affectionately known to her family as "Grans," Kay lived all her days with love and happiness. She never had a bad word to say about anyone, and she would help you any time you needed something. She baked the best apple pies in the whole world, and she could play a mean game of Scrabble. Kay enjoyed sewing, watching *I Love Lucy* reruns, and feeding her outdoor

birds. She filled her bird feeders at least three times a day and was the most popular house in town among her feathered friends. The cardinals were her favorites!

Kay leaves several people in this world who loved her very much and will continue to do so. They include Kay's sister, Dottie, her daughter-in-law, Sarah, her granddaughter, Katie, and many friends. Though they will miss her very much, they know that one day they too will be reunited with her. They are grateful for everything she taught them. Everyone who knew Kay was blessed by her. Praise God!

There will be a service on Tuesday, August 25th to celebrate her 87 years on earth and her eternity in heaven. Please come and pay tribute to Kay beginning 10 a.m. for a visitation and 11 a.m. for the service. Both events will take place at Union Bridge Church in Bakersville.

"I like it," Katie said with approval. "It's *much* better than the one you started." Katie nudged her mother lovingly.

"You know what? You're right. And you know what else?" her mother said as she stroked Katie's long hair. "Your Grans would love it. And your father would be very proud of you."

Katie's heart warmed.

"And speaking of your father, I have something for you. Stay here." Katie's mother momentarily disappeared down the hall into her bedroom. When she returned, she placed something on the kitchen table in front of Katie. It was a tiny box, no bigger than the palm of Katie's hand. Katie looked at her mother expectantly.

"Go on, open it."

Katie removed the lid and retrieved a delicate gold necklace. From the chain dangled an initial, "K," written in cursive and embellished with a single emerald and diamond.

"It's so beautiful." Katie held the necklace in front of her and admired the shimmering charm as the gemstones caught the light.

"It belonged to Grans. When you were born your father had it made special for her. The "K" represents you and Grans, since you both have the same first initial. And those are your birthstones—the diamond is yours and the emerald is hers."

Katie had never seen anything so magnificent.

"Grans wore it on special occasions. I know she would want you to have it, Katie. It belongs to you now." Katie was speechless. So many emotions were coursing through her young body that she didn't know how to process them all. The sadness of having lost one of the people she loved most in the world. The joy at being able to have some small token of remembrance. The love she felt for her mother at that moment. It was a kaleidoscope of feelings running through her mind all in one big jumble.

Katie's mother carefully unclasped the exquisite piece of jewelry and placed it around Katie's neck as she lifted her hair out of the way. The moment the charm rested on her chest she touched it, feeling a love that defied explanation.

"Thank you so much, Mama, this is the best present anyone could have ever given me. I promise I'll take good care of it."

"I know you will, sweetie, I know you will."

And in some small way, Katie felt that the connection she had with both her grandmother and her father was stronger than ever before.

In the following days Katie helped arrange every last detail of Grans's service. At first Katie's mother protested that an eleven-year-old girl shouldn't be thinking about things such as planning a funeral, but Katie insisted on being involved.

"I want it to be special for Grans," Katie announced emphatically. And her mother, grateful to have someone share the burden of what is usually an exhausting few days of preparations, gratefully accepted the help.

The morning of the funeral arrived. Katie braided her hair and pulled her flowing yellow-and-white checkered gingham sundress over her head. It was Grans's favorite dress of hers, and it was one of the many small details that was so important to Katie. They had put word out for anyone coming to the service to please wear yellow, Grans's favorite color.

"I don't want black," Katie said. She had heard that people usually wore black to funerals. "It's just so dark and dreary. No black!" The necklace that had belonged to Grans hung around Katie's neck. She looked absolutely beautiful. Within moments she heard a knock at the door, and navigating past Trouble, who was batting around a toy mouse in the hallway, she greeted Benji at the door. He looked quite dapper in his too-short khakis and a pale yellow Oxford shirt with a clip-on tie that was dotted with sunflowers among a navy blue background. His wavy hair was slicked back with some gel or other goo that made it look crunchy, obviously his mother's effort at controlling his uncontrollable hair.

"You look nice," Katie offered as she welcomed him inside.

"Thanks, so do you."

Katie had asked permission for Benji to join them for the day. His mother had planned to attend the service, but she wouldn't arrive until later and Katie needed the moral support. She had never been to a funeral before, and although the last few days of arranging details had been cathartic to Katie, she was still understandably nervous about what lay ahead. They were the first ones to arrive at Union Bridge Church, and Katie sighed noisily as they approached the old brick structure. Her mother, sensing Katie's anxiety, caught a glimpse of her from the rearview mirror as she parked the car.

"Are you okay, sweetie?"

"Yes, Mama, I'm okay."

Benji squeezed her hand in a show of support as they entered together through the sanctuary doors. Katie scanned the modest room adorned with wooden pews, burgundy carpet, and wall-length windows made of "wavy glass," as Katie called it. On the altar hung a plain wooden cross. The cross of a carpenter. But the cross kept Katie's attention only momentarily. It was the casket in the front of the church at which she couldn't help but stare. It was cream-colored with a beautiful arrangement of yellow roses draped over the closed lid, and Katie approached it without thinking. Benji began to follow, but her mother gently touched Benji's arm to halt him. "Katie needs a moment alone with her grandmother," she warmly said to Benji. And Benji understood.

Katie touched the cold metal of the casket with her fingertips and leaned over, breathing in the fragrant sweetness of the roses. Then she looked over at the framed 8x10 picture of Grans that had been taken only the year before when her church was completing their new directory. Grans looked just like Grans in the picture, smiling and full of life. And in it she wore the necklace.

Katie whispered to the picture. "Thank you for the necklace, Grans. I love it. I will always wear it and think of you. I love you. And I'll miss you." Katie swallowed hard and wiped a single tear away with the back of her hand. Taking a deep breath, she joined Benji in the last pew, finding indescribable comfort in the presence of her friend.

Before long the church filled with visitors wishing to pay their respects. Katie and Benji had volunteered to remain in the back of the sanctuary during the visitation period to ensure that everyone signed the guest register when they entered. Once each person signed in, the two friends had a very special token for each visitor. You see, Grans had loved pansies ever since she was a little girl. And what better way to honor her than to blanket the town with pansies, Katie had decided. Each person was presented with a packet of pansy seeds along with a note encouraging them to plant them and nurture them in tribute to her grandmother. Katie and Benji each carried a basket filled with packets of seeds, and they gave away every last one.

As the visitors continued to fill the church, it made Katie's heart smile to see how many people loved her Grans. After shaking hands, hugging, or being kissed by what seemed like at least a million people and hearing the typical "my how you've grown" or "aren't you so sweet?" comments, Katie turned to greet the next visitor and looked up. And up, and up, and up. There he stood, towering above everyone else in his debonair three-piece suit.

"Brother Washington?" Katie asked, completely taken by surprise.

"Yes, young lady." He nodded.

"I didn't know you knew Grans."

"I didn't know her personally, but I do know you and I do know your mother, and I wanted to pay my respects." He took Katie's small hand and cupped it in both of his massive ebony hands. "I'm very sorry for your loss."

"Thank you." It was the only thing Katie could think of to say. And once again with very few words and a wisdom that defined him, Brother Washington moved forward in the line to sign the guest book. Benji looked over to Katie and smiled.

Next in line was Grans's sister, Dottie. She immediately wrapped Katie in a huge bear hug. Katie, when pulled close to the elderly woman, detected a very distinct scent coming from her, although she wasn't exactly sure what it was. (Katie would later learn that the scent was mothballs after she described to her mother that it "smelled the way a lot of old people smell.") Dottie clearly resembled her older sister in many of their facial features, but Dottie was short and stout while Grans was very tall and lanky like Katie.

"Dear sweet Katie, how are you holding up?"

"Oh, I'm okay, Aunt Dottie," Katie replied. Even though Dottie was actually her *great*-aunt since it was her grandmother's sister, when have you ever heard of someone saying "Oh, hello, Great-Aunt So-And-So"?

"Well, I have something for you." She pulled out of her pocketbook (Katie learned that from her mother too—old people have pocketbooks, not purses) a shiny black-and-white photograph with white rims around the edges.

Benji, who had peered over Katie's shoulder to get a glimpse of the picture, was in complete awe. "Wow! That's amazing! Katie . . . it's you!"

It was Katie in the picture all right. Same long legs and pencil-thin frame. Same light hair with white streaks that fell flawlessly to her waist. Same sparkling eyes and glowing skin. Even the same tomboyish grin. If the vintage cars in the background and the graininess of the photograph itself hadn't given the secret away, you would've thought for sure the picture had been taken of Katie only yesterday. Except it wasn't Katie at all.

"That picture was taken when your grandmother was almost thirteen, so she was right around your age now," Aunt Dottie shared.

Katie incredulously stared at the picture as if she were looking straight into a mirror. She was completely captivated that this beautiful young woman was *actually* her grandmother. Katie had been told more than once that she resembled her grandmother, but Katie never really thought much of it. I mean, aren't people *supposed* to tell you that you look like one relative or another? But this was much more than Katie just *resembling* her grandmother. They could have been twins. Different generations, but the same person. It was even more than that. As far back as Katie could remember Grans always had white hair and wrinkles. The thought had never seriously occurred to Katie before that Grans herself had once been a young girl with her whole life ahead of her. Katie stared at the girl in the photograph and wondered what Grans's dreams were when she was a girl and whether she ever had a Benji in her life like Katie did.

Aunt Dottie patted Katie on the shoulders and jarred her attention back to the procession of visitors as if she were releasing Katie from some hypnotic trance. "I want you to have it, dear," she said as she tucked the picture in Katie's dress pocket. "It can be a reminder to you that your Grans isn't really gone at all. She still lives on very much right here," she gestured, lightly touching Katie's chest. "Inside of you."

The next several hours passed quicker than Katie had anticipated. The church was packed to the brim with friends and loved ones, and the service was beautiful. It was everything Katie had hoped it would be for her Grans. Several people shared loving tributes, everyone sang her favorite hymns and read her favorite scriptures, and Katie even mustered the courage to read the Twenty-Third Psalm. Best of all, the church looked like a sea of yellow buttercups. After an emotionally exhausting day, they dropped Benji off at his house and headed home to change into some comfortable clothes and unwind. Katie settled into the couch, and Trouble jumped up on her lap almost immediately, always eager for affection.

"I think we're going to call it an early night, sweetheart," Katie's mother told her, "but first there is one more thing we need to do." She pulled out a packet of pansy seeds from the various items she had brought home from the church. "I've got a small window box in the garage that I didn't use this spring. What do you say we get these little guys planted?"

"Yes, definitely." Katie smiled. "But can I keep it in my room? I'll put it right in my windowsill where it'll get lots of sunlight and I'll make sure to water it. Please?"

"I think that sounds like a great idea." And as tired as they both were, they found a renewed energy from honoring the woman they loved so much by spending the last few hours of their day creating new life.

"Grans is like this seed, you know."

"She is?" asked her mother.

"Yes, Benji told me about it. How when she died it was kind of like this tiny seed that will eventually go on to become something much more beautiful."

"You mean the flower," her mother offered.

"Yes, something like that." Katie was still processing it all. But she was beginning to find peace with the fact that although she would never see her grandmother again in this lifetime, she had a wonderful reunion to look forward to someday in paradise.

"I think Benji explained it beautifully. And I'm very glad he was there to help you through these last few days."

"Me too," Katie agreed. "I would definitely be lost without him."

"Well then," her mother smiled, "you'll just have to make sure that he's always a part of your life. Then you won't ever have to worry about being lost, will you?"

Three months later . . . Thanksgiving Day. Katie awoke that morning to the most beautiful discovery. She had almost missed it completely, but as she rushed out of her room she was practically blinded by the light penetrating her blinds. She hurriedly opened them and was greeted by the first snow of the season that had quietly blanketed God's creation overnight. It was probably no more than an inch, but everything outside from the ground to the trees to the rooftops glistened brightly in the morning sun. Winter had arrived a bit early in Bakersville.

Inside, however, Katie discovered something even better. She stopped dead in her tracks and stared at the window box in her sill. Her heart pounded with exhilaration. Poking through the soil, no more than an inch high, were half a dozen tiny green stems.

The seeds had died. The flowers would soon bloom.

Katie smiled. "Thanks, Grans."

CHAPTER 6
STICKS AND STONES

"Love your enemies and
pray for those who persecute you."
Matthew 5:44

Every middle school has one. *That* girl. It doesn't matter if you were in middle school decades ago or just yesterday. Doesn't matter if you went to an overcrowded school in the city or a sparsely populated one in the country. Doesn't matter if they called it middle school or junior high. Ever since middle schools have existed, in every school everywhere, there was always that *one* girl everybody remembers for the rest of their lives.

Maybe you didn't know her personally, you just gazed upon her from afar. Or maybe you were lucky enough to be friends with her so that you were actually graced by her presence. If you were a girl, chances are you never wanted to stand too close to her for fear there might be some comparison (which you knew, of course, there *was* no comparison—it was pointless). If, on the other hand, you were a boy, you probably couldn't get close enough. The girls wanted to *be* her, and the boys wanted to be *with* her. Even through the years as you grew older and had kids of your own who then went to middle school, you can still remember *that* girl's name. Everyone in your class can. Her name itself was almost like magic. It's been a vicious cycle since the very beginning of middle school existence. There is always *that* one girl.

You see, *she* was the one who, by some miracle of God, never had to suffer through the awkwardness of the "tween" years or the pitfalls of puberty. When most other middle school children were popping pimples and visiting dermatologists, *she* had flawlessly smooth skin. When their buck teeth were masked by a face full of metallic braces, *she* had a natural million-dollar smile. When the growth in their bodies couldn't keep up with the coordination in their minds and the clumsiness overtook them, *she* had the grace of a swan. When the girls experimented with makeup and ended up looking like Frankenstein's bride, *she* wore only a bit of gloss on her lips. And when she passed you in the hallways, she took your breath away. She was the one who would (to no one's surprise) go on in high school to become homecoming representative, prom queen, head cheerleader, or maybe all three. No matter the time or place, *that* girl has always been there to remind us just how unfair life can sometimes be for the rest of us. That freak of nature, that anomaly where all the stars aligned perfectly to form this exquisite human specimen. I'll bet you can picture her now just like it was yesterday.

Well, at Bakersville Middle School, Katie Kirby was *that* girl. By the end of the seventh grade Katie was hands down the most captivating young lady not only in her grade but also in the entire school. She had bloomed. And what a flower she had become! Her father's genes had served her well. She was tall and lean with legs that stretched on for miles. But the lanky body of her childhood years disappeared somewhere between twelve and thirteen. In its place were the beginning curves of a young woman. As Katie grew, her dirty blonde locks lightened to vanilla blonde that created an angelic glow around her face. Her blue eyes were wide and brilliant. And her cheeks betrayed the slightest hint of pink, not from any overly applied blush but rather from the natural glow that resonated inside Katie. Yes, the boys loved Katie, fresh off of their pubescent doses of testosterone. Unfortunately though, many of the girls felt very differently, and for no other reason than because of her overwhelming beauty. They were green with envy.

For a long time Katie herself was oblivious to it all. Even as the outside transformed into this rare flower, on the inside she was still the same old Katie. She spent all of her time with Benji, she was a tomboy at heart, and she loved her T-shirts, blue jeans, and flip-flops. While most middle school girls tested the boundaries of decency with their miniskirts and midriff-bearing tank tops in order to *get* attention, Katie preferred to blend into the crowd. The only problem was, Katie was just too stunning to blend. Even parents often remarked to Katie's mother that she should go into modeling or at the very least enter the local beauty pageant. But Katie would have none of it, so she ignored the superficial attention. She had no desire to be part of the "in" crowd. She shunned participating in the current social media fads that just about every other teenager had become addicted to by their middle school years. No Facebook, no Snapchat, no Twitter, no Instagram. In fact, by the time she was thirteen Katie didn't even have a cell phone. It was nothing short of scandalous! While every other tween or teen clutched cell phones in their hands like a fifth appendage, Katie preferred the old-fashioned method of communication—having an actual conversation. She was beautiful, intelligent, and *definitely* her own person.

Now in middle school, I'm sure many of us can say from personal experience that it's not easy being the ugly duckling. That gangly creature who hasn't yet come into her own and waits impatiently for that glorious moment when the outside will finally catch up with the inside. But Katie was about to find out that sometimes it can be equally hard if you are the swan. Especially if you're a swan swimming in a pond with an alligator.

Katie had managed to fly under the radar at Bakersville Middle School for more than half of her time at the school. She worked hard, volunteered for several school-wide service projects, and she never caused any of her teachers the slightest hint of trouble. Thus, while most girls at Bakersville Middle would have loved nothing more than to expose Katie's flaws to the world, they had a small problem. They couldn't *find* any flaws. But one day, that changed. Someone decided that if she couldn't find an actual flaw about Katie, then she would just have to make one up. Simple as that.

Enter Madeline Taylor, or Maddie as everyone called her, the most popular girl in the middle school only one town over. Oh, even Maddie had heard *of* Katie. That happens to be another thing about *that* girl in each middle school. They all know of each other. Word spreads when you're that perfect. When Maddie's father unexpectedly transferred jobs and the Taylor family relocated to Bakersville, Maddie soon found herself the *second* most beautiful girl in Bakersville Middle School. And Maddie was having none of that.

Within the first month of her arrival, Maddie had ingratiated herself to every student, teacher, and administrator at the school. She dripped with a sweetness that virtually no one could resist, so they flocked to her like flies to honey. Except her sweetness wasn't the natural kind at all. It was more like the antifreeze type of sweetness— deceptively alluring to unsuspecting creatures, but dangerously toxic. Yes, Maddie sucked them all right in. She batted those hazel-green eyes, tossed her thick auburn hair over her shoulder, giggled ever so slightly, and they were putty in her hands. She was the quintessential expert at manipulating people. Perhaps that trait (for better or worse) came from her father. Mr. Taylor, or more appropriately Sergeant Taylor, was a detective on the county police force who specialized in interrogations. He would spend hours locked in a stuffy room with a suspected criminal, and he wouldn't come out until he had a full confession in hand. Sergeant Taylor would do whatever it took to get that confession from his suspects— he would pretend to be their buddy, he would sympathize with them, he would paint a picture of a bright future for them if they confessed. In fact, word on the street was that Sergeant Taylor even had a heavy hand at times, but only when it was absolutely necessary. Of course some of the suspects complained about the alleged brutality, but who are you going to believe? A decorated police officer or some good-for-nothing, lying criminal? *Exactly.* For every person he interrogated, he had an uncanny ability to discern what would break them and give him what he wanted. Not coincidentally, his daughter was no different. Bakersville Middle School was Maddie Taylor's own little interrogation room.

Even though it was well into spring and the school year would soon be winding down, Maddie got involved in just about everything she could. She joined the morning announcements team, and she even volunteered to spearhead the "Ban Bullies" assembly series scheduled for the last few weeks of school. She had told Miss Teasley, the English teacher who was in charge of organizing the assembly (and in case you were wondering, yes, the very same Miss Teasley who had infamously "lent a hand" to Mr. Callahan at the communion rail one Sunday morning at St. Paul the Apostle Church) that she had once been bullied herself. Maddie vowed that after she had experienced something so horrific she would never let anyone else suffer through what she had. And dear Miss Teasley, God bless her kindhearted nature seeing the good in everyone, bought it all—hook, line, and sinker.

Katie and Benji were well aware of all the commotion when Maddie arrived at Bakersville, but at first they were largely unaffected by the hubbub. Katie had music class with Maddie, so they had officially met when Katie introduced herself and welcomed the newcomer to the school. Benji had never actually met Maddie but only passed her on occasion in the hallways. But unlike every other middle school boy at Bakersville, he never took a second look when she passed by. Benji just kept right on going. And believe you me, Maddie noticed.

Memorial Day weekend arrived to the glee of hundreds of middle schoolers for two reasons. First, it meant a long weekend. Second, it meant that the end of the school year was right around the corner. Maddie had finally assimilated herself into the school, and it appeared as though Bakersville Middle School had returned to its usual, uneventful self. Unfortunately, appearances can sometimes be deceiving.

The first time Katie noticed it was the Tuesday after the holiday weekend when she returned to school. Initially she wasn't even sure *what* she sensed so she brushed it off, thinking her mind was playing tricks on her. She didn't think of it again, and she never mentioned a word to Benji. But then it happened again. And it kept happening. They were the smallest of things. Katie would be walking the hallways of school, and out of the corner of her eye she would catch girls huddled around their lockers staring at her and whispering. In the cafeteria she felt everyone's eyes on her as she headed to her lunch table with Benji. On the afternoon bus everyone sat a bit further away from her. She would catch some of her classmates texting until Katie joined in, and they would abruptly put their phones in their pockets. And in her classes where she normally chatted with other students, there was instead an uncomfortable silence. Now mind you, Katie had gotten used to the stares and whispers of her many admirers. In fact, she got so used to *those* kinds of stares that she tuned them out altogether. But this was different. These weren't stares of awe. They were states of pity, or maybe even indignation. Whatever it was, Katie felt a tension growing inside of her.

Most of the week passed quietly, and Katie began to wonder if her feelings of being watched were simply her mind playing tricks on her. But then every last suspicion she had was confirmed when Jenna Williams, her friend from second period history class, approached her while she was retrieving homework from her locker.

"Hi, Katie," Jenna offered warmly.

"Oh, hi, Jenna, what's up?"

"Hey, listen," Jenna began. She paused more than once, and it was immediately obvious that Jenna was struggling for words. Jenna fidgeted and twirled her hair with her finger. "I'm real sorry to hear about your dad."

Katie's nose crinkled. "Umm, thanks."

"I mean, that really stinks." And before Katie could get a word in, Jenna shot down the hall joining a group of girls.

Katie was totally perplexed. She had been friends with Jenna since kindergarten, and Jenna had known for years that Katie's dad died when Katie was only two. Why would she be offering her condolences now? Something didn't add up. Katie searched for Jenna the rest of the afternoon to find out what that was all about but with no luck. It would have to wait until tomorrow. It was the only thing on Katie's mind for the rest of the day.

Katie arrived at second period early the next morning and watched as the students filed into the classroom. As soon as she saw Jenna enter she approached her.

"Hey Jenna, can I ask you something?"

"Sure," Jenna offered, looking the slightest bit nervous.

"Yesterday when we were talking at my locker, what did you mean when you said you were sorry to hear about my dad?"

Jenna stared at Katie. A deer caught in headlights. "Um, well, you know, about what *really* happened to him." The word "really" lingered on Jenna's lips.

"What *really* happened to him? What do you mean? You mean how he died? Jenna, you have known about that for years."

"No, Katie, it's okay, everyone knows now. You don't have to cover it up anymore."

"Cover *what* up?" Katie was becoming frustrated and desperate. "Jenna, what did you hear? I need you to tell me the truth."

Jenna took a deep breath and then explained to Katie every last detail of why people had been staring at her all week. As Katie listened to her friend, her heart sank. Apparently over the holiday weekend Facebook had exploded with the "true" story of what really happened to Katie's father. No, he didn't actually die in a horrible boating accident. In fact, he didn't even *die*. According to the post, Katie's father had never wanted children. When her mother became pregnant, her father was miserable. He gave her an ultimatum which she refused, and then little Katie came into the world. He tried to live with this "mistake" for as long as he could, but by the time Katie was two he just couldn't take it anymore. So he up and left. Deserted the mother and daughter. Packed his things, left a cryptic note for Katie's mother, and headed to the other side of the country where he could live the way he wanted to live, unburdened by a wife or a child. At that very moment Michael Kirby was allegedly gallivanting somewhere on the beaches, childless and carefree.

When Jenna finished explaining, Katie was completely speechless. She felt so many things all at once that she didn't know where to begin. Angry that someone would create such an ugly rumor. Sad that someone meant to hurt Katie. And somewhere deep down even a little wishful that the rumor had been true, because at least that would mean Katie's dad was alive somewhere, and she might see him again one day.

"That's ridiculous," Katie defensively told Jenna. "How could anyone believe that? Everyone knows my dad died."

"Well, we all *thought* he did," Jenna replied. "But I mean, we did hear that no body was ever recovered, so it all kind of made sense."

"Made sense? *Made sense?* This is the craziest thing I have ever heard!" Katie was furious. "Who told you this?"

"I told you," Jenna answered sheepishly, "I heard that someone posted it on Facebook. I didn't actually see the post myself, but everyone is talking about it. I'm surprised you haven't seen it by now."

"I'm not *on* Facebook," Katie shot back.

The rest of the afternoon Katie talked to no one. All she wanted to do was ball up into a little cocoon and vanish from the face of the earth. But the sadness she felt that morning at being the butt of some ludicrous rumor had turned into anger by that evening. How could anyone dare say that her father didn't love her? That he ran off to live some other life? Why, if there was one thing Katie knew without a doubt it was how much her father had loved her, and if it had been his choice he never would've left her and her dear mother widowed at such a young age. And besides that, how could her *friends*, the people she had grown up with, believe such a ridiculous story? Katie was amazed at how quickly her peers could fall prey to a juicy rumor, regardless of how far from the truth it may have been.

"Benji!" she said aloud even though she was alone in her bedroom. Did he know too? she wondered. Had he been hiding something from her all week just like the rest of the seventh grade had? There was only one way to find out. Katie called Benji straightaway and asked him to come over. When he arrived moments later, Katie was waiting for him on the front porch swing. She was determined not to let her mother find out what vicious rumors had been circulating, so this was a conversation that Katie could not afford to have anyone overhear.

"What's up?" Benji asked as he climbed the front porch steps. "You sounded kinda upset when you called."

"Benji, did you hear what people have been saying about me? Well, I guess I should say what people have been saying about my dad?"

"Your *dad*?" Benji asked. Katie could tell from his confused expression that he knew nothing about it. Katie was relieved. At least he wasn't part of it too.

Katie then proceeded to relay the entire story to Benji. How she had felt strange all week at school after the holiday, like people were looking at her or talking behind her back. How Jenna told her about the Facebook post of what had "really" happened to her dad. She didn't spare Benji any detail. And the more she shared, the angrier she became. Retelling it to her best friend was like reliving it all over again.

"How could someone say such terrible things, Benji? And *why*? I don't understand why anyone would want to make something up like that. I mean, what have I ever done?"

"I don't know, Katie, it doesn't make sense. And you're right, you never did anything to deserve it. Do you know who originally posted the story?"

"No, Jenna didn't actually see the post, she had just heard about it. And I'm not on Facebook."

"Well, you know I'm not either," replied Benji.

"So that's what we need to do. We need to find out who posted it and then—"

"And then what?" Benji interrupted.

"I don't know," Katie answered, a look of determination on her face. "I haven't figured that part out yet, but I can tell you it's not gonna be good."

"How are you going to find out who posted it if neither of us is on Facebook?"

"Because I know someone who is. And I think she'll help."

Katie wasted no time tracking down Jenna before school even started the following day. "Jenna, I need your help." At first Jenna was reluctant. She didn't want to get in the middle of anything, and she certainly didn't want to get on anyone's bad side. Whoever had originally posted the story obviously had something against Katie and wasn't afraid to resort to some pretty low blows. Jenna was afraid that if she helped Katie she too might become a target. But the pleading look in Katie's eyes convinced her otherwise. Katie had been her friend for years and had never done anything to warrant such a cruel rumor. Later that Friday afternoon Katie visited Jenna's house, where they immediately headed to Jenna's bedroom and shut the door behind them.

Like Hansel and Gretel following a trail of breadcrumbs, it took Katie and Jenna no time at all to trace the post back to its original source. One post from an eighth grader named Bobby Miller cryptically read, "well I guess u oughta know the truth since ur dad iz a cop, lol." Katie and Jenna looked at each other knowingly. "Maddie," they said simultaneously.

"Keep searching," Katie beckoned her. With only a click or two of the mouse, the two girls were reading the original post, word for word. It was from none other than Madeline Taylor. Jenna was absolutely right in everything she had told Katie the other day, but that wasn't all. At the end of the post Maddie went so far as to make it sound like she was sharing this information for Katie's benefit.

"So the next time you see Katie, instead of looking up to her like she's perfect maybe you should feel sorry for her instead. And maybe she's so quiet because she is emotionally unstable from everything her dad put her though. All I'm saying is you probably don't want to get too close to her for her sake." Katie read the words and her eyes widened like saucers. She couldn't believe that Maddie would have the gall to write the words she was reading.

"That's it," Katie said. Enough was enough.

Had it not been for the intervening weekend, this story would've probably had a much different ending. You see, Katie left Jenna's house that Friday afternoon fuming and ready for war. As Katie lay in bed she thought of all the possibilities how she could get even with Maddie. Should she make up some far-fetched rumor about her family, just like Maddie had done to Katie? Should she go straight to Maddie's parents and let her suffer the consequences? Or should she tell all of Maddie's friends what a lying, manipulative person she really was? Katie pondered all of the possibilities. And Katie wasn't just angry for herself anymore. Maddie could say anything she wanted about Katie, but to desecrate her father's memory was taking it too far. Nevertheless, the more Katie thought about her method of revenge, the more hesitant she became. You see, somewhere deep down Katie didn't really want to do *any* of those things. Katie wasn't that type of person. She didn't go around hurting people purposefully, so even Katie felt this was very out of character for her. But the second Katie's conscience started to get the better of her, she dismissed it. Maddie had crossed a line, and Katie had to teach her a lesson.

Thankfully, God always has impeccable timing even in spite of ourselves sometimes. The weekend days of respite from the rumor mill at Bakersville Middle School was just what Katie needed to clear her thoughts and regain her composure. Well, Katie needed two days without school *and* a heart-to-heart talk with Benji. Saturday morning dawned a glorious day with birds chirping and the sweetness of honeysuckle lingering in the air. They arrived at their willow tree just before noontime as the sun reached its apex in the cloudless sky. Katie proceeded to fill Benji in on the events at Jenna's house the night before.

"So, you're sure it was Maddie?"

"Yep, positive," Katie assured him.

"Why do you think she did it?"

"Who knows, and who cares?" Katie answered flippantly. "I mean, what gives her the right to make up such mean things about my dad?"

"You're right," Benji agreed. "She doesn't have the right. But have you thought about talking to Maddie to see why she said those things?"

"Talking to her?" Katie was shocked at Benji's suggestion. "Why would I talk to her? So she can make up more stuff about me?"

"Well, when two people get into a disagreement, shouldn't they first try to talk it out?"

"Benji," Katie scolded him, "Maddie and I aren't in a *disagreement*. I never did *anything* to her. She is flat-out bullying me. Funny too," Katie laughed sarcastically, "Maddie is in charge of the anti-bullying assembly and look who is being the bully! We need to do something!"

"And what exactly are you planning to do?"

It didn't escape Katie's notice that while her invitation was in the plural, his response was in the singular. Apparently Benji was not going to be a co-conspirator. Katie was on her own this time.

"I'm not sure," Katie replied. "I mean, I was thinking that since she started some rumor about my family it would only be fair to start a rumor about her family. I'm not on Facebook like she is, but I'm sure I could get something started easily enough. And heck, I would be even smarter than she was and make sure no one could trace it back to me! Or, I was thinking I could tell all of her friends just what a mean person she is and how she can't be trusted so they will all stop hanging out with her. Then she won't have *any* friends." Katie smiled, quite satisfied with herself. When she had finished her mini-rant and focused her attention on her friend, she could feel the genuine concern emanating from his eyes. "Why, what do *you* think I should do?"

Benji stared at Katie in silence.

"Benji?"

"What?"

"Didn't you hear me? I said, 'what do you think I should do?'"

"Do you want the truth?"

"Of course I want the truth."

"I think you should pray for Maddie."

"*I should do WHAT?*" She practically had the wind knocked out of her. Benji must have completely lost his mind.

"I think you should pray for her. Well, actually I think you should try talking to her first, but I also think you should pray for her."

"Why on earth should *I* pray for *her*? She's the one who made up those terrible things about *me*! If anything I'm the one who needs the prayers, not *her*!"

"Well, you're right about the fact that you need prayers. Yes, she definitely did something wrong and it hurt you a lot, so we should pray that you can get past this and somehow forgive her. But I really think that Maddie must need the prayers too."

Katie's eyes narrowed. "And why exactly do you think *she* needs our prayers?"

"Because I don't think Maddie would have done this if something weren't very wrong in her life. My father always taught me, just because someone hurts us it doesn't mean we have the right to hurt them back. Plus, we really don't know what's going on in someone's life. I mean a lot of times we *think* we do, but maybe there is something going on in Maddie's life that we don't know about. Instead, I think you should pray for her and try to get along with her as best you can. Maybe if you talked to her and told her how much she hurt you, she would understand how you feel and even be sorry for what she did. I also think you need to remember that it's not your job to get back at someone. God sees everything that happens, and God will set it all straight with Maddie in the right way and when it's the right time. We shouldn't let our anger get the best of us so that we do bad things. Instead, we should show the person who hurt us what it feels like to love someone even if they don't really deserve love at that moment."

"That's crazy," Katie replied, although not as convincingly as she would've liked.

"Is it really crazy?" Benji challenged her. "Think about it, Katie. None of us is perfect. We *all* make mistakes. And God constantly forgives us for those mistakes. So who are we to say someone else doesn't deserve to be forgiven when they do something wrong? And even more, who are we to say what someone else's punishment should be? We don't know the whole story." Benji paused. "It's not our job, Katie, that's God's job."

Katie stared at the ground. She couldn't look her friend in the eye. She was ashamed of herself.

"Katie, I really do think that for Maddie to have made up something like that about your family, she must be hurting in some way. I'm not sure how, and I definitely think that what she did to you was very wrong. But I think the best thing you can do is let her know that you forgive her and you want to get past it all. I think that will be best for both her and you. And God will take care of the rest."

Katie sat for a while without saying a word, staring at the minuscule ants wandering aimlessly over the roots of the tree. She finally spoke, barely in a whisper.

"I know you're right, Benji, but it's so hard. For one thing, I don't want all of my friends to think those things about my dad are true."

"Yeah, I know. But just as quickly as the rumor spread, we should be able to spread the truth."

"Well, for another," Katie offered, "I don't want her to hurt someone else like she hurt me. What if she keeps on making up rumors about people?"

"No, I agree, I don't think she should be able to do that either. But maybe if you talk to her and show her you will still be her friend, maybe she won't feel like she needs to spread rumors anymore. And maybe you'll even understand why she did it in the first place."

"You're right, Benji, I know you are. It's just so hard. I know it sounds terrible of me and I'm sorry, but in some ways I don't *want* to let go of it. I *want* to keep being mad at her and get back at her. It's not fair what she did. I'm not sure how to get past the way I'm feeling."

Benji put his arm around his friend. As soon as Katie felt his touch, she knew everything would be all right. "You just need to give it over to God. I know it's not easy. But God loves you so much, Katie, and he loves Maddie too. You need to trust God that he will make sure everything is okay for both of you. And if it's hard for you to let go, then you need to pray about it. Ask God to give you the strength to see Maddie for who she really is on the inside, not for some mean thing she did on the outside. Ask God to help you let go of it. All you have to do is ask."

That whole weekend Katie did exactly what Benji had suggested. She prayed. And prayed, and prayed, and prayed. She prayed when she went to bed Saturday night that God would help her forgive Maddie. She prayed in church on Sunday morning that God would help Maddie want to stop spreading rumors. She prayed when she rocked on the porch swing with Trouble that God would help her not be angry anymore. She prayed when she went to bed Sunday night that her friends would believe the truth about her father. And she prayed when she woke up on Monday morning that she would be able to talk to Maddie honestly and openly. That whole weekend and into the next school week, Katie prayed non-stop. And just like Benji had said, God answered her prayers.

The conversation with Maddie on Monday morning could have gone better, but it also could've gone much worse. Katie confronted Maddie about the Facebook post. Initially Maddie denied everything, but then when Katie explained how she traced the post back to its original source (without even mentioning Jenna, for there was no need to unnecessarily bring anyone else into it) Maddie couldn't deny it any longer.

"Yeah, so what?" That had been Maddie's initial response to Katie.

But then, when Katie dug a little deeper she struck a nerve. Katie was able to extract just enough out of Maddie that she could read between the lines.

"Your life is so perfect," Maddie sulked. "Do you know how hard it is coming to a new school with no friends and everyone compares you to some girl who's perfect?"

"Maddie, I'm definitely not perfect," Katie tried to explain, thinking back to her conversation with Benji when all she had wanted to do was seek vengeance against Maddie. "And no one was ever trying to compare us."

"What do *you* know?" Maddie replied sarcastically.

Katie could tell it was no use. Something deep inside of Maddie was eating away at her, but Maddie had built a wall and she certainly wasn't about to let Katie in. As much as Katie genuinely wanted to be friends, she knew it wasn't going to happen. Not then, anyway. Katie opted to answer Maddie's question honestly and speak her piece.

"Well, one thing I know is that your rumor really hurt me. I miss my dad a lot and to say that he left me and my mom on purpose was just mean. And I really hope you don't say things that aren't true about me or anyone else ever again. And I know that there are plenty of people at school who would like to be your friend if you gave them the chance. And no matter what you said, I want you to know that I forgive you."

Maddie remained stoic. Her expressionless face let Katie know the conversation was over. It wasn't exactly the outcome she had hoped for. Maddie never offered an apology and she never explained why she had chosen to attack Katie the way she did. Still, she admitted having made the original post. All in all, Katie was at peace. She had spoken her mind, she had forgiven Maddie for her sin, and she had moved on. Most importantly, Katie learned in the process that it can be truly freeing when you give something over to the Lord and don't try to carry it all yourself. Katie realized that whatever had prompted Maddie to do what she did, it wasn't Katie's place to judge. Benji was right, and Katie was thankful she had listened to her friend.

Yet Katie couldn't help but carry sadness in her heart for Maddie. Maddie was certainly beautiful on the outside, but there was an ugliness on the inside. Something lurking far below the surface that Maddie kept safely hidden away under lock and key. Some unspeakable secret. Katie didn't know what it was, but she knew it was a burden beyond what Maddie could bear on her own. To the rest of the world Maddie put forth this picture-perfect life. Katie wondered how long the charade would continue until, somehow, her secret was exposed. Turns out, it wouldn't take long at all.

The last day of school had finally arrived. Katie was cleaning out her locker before the morning bell rang when Jenna approached.

"What goes around comes around, huh?" Jenna said with a smirk.

Katie was completely perplexed. "What are you talking about?"

Suddenly Jenna's eyes widened. "Oh, you must not have *heard*."

"Heard what?"

"Heard about Maddie."

"What about Maddie?" asked Katie, still confused.

"It's all over social media, and it even made the front page of the morning newspapers." Jenna pulled out her cell phone, swiped the screen a few times, typed something in, and handed it to Katie. "Here, see for yourself."

Katie stared at the rectangular screen and couldn't believe her eyes. It was written in bold block letters and plastered across the front page of *The Daily Journal*, Bakersville's only newspaper: *COUNTY SHERIFF ARRESTED FOR SPOUSAL, CHILD ABUSE; CHARGES PENDING.*

Katie gasped. "Oh, no." Her heart sank. So *this* was the secret Maddie had been keeping from everyone. Just as Katie started to read the article the first morning bell rang, signaling to students they had two minutes before homeroom would begin. Jenna reached for the phone but Katie held onto it.

"Hang on, just give me one sec."

Katie hurriedly skimmed the article. The bits and pieces she read put the whole puzzle together. *"Police called to a domestic disturbance . . . 409 Sheltham Way . . . Sergeant Charles Taylor . . . fifteen years on force . . . recipient of Distinguished Service Medal . . . detective in Interrogation Unit . . . wife questioned on the scene . . . visible injuries . . . daughter suffered minor injuries . . . treated at local hospital and released . . . resisting arrest . . . suspended without pay pending departmental inquiry . . . being held in local detention center . . . formal charges to come."*

Katie felt nauseous. She returned the cell phone to Jenna.

"See," Jenna said, "I guess she got what she had coming to her, didn't she?"

The second bell rang and Katie closed her locker door. She would be late to homeroom, but she didn't care. As she mindlessly crept down the hallway with several other stragglers, she couldn't help but overhear the whispers about Maddie, and the same scene unfolded as only a few weeks before. Déjà vu. Except *this* time they weren't talking about Katie. And *this* time what they were saying was true.

Traditionally speaking, the last day of school is always a joyous day. Teachers wouldn't dream of actually *teaching* anything, but instead the time was spent cleaning out lockers and desks, collecting books, watching movies to bide the time, and sometimes enjoying a little extra fresh air during recess. Some of the classrooms even splurged for pizza parties at lunchtime. Katie couldn't enjoy any of it though. No, all she could do was think of Maddie and what she must be going through. By the end of second period Katie had looked everywhere for Maddie until she finally learned that Maddie was absent from school. The last and best day of the entire school year and Maddie couldn't bear to come. It weighed heavily on Katie, and it seemed like the school day would never end. Finally, 3:15 arrived and the buses began pulling out of the school parking lot to deliver all the middle schoolers home for their summer vacations.

"Benji, did you hear?" Katie took her usual seat next to Benji on the second row of the bus.

"Yeah, I did. It's terrible."

"I'll say. Poor Maddie, I can only imagine what she's going through right now." Neither of the two friends shared the same exuberance that permeated the rest of the bus. The paper airplanes had already begun flying about. One even shot right out an opened window so that Mr. Parker, the bus driver, was forced to give a warning to the entire bus.

"Benji we *have* to go see her." Katie's voice held an urgency Benji had never heard before.

"Okay," Benji agreed, "but do you even know if she's home?"

"Well, the paper said that she was treated and released from the hospital, so I guess that means she's home. We at least have to *try*, Benji."

The two agreed. As soon as they arrived home they would ask their mothers for permission to ride their bikes the four blocks to Maddie's house on Sheltham Way. Katie wasn't exactly sure what she would do or say once she got there, but she knew she had to go.

Benji met Katie at the end of her driveway, ready to make the trek.

"Hey, Benji," Katie began, "do you think that God made this happen to Maddie on purpose? You know, to get back at her for what she did to me?"

"No, I don't think that at all. Why do you ask?"

"Oh, I don't know. Just something Jenna said to me earlier."

Benji mounted his bike. "God wouldn't do that to Maddie. He wouldn't make something bad happen to her on purpose just to get even. I think that God is sad about Maddie just like we are. But I also think that God can take anything, no matter how bad it is, and make something good come of it. So I think that God will get Maddie through this, and in the end he'll make sure some good comes from all this, no matter how terrible it may be right now."

"I sure hope so," Katie replied.

They biked silently next to each other for the brief journey. Katie thought the whole time about what she would say when she saw Maddie, but nothing was coming to her. Her mind was completely blank. Within moments they pulled their bikes up on the sidewalk next to 409 Sheltham Way, a perfectly manicured brick colonial with an American flag dangling from the entranceway pillar. Katie sensed the irony in the whole thing as she stared at the house. It looked flawless on the outside, but inside a much different story unfolded. And although it was only a few short blocks from her house, in might as well have been a million miles away.

They both dismounted and Katie hesitantly approached the house. When Benji followed, Katie stopped him.

"Benji, it's not that I don't want you here, because *believe me* I do. I need you here. But I kinda feel like I need to talk to Maddie alone. Would that be okay?"

Benji more than understood. "Sure thing, I'll just hang out here at the curb. You know I'm right here if you need me for anything." And Katie did know.

Katie methodically approached the house and rang the doorbell, half hoping that Maddie would answer, and the other half hoping that no one would be home. Her heart pounded so hard within her chest that Katie was sure you could actually *see* it beating.

A few moments passed. Katie had just turned to check on Benji when she heard the doorknob turn.

"What are *you* doing here?" Maddie asked accusingly. Her squinting eyes were red. Her hair was pulled up in a high ponytail, and she was wearing what looked like pajamas. Her arm was in a sling.

"I came to see you," Katie answered honestly.

"Why? To give me a hard time? To rub it in? *Why* did you come?" Maddie had tried to sound sarcastic and uncaring, but she only really succeeded in sounding dejected.

Why *had* Katie come? It was a valid question, and it was one Katie wasn't even sure she knew the answer to. How would she answer Maddie if she didn't even know herself? But then, as Maddie stared coldly at Katie, and as Katie nervously glanced back at Benji, everything clicked. Every last word of what Benji had said to her that afternoon under the willow tree penetrated her mind and her soul. She felt a revelation within her. Katie suddenly knew *exactly* why she had come.

"I came to pray for you."

"What?" Maddie asked skeptically, positive that Katie was joking.

"I want to pray for you . . . if it's okay."

"And why do *you* want to pray for *me*?"

"Because I think it might help you, and because I think you need it."

Maddie stood in the doorway like a statue, completely stunned and motionless. But as she looked into Katie's caring eyes, the initial disbelief in her own eyes softened. Katie sensed the slightest bit of wall being torn down within Maddie.

"Well, no one has ever prayed for me before."

"Then I think this would be a good time," Katie offered.

Maddie shifted her weight and stumbled over her words. "What do I do?"

"You don't have to do anything. Just stand here and listen."

And with that, Katie bowed her head, folded her hands, and began. She didn't know what she was going to say ahead of time, and when the prayer was over Katie couldn't remember a single word of it. But it was the most beautiful, heartfelt prayer you could ever imagine. Katie finished, looked up to the sky, and said, "Thank you, Jesus. Amen."

"Amen," Maddie echoed quietly.

"I want you to know I'll keep praying for you." Katie left Maddie standing on her front doorstep and rejoined Benji at their bicycles. Maddie didn't say a word.

But then, just as Katie mounted her bike and they were about to depart, it happened.

"Katie?" Maddie called.

"Yes?"

"Thank you."

For the very first time, Katie saw Maddie smile. Not the fake smile of a manipulative and conniving middle schooler. No, the genuine smile of a young girl who had just been touched by God. Maddie hesitated for a second. Then she found the inner strength to say what she needed to.

" . . . And I'm sorry."

"It's okay." Katie smiled back.

And it was okay.

CHAPTER 7
TICKET TO RIDE

*"There is a time for everything, and a
season for every activity under heaven."*
Ecclesiastes 3:1

*How did it get so late so soon? It's night before it's afternoon. December is
here before it's June. My goodness how the time has flown. How did it get
so late so soon?* Ah, the ultimate question we all wish we could
answer . . . How does time pass us by so quickly? Our youthfulness
vaporizes into oblivion in the blink of an eye, swallowed by a world
of adulthood where it's impossible to turn back the hands of time.
Philosophers, sociologists, psychologists, and theologians (to name a
few) have all grappled with the question. And although they with
their fancy degrees have tried mightily to articulate the nature of the
beast, I think a very wise doctor and friend of ours put it best when
he said, *How does it get so late so soon?* Thank you, Dr. Seuss, for so
eloquently hitting the nail on the head.

For Katie, her Decembers rolled into her Junes like a snowball,
starting out no bigger than the palm of her hand but quickly growing
into a monstrous white sphere careening down a hill. And in
amongst the Decembers and Junes hid tucked away the last years of
middle school, the beginnings of high school, clubs, activities,
homecomings, youth group, summer jobs, driver's licenses, college
applications, graduation, and all of the other joys of the teenage
years. All balled up into this gigantic mass that sped out of control.
That is, until the snowball smashed at the base of the hill, Katie
blinked, and she found herself at the end of her senior year in high
school.

Katie stood bravely at the precipice, unsure of which way to go.
To turn back would bring her the comfort of her childhood years.
The love, the familiarity, and the innocence of a much simpler time.
Like a warm blanket that Katie could huddle around herself, her

yesterdays brought her that much needed sense of security to which the little girl in her still desperately clung. Yet, to venture ahead into an unknown tomorrow that awaited her was exhilarating. Scary yes, but exhilarating. To borrow once again from our beloved doctor,

Today is your day!
You're off to great places!
You're off and away!
You have brains in your head.
You have feet in your shoes.
You can steer yourself
any direction you choose.
You're on your own.
and you know what you know.
And YOU are the one
who'll decide where to go . . .
OH! THE PLACES YOU'LL GO!

The only problem was, Katie wasn't quite sure whether she wanted to proceed forward or turn back. What a dilemma!

But of course we all know there *is* no turning back. With one foot steadily in front of us, we must boldly step off that precipice of childhood into the uncharted territory of "real life," and from that point forward we take our chances. Katie had bought her ticket, and now it was time to take the ride.

And what a ride it would be. You see, Katie would, without a doubt, "*go* places" as they say. Indeed, she had a bright future just waiting to greet her on the horizon. Katie possessed not only an unparalleled physical beauty, but she had also been blessed with the brains to match. Yes, Katie was the whole package. She had always been a gifted student who worked diligently in every class, whether advanced calculus or painting and drawing. And by the beginning of her senior year she found it had paid off. Her straight A's and advanced classes caught the attention of quite a few colleges, some even Ivy League. And with high scores on her college entrance exams the likes of which Clark County High School hadn't seen in years, she was further enticed with full scholarships at more than a dozen prestigious universities. The possibilities were limitless.

After several college visits and appointments with her high school guidance counselor, Katie opted for the well-respected nearby State University. She made the decision for several reasons. For one thing, it boasted a nationally recognized pre-law program. Katie hoped eventually to continue her education in law school, so she knew this would keep her academically pointed in the right direction. But Katie chose the state school of about 20,000 undergraduates for another very important reason. His name was Benji. Katie wouldn't admit it to anyone, but she and Benji had grown so close over the almost decade since they had first met that Katie couldn't bear to be too far from his side. The university was only an hour away, and after her freshman year when she was permitted to have a car on campus she rationalized that she could visit Benji whenever she wanted. *Maybe* even make some quick trips to their willow tree. Or so she thought.

While Katie spent the summer after high school preparing herself for roommates, professors, cram sessions, and college life, Benji had decided his place was to remain in Bakersville. Now don't get the wrong idea, Benji was equally bright and could have also chosen the four-year college plan had he wanted. But during his junior year when he needed an elective and registered for Mr. Fox's carpentry class, there amongst the band saws and drill presses he discovered a passion quite different from textbooks or essay papers— woodworking. Benji loved to work with his hands, and he had a gift. He could take the most ordinary piece of wood and transform it into the most extraordinary—well, *anything*. Benji crafted furniture so breathtaking it rightfully belonged in any mansion. He whittled birds so lifelike you half expected them to take flight. His finished products were so unique that they were almost other-worldly. Following in the footsteps of his father, who was also a carpenter, Benji elected to open a small shop on the main drag through town and to take up residence in the unpretentious studio apartment above. Benji knew his choices would likely never bring him untold riches or fame, for of course one only had so much potential if they remained in Bakersville. Nonetheless, he was content to live a simple life in a small town where his hands would quite literally sustain him each day.

Faced with very different paths ahead of them in only a few short months, Katie and Benji seized every opportunity to spend that last summer together. That's one thing which hadn't changed in the least since the third grade. In fact, they spent *so* much time together that practically everyone assumed they were an item. Like when Jenna Williams prodded Katie one day during a pep rally their sophomore year. "Come on, Katie, give it to me straight," Jenna said, "you and Benji are together *all* the time. You *must* love him." Or when Maddie Taylor, whom Katie had actually become quite close with during their high school years, asked Katie why they weren't going to the prom together since it was obvious they were "meant to be." In their high school yearbook superlatives Katie and Benji were voted the "couple most likely to end up together." Even Pastor Haddock, who regularly observed the two teenagers together at worship services on Sunday mornings and youth group Wednesday evenings, asked them to portray Mary and Joseph in the Christmas play because, in his words, they "fit the part so well." It seemed as though everyone in Bakersville *wanted* to be right about Katie and Benji. And in a way, they were.

Katie did love Benji. Without question. In fact, she loved him more than she had probably ever loved anyone in her whole life. When Katie was with Benji, she knew she was loved, and she knew she was safe. There was never any pretense about their relationship—she could say whatever was on her mind and Benji would never judge. She was completely and wholly free to be herself. She shared her innermost secrets with him. He was her rock and her strength. When Grans died and she questioned the very core of her faith, Benji led her through that valley. When Katie was hurt, Benji healed her. When she was confused, he guided her. When she was angry, he soothed her. When she was distraught, he comforted her. When she was sinking, he rescued her. Benji was always patient and kind with her. In spite of all the attention Katie received, Benji never once became jealous or envied her. All he ever wanted was what was best for Katie.

So yes, Katie *did* love Benji. One could even say that she was *in love* with him. But not in the way that everyone wanted her to be in love. It wasn't a passionate kind of love that teenagers experiment with as they charge fearlessly into the world of dating. None of that "Katie and Benji sittin' in a tree," kind of nonsense. No, it wasn't that at all. The love that Katie felt for Benji was more than that. It was deeper. It was something pure and untainted and incomparable to the flirty and shallow love that most of us experience in our teenage years. This was a love from the deepest parts of her soul, a love that Katie couldn't even articulate in words. And it was a love that, were it ever taken away, she would never be the same. Benji wasn't just part of Katie's life. He was a part of *her*.

The only person who understood the true nature of their relationship was Katie's mother. Perhaps because she had introduced them all those years before, Katie's mother had watched the two develop a bond that many people never experience in an entire lifetime. Yet, she could sense her daughter's uncertainty as to what the future would hold for them.

One evening as mother and daughter rocked gently on the front porch swing, a cool July breeze provided refreshment from the typical sweltering summer day. Trouble, who had entered her lazy middle-aged years and was probably on life number six of her nine lives, sprawled out on the decking at their feet.

"So," her mother began, "next month this time we'll be unpacking your dorm room."

"Yep," Katie replied rather flatly.

"Are you excited?"

"Sure I'm excited." Katie's tone betrayed her.

"But . . .?" Her mother asked.

"But what?"

"I feel like there's some 'but,' that you're holding something back."

"I don't know," Katie answered blandly.

Katie's mother didn't want to pry, but she also knew that Katie wasn't likely to reveal her doubts. So she took the lead.

"Are you worried about what's going to happen between you and Benji when you go away to college?"

"No," Katie quickly answered. "Well . . . maybe a little."

"Sweetheart, it's totally natural to feel that way. This is going to be a big change for both of you. I mean gosh," her mother smiled, "you've spent practically every moment together since you were nine years old. It's okay to feel a bit of trepidation."

"Mama, I'm not going to see him every day." The pained expression on Katie's face made her mother's heart ache for her. "I can't even imagine that. I might not even *talk* to him every day. I just don't want to lose what we have. He's the most important thing in my life. More important than college even."

"I know, Katie," her mother reassured her. "But let me explain something to you. When you have someone special in your life, like Benji, the nature of that relationship will change over time as you change. Not necessarily how you feel about one another, but the aspects of your relationship will change."

"What do you mean?" Katie asked her mother.

"Take your father and I, for example. We first met when we were in high school, and much like you and Benji, we were inseparable. Then your dad went to college, and since he was about six hours away we saw each other only on holidays and summer break. At first it was very difficult. Back in those days we didn't have email or texting or Skype—all of those good things you have today where you can be in touch with someone in just a click. We had to mail letters to each other, and we made long-distance calls where we literally counted how many minutes we could talk because each minute cost money. But over time your father and I got used to it. And you know what? During those four years away we actually grew closer."

"Really?" Katie asked.

"Really. Even though we didn't see each other as much, we found ways to stay close. And during those times when we were together, we appreciated one another that much more. Then when your father graduated, he came home and we got married. And shortly after that we had you. Again, our relationship changed. We still loved each other in the same way, but we shared our love not only with each other but with our new daughter as well."

Katie smiled at the thought of her parents, young and in love with a baby in arms. Katie's mother grew serious. "And even now," she continued, "your father and I still have a relationship. I talk to him every day, I ask for his help in raising you, and I ask him to watch over you. It's a very different relationship since he can't answer me back the way I'd like for him to sometimes, but I still love him and I know he loves me. Now I know you and Benji don't have that romantic love like your father and I did, but in many ways love is love. So you see, Katie, as you grow older and find your path in this life, you can't expect that your relationship with Benji will be *exactly* the same as it has been. It wasn't meant to be the same. Life is continually moving forward and things are constantly changing, no matter how you feel about it. But you have a love for Benji that will endure through whatever the future may hold. And while you need to be ready for your relationship with him to change as you go to college and whatever comes after that, you don't have to be afraid of it. Those changes won't necessarily be bad, just different. And if you put your love for him above everything else, that bond will never leave you. You just need to trust in that and be willing to try to make it work."

"Oh, I will, Mama, I definitely will. He means the world to me."

"I know he does," her mother replied as she tickled Trouble's exposed belly. "And you should know by now that Benji will always be with you. Even if he isn't physically standing next to you, he will be there for you, guiding you and showing you the path to take."

"He's just so different from anyone I've ever known."

"In what way?" Katie's mother inquired.

"I'm not even sure how to explain it. He just *is*. I mean, for one thing, I feel like he knows me better than I even know myself sometimes. He knows what I'm thinking or feeling even before I tell him. It's kind of strange. And for another, he always knows exactly what I need. I feel like he's known me ever since the day I was born, even before that. He just *gets* me."

"Well," Katie's mother replied as she brushed a strand of Katie's blonde hair off her shoulder, "you should be very thankful to have someone like that in your life."

"Mama?"

"Yes, sweetie?"

"Did you ever have a Benji when you were growing up?"

"Actually, I did." She smiled. "And I felt very much the same way about him as you feel about your Benji."

"Whatever happened to him? I never hear you talk about anyone."

"Oh, my friend is still around and very much in my life. In fact, just like Benji, he has gotten me through some of the most difficult times I have experienced, like when I lost your father or Grans died. Like I told you, sweetheart, relationships change by their very nature. He is there just as much for me as he's always been."

"Cool." Katie was encouraged by the fact that her mother truly understood. *Maybe everybody had a Benji*, she thought. Or at least if they didn't, they should.

That evening Katie lay awake in bed for what must've been hours, stroking Trouble while fondly reflecting on those early years with Benji and the precious memories they'd made. She replayed the events in her head like a slideshow clicking through different scenes, each picture as vivid as the last as if each memory had happened only yesterday. Some of the memories made her laugh (dear Miss Teasley, God bless her soul), some made her cringe (her initial difficulties with Maddie) and others made her wince (finding solace in Benji's arms when Grans died). Each memory was a perfect gift that could never be altered, destroyed, or taken away from her. She wished she could bottle them all up and save them. But Katie knew that reflecting on the past and living in the past were two very different creatures. Katie couldn't live in the past, nor did she want to. And after the heart-to-heart conversation with her mother, Katie came to a realization. The time had come for her to venture forward. To take that leap of faith off the precipice and give adulthood her best shot. She was on the cusp of a whole new chapter of her life, filled with promise and potential. It was time for Katie to take that first step. She was as ready as she'd ever be.

One of the main staples of life in Bakersville had always been the county fair. Held the first week of August each year, the small town prided itself on this decades-old tradition where all of the locals could showcase their talents and enjoy one another's company. In fact, the fair had become such an integral part of its culture that you would expect the earth to stop revolving if it didn't happen. Bakersville without the county fair would be like the Fourth of July without fireworks, Valentine's Day without a heart-shaped box of chocolates, or Thanksgiving without a turkey. You get the drift. Oh, there were a couple of close calls over the years. Back in the fifties a hurricane set its sights on Clark County for that very same week, so county officials decided to end the fair a few days early. And believe me, that was tragedy enough. Then a couple of decades later during the war tensions were so high that many concerned citizens feared the fair would become a staging area for violent protests. An emergency meeting was held at which some people argued that the safest course of action would be to cancel the fair for that year. But oh no! Bakersville would not cave to political pressures! They hadn't let Mother Nature stop them, and they certainly weren't about to let a few rowdy protestors ruin it for the entire town. Thus, a compromise was reached. Extra police were posted throughout the week-long event to ensure everyone's safety, and the fair went off without a hitch. Yes, it would take nothing short of an act of God (and maybe not even that!) to stop the county fair.

Two things you could pretty much assume as a given whenever you went to the fair. First, it would inevitably be the hottest week of the entire year. You know, that brutal August heat when the humidity is so high you constantly feel moist and you can practically see the condensation hanging in the thick air. When even breathing was an effort. And second, you will see absolutely everyone in town at some point during the fair. The mothers pushing strollers of their toddler children; the teenagers moving in designated herds depending upon the clique they belong to; the twenty-somethings casually strolling through the fairgrounds, still in the hand-holding stage of their courtship; the middle-agers looking relieved to be free of children for an evening, who were by then old enough to explore the fairgrounds unsupervised; the retirees keeping watch over their young grandchildren like hawks; and the elderly individuals precariously navigating the uneven terrain with their canes or walkers, more focused on not falling than enjoying the sights. Yes, they are all there, every last one of them. The person you hadn't seen in months and happily encounter at the hot dog stand, and the person you've been purposefully avoiding whom you literally run right into even with a crowd of hundreds. Doesn't life always have a way of working like that?

Just like everyone else in Bakersville, Katie and Benji wouldn't dream of missing out on the annual custom. They too had been regulars ever since elementary school, at first with their mothers at a close but comfortable distance. Then in the middle school years they would be dropped off and collected at a designated place and time with a few dollars in their pockets for lunch and some amusement rides. And finally as high schoolers complete with the independence a vehicle brings (not actually their own vehicle but their parents') they could come and go as they pleased. But this year's fair was bittersweet for Katie, because she knew it would be their last. Oh, maybe not the last time they ever visited the fair together, for Katie had every expectation of returning to Bakersville to find Benji and picking up right where they left off. But still, it wouldn't be the same.

They paid their nominal $5 entrance fee (this was the first year they had to pay the "adult" prices as they had celebrated their eighteenth birthdays in the spring), and began their usual trek through the attractions. First to the display of mile-high tractors, combines, and other farm equipment, then to the animal stalls where they petted pigs, sheep, horses, and cows, then to the arts and crafts display, and finally to the concession stands where they treated themselves to everything from soft pretzels and French fries to cotton candy and candy apples. Whoever said the fair was supposed to be a health club? They were young, had great metabolism, and could afford to splurge.

They sat together on one of the dozens of picnic tables in the designated eating area. Katie watched as Benji intently pulled chunks of fried dough off a funnel cake and made a complete mess of himself. Powdered sugar littered his T-shirt, and when Katie tried to brush it off for him she only succeeded in smearing it into the fabric even more. Benji didn't care though. He had never been one for appearances, and his teenage years hadn't changed a thing.

"So," Benji said with a mouth full of dough, "in a couple of weeks you'll be off to college." There wasn't any sadness in Benji's voice. He was just stating a fact.

"Yep, two weeks."

"You all packed?"

"Pretty much." Katie thought of the growing pile of "college necessities" that had overtaken their extra bedroom during the summer months—comforter, towels, sheets, laundry basket, throw rug, storage containers, and much more. All of the essentials and then some. Trouble apparently even approved of the new décor and decided she would sleep amongst the supplies, usually either on the blankets or in the laundry basket. Katie found Trouble contently nestled there each morning and started to joke that the cat would become her college stowaway. Oh, how she wished. Trouble was just one more tie to home that Katie would be forced to leave behind in a few short weeks, and she couldn't bear the thought of not having her faithful friend curled up at the foot of her bed each night. Making matters even worse, Katie feared the cat would think she had been abandoned. It made her heart break all over again, just like that day years ago when she temporarily lost the tiny little fur ball of a kitten. That is, until Benji saved the day.

Katie tore a small piece of the cake from the paper plate and, quite unlike her friend, she successfully deposited it into her watering mouth without a single drop of powdered sugar finding its way to her blouse. "Benji, I want you to promise me something."

"What's that?" Benji asked as he chewed with his mouth open.

"I want you to promise me that we'll always be best friends. That no matter how often we see each other or talk to each other, we will always be as close as we are now." Katie waited somewhat impatiently until Benji pried his attention away from the diminishing treat on his plate and focused on her. "Benji, you're the best friend I've ever had. I can't even imagine what growing up would've been like without you. I hope you know that. I hope you know how much you mean to me. And I just don't want to lose what we have."

Benji sopped up the remaining powdered sugar with the one final piece of funnel cake left on the plate. "I can't promise you that, Katie."

"What?" Katie was shocked. At that moment all she had wanted was a little reassurance. You know, the *"everything will be just fine"* line, or the *"don't worry, Katie, we'll always be the best of friends"* response. But one of Benji's greatest strengths (and sometimes, like now, one of his greatest downfalls) was that he *never* lied. Never. Not when he and Principal Wexley went at it about the Pledge in the fourth grade, not when he defended himself from his visit with the psychiatric patients when Katie had her tonsils out in the fifth grade, not when he lovingly reminded Katie how vindictive she was being toward Maddie Taylor in middle school, and certainly not now. Katie could always count on her friend for complete and total honesty. The only thing is, sometimes it's not really honesty we want. We might think we do and we might even say we do, but sometimes a good ol'-fashioned little white lie is what we're looking for deep down. But with Benji those white lies never came. One time when Katie asked why he never lied he offered some excuse about being afraid of getting caught. But Katie knew it was more than that. It was almost as if Benji, by his very essence, was programmed *not* to lie. The hardwiring for it just wasn't there. Like a lie was something so foreign to him that if he even attempted it, his body would immediately reject it. Benji did more than just *tell* the truth, he *was* truth. So, the truth it would be. Katie knew immediately upon hearing his response that their conversation was about to take a sharp left turn and head in a much different direction than what she had anticipated.

"What do you mean you can't promise me we'll always be best friends? Do you plan on forgetting about me as soon as I go away to college? You know, out of sight out of mind?" Katie tried to appear nonchalant, but she never could fool Benji.

"Of course not, that's not what I mean at all. You asked me if I would promise that *we* would always be best friends. I know how I feel about you," Benji continued, "and I know that I will *always* feel about you the way I do now. But I can't promise you how you'll feel. Once you go to college and even beyond that, *you* might change how you feel about me."

"That'll never happen," Katie emphatically replied, frowning.

"I know you don't think it will, Katie, but you're going to meet a lot of new people and there will be a lot of things competing for your time and attention."

"I don't care how many people I meet or how busy I am, nothing will ever change the way I feel about you!" Katie was fully convinced of what she was saying to her friend.

"Well, I hope you're right," Benji offered as he deposited the paper plate in a trash can and tried unsuccessfully to wipe his sticky fingers on his shorts. They stood together with masses of townspeople milling around them, but as Benji's eyes penetrated deep into Katie's, they might as well have been the only two people on the planet.

"I want you to know something, Katie. *I* won't change. I am going to be the same Benji that I was yesterday, that I am right now, and I will be that same person tomorrow. I will always be here for you, Katie, just as I am today. I know that a lot of things are going to be changing in your life when you go to college, but I can promise you that *I* won't change. So as long as you want me to be a part of your life, I'll be here. And I want you to know something else. I'll be with you wherever you go. I might not be there in person, and there will probably be times when you don't even realize I'm there. But I will be."

Benji took Katie's hands in his. "So, no, I can't promise you that we'll always be best friends, because only *you* can answer that, Katie. But I can promise you that I will always *want* to be your best friend."

Katie smiled as the relief washed over her. "Well then I guess it's settled, because I *know* I will feel the same way too. So it looks like you're stuck with me!" Katie felt as though she was stating the obvious.

"Looks like it." Benji smiled back.

The pair spent the rest of the evening visiting with other friends, and they also stopped in to say hello to Brother Washington, the official hamburger flipper at the men's club concession stand. As usual, he spoke little, but he did manage to slip Benji a courtesy cheeseburger, which Benji quickly inhaled. He was, after all, a growing boy.

As darkness overtook the fairgrounds and the lights from the carnival rides created an iridescent glow over the entire area, many of the young children and older adults departed for home. At the same time, the teenagers emerged from the woodwork and multiplied like bunny rabbits until they soon overtook the entire park. Benji purchased a handful of tickets from Mr. Smith, owner of the local hardware store, and they spent the next hour riding the Ferris wheel, swirling back and forth in the giant teacups (which almost made Benji sick given all he had eaten that afternoon), and crashing carelessly into one another on the bumper cars. Katie hadn't laughed so hard in months, the anxiety of her upcoming transition the farthest thing from her mind. Just like they had managed to do so many times before and in a way that children can only do, Katie was living one hundred percent in the moment. And what a beautiful moment it was.

Mr. Parker weaved his way through the throngs of teenagers announcing on his megaphone that the fair would close for the night in fifteen minutes. The lights began to dim on several of the concessions, and the local farmers ensured their animals were bedded down for the night. Katie knew the evening was almost over, but there was one thing left that Katie and Benji *had* to do before their time at the county fair would be considered complete. It *was* a tradition, after all.

Katie grabbed Benji by the arm and led him to the "Crazy Coaster," Bakersville's version of a thrill-delivering roller coaster. Of course, on a scale of one to ten in theme park land, the Crazy Coaster would rank maybe a three. It didn't climb that high, it only had two good turns, and no self-respecting roller coaster can even think about claiming to be a five or higher unless there is at least one loop-de-loop. And well, the Crazy Coaster just wasn't that crazy. But it was fun nonetheless, and there were always a few fleeting moments when Katie would get that rush of adrenaline as it barreled down the steeply sloped tracks. They gave their last two tickets to Miss Teasley (God bless her dear soul, that woman was absolutely everywhere!), and voluntarily surrendered themselves to the captivating rush of the moment. Up and down and over and around, up again and down again, tilting this way and then that way. And then, within a few minutes at most, it was over. Quick and satisfying, but over.

They extracted themselves from the worn seats of the coaster, and Katie glanced over at Benji, still exhilarated from the ride. Even though she was a bit disheveled with her windblown hair and blouse hanging slightly off of one shoulder, Katie was beaming. She was more at peace with her life in that one single moment than ever before. Revisiting the past, she was comforted by the blessings of a wonderful life in this small town with a loving family, good friends, and the comforts of home. In the present moment she had Benji by her side, which was all she needed. And looking to the future, she had a glorious destiny just waiting to meet her. The peace she felt became a radiance that emanated from within her. Benji returned her gaze, but for the briefest of moments his smile faded ever so slightly and transformed into a look of sadness. A look that Katie didn't even notice. Why would she, after all? How could she know what he knew? That while she had just gotten off one roller coaster, she was about to get on a much larger one. Gigantic, in fact. One with hairpin turns and sharp corners that you never see coming and will change your direction in a heartbeat. One with bumps that immediately jolt you back into place. One with the highest peaks imaginable, so high you feel as though you're on top of the world. One with the lowest of valleys, so low you think you may never recover or see daylight again. And one with more loop-de-loops than any coaster Katie could ever envision in her wildest dreams, which would turn your entire world completely upside down in a flash. This was a roller coaster that once you got on and buckled in, it was nearly impossible to slow down, and there was no getting off no matter how much you may want to. *This* was the roller coaster called *LIFE,* and it was waiting for Katie to turn in her ticket and take the ride.

Part II
Benjamin

"When I was a child, I talked like a child,
I thought like a child, I reasoned like a child.
When I became a man,
I put childish ways behind me."
1 Corinthians 13:11

CHAPTER 8
THE FAST LANE

"Who of you by worrying
can add a single hour to his life?"
Matthew 6:27

"Everyone, look to your left. Now look to your right. In three years, one of you will be gone."

Katie remembered the words from her contracts professor like they were only yesterday. It had been her first day of law school. She fidgeted nervously in the spacious lecture hall and looked around among ninety-some other aspiring attorneys. For the most part everyone else looked exactly the way Katie had felt—downright petrified but trying their best to mask it. They unpacked laptops or flipped through thousand-page textbooks as if they had any clue what the hieroglyphics inside said. A few people confidently chatted with their neighbors, and a few others sat stone cold silent staring ahead at the whiteboard. Professor Forsythe entered the room at precisely 8 a.m., and an immediate hush fell over the body of fledglings. He was younger than Katie had expected, maybe in his mid-forties at most. He wore a shirt and tie with a pair of jeans, his hair slicked to the side in a feeble attempt to divert attention from his slightly receding hairline. He carried a yellow tablet, a pen, and what looked like a class roster. Katie thought he appeared harmless enough. Just another ordinary man that she might encounter on the street. Maybe law school wasn't going to be so bad after all.

But that was before he opened his mouth. Instead of the *"this is going to be a great semester"* first-day-of-class pep talk to which she was accustomed from her years of college classes, she was greeted by the harsh words that in three years, *"one of you will be gone."* A dropout. A failure. One-third of the entire class never having made it through boot camp or basic training or whatever they called it in law school. Nope. Couldn't cut it so you threw in the towel and settled for a second-rate position as a legal secretary or paralegal. Or maybe you were so ashamed at having been one of the weeds so callously discarded that you changed direction entirely and opted for a whole new vocation. *One of you will be gone.* Those were Professor Forsythe's words of welcome to his overly anxious 1L class. Lovely.

Of course, as soon as he said it his students all diligently followed instructions like baby ducklings following their mother through a dangerous intersection. Katie looked left and smiled warmly at a young African-American woman around her age with a short afro and smooth ebony skin. Her features were striking, and she smiled graciously in return. *An ally*, Katie thought. Then she looked right and met eyes with an older gentleman, perhaps in his late fifties, who was a bit disheveled but dignified in his dark-rimmed glasses and Oxford shirt with three designer pens at the ready in his pocket. The man nodded slightly and then returned focus to his laptop screen plastered with the world news. Katie looked forward and sighed. One of them. One of them wouldn't make it through the rigors of the next three years. As the words sunk in, Katie sensed her blood pressure rise and heat fill her cheeks until they flushed. She didn't wish the least bit of harm on either student sitting next to her, but it would just *have* to be one of them. She had come too far to be that *one*.

You see, after high school Katie eagerly boarded that roller coaster of life, and for four years she had one heck of a ride. She took college by storm and conquered it like the most skilled climber conquers Mount Everest—one step at a time with precision and an unyielding determination that couldn't be underestimated. True to form for Katie, she graduated college summa cum laude with all the top honors and even received the "distinguished undergraduate student" award for the entire college of arts and sciences. Not only did Katie excel academically, but she was also president of the Pre-Law Society, she volunteered once a week at a local homeless shelter, and she played intramural volleyball to keep in shape. In her graduating class of almost 5,000 students, Katie once again stood out.

Acceptance into law school was a cinch. She had taken hold of her future, and she was in the driver's seat.

But somewhere amidst the words *"one of you will be gone"* that constantly echoed in her mind and the textbooks and legal pads, Katie's confidence began to waver. She spent those first six months of law school working tirelessly to keep up with the grueling expectations of a 1L while watching in horror as some of her fellow comrades sunk helplessly into the quicksand. Apparently Professor Forsythe wasn't kidding. When second semester began in late January, ten of the ninety seats in the lecture hall were vacant. Of course, attached to each empty seat was a story of validation—one student decided to take a semester off and travel; another allegedly transferred to another school; a few others postponed law school for a few years. But everyone knew the truth—*they* were all part of that thirty-three percent doomed to fail. *They* couldn't cut it. The weeds were being pulled left and right. Survival of the fittest.

Katie awoke well before dawn that first Saturday in February. Even though it meant over an hour commute each way into the city, Katie had decided to move home for the three years of law school so she could save money and forego the headache of maintaining an apartment. At the time she also thought it would be wonderful because she and Benji could catch up on lost time from her four years away at the university. Of course they had kept in touch regularly, and in spite of Katie's initial fears, they stayed the closest of friends. But the demands of college life and the distance made it impossible for them to see each other as often as Katie would've liked. They were relegated to visiting mostly on holidays or a quick weekend here and there. With Katie living at home again for law school that would all change. Katie and Benji would be the exact same Katie and Benji they had been in the third grade, albeit all grown up. Yet even though Benji lived only a few miles down the road, in the first six months of law school she saw less of him than she had during her entire first year of college.

She crept quietly downstairs in the pitch-black house, groping for the banister to avoid missing a step. When she hit the landing she shuffled into the kitchen, flicked the switch for the light over the table, and brewed a large pot of fully leaded coffee. She then began her Saturday morning ritual of spreading books, papers, pens, highlighters, Post-it notes, and laptop on the circular table. Textbook was piled atop textbook, law dictionary, restatements, flash cards—you name it, the table was a cluttered mess. Katie wasn't quite sure how she was going to pull it off, but somehow or other she had to read six chapters, write fifteen case briefs, and successfully complete an online tutorial for electronic legal research all before her Monday morning 8 a.m. class. There just weren't enough hours in the day.

Katie worked furiously as the minutes ticked by. She barely even noticed when the sun came up, when her mother joined her in the kitchen with a kiss on top of the head, or when the aging Trouble rubbed affectionately against her legs. These were all minor distractions which she had neither the time nor the energy to acknowledge. Katie only stopped working when she needed to refill her mug with more coffee.

Just as Katie became fully engrossed in outlining *Palsgraf v. Long Island Railroad Co.*, she suddenly bolted upright as the front doorbell startled her. Half annoyed, she called several times for her mother to answer it only to realize that she was alone in the house. Glancing at the clock across the kitchen, she couldn't believe it was almost noon. Katie had been at it non-stop for more than six hours.

She stood and stretched her legs to work out the stiffness. "I'm coming," she said as she headed to the front door.

A familiar face.

"Hey, Katie."

"Hi, Benji," Katie replied, stifling a yawn.

"I just thought I'd come by to see if you want to grab some lunch with me in town."

"No thanks. I have a ton of work I've got to get done. I don't have time to go out."

"Yeah, well you have to eat, don't you?"

"I'm sorry, Benji, I just don't have time."

The disappointment was evident on Benji's face. "Well then, how about if I go pick up a pizza and bring it back. You don't have to come with me. You can stay here and keep working while I go."

CRASH!!!

Before Katie could answer they both heard an enormous explosion from the direction of the kitchen.

"Crap!" Katie rushed back into the house to find quite the disaster waiting. Apparently Trouble had decided she wanted to be a part of Katie's study routine, so she took a flying leap from the kitchen counter onto the table. The only problem was, she slid about two feet in the process and pushed everything off the table except the laptop. Papers were strewn across the floor, books were flipped over with pages bent at awkward angles, and flash cards were in complete disarray. Trouble sat atop the practically bare table like the innocent cat who had swallowed the canary.

"*Trouble!*" Katie snatched the cat and dropped her onto the floor with a thud. "Now look at what you've done! Can't you stay out of my way for five minutes anymore?" The irritation permeated her voice as she collected the jumble of papers from the floor. Benji knelt next to her and began to help. Trouble sulked out of the kitchen and headed for the stairs, eager to find safe harbor.

"Just leave everything," she abruptly told Benji. "You don't know what order they were all in. You'll just make it worse."

"Sorry," Benji replied. "I was only trying to help. And Trouble didn't mean any harm either."

Katie sensed his hurt tone, and it stopped her in her tracks. "I'm sorry, Benji, I just have so much going on right now. I don't know how I'm ever going to get it all done."

"It's okay, I get it."

Katie couldn't help but laugh. "Please don't take this the wrong way, but how could you *possibly* get it? I mean, you sit in your shop all day and whittle things out of some old wood. You can take a break whenever you feel like it and quit working for the day whenever you want. It's totally not the same." Whether she had intended to be offensive or not, she was.

"I didn't mean 'I get it' like I'm comparing my life to yours, because I'm not. I know how busy you are, Katie, and I know it's a really stressful time for you right now. I know you're under a lot of pressure. That's why I came by today. We haven't seen each other in weeks, and I figured that maybe if you took a quick break it might make you feel better. You know, get away from it all for a while and then come back refreshed and ready to go."

"Thanks for trying to help," Katie offered, "but I really can't take a break. If I do I'll get even more behind than I already am. I can't afford to have that happen. Do you have any idea how hard it is?" Katie settled back into her chair and, without even realizing it, for the first time ever she threw herself a pity party.

"I mean, they give us more reading than there are hours in the day. And if all we had to do was actually *read* the books that'd be one thing. But then we have to brief all of the cases we've read, *and* be ready to discuss them in class if we're called on—like we actually know what we're talking about."

Benji listened sympathetically as Katie let it all out. "Do you know I have this one professor for my property class who picks three students every class and grills them the whole time? You never know who he's going to call on. He walks in with his class roster, literally closes his eyes and randomly puts his pen down on the paper next to a student's name. It's like pin the tail on the student. I sit there during the entire class petrified that he's going to call on me."

"Well, I'm sure you'll do great if he calls on you. You're one of the smartest people I know."

"Yes, but it's not like that. He asks these totally off-the-wall questions trying to confuse us. Like he wants everyone to realize how smart he is and how stupid we are. A lot of the professors are like that. They act as if they're all part of some secret fraternity and we're just the lowlife pledges who have to prove ourselves worthy to be a part of it too. It's not just the professors either. At the end of last semester we had to complete this research assignment in the law library. It was kind of like a scavenger hunt where we had to answer questions by finding the proper books to use. Well, do you know that when some of the students found the right book, they would write down the answer and then either hide the book or rip out the page so no one else could answer it? How crazy is that?"

"Didn't the school do something about it?"

"They tried, but they could never prove who actually did it. Plus, all anyone talks about is having an impressive resume. Good grades aren't enough. That's one of the things I was going to work on this weekend. I am trying to write onto the school's *Law Review*."

"What's that?" Benji asked.

"It's a prestigious journal that law schools publish a couple of times a year. It has all kinds of research articles in it. The upperclassmen say that if you're on *Law Review*, you've got it made. You need a certain grade point average to be eligible, and then once a semester the editors hold a writing contest. You can submit an article, and whoever writes the best article is invited to join the *Law Review* staff. Benji, I've just *got* to get on it! If I don't I'll never get a job with one of the big firms when I graduate."

"Katie, slow down. That's almost three years from now. Why don't you focus on today instead?"

"I know it's three years away, but it'll be here before you know it and I've got to start preparing now and building up my resume."

"Is that what you want? To work for one of the big firms?"

"Well, yeah," Katie replied, rather unsure of herself. "That's what pretty much everyone in law school wants I thought."

Katie sighed and patted Trouble, who had since cautiously returned to see if it was safe to show her face again. Katie had felt horrible for scolding the feline and was thankful Trouble had decided to give her a second chance.

Benji knelt next to Katie and gently rested his hand on her knee. "Can I give you some advice?"

"I guess so."

"Just try to take it one day at a time. I know you have a lot going on. But try not to think about three years from now or even next month for that matter. Just think about what you have to do today. The rest of it, well, you need to give that part over to God, Katie. Remember that God is in control of everything, not you. God will guide you through this and show you the path to take. Don't feel like you have to do it all yourself, because you can't. Give it over to God and let him take care of it for you. And instead of constantly worrying about tomorrow and the next day and the next day, focus on today. If you're stressed then be honest with God and tell him that. Don't be anxious, but instead pray to God for exactly what you need. Thank him for getting you where you are to this point and pray to him for what you need today. God is faithful, Katie. He will give you what you need each and every day."

"What I *need* is to get on *Law Review* and to get good grades this semester and to get an internship with one of the firms in the city. That's what I *need*."

"Well, maybe you *will* need all of those things, but do you need them right now?"

"Not exactly right now, but I will need them."

"I get that, Katie, but my point is you don't need all of that today. Focus on the here and now and let tomorrow worry about itself. Remember in the Bible when the Israelites were wandering in the desert after Moses had rescued them from slavery in Egypt?"

"Yeah," Katie replied, unsure of what Benji was getting at.

"Well, God rained manna down from heaven each day to feed them."

"Okay, so?"

"So, he gave them enough only for each day. In fact, he had Moses tell them not to store up extra, and a few people who did found that the manna had gone rotten and was infested with maggots. But then the next day he rained manna down from heaven again. And the next day. And the next day."

"Benji, what's your point?" Katie asked, glancing impatiently at the clock.

"My point is that God wanted the Israelites to trust in him to provide for their needs each and every day. He wanted the Israelites to know that he was in control, and that if every day they gave over their worries to God, they would never have to fear. So Katie, if you focus on asking God for what you need today and give the rest over to him, God will make sure you have what you need. He will give you that manna to sustain you."

"So, I'm supposed to do nothing and just give it all over to God so that he can take care of me? I can quit reading and writing case briefs?" Her tone was laden with sarcasm.

"I never said that. The Israelites still had a lot of burdens when they were in the wilderness. They had to do their part to show their faithfulness, and so do you. But if you do your part by showing God how important law school is to you and you give the rest over to him, then he will reward you for your faithfulness just like he did them."

"It all sounds great, Benji," Katie half laughed, "but that's a lot easier said than done."

"I never said it would be easy, that's why you have to pray. Katie, when is the last time you prayed?"

Katie shrugged and ran her finger along the rim of her coffee mug. "I don't know. It's been a while I guess."

"Well, maybe that's where you should start. Tell God how you're feeling. I'm sure he'll be very happy to hear from you." Benji leaned over and kissed Katie tenderly on the cheek. "I'll tell you what, I'm going to run into town and pick up some sandwiches from the deli. I'll swing by and drop yours off. I won't stay so you can get your work done. You can eat when you're ready, but you're never going to get anything done on an empty stomach."

"Thanks, Benji, for everything. I needed to hear this." Katie was truly grateful. "Oh, and get me a tuna sub with—"

"—extra pickles and hot peppers." Benji finished her sentence. He knew.

As it turned out, Katie did write onto *Law Review* that winter. Not only did she manage to add another bullet point to her resume by joining the editorial staff, but she also gained something else. She met a third-year student, Griffin Harris, who was two years her senior. "Griff," nicknamed by friends, was, how should we put it? Well, he was the male version of Katie. He was handsome beyond words, with silky hair so dark it appeared black. His light blue eyes glistened like glaciers in the sunlight. He stood well over six feet tall with a chiseled physique, remnants of his days on the college swim team, and his olive skin was always tanned no matter the time of year. He wore reading glasses which gave him that brainy-yet-irresistible look. Griffin was at the top of his class, editor-in-chief of *Law Review*, and already had offers from four of the top five law firms in the city waiting for him after graduation. Katie, of course, had known *of* Griffin well before she joined the *Law Review* staff. *Everyone* knew of Griffin. But when she joined the privileged few on the journal who worked out of a small yet comfortable office on the third floor of the law school where only the brightest of the bright were granted access, she had the pleasure of actually meeting Griffin for the first time. Katie, of course, had only grown more beautiful with each passing day, and Griffin was immediately enraptured by her. Predictably, it didn't take long at all for Katie and Griffin to become, well, "Katie *and* Griffin." It was a real-life Barbie and Ken. Picture perfect, bright, and beautiful. So Katie received one very unexpected and pleasant bonus for the many hours she spent poring over her *Law Review* submission.

Also on the bright side of things, Katie's resume was growing more and more every day. Not only was she an editor on *Law Review* with grades in the top five percent of her class, but she had also started volunteering a few hours each week at a small firm down the street from the school, and by her second year of law school she began tutoring underclassmen on their writing skills. Yes, her resume was certainly expanding, but so were her obligations. Katie was being pulled in every direction, barreling forward at a thousand miles an hour. *Literally.* More than once on her commute to school Katie had been pulled over by the state police for excessive speed. She kept a collection of tickets in her glove compartment that she would pay when she had the time. And there they sat, some of them months overdue.

On the not-so-bright side, the conversation between Katie and Benji that day in her kitchen vanished from her mind not long after it had taken place. After all, how could Benji *possibly* understand all of the pressures she faced? Here he was with a simple job where he could come and go as he pleased. He didn't have to worry about research papers or final exams, and he certainly had no resume to build. It was like comparing apples to oranges. And no offense to God, but Katie was firmly in control of her destiny. If she had any hopes of succeeding as a lawyer she had to remain in the driver's seat. She couldn't afford to give any*thing* over to any*one*, especially when it came to her future.

By her third and final year of law school, Katie had fully immersed herself in the culture of the legal world—a culture very different from the simple childhood she and Benji had shared. It was a world where the single most important objective was to get ahead. The words "do unto others . . ." had no place in this culture. Nope, every man for himself. It was a world where feelings mattered little, where every argument could be counter-argued, and where every law had a loophole. It was a world of deadlines and rules, devoid of forgiveness or grace. It was a world where doing the right thing morally and doing the right thing legally could easily be polar opposites. It was a world where gray permeated the black and white. And it was also a world where the more sophisticated you were, the better. Katie had long since traded in the jeans and flip-flops she wore on her first day of law school for khakis and crisp button-down blouses with blazers.

Slowly but surely, everything about Katie was changing. Why, even her *name* changed. Not literally, of course, but it changed nonetheless. You see, law school isn't a place full of Jims, Bills, Tims, Beths, or Jennys. Oh no, those names are far too ordinary for the legal profession. Attorneys must be extraordinary! So the men were either "the third" or "the fourth" to proudly showcase their esteemed lineage. Or, if they couldn't use family history to elevate their stature, instead they insisted on using their middle name, usually a family name, and their ordinary first name hid behind an initial. So Jim became James E. Wallingford, IV, Bill became William T. Marshall, III, and Tim became T. Crandall Evans. Of course, their female counterparts were equally deserving of acclaim. So Beth transformed into Elizabeth A. Banks, and Jenny was no more, instead replaced by Jennifer V. Richmond.

During the fall of her second year, Katie learned that her first article would be published in the *Law Review*. She was ecstatic! All of her hard work had paid off, and her name would finally be in print. But what name would it be? When the production editor asked Katie how she would like her name to appear on the byline, Katie considered her options carefully. She decided she needed every last edge in this new legal world to which she was so quickly assimilating. So from that day forward, Katie was no longer Katie. She was Kathryn. Of course Katie hadn't been called Kathryn in she couldn't remember how long. Usually only when her mother was annoyed with her (which was rare) or if she was filling out some type of official document. But it just *looked* better on paper, and it *sounded* better. It sounded more lawyerly, so that was that. It all happened so subtly that Katie never saw it coming. But at some point during those three years of law school, Katie, the little girl from Magnolia Lane, disintegrated like the Phoenix unto the ashes. Out of those ashes arose Kathryn Ann Kirby. Though in theory they were the same person, Kathryn hardly resembled her predecessor at all.

When it comes right down to it, what's in a name anyway? We name our children sight unseen. As we get older we adopt nicknames that sometimes bear absolutely *no* resemblance whatsoever to our given names (whoever came up with "Peggy" from "Margaret" anyway?). Does our name actually have any real significance in the grand scheme of things? Benji was about to find out.

Kathryn methodically weaved through the throngs of people, a controlled chaos of proud families trying to find their newly minted attorneys-at-law in the courtyard among a sea of black robes and purple sashes. She greeted her friend Alicia, the African-American woman who sat next to her that very first day of class, and she pushed past a few other graduates who were already celebrating with their loved ones. The ceremony had lasted well over two hours in the stuffy auditorium, so now everyone, eager for some fresh air, milled about rather aimlessly hoping to be reunited with their graduate among the almost 300 others who all looked identical. Kathryn excused herself more than once after bumping into various people and almost ran over a toddler barreling unsupervised through the crowd when she spotted the two of them.

"Mom!" Kathryn shouted as she waved her diploma overhead trying to get their attention. "Over here!"

I think it's a proven fact that once you are a mother and someone calls out "mom," you automatically look for the rest of your life. No matter where you are, no matter how old you are or your child is, and no matter how many other moms are around, you look. It's instinct. So as soon as Kathryn called out, at least a half dozen women looked her way. Fortunately for her, so did her mother. Kathryn ran over, wrapped her arms around her mother, and presented her with the honors diploma safely tucked under her arm.

"I did it!" Kathryn exclaimed with a mixture of pride and relief.

"Yes, you did, sweetheart. Was there ever any doubt?"

"Of course not." Kathryn looked at Benji and smiled. If her mother only knew all of the worry and tears that had gone into this one piece of paper. Oh, there was *plenty* of doubt along the way, but that was Kathryn's secret to keep. All she knew was that Professor Forsythe might have been right on that first day of law school, but *she* wasn't part of that one-third. *She* had made it.

Benji was just about to congratulate her when out of nowhere someone came from behind and wrapped Kathryn in a huge bear hug, literally sweeping her off of her feet and swirling her around before depositing her in the exact spot where she had been standing. Kathryn giggled like a school girl and threw her arms around him in utter joy.

"You did it, babe! I'm so proud of you."

Kathryn beamed while lost in his sea of blue eyes.

"Oh, I'm sorry," Kathryn pardoned herself, "I don't think you've met yet. Griffin, this is my good friend Benjamin; Benjamin, Griffin."

"Nice to meet you," Benji offered as he extended his hand. The two men shook and exchanged pleasantries. Even in that brief moment the contrast between them was striking. Griffin, who for the last two years had been a rising associate at the upscale firm of Doyle, Bendermann, Richards & Schwartz, filled out his navy pinstriped suit flawlessly. His hair was perfectly slicked back, and despite the unusually high temperatures for early June and the fact that everyone else was fanning themselves with their graduation programs, he didn't appear the least bit uncomfortable. Yes, Griffin looked like he had been born in a suit and tie. Benji, despite a valiant effort, still couldn't manage to tuck his shirt in completely and his tie was crooked. Griffin stood a good six inches taller than Benji, and for that matter even Kathryn, in her four-inch heels, was taller than her friend. In many ways Benji was hardly noticeable.

"Nice to see you again, Mrs. Kirby." Griffin took her hand.

"Nice to see you too, Griffin." Kathryn's mother smiled approvingly.

Griffin wrapped his arm around Kathryn and addressed her mother and Benji. "The *Law Review* is holding a small reception in a few minutes for all of the graduates and alumni who were on the journal. We'd love to have you join us if you can. It's nothing fancy, just some hors d'oeuvres and champagne. A bit of a victory celebration."

"That's very kind of you," Kathryn's mother offered, "but as soon as we take a few pictures I'll be heading home. You both enjoy your afternoon together!"

"Benjamin?" Griffin shifted his focus. "You are more than welcome to come."

Benji was struck by Griffin's genuineness. "Thanks very much for asking, but I think I'll head back home as well."

The four chatted for a while longer while taking plenty of pictures to memorialize the occasion before Kathryn and Griffin departed for the reception. A few hours later, while Kathryn was on her third shrimp cocktail and nursing her second glass of champagne, she received a text from Benji.

Stop by workshop on your way home if u have time. Have something for u.

Kathryn was intrigued, but it would have to wait. First she had celebrating to do.

It was well after 10:30 p.m. when Kathryn drove down Main Street in Bakersville. The *Law Review* reception had lasted much longer than anticipated, and time had gotten away from her. For a Saturday evening the town was desolate. The neon sign of Guido's Pizzeria and the sole traffic light in the center of town flashing yellow due to the late hour cast an unnatural glow on the row of miscellaneous stores closed for the night. Kathryn laughed to herself. She had left the city only an hour ago, where at 9:30 couples were just starting to venture out to dinner, and clubs were welcoming their first few patrons. Yet here she was in good ol' Bakersville, a town that hadn't changed a bit since as far back as she could remember, where by 9 p.m. on a weekend everything was locked up tight and the occasional bat fluttering overhead was the only sign of life.

Kathryn glanced at the storefront of Benji's shop, a two-story brick building at least a century old with a faded green wooden door revealing flecks of various colors underneath where the chips of green paint had peeled away over the years. An oversized bay window with a handwritten sign propped in the sill read "CLOSED" in red letters. Unlike the other shops in town, Benji didn't even have a storefront sign designating what kind of shop it was. Next door on the corner was "Francine's Florist," and several doors down was "The Early Bird Bakery." In between that were a bank, a small real estate business, and a deli. But Benji's shop sat among the catchy titles completely barren—signless. He didn't need one. Everyone in town knew of Benji's skilled craftsmanship. Word of mouth was good enough, and somehow or other his customers managed to find their way through that old green door. The first floor was completely dark, but Kathryn was relieved when she glanced up and noticed the light on in the second-floor studio apartment. Benji was still awake. She parked along the empty street next to a meter and rang the bell. Benji buzzed her upstairs only seconds later.

"I thought you'd forgotten about me," Benji said as he retrieved two cans from the fridge.

"I'm sorry. The reception went on longer than I expected, and I lost track of time."

Benji handed Kathryn a soda. "The place looks nice," she said as she glanced around at the sparse furnishings. A pull-out couch in the center of the large room was accompanied by an end table, a coffee table, and a single bookshelf along the wall with the two windows overlooking Main Street. The glow of the flashing yellow street light pulsated through the sheer curtains. On the far side of the room a microwave, Bunsen burner, and a small fridge were Benji's version of a kitchen. His lifestyle was meager to say the least.

"Thanks. It's not much, but it's home. And my commute to work isn't half bad either," he chuckled. "Listen, I know it's late and you're probably tired, but I got you a little something as a graduation gift. Well, actually, I made you something."

Kathryn looked at him curiously. "What is it?"

"It's nothing much really. It's just something I figured you'd need. Come with me." Benji led his friend down the stairs into the dark workshop. He turned on the iridescent overhead lights which revealed a large object in the corner of the room with a sheet draped over the top.

"What is it?" Kathryn asked again.

"Go see for yourself."

Kathryn walked over to the mysterious object and carefully removed the sheet. She gasped. It was a large desk, unlike anything she had ever seen. She ran her hand along the rich mahogany desktop, so flawless and smooth, tracing the grain of the wood with her fingertips. She then felt the pattern that Benji had meticulously carved along the edges of the desktop. "They're willow tree leaves," Benji explained. The drawers each had a polished bronze knob and the legs of the desk had been carved to look like tree roots winding upwards. It was breathtaking.

"I can't believe you did this for me." Kathryn was speechless.

"It's no big deal. I figured now that you're a big city lawyer you're going to need a desk and, well, I had a little extra time between projects."

"How long did it take you to make this?"

"I don't know, not that long. And I know you don't have anywhere to put it right now, so it'll be fine here in the shop until you start your job at the firm. You can come get it whenever you're ready."

Kathryn wrapped her arms tightly around Benji, astounded at the amount of effort and love he had put into creating her gift. "This is one of the nicest things anyone has ever done for me. Thank you so much." Kathryn started toward the entranceway, ready to head home after a wonderful yet exhausting day.

"Hey, one more thing before you go."

"Sure."

"Today at graduation, when you introduced me to your boyfriend."

"Griffin?"

"Yes. Well, you introduced me as Benjamin."

"I know," Kathryn answered.

"How come? No one ever calls me that."

Kathryn thought for a minute about how to explain it in a way that he would understand. "Well, no offense, but Benji just sounds so . . . so *childish*. And we're not kids anymore. I haven't been Katie for a couple of years now. Everyone at school and at the firm calls me Kathryn. It's so much more mature and, I don't know, worldly. And if I'm going to expect people to respect me as an attorney I can't have a little girl's name like Katie."

"Okay, I get that, you want to be called Kathryn. But why me? Why Benjamin?"

Kathryn tried to articulate her feelings as delicately as she could. "Well, I've grown up, and maybe it's time that you should too. I mean, you've got this great business here, and you have such a talent for carpentry that you could easily make a fortune. But with a name like Benji do you really think people are going to take you seriously? Benjamin sounds so much more professional. And who knows? You might even get more business."

"But Katie—I'm sorry, *Kathryn*—I'm not interested in being a part of *that* world. I'm perfectly content living in Bakersville and making people happy when I can sell one of my pieces. I'm not looking to get ahead or gain someone's respect. I just want to be me."

"Regardless," Kathryn answered, "I just think Benji sounds a little silly now that you're twenty-some years old with your own business."

Benji looked into Kathryn's eyes and immediately he knew. Something had changed. Something deep within her that she hadn't even noticed herself. The girl sitting under the willow tree without a care in the world was gone. And not only was that girl gone, but so was the closeness that the two of them had once shared. Oh, they were still friends, and every now and then a trace of the old Katie might surface. But they were entering uncharted territory in their relationship, going down an entirely new path. It wasn't the same old Katie and Benji. It never would be. Even though it saddened Benji beyond words, in his great love for his friend he would take whatever he could get. He dismissed the ache in his heart, and instead of trying to make her see what was happening, he let it go. Kathryn wouldn't understand if he told her. It would only push her further away, and that was the last thing Benji wanted.

"You can call me anything you want, but I hope you know that I'm still going to be the same person I've always been. And I'll always be here for you, no matter what."

Kathryn smiled, thinking she understood. Benji walked her out and then watched from the doorway as she crossed the empty street to her car, her heels clicking against the asphalt. A haze had begun to settle in after the heat of the day.

"Thanks again. Goodnight, Benjamin." She waved.

"Goodnight, Kathryn," Benji called in reply as she got into her car and closed the door.

"And goodbye, Katie."

CHAPTER 9
PRIZED POSSESSIONS

"Everything in the world —
the cravings of sinful man,
the lust of his eyes and the boasting of what he
has and does —
does not come from the Father
but from the world."
1 John 2:16

Being a lawyer is a lot like being a boxer. You start out as an amateur, sparring with unknown opponents in order to get some experience under your belt. Gradually, you work your way up to the more formidable adversaries. After your defeats you pick yourself up and learn what not to do the next time around. With each victory you put a check mark in the "win" column and watch your ratio of wins to losses increase. And with each notch in your belt you get to enjoy the spoils a little more — your lifestyle becomes more comfortable, and you don't worry about that next fight quite as much. Then, after all the grueling hours of sweat and tears you find yourself standing ringside at the championship match. The opportunity of a lifetime. The fight that will make or break you. You've trained for this moment your entire career, and you're ready to unleash every weapon in your arsenal and every trick up your sleeve. But take heed, because you can become so obsessed with winning the prize dangling in front of you that you just might cross that paper-thin line. The line between taking your opponent down with a good, clean knock-out and pulverizing him within an inch of his life while you surrender your own self-worth in the process.

"Your attention, please. I'd like to propose a toast." He lifted the Waterford crystal high above his head along with a dozen other attorneys milling about the plush conference room on the twenty-fifth floor of the city's tallest building. Darian Wallingford was slender and tall with facial features so sharp that, even in his advancing age, he resembled an exotic bird more than a person. His snow-white mop of plumage fluffed up á la Albert Einstein. He cleared his throat dramatically to ensure he had every last person's undivided attention and paused several seconds before continuing. "It's hard to believe that only three short years ago she graduated at the top of her class and successfully passed the Bar. Today we celebrate a major milestone in her legal career. She has achieved the rank of partner in less time than any associate in our firm's one-hundred-and-fifty-year history. She has worked harder in those three years and accomplished more than most attorneys do in their entire careers. She has received the distinction of being named one of the top ten attorneys among Who's Who in the Law. The *Bar Journal* recently published an article about her and said, and I quote, 'She's the litigator to keep your eye on for the New Year.' I can say without the least bit of reservation or hesitation that she will soon be one of the leading criminal defense attorneys in the entire state. Ladies and gentlemen, please join me in welcoming our newest partner to Engel, Wallingford & Driscoll, Ms. Kathryn Ann Kirby. Cheers!"

"Hear! Hear!" Applause erupted and glasses clinked. Kathryn sipped the finest champagne while the young associates took turns shaking Kathryn's hand or hugging her, some genuinely happy for her achievement while others scoffed under their breaths. How did *she* manage to make partner so quickly in the top firm of the entire city? *They* had been associates for years now, *they* worked hard, and *they* won court cases just like she had. They thought they had it all figured out. One look at Kathryn—her tailored suits accentuating her flawless figure, her mile-long legs, her golden blonde bob that never saw a hair out of place, the confidence she exuded—and they all assumed they knew how she got to the top so quickly. But their assumptions were wrong. Deep down most of them knew they were wrong too. It was just easier for them to justify her rise to the top with some sordid tale rather than admitting that she was better than they were as they struggled to make their billable hours each week. Of course, Kathryn was no dummy either. She knew what they said about her behind her back. But somewhere during those three years of law school she had stopped caring about the rumor mill. She had one objective and one objective only—to get ahead.

Kathryn graciously accepted the accolades even when she knew they weren't genuine, and she basked in the attention. That had changed quite a bit since the foregone days of Katie. In middle school and high school she had shunned the spotlight, but now she deliberately sought it. The more attention, the more clout. And the more clout, the better.

The celebration continued for some time until, one by one, the attorneys excused themselves for the more pressing demands of filing depositions or replying to emails. Darian approached Kathryn to congratulate her personally. As the sole remaining partner claiming a direct lineage to the firm's founders (Darian's great-great grandfather, Horace Wallingford, first conceptualized the law firm with his two best friends out of a one-room office above a hardware store in the city), it was indeed an accomplishment if Darian even knew you existed. To be addressed personally by the legal legend was beyond anyone's hopes or expectations. Yet here he was, engaged by Kathryn's presence like a school boy.

"Kathryn, congratulations. It is indeed an honor to have you among the ranks of partner in this firm."

"Thank you so much, sir, but the honor is all mine. This is something I've been dreaming about ever since my first day of law school. I can assure you that I will do my best to represent the firm with dignity and fortitude."

"I have no doubt you will, I have no doubt at all." Darian took the last few gulps of his champagne and set the empty glass on the conference table. "Along those lines, I have a very special case that I am going to assign to you. The family contacted us about a week ago for representation. It's a case that could bring our firm a lot of publicity if handled properly. I am counting on your prowess."

Kathryn was both intrigued and nervous. "Sir, I am humbled that you would even think of me. I will look at it first thing in the morning."

"Yes, I would appreciate it if you would. And Kathryn," Darian began.

"Yes?"

"Do whatever it takes for this one."

"Yes sir," she immediately replied. She wasn't sure why, but for the briefest of moments Kathryn got a sinking feeling in the pit of her stomach. It must've been all the champagne.

Kathryn excused herself from the remaining two associates, deep in conversation about a case set for trial the next day, and headed to her office. Well, it would be her office for only a few more days anyway. Granted, it was spacious and more than she needed, but as the newly minted partner she would inherit a corner office with coveted views of the city skyline. She quickly fumbled through some papers on her desk until she found her cell phone. She had one text message waiting for her from Benjamin.

> *Congrats on officially being named partner. You deserve it*
> *for all the hard work. Want to take you out to celebrate one*
> *night soon. Let me know when you're free.*

Kathryn clicked over to her favorites list and hit speed dial for Griffin. She would reply to Benjamin later.

He picked up on the fourth ring.

"Hey, babe, it's official." She smiled. "You are now talking to the newest partner at Engel, Wallingford & Driscoll."

"Well, congratulations, partner. How did it go?"

"It went great. You know, the usual. Couple glasses of champagne here, handshake there. But something very interesting happened. Darian Wallingford approached me afterwards and said he has a special case he is assigning to me. He specifically said I should, quote, do whatever it takes."

"What's the case?"

"I don't know yet."

"What did he mean when he said you should do whatever it takes?" Griffin asked.

"I'm not exactly sure. I haven't had a chance to look at the file, but I told him I'd start on it first thing in the morning." Kathryn glanced at the thick manila folder on the far side of the mahogany desk Benjamin had made for her. The name on the corner was obscured by some other papers, but it hadn't been there when she left for her celebratory soiree, so she assumed that was the case Wallingford was telling her about. "So what's the game plan for tonight anyway?" she asked.

"I've got to work late again, babe. I've got pretrial motions the rest of this week, so I need to be sure I'm ready. I probably won't get home till close to ten."

"That's fine," Kathryn replied. "I've got a few things to do here at the office anyway, so I'll probably work late too. I'll just see you at home later tonight."

"Sounds good. Hey, I'm real proud of you. I knew you would do it!"

"Thanks, Griff. Love you."

"Love you too."

Kathryn placed the phone back on her desk and reached for the folder. She had no intention of looking at it until morning, but curiosity got the best of her. As soon as she opened it she read the case caption in capital letters: THE STATE VERSUS GERALD NORMAN LYONS. She stopped in her tracks. She couldn't believe it. She frantically flipped through the pages of legal documents looking for the police report to see if it was the same person. *It couldn't be*, she thought. There was no way on earth *she* would be representing him. But when she located the report buried at the bottom of the stack she realized it was, indeed, one and the same. The days of sparring with amateurs were long over. She was about to fight in that title match a lot sooner than she had anticipated.

Two Years Prior . . . To say that their ceremony was lavish would be a gross understatement. Kathryn and Griffin married one year after she graduated law school, on her twenty-fifth birthday, amidst all the pomp and circumstance of the most talked about wedding of the year. Griffin's family shouldered the bulk of the expense since his family had more money than they knew what to do with, and Kathryn's mother could contribute only so much as the Bakersville town librarian. The prominent guest list of over 300 included all of the high-profile attorneys in town, politicians, and judges. Anyone who was anyone was invited.

Kathryn's mother had hoped that her daughter would be married at Bakersville's St. Paul the Apostle Church. After all, the quaint church was where Kathryn's faith had blossomed as a child. But Kathryn wouldn't have any part of it. For one thing, she needed a sanctuary large enough to accommodate her impressive guest list. And for another, what on earth would they do for a reception in Bakersville? Guido's Pizzeria or Dan's Deli and Dogs? Could you even imagine a federal judge noshing on a chili dog after their elegant wedding ceremony? Hardly! High society and Bakersville was a contradiction in terms. Instead, Kathryn and Griffin took advantage of their connections with one of the local judges who also happened to be a deacon at St. Mary's Cathedral in the city, and within a few days their reservation was booked. The Gothic cathedral built at the turn of the century boasted three-hundred-foot ceilings with countless arches and wall-to-wall stained glass windows reflecting a rainbow of colors in the sanctuary. One step in this magnificent holy structure and you felt as though you had set foot within God's personal dwelling place. And, of course, the crimson carpet that stretched down the center aisle for what seemed liked miles was any bride's dream come true to walk down on her special day. Benjamin did the honors of standing in for Kathryn's father. It was the first time Kathryn had ever seen him in a tuxedo. He was handsome indeed, although Kathryn couldn't help but notice that he still looked at bit out of place. Tuxedos and cathedrals just weren't Benjamin's world.

Following the evening ceremony the wedding guests were escorted a few blocks away to the Officers' Club where they dined until the wee hours of the morning on lobster tail, filet mignon, and ganache-filled wedding cake. The guests sipped their bourbons and water or brandies while puffing on cigars and enjoying the magnificent views of the harbor and city life. Yes, Kathryn and Griffin spared absolutely no expense. After all, they were two of the most up-and-coming attorneys at the most powerful law firms in the city. They had an image to maintain. Money was no object, and this day was all about them.

Kathryn was truly in her element. The attention she had once shunned was now a welcomed and almost expected part of her daily existence. And she was absolutely, completely, one hundred percent in love. In love with Griffin? Well yes, sure. But she was also in love with *being in love*. With wearing a vintage white satin gown and carrying a fragrant bouquet of daylilies and freesia; with being the object of everyone's envy for having such a picture-perfect life; with putting a down payment on one of the most sought after condominiums in all of the city. That was what Kathryn was really in love with—with playing wife to the city's once most eligible bachelor and being a high-profile attorney in the most respected firm. And in Kathryn's mind, somewhere down the road that fantasy of married life would eventually become a colonial house in the suburbs with manicured lawns, a sprinkler system, pool in the backyard, white picket fence, some sort of Lab or retriever, and 2.5 kids. *That* was what Kathryn was in love with more than anything. Sure she loved Griffin, no question about it. But she loved the *idea* of Griffin even more.

The morning after her official welcoming at the firm, Kathryn drove the fifteen-minute commute through the congested city streets in a fog. She stopped at several traffic lights but never noticed them change. She yielded to a flock of preschoolers led by their caretakers through a crosswalk but never heard the rhyme they were singing. She even pulled to the curb to let an ambulance pass, but she never actually *saw* any of it. All she could see was his name printed in bold letters on the file: **GERALD NORMAN LYONS**. College professor ... department chair ... author ... philanthropist ... husband ... father ... Little League coach ... predator ... murderer.

It had happened in late spring only a week before Kathryn was set to graduate from law school. Nineteen-year-old college freshman Emily Porter had just completed her last final exam, and she had planned to meet several of her girlfriends to commemorate the end of the semester. That was when she ran into her favorite professor while walking across campus to her car. "Allow me the honor of buying you a celebratory drink," he said. "Oh, but Professor Lyons, I'm underage," she replied. "Please, call me Gerald. And not to worry, you're with me, remember?" Emily blushed and ignored the little voice inside of her warning her not to go.

He took her to an obscure bar on a dark corner several blocks from the college. It was a bar Lyons knew well. Only the locals patronized it, and those who did would never in a million years breathe a word that an astute college professor was one of the regulars. The college students didn't even realize the establishment existed. Yes, he knew they would be safe there. As promised he bought Emily only one drink, and he kept the conversation casual and platonic. But as they left the bar together less than an hour later, she could already feel her body changing. Her vision began to blur, her tongue felt fuzzy, and she was convinced that two cinderblocks were tied to her feet. She stumbled down the steps onto the sidewalk. "Here, let me help you," he said as he gingerly deposited her into his Lexus sedan. It was the last time Emily Porter would see the light of day. He drove her to a vacant lot where he did unspeakable things while she was unconscious and dumped her in a roadside ditch. There she lay, face down, full of promise and potential, discarded like a piece of trash.

He had been careful not to leave any tell-tale signs. He was, after all, a criminal justice professor, so Gerald knew all the nuances of DNA and trace evidence. When she awoke the next morning she wouldn't remember a thing—he had made sure of that—and she would either be too embarrassed or too scared to do anything about it. He had planned everything perfectly. Except there was *one* thing that Gerald hadn't planned on happening. A thunderstorm. One of those freak storms that doesn't appear on the radar until it's right on top of you. The kind of thunderstorm where God unleashes his fury over creation for the briefest of moments just to remind us all who is really in control. The unexpected storm came barreling through in the middle of the night and saturated the entire area with almost two inches of rain. The next morning a jogger found Emily's body in the flooded ditch. She had drowned.

Although Gerald was confident he had covered his tracks, he also wasn't aware of the brief text Emily sent her friends from the ladies' room of the bar:

> *Prof. Lyons asked me out for a drink!!! OMG!!! At a bar w/him now. Don't wait up!*

She had deleted it as soon as she sent it, so when Gerald scrolled through her texts during her state of unconsciousness later that evening, he found nothing. His fatal flaw.

With the help of Emily's friends it took homicide detectives less than a week to make the arrest. He was formally charged with felony murder and a laundry list of other crimes. Gerald pleaded not guilty at his arraignment, and as he left the courthouse in shackles and flanked by several sheriff's deputies, the reporters descended upon him like vultures hungry for fresh meat. They shoved their microphones in his face. "Are you concerned about your fate?" "Did you kill Emily Porter?" "How do you feel about the prospect of spending the rest of your life behind bars?" They fired questions at him a mile a minute. Gerald smiled and made eye contact with an attractive female reporter who stood closest to him. "Sweetheart, I'm not worried about a thing. They'll never touch me," he replied arrogantly. The following morning the papers ran a full-page color photo of Gerald Lyons smiling for the camera. Above it was a single word for the headline: *UNTOUCHABLE.*

That had been three years ago. After the initial barrage of publicity, the frenzy died down amidst more pressing problems like the city's gang and drug culture. All the while, Gerald, who had been denied bail, quietly sat in jail. Quietly, patiently, strategically. Waiting for just the right time and just the right person. Someone gifted, someone ambitious, and someone who would put the letter of the law above any moral or ethical issues that might threaten to get in the way. Someone who could set him free. That someone was Kathryn. She had been a practicing attorney for little more than three years and partner for less than a day, yet already she found herself on the cusp of that championship match. If she won the case, it would bring Engel, Wallingford & Driscoll untold publicity. As for her, it would propel her into an entirely new stratosphere of attorneys. Those few and far between who had won the title and could hold the gold belt high above their heads in victory. A small yet prestigious few. Kathryn knew she had to give this fight everything she had, and she was ready.

The entire day Kathryn buried herself in the case, reading every last detail and educating herself as to who Gerald Lyons was. Benjamin texted her twice to follow up from the previous day's celebration, only to be curtly dismissed.

> *Benjamin: Hi Kathryn, just checking 2 see if you got my text yesterday. Want 2 take you out 2 celebrate.*

> *Kathryn: Got it. Sorry. Busy.*

> *Benjamin: No prob, hope we can catch up soon. It's been ages. I miss my friend.*

> *Kathryn: Will text soon.*

The more Kathryn read in the file, the clearer she could see the truth buried in all the legal documents. Yes, it was crystal clear. The evidence against him was overwhelming. Her client was guilty.

One Year Prior ... Kathryn and Griffin celebrated their first anniversary by defrosting that last slice of wedding cake and deciding that the tradition of eating the stale cake definitely wasn't what it was cracked up to be. They were each earning six figures at their respective law firms, and Kathryn had successfully sparred with countless opponents. In fact, she was so gifted at her sport that she quickly accumulated dozens of wins and was challenged by a higher class of opponents. No matter though. Kathryn could gracefully navigate a courtroom and take witnesses down with a ferocious left hook on cross-examination that they never saw coming. Indeed, the courtroom was Kathryn's ring, and she could deliver one hell of a beating.

With her daunting reputation also came the plunder to go along with it. She and Griffin had already moved into an even larger condominium with an elevator opening directly into their living room. They owned a speed boat docked less than a mile away, an oceanfront beach house, a time share in the Caribbean, and season tickets with box seats for all of the city's top sporting events. The only problem was, they were both so busy *making* money in order to purchase even bigger and better baubles that they never had the time to enjoy the things they already had. When the sporting events came or their week at the time share approached, they inevitably had business meetings or social engagements that just couldn't be postponed. So the tickets to the ball games or the week in the Caribbean went to some indebted friend who got a brief taste of how the other half lives. The beach house remained vacant no matter the time of year. Even their two-story condominium with gorgeous views of the city harbor sat largely unoccupied, except when they briefly escaped from their offices at all hours of the night (or sometimes well into the morning) to catch a few hours of sleep before they headed back to their respective firms to do it all over again.

They hired professionals to take care of all the daily chores that they had neither the time nor the desire to fool with—a maid service, a dry cleaning service, hired hands to wash their cars and maintain their boat, and even a personal chef service to deliver meals on weeknights. Kathryn's clothes were designer, her car was a customized convertible Benz, and any piece of jewelry she wore cost at least in the thousands. Her engagement ring alone, which was blindingly huge at over three karats, cost more than most people pay in rent for an entire year.

Yes, they had it all. But the more they had, the more Kathryn wanted. She couldn't wait to step into that ring, decimate yet another unworthy opponent, bask in the fame it brought, and enjoy the spoils from her victory. It had become addictive. The bigger the case, the bigger the reward she would lavish upon herself. After all, she worked sixty, sometimes seventy hours a week. She was unstoppable. What was wrong with indulging in the nicer things in life, especially when you work hard to earn them? She deserved it.

For the next several months the Lyons case consumed Kathryn. She stopped eating anything other than quick take-out meals, and she guzzled coffee like it was her lifeline. Most nights she made it back to the condo for a few hours of restless sleep, and some nights not even that. She would take a quick catnap on the oversized couch in her office, set the alarm on her cell for twenty minutes, and awaken on her own thinking about the case before the alarm ever sounded. She had lost weight and dark circles were painted under her eyes. Even Griffin, who knew the demands of a rising attorney's schedule better than anyone, had shared his concern for her more than once. "You need to take better care of yourself, babe, I never see you anymore," he would tell her, only to have her snap back that he of all people should be supportive and not judgmental. He wasn't being judgmental, though, he was just worried and tired of having a wife in name only. But he never pushed. And she never caught his drift.

This was, after all, the big event. It was her chance to claim the heavyweight title of defense attorneys in the entire city, maybe even the entire state. She scoured the witness reports, scheduled meetings and phone conversations with her client, read over the depositions, examined the exhibits, studied the autopsy report, interviewed expert witnesses, researched the law, and reviewed the procedures. She did it all. Attorneys are obligated to represent their clients effectively and diligently, and Kathryn had met this obligation by more than a thousand percent. Lyons's trial date would arrive before long, but no matter how deep she dug she just couldn't seem to find a sliver of hope that her client would be found anything but guilty as charged and rot in prison for the rest of his life. Kathryn was relentless though. She hadn't lost a case in she couldn't remember how long, and she wasn't about to lose this one. You don't get all the way to the final round of the championship match only to throw in the towel and admit defeat. She would go down swinging. And before she knew it, just like that roller coaster she had boarded, life took a sharp left turn that changed everything.

It happened one afternoon after Kathryn had already been working on the case for months. She reported to Darian Wallingford weekly on the status of the case, but even those brief meetings were stressful since each time she had little hope to offer and it looked as though she couldn't salvage the biggest case in the history of the firm. She grabbed her wallet and headed down the elevator into the lobby to grab yet another espresso. As she crossed the street to the local Starbucks next to the courthouse she saw the protestors. They were picketing in front of the courthouse with signs that read "My gun, my right," and "Arm the people," the latest response to a bill proposing the severe limitation on privately owned firearms. She passed the chanting protestors with little interest until one of them shoved something in front of her face. It was a small booklet, no bigger than the size of a passport. "Our Constitution, our rights!" the person shouted. Kathryn grabbed the booklet and shoved it in her pocket, happy to escape the commotion. When she returned to her office and went to dispose of the booklet, she missed the trash can and instead it landed opened on the floor. As she bent over to pick it up the words on the page jumped out at her—The Sixth Amendment. She read it and smiled. The thought had already crossed her mind. After all, Lyons had been incarcerated for three years—the same amount of time she had been out of law school. She figured that somewhere down the line, one of the previous defense attorneys representing him in the case had already raised the issue. She was wrong. She pored through every last motion, but it was nowhere to be found. Kathryn had just discovered her saving grace, the knock-out punch that the State would never expect and would be completely defenseless against. She could taste the victory already.

Kathryn hurriedly ran down the hall and barged into Darian's office, interrupting what appeared to be a somewhat unpleasant conversation with his wife.

"I'm so sorry, sir, I didn't meant to interrupt, but I need to talk to you immediately about the Lyons case."

Darian glanced at Kathryn and then redirected his attention to the phone conversation. "All right, dear, let me call you back. No, no, I'll call you. Goodbye," he said quite stiffly and hung up the phone on his desk, not appearing the least bit annoyed by the intrusion. "Yes, Kathryn, you have my attention. Go ahead."

Kathryn sat on the edge of the armchair positioned across from his desk. "As you know, I've been working exhaustingly on the case for months. And while initially it appeared as though we had very little chance of success in the case, I think I have found something that will change everything. In fact, if I'm correct on this, and I'm quite sure I am, it could mean he goes free."

Darian looked at her with a puzzled expression on his birdlike face. "You mean he may not face life imprisonment?"

"I mean he could go free."

"You mean he might have some of the charges dropped?"

"I mean he could go free."

"You mean a jury would likely find reasonable doubt?"

"Sir, I mean he could go free. As in walk out of prison, never have to spend another day in jail, and have a record that is one hundred percent clean."

Darian leaned forward with his elbows on the desk and his fingertips pressed against each other. He studied her eager face carefully, debating whether to give credence to her sudden outburst of confidence. "Well, you certainly do have my curiosity, considering only last week you were suggesting the possibility of entering into a plea bargain with the State because it would be the only way to prevent his life imprisonment. And now you are telling me he is going to walk out of jail scot-free. So what exactly is this trick you have up your sleeve?"

"It's no trick at all, sir. It's the Sixth Amendment right to a speedy trial."

Kathryn sat in Darian's office for over an hour discussing strategy. The more she talked, the more he agreed that her position was based on sound legal doctrine. You see, the Sixth Amendment is part of the Bill of Rights to the United States Constitution. And the Bill of Rights was enacted to protect the citizens from an overzealous government abusing their rights. In order to keep the system from locking up criminals for years on end without the benefit of a trial to prove their innocence, the right to a speedy trial was incorporated, basically warning the government that it had to bring a defendant to trial in a timely manner; otherwise, all charges would be dismissed. Of course, what exactly "speedy" means has always been open to interpretation and debate, but Kathryn knew without a doubt that the three years Gerald Lyons had been sitting in jail was far beyond a reasonable amount of time in any court's eyes. Trial dates for Gerald Lyons had been set and postponed countless times, almost always because the courts were too crowded and there was no courtroom available to hear his case. For as much publicity the Lyons case received in the months following his arrest, somehow it had managed to slip through the cracks of an imperfect system where State's Attorneys had too many cases and too little time to prosecute. Somewhere between the ninth and eleventh postponements and changing of prosecutors the State's Attorneys' Office forgot completely about Gerald Lyons sitting patiently in his jail cell. And Kathryn was more than happy to point out their lapse. What made this strategy even more glorious was the fact that if she succeeded, the prosecutor could not initiate new charges. It wasn't at all like losing a boxing match where the opponents can still fight each other another day. No, if Kathryn won then this fight was over once and for all.

"So it's settled then," Kathryn said to Darian as she arose from the chair in his office. "By the end of the week I will file a Motion to

Dismiss requesting that all charges be dropped. I will call my client in the morning and let him know of the course of action."

Darian looked at her pensively, not sharing the least bit of exhilaration that was coursing through her body at this incredible breakthrough.

"Kathryn?"

"Yes, Mr. Wallingford?" she replied as she opened the door to his secretary's office.

"I want you to know this was very well done. I knew I put you on this case for a reason, and I am glad you proved me right. But I also want you to know that you should expect some degree of fallout from this if we do succeed in having the case dismissed. It will mean a great deal of publicity indeed, and I believe you will achieve a degree of stardom from your successes. But there will be those who take issue with our actions and believe that his release is unjustified."

Kathryn had already thought about everything he was saying. "Thank you, Mr. Wallingford, I realize that. But don't we have an obligation to represent our client to the best of our ability? And besides, you told me from the get-go to do whatever it takes. That is exactly what I'm doing."

Darian smiled at her, a cold, callous smile, and she exited his office, shutting the door behind her.

That night Kathryn left the office early and was home by 8 p.m., plenty of time for her and Griffin to enjoy a steak dinner with a few glasses of wine. It was the most she had eaten or relaxed in months. She filled Griffin in on the legal strategy with little comment from him, mainly because he was more excited to have his wife back than to care about yet another guilty defendant.

It was past midnight when she crawled into bed. She spent the next hour staring at the ceiling, tossing and turning, wishing sleep upon herself. But it wouldn't come. She was too excited to drop this bombshell on the prosecutor's office, and she couldn't wait to get up in front of the judge and argue that Gerald Lyons should be a free man. A free man. A free yet guilty man. Kathryn wouldn't let herself consider that a victory in the courtroom meant that a lying, detestable murderer would once again be prowling the streets. That perhaps another unsuspecting college student might cross paths with him and end up as yet another statistic on an end-of-year report. That her obsession with representing her client to the letter of the law might mean compromising everything she had believed in her entire life. That it might blur the line between right and wrong that she wasn't ready or equipped to handle. No, she couldn't let herself go there in her mind. After all, her legal argument was completely legitimate. She wasn't doing anything dishonest or illegal, and she wasn't withholding anything she was obligated to disclose. She told herself that any other defense attorney representing Lyons would make the exact same argument, and she was right. So why should she give up all the fame and glory when it would go to some less deserving attorney trying to fight their way to the top like she was? She was only zealously representing her client, which was exactly what she swore an oath to do when she was inducted into the State Bar. This win was all Kathryn's, and she wasn't about to share it with anyone else.

Six Months Prior . . .

"Hey, stranger! It's good to hear your voice."

"Hi, Benjamin, same here. It's been a while."

"Yeah, well that's 'cause someone I know is always so busy. You're next to impossible to get hold of these days. So how is life in the big city anyway?"

"It's amazing. I have so much to tell you I don't even know where to start."

"Well, why don't you start with your job? I read about you in the paper the other day. Something about your defending a doctor who was on trial for illegally prescribing pain meds to addicts."

"Wasn't it great? Only an hour of deliberation and the jury acquitted him."

"Yeah, great," Benjamin replied, although less enthusiastically than Kathryn.

"And you'll be seeing my name in print again very soon!"

"Oh yeah? Tell me about it."

"I was just interviewed by the *Bar Journal* last week and they are going to write a feature article about me in their monthly magazine. Apparently they're doing a series of articles on the most up-and-coming litigators in the city, and they picked me for the spotlight on criminal defense attorneys! I have to admit, I'm not surprised. Not to sound conceited or anything but I do have one of the best records for acquittal in the entire city and that's in less than two years after graduating law school. I don't want to pat myself on the back, but that's pretty good."

"That's amazing, I'm really happy for you."

"What can I say," Kathryn replied with a chuckle. "When you've got it, you've got it! Oh, and speaking of having it, did I tell you that we just bought a cabin in the mountains?"

"No, you didn't. I didn't even know you went to the mountains."

"Well, we don't, at least not that often. But a few months ago Griffin and I went to this weekend conference for work, and it was at this amazing chalet in the mountains. We both fell in love with the area so we decided to buy a cabin there. You know, for weekend getaways and things like that. And well," she again chuckled, "we already have a place at the beach so we figured we had to even it out and get someplace in the mountains too."

Benjamin paused for a few moments, unsure of what he should say. "Well, I'm really happy for you. Sounds like you're working hard and enjoying life. How is Griffin anyway?"

"Griffin who?" Kathryn laughed yet again. Benjamin couldn't help but notice it was an artificial laugh, like the way she would laugh in front of judges or other attorneys she wanted to impress. It didn't sound anything like the laugh of the friend he once knew. "Oh, I'm teasing. He's good. We're just both so busy right now it seems like sometimes we're ships passing in the night. But that's okay, we made a pact that while we're young we're going to work as much as we can and then in a few years we'll take a break to relax a little."

"That sounds like a good plan," encouraged Benjamin.

"So what's new in Bakersville?" Kathryn asked sarcastically. She well knew that nothing was *ever* new in Bakersville.

"Not much I suppose. Actually, they did decrease the speed limit going through town from thirty-five to thirty. And I ran into your mother the other day in town. We had a nice lunch together. She misses you too."

"Yeah, I've been meaning to call."

"I just hope that you're doing well, being so busy all the time."

"Are you kidding me?" answered Kathryn somewhat defensively. "I've never felt better in my life. I finally feel like I know where I'm headed and what I'm supposed to be doing with my life."

"And what's that?"

"Is there even a question about it?" Kathryn asked him incredulously. "To make partner, of course! I am going to be the youngest, best, and most sought after defense attorney this city has ever seen!"

The more their conversation continued the more excited Kathryn got, and the sadder Benjamin became.

"Well, I hope you get everything you wish for, Kathryn. You definitely have a gift for the law. Just don't ever forget where that gift came from."

"Oh, I won't forget it for one second."

"Good," Benjamin replied, relieved.

"It came from three years of my dedication and hard work while in law school. It came from me never letting it get to me and pushing through. It came from all of my *Law Review* articles and my 3.89 grade point average."

"That's not exactly what I—"

Kathryn interrupted. "Oh hey, one of the partners from the firm is beeping in on the other line, I've got to take this."

"Okay, sure," Benjamin quickly replied. "But before you go, if you ever have time for coffee one morning let me know. I could meet you in the city and—"

"Sure thing," Kathryn quickly replied. "I'll call you soon, sounds great."

"It was really great talking to y—" With that the line went dead. She was gone.

She never did call him back.

It was the slap heard 'round the world. Kathryn descended the courthouse steps among throngs of reporters from every local news station and some not so local. Most of them followed the handsome man in the navy suit who walked about a dozen steps ahead of her. "How does it feel to be a free man?" "What are your plans now?" they all asked him. He stopped on the steps and happily answered every last question. "It is a new lease on life," he declared. "It has restored my faith in the criminal justice system," he said, choking back crocodile tears. Yes, he was the man of the hour, but one or two reporters followed Kathryn instead. And they captured the moment on film which would be played during the six o'clock news, replayed during the ten o'clock news, and then plastered on every newspaper in the metropolitan area. That was when Charlotte Porter, Emily's mother, walked right up to Kathryn and slapped her across the face.

"That was for Emily," she hissed. Then, before Kathryn could even react, she slapped her a second time. "And that was for his next victim." She didn't give Kathryn an opportunity to respond, she simply walked away. Her cheek stung and it reddened immediately. She fought to maintain her composure.

After testimony and arguments that lasted almost an entire day, Judge Horne ordered that all charges be dismissed effective immediately. The judge, visibly agitated while delivering his ruling from the bench, chastised the system for allowing someone to be released who was, in his words, "a cowardly predator believing himself above the law." "Might this be a lesson to all of those participants in the process who seek justice for the voiceless. Today marks not a victory, but instead a failure of our system." Lyons gazed upon the judge smugly as the courtroom artist furiously sketched the expression on his face. Kathryn outwardly remained stoic but inside she was ecstatic. She had finally captured her most prized possession of all—the pinnacle of fame.

The same reporter who had captured Charlotte Porter's outburst approached Kathryn. "So, Ms. Kirby, how does it feel to know that you will likely be the most sought after criminal defense attorney in the entire city?"

"I don't have any feelings about it one way or the other," she lied. "I was simply fulfilling my obligations to represent my client to the best of my ability." Kathryn had learned how to play humble very well when in front of the cameras.

"Excuse me." A young reporter with a Channel 2 name tag pushed through the crowd to get closer to her. "How does it feel to know that a murderer is walking the streets tonight because of you?" Kathryn looked him straight in the eye, pushed the microphone out of her way, and walked briskly to the car waiting for her at the curb. She wouldn't dignify such a ridiculous question with an answer. But for some reason she couldn't get the question out of her mind.

That evening Kathryn arrived home to find Griffin waiting for her with a bottle of champagne, a dozen red roses, and an intimate evening that was long overdue. She received several congratulatory phone calls from colleagues. Darian Wallingford also sent word that the next day he would expect her company at a dinner in her honor. She was the star of the hour.

Later that evening as Griffin settled on the patio to read the latest legal updates, Kathryn retrieved her cell phone from her purse and texted Benjamin. It was the first conversation she had initiated with him in months. Perhaps she was looking for his validation, perhaps she was looking for reassurance. Or perhaps she was looking for some part of the foregone Katie that only he knew. Benjamin replied within a few minutes.

Kathryn: Hey, did you hear about the case?

Benjamin: Yep, all over the news.

Kathryn: What did you think?

Benjamin: I think you had to do what you felt was right.

Kathryn: So you don't think I was right?

Benjamin: Never said that. I don't understand the law like you do. I'm sure you did your best to represent him. I just hope you did it for the right reasons.

Kathryn: What's that supposed to mean? I was doing my best to help him. Why else would I have done it?

Benjamin: I don't know. But I hope he never harms anyone else.

Kathryn: That's not my problem. Gotta run.

Benjamin: Okay, goodnight.

Whatever hope or comfort she was looking for, she didn't receive from Benjamin. She could still feel the stinging on her cheek from Charlotte Porter, but now she stung deep inside as well. Benjamin may never have explicitly said she had done anything wrong, but she could tell from his brief texts that he didn't approve. Kathryn had succeeded in having the case dismissed, her client walked free, and she could finally claim the title she had coveted for so long. She had won the case and rightfully claimed the prize. But what had she lost of herself in the process?

CHAPTER 10
THE SOUND OF SILENCE

"Do not let the sun go down
while you are still angry,
and do not give the devil a foothold."
Ephesians 4:26-27

As everyone had anticipated, the floodgates opened after the Lyons victory and Kathryn was inundated with cases. Clients would ask not just for the firm, but they would specifically request her. And she loved every minute of it. Her work weeks became even longer and her resume grew with each success in the courtroom. Gerald Lyons might have been "untouchable," but Kathryn Kirby was *unbeatable*.

She had represented them all—embezzlers, drug kingpins, tax evaders, drunk drivers, murderers, and so on. They were millionaires and sometimes even billionaires. They owned companies, yachts, mansions, and more jewels than what was stored in the Tower of London. Regardless of the client, Kathryn had one firm policy—*don't ask, don't tell*. Well, let's qualify that remark. Yes, she would ask them all kinds of questions in preparation for their cases—that was her duty as their legal counsel. But there was one question she would never ask, and she made it quite clear during her initial interviews that she would not take the case if they volunteered the information. The question . . . *Did you do it?* Kathryn watched drug kingpins arrive in their Rolls Royces wearing Rolexes around their wrists without having had any steady employment history for the past ten years. She took calls from her tax evaders vacationing in Dubai or Bora Bora. Where did they all get the money to afford such grandeur? Maybe they inherited it, she rationalized. Maybe they won the lottery. Sure they did. As much as Kathryn knew the truth in her heart, she allowed herself to overlook the obvious as long as she had that scintilla of hope that they might be innocent. Within two years of her victory in the Lyons case, she was lauded as the best criminal defense attorney in the state.

Christmas snuck up on Kathryn that year like a cat stalking its prey. She barely managed to purchase gifts and wasn't sure if she had time to take off. Nevertheless, since the holidays were typically a very slow season for trials, she managed to squeeze in a few days and head to Bakersville. Christmas fell on a Friday this year, so Kathryn would return to her childhood neighborhood for the weekend and then head back to the city by the crack of dawn Monday morning. She and Griffin had decided to pay holiday visits to their respective families solo this year. He would make the three-hour commute south of the city to visit his parents and siblings while she would travel north for an hour. Actually, Kathryn and Griffin had been spending a lot of time apart in recent years. It had been a gradual thing, starting not too long after she had graduated law school. It was so gradual, in fact, that neither one of them had seemed to take much notice of it. At least Kathryn hadn't anyway. Rumors circulated that they were each engaged in extramarital activities, but the thought alone was laughable. They didn't even have time for each other, let alone someone else. No, Kathryn wasn't having a love affair in the sense that everyone thought. Her only love affair was with herself.

Kathryn arrived in Bakersville around ten on the morning after Christmas. The commute took her no time on the desolate roads. As she drove through town, she noticed the light in Benjamin's studio, so she pulled to the curb and let herself in. She found Benjamin hunched over what looked like an unfinished credenza, carefully sanding it.

"Good morning," she said as she shut the door rather loudly to get his attention.

Benjamin was startled. He looked up and smiled warmly when he saw his visitor.

"Hi, stranger, it's so good to see you! I wasn't sure if you were coming home this weekend or not."

"Yeah, well, I wasn't so sure either, but I managed to sneak away for the weekend. I'm the top biller at the firm so what are they going to do, tell me I can't go home to see my family for Christmas?"

"I certainly hope not," Benjamin replied. "Is Griffin with you?"

"No, he went home to see his family for the weekend. We figured we would divide and conquer to get it over with quicker."

"Get *what* over with?" Benjamin asked.

"You know, the visits with family, the pleasantries, all that kind of stuff."

"Oh," Benjamin replied with resignation. "Well, I know your mother is really excited that you're going to be spending a few days at home. She's been talking about it for weeks."

"I am too," Kathryn immediately backtracked, realizing how her comment had sounded. "Don't get me wrong, it just makes for a tiring couple of days and I don't think I could handle an entire weekend with the Harris family, if you know what I mean." Benjamin didn't know what she meant, but he also didn't *want* to know so he didn't ask.

"So what are you doing working the morning after Christmas anyway?" Kathryn asked as she gestured at the credenza.

"Oh, I just have this one project to finish up before the New Year. But hey, that can wait. Let's head upstairs and chat for a few. Do you have the time?"

Kathryn glanced at her watch as if she had someplace important to be at that very moment. Not because she did have someplace to be mind you, but rather out of habit.

"I could definitely spare a few moments," she replied.

They ascended the narrow staircase through another beat-up door into Benjamin's studio apartment. Kathryn couldn't help but notice that everything looked exactly the same as it had the last time she was in his apartment over three years ago. She sat on the couch next to him somewhat stiffly. The mismatched cushions were out of place, and the fabric on the arms was ripped. Kathryn was used to only plush leather couches.

"Do you have any wine?" Kathryn asked.

"Um, no," Benjamin answered, somewhat surprised. "It's only ten o'clock in the morning."

"Oh, it's always a good time for wine," Kathryn replied, completely oblivious to the look on Benjamin's face.

"How about some water instead?"

"That sounds great."

Benjamin retrieved a tinted plastic cup from the cabinet, plunked a single ice cube in it, and filled it with tap water. He gave it to Kathryn. She looked at it suspiciously and set it on the coffee table without drinking any of it.

"So, I see you're still living in the lap of luxury." Kathryn smiled.

"Yep, you know me. I live like a king."

They chatted for almost an hour while listening to the hum of the space heater in the background, the conversation cordial but hollow. It was like an electrical connection flickering in an effort to sustain itself but never quite succeeding in making the connection. There were sparks of honest to goodness joy and companionship, but those sparks never ignited. The conversation was mostly awkward and forced. The more they chatted, the more they realized that they were from two different worlds; worlds which did not connect and rarely even crossed paths. Worlds of different interests and especially of different priorities.

Most of the conversation centered around Kathryn. Her cases, her life, her rise to success. After all, what was there to say about Benjamin? The same job in the same town with the same apartment ever since high school. Why, the only difference Kathryn could detect was the new painting of a set of praying hands that hung on his wall. When she commented about it (it really was an exquisite piece of art), Benjamin told her that one of his clients had painted it for him as a thank-you for his craftsmanship. Other than that, there really wasn't a whole lot to say about Benjamin, except the one thing that Kathryn probably *shouldn't* have said.

"Benjamin, why don't you move to the city? You could get a small apartment and open your studio there. You could make *so* much more money than you are making here in Bakersville. With your talent and the pieces of furniture you create, you could be making two, even three times what you're making here. And just think of the clientele you could have. I could even put in a good word for you with some of the judges and attorneys. They would be coming to you in no time flat. And if you need help with rent, I could always pay—"

Benjamin cut her off before she could finish. He could see her wheels turning and the excitement over a life that *she* thought he should have, not a life that he wanted. "Kathryn, I really appreciate the offer but I'm happy here in Bakersville."

"But *why*?" Kathryn asked, truly befuddled as to how on earth Benjamin could find contentment in such a humdrum existence.

Benjamin thought for a minute. "Well, let me see. For one thing, I like it here because these are the people I've known all my life. They are who they are, and they don't pretend to be anything else. They stop on the street to wish you good morning, and they would give you the shirts off their backs if you needed it. For another, it's a place where you can take the time to enjoy life. It's not so fast-paced here that everything passes you by without even realizing it."

Kathryn unknowingly crinkled her nose. Some things never changed.

"You know, like the Fourth of July parade each year, or the farmer's market where the locals sell their fresh produce hand-picked the day before, or the bakery that gives free donuts to toddlers, or the bird watchers' club that meets every Tuesday morning in the park."

"So what does all of that have to do with you?" Kathryn asked.

"It doesn't, not directly anyway. But it's the little things that make life the experience that it is. I just feel like if I went to the city I would get so caught up in the *process* of living that I wouldn't enjoy the *substance* of it."

Kathryn looked at him again in bewilderment. Benjamin knew his words were completely lost on her.

"I do appreciate your wanting what's best for me, but really, I am very happy here."

"Suit yourself," Kathryn replied aloofly.

"So, what are you doing tomorrow morning?" he asked her.

"Nothing that I know of, why?"

"How about if I pick you up for church around nine thirty? I'm sure everyone at St. Paul's would love to see you again."

Kathryn felt a wave of panic wash over her, something she wasn't used to at all. Put her in any courtroom and she was cool as a cucumber, but church was a place she hadn't visited regularly in several years. She had simply been too busy.

"Oh, I don't know," she balked.

"Come on, it'll be fun. We have a new pastor who's been there a little over a year. Pastor Richardson, although he insists that everyone call him Pastor Matt. He's very informal. And let me tell you, he can preach one heck of a sermon."

The thought of returning to her home church, or *any* church for that matter, was simultaneously terrifying and comforting. She wracked her brain for some excuse as to why she wouldn't be able to make it, but she couldn't think of a single one. She might be able to pull brilliant legal arguments out of thin air like a magician pulls a rabbit out of a hat, but in this instance she was at his mercy.

"Okay, I'll go," she answered hesitantly.

Benjamin didn't give her the opportunity to back out. "Great, I'll pick you up tomorrow morning. Enjoy the night with your mother."

Benjamin escorted Kathryn to her car and watched her disappear down the road, all the while thinking hopefully about Pastor Matt. When he shared the Word of God, he could make you stop dead in your tracks and take a good hard look at your life. He could make you turn 180 degrees and want to give everything you had to the Lord. He could make you feel alive and even on fire for God. Yep, Pastor Matt could preach one heck of a sermon. And Benjamin was counting on his faithful servant more than ever.

The rest of the afternoon Kathryn spent at her childhood home acquainting herself with Oreo, a black and white rescue cat from the shelter her mother had adopted a short while ago. The cat was very friendly, obviously aware of the fact that it had beaten the odds of most unwanted animals and found a "forever" home, but this two-year-old feline was no substitute for Trouble. No, Trouble was one of a kind. She was wonderful yet horrible, mischievous yet well behaved, free-spirited yet dependent, and aloof yet loving all at the same time—which doesn't make the least bit of sense unless you've ever had the honor of being owned by a cat at some point in your life. Then, it makes *perfect* sense. Trouble had lived all of her nine lives to the fullest and departed this world as an elderly lady at the ripe old age of eighteen. As Kathryn stroked the purring Oreo she thought back to that day when young Benjamin cradled the tabby kitten in his arms on the front porch and Trouble inherited her name. That day felt like a million years ago.

After dinner Kathryn welcomed the contentment of a familiar scene. She and her mother sipped hot tea at the kitchen table in their pajamas and enjoyed something they had not shared in months—each other's company.

"So tell me," her mother asked, cherishing every moment of her daughter's presence, "how are things with you and Griffin?"

"Oh he's good," Kathryn replied while nibbling on a sugar cookie. "He has a big case coming up right after the New Year, so he's been spending a lot of time on that. But otherwise he's good. He still works out each morning, and he bikes on the weekends whenever he can."

"That's wonderful, sweetie, but that's not what I asked."

Kathryn stared blankly at her mother.

"I asked, how are things with *you* and Griffin?"

"They're fine, why?"

"You two both seem to be going a hundred miles an hour. I just hope you're making time for each other in the process."

"Mom"—Kathryn rolled her eyes—"everything is fine. You remember when you and Dad were young and just getting started? I'm sure you were busy too."

"Yes, you're right about that, we definitely were. But it was a very different world then, and we always made each other our first priority. No matter how busy we got with work or even once you were born, we always made time for each other. And now, looking back on how little time we actually had, I'm so glad we did. If I had known I was going to have your father for only a few short years I probably would've spent every waking moment with him. You have to be so thankful for the blessings you have while you have them, Kathryn, I hope you know that."

"Of course I do," Kathryn answered defensively.

"And how was your morning with Benji? I heard that you two were able to spend some time together at his studio. He sure does beautiful work, doesn't he?"

Kathryn sighed heavily. "Yes, he does do beautiful work."

"But?" her mother asked.

"But I just don't understand him anymore."

"Why not?"

"He has this amazing talent, and if he would just put a little effort behind it he could have something huge. I've tried to convince him more than once to move to the city, but he won't have any part of it. I just feel like he's so . . . so, stagnant. That the world is out there passing him by while he just sits in his little studio apartment in Bakersville. He's so *different* than he used to be."

Kathryn's mother smiled at her knowingly, in a way only a mother could understand a child she brought into the world. "Are you sure *he's* the one who's different?"

"Of course I am. What does that mean anyway?"

"Kathryn, maybe you are the one who **has** changed."

"Maybe I have a little," Kathryn admitted, "but I mean, how could I not? I'm not some teenager anymore. I'm a grown woman."

"Indeed you are," her mother agreed. "I don't know if you remember, but several years ago when you were a senior in high school you were so worried that you and Benji would grow apart. We talked then about the fact that your relationship *would* change over the years. That you would both grow into adults, and your focus for life would change, but that if you really meant something to one another, you would allow your relationship to grow even in the midst of those changes."

"So what are you trying to say?" Kathryn asked.

"All I'm saying is maybe you should embrace your friend for who he is and not try to see him for who you want him to be. Maybe there are things about you that he wishes he could change, but rather than forcing you to be something you're not he accepts you and loves you for the person you have become."

Kathryn finished the last of her tea and stared out the window as the moonlight danced across the bare branches of the trees.

"Just don't give up on what you two have. Sure, you may go through some growing pains along the way, everybody does in their relationships. But don't ever lose sight of what truly matters in this lifetime."

Kathryn's mother arose, put her mug in the sink, and kissed her on top of the head before heading upstairs for the night. "Goodnight, sweetheart, it's good to have you home for a few nights."

"Night, Mom."

Kathryn followed shortly behind her mother, surprisingly tired even though it wasn't even ten o'clock. She had to laugh about it. If she had been in the city she would likely either be at her office (yes, even on a Saturday night) or getting ready to go out to dinner with Griffin. Yet here she was in Bakersville where Mr. Sandman sprinkled his potion over the town not long after sunset. Kathryn clicked the lamp on her bedroom dresser which dimly illuminated her lemon yellow walls. Same room, same patchwork quilt, same furniture from her days in high school. She lingered in front of her dresser and contemplated each of the photos—cherished memories ornately framed to preserve their importance. Grans, wearing her favorite yellow sweater and initial pendant that Kathryn hadn't dug out of her jewelry armoire in years. A picture of Kathryn's father, young and handsome and larger than life with his precious two-year-old daughter perched atop his shoulders grinning from ear to ear. Kathryn and Benjamin at their high school graduation, he in his royal blue gown and she in her white gown with various gold cords and emblems signifying all of her accolades. She touched the photo and smiled at his lopsided mortar board. God bless him, he couldn't even wear graduation apparel without somehow getting it wrong. And finally a picture of Kathryn in her middle school years, rocking gently on the front porch swing with Trouble faithfully curled up next to her, the best of friends. The pictures all brought back so many feelings and memories it was difficult to know how to process them all. As she turned the light out and pulled back the covers, she couldn't help but wish that for just a little while she could be Katie again.

Have you ever been to church one Sunday when the pastor preached a sermon that spoke so perfectly to your life that you'd swear it was written just for you? Like the pastor had some sort of crystal ball and was looking into your innermost thoughts and feelings? It's that eerie feeling in a Twilight Zone kind of way, where you think to yourself, "*How on earth did he know?*" That was exactly what Kathryn was about to experience, and she wasn't the least bit prepared for it.

When she first entered St. Paul the Apostle Church, it seemed like she was stepping back in time. She was warmly greeted by several familiar faces, yet in spite of the hospitality she felt very out of place. It was a world that Kathryn had left behind long ago, a world of country folk and simple conversations where resumes or status mattered little. She felt very conspicuous and self-conscious.

Benjamin escorted her into the sanctuary in the same pew they had claimed as their own through so many years of their childhood. She assumed that Benjamin still sat in that same pew every Sunday, unfazed by the changing world around him. It impressed and offended her all at the same time. Brother Washington, who walked a little slower than the last time she had seen him and was white around his temples, greeted her with a smile and bow of his head but did not stop to make conversation. As the churchgoers filled the pews and the organist began a soft medley of traditional hymns, Kathryn visited that foregone world ever so briefly in her mind. She thought of the days when Benjamin would tell her stories about the people in the church, their intentions and innermost feelings. She smiled, her heart strangely warmed. How simple life was back then. But then her smile faded into a grimace when she wondered what kind of stories people would tell about her if they could see inside her heart. She wasn't sure she wanted to know.

For most of the service Kathryn appeared attentive with her legs crossed and hands folded neatly in her lap, but the whole time her mind wandered. First it wandered to cases she was working on, then she wondered what Griffin was doing with his family for the weekend. Then she thought about Benjamin and how even though they were sitting right next to each other there was a distance between them, a distance that she wasn't sure how to bridge. She barely heard the layperson announce that the scripture for the morning could be found in Chapter 14 of the Gospel of Matthew, the story of where Jesus walks on water. She had heard the story before many times and nothing specific registered with her except how cool it would be to *actually* walk on water. Kathryn daydreamed, her mind floating in and out of consciousness, right up until Pastor Matt stepped down from the transept and stood adjacent to the first pew in the sanctuary. Apparently Pastor Matt wasn't a pulpit kind of preacher. He wanted to be right there with the flock of his pasture.

"When I was a little boy," he began, "I was deathly afraid of the water. I loved going to the town swimming pool each summer and I would spend my entire day there, but the most I would ever do is wade in the water about knee-deep and that was it. I looked out at the vastness of the water and how small I was in comparison, and I thought I had better stick close to the edge just to be safe." Kathryn was mildly interested in his childhood story, and as she looked around she could tell that the entire congregation was transfixed.

"Then one day," he continued, "my father decided he was going to teach me how to swim. At first I didn't want anything to do with it. I was perfectly content playing in the shallow end. But every once in a while I couldn't help but look out into the deep end of the pool at the older kids—playing their games of Marco Polo or sharks and minnows and having a glorious time. And I have to admit I was a little jealous. But even still, the water looked so sinister to me. Well, my father went out into the water just a few short steps with his back towards the deep end and had me paddle out to him. Just a couple of strokes. I was scared, but I figured how hard could it be? It was only a few strokes. And before I knew it I was safely in his arms. Then we did it again, but this time my father took a few more steps farther out into the water. I looked at him anxiously, but he just smiled and winked at me. Again, I took a few more strokes and flung myself into his arms as he spun me around with joy. The third time, though, something quite interesting happened. My father went out a little bit farther, just as he had done before. Nothing changed at his end of things. But since I had already swum out to him twice before, I became a little too confident. Cocky even, we might say. I didn't think twice about it, and I began to swim out to him. But about midway in my journey I took my focus off of him. Instead, I looked at the water and suddenly realized how far I was from the safety of the edge, and I panicked. I started flailing my arms wildly, I took a huge gulp of water, and I sunk like a rock. I can still remember that moment like it was only yesterday—I could see the sunlight from beneath the water, yet no matter how hard I tried to swim towards the light, it seems as though I was only sinking farther down. Of course my father was right there within seconds to pull me up and to give me a good pat on the back as I coughed up water. And he said something to me that day that I'll never forget. He said, 'Son, you never should've taken your eyes off me. If you had kept your focus on me the whole time, everything would've been fine.'"

Pastor Matt paused for a moment while he flipped through his Bible to let the meaning behind his story sink in. Kathryn looked sideways at Benjamin and felt the slightest twinge in her stomach. Pastor Matt continued.

"I think Peter suffered from very much the same problem that I did when I was learning how to swim. You see, when Peter first gets out of the boat he is able to walk on water with no problem. He has his eyes set on Jesus, and as a faithful disciple of the Lord, Peter knows in his heart that Jesus would never harm him or lead him astray. But then, only for a moment, Peter takes his eyes off of the Lord. And what does he see? The huge waves that are churning all around him. What does he feel? The wind shaking him off balance. He knows that he is walking on water in the middle of a storm. And just like I did, Peter panicked. He set his eyes on something other than Jesus and as soon as he did that, he began sinking. Peter became so scared that he shouted out to Jesus, 'Save me, Lord!' There's no doubt in my mind that at that very moment Peter thought, *'That's it, I'm a goner.'* But of course we know that's not the end of the story. Because just like Jesus always has, he comes to the rescue. Jesus reached out for him and pulled him to safety."

Pastor Matt paused once again. He looked at his congregants very seriously and lowered his voice, almost to a whisper. "Let me ask you, how often are we guilty of doing exactly what Peter did? The Lord promises us that if we follow him, we can never go wrong. The Bible tells us that if we acknowledge him in all of our ways, he indeed will make our paths straight. But how often do we allow ourselves to become preoccupied with the things of this world that take our eyes off of Jesus? How often do we turn our attention to those things only to realize that, like Peter, we have totally lost our bearings? I want you to ask yourselves something, and I want you to pray about it. What are *your* sights set on? Are they set on the things of this world? The wealth? The pleasures? The material things that we feel like we *have* to have? Or perhaps the influence? The power? The fame? I promise you, brothers and sisters, if you have your sights set on those things you will surely be disappointed. They are all temporary and will be gone one day. Vanished."

The more he spoke, the more Kathryn fidgeted nervously in her pew. Her heart began to pound, and she could feel her breath quickening. She felt as though this pastor had been watching her every move for the past five years and was looking directly at her as he delivered his sermon. *That is ludicrous*, she assured herself. Pastor Matt didn't know her from Adam, and surely his "warnings" were just a bunch of Biblical mumbo jumbo. The only problem was, Kathryn knew in her heart that every word Pastor Matt said was unequivocally true about her. She had taken her eyes off Jesus years ago, and instead she had set her sights on the things of the world which she thought would bring her pleasure and success. If she had everything she had ever hoped for, then why did she feel so empty inside? She was beginning to panic. *Keep it together*, she told herself. *The sermon will be over soon, just keep it together.*

"Let me share one other very important point that I think this particular story teaches us," Pastor Matt said. "You see, Peter never would've been able to walk on water in the first place if it hadn't been for Jesus. And Peter sure as you-know-what would not have been able to save himself from the storm once he began to sink. He *needed* Jesus. And so do we. Sure, we all have times in our lives when we might *feel* like we can walk on water. When everything is going so well for us, we're on top of our game and feel like we're '*all that*' if you know what I mean. But is it really our own doing? No, not at all. The Word tells us that every good gift we have is from God, not from ourselves. So we also need to give credit where credit is due. All glory should go to the Lord. So please," Pastor Matt concluded as Kathryn felt her heart racing and the sweat collecting on her forehead, "keep your focus where it should be. As a little boy I learned that day in the pool never to take my eyes off my father. He loved me, he would never let me down, and he would always be there for me. Does that sound like anyone we know? Furthermore, because I trusted my father I soon learned to swim and within a few weeks I was out there playing sharks and minnows with the big kids in the deep end. So please, don't make the same mistake I made and that Peter made. Don't ever take your eyes off the only thing that really matters. Because Peter can tell us from firsthand experience, and so can I—if you set your sights on anything else, you will undoubtedly sink."

"Amen!" shouted several of the churchgoers. They bowed their heads, and a few even applauded. Pastor Matt ignored it all, obviously not wanting the glory for allowing himself to be the vessel that God had used to deliver his message. He called for the ushers to come forward, and as hard as Kathryn tried to pretend like nothing was wrong, she couldn't do it. She was on the verge of an all-out panic attack right in the middle of the service. She leaned over to Benjamin.

"I've got to get out of here," she whispered.

"What?" Benjamin replied. "Is everything all right?"

"Just take me home. Please! Can you take me home right now?" Kathryn didn't wait for a reply. She grabbed her purse and quickly exited the pew. She could feel herself begin to hyperventilate. She was suffocating. *God, please just make it stop,* she told herself, *please let me get out of this church without making a scene.* She fled past the pews filled with people, pushed the ushers aside without making eye contact, and practically ran toward the doors leading from the sanctuary into the parking lot. *I don't belong here,* she told herself. *Not with all of these Godly people. These holier-than-thou Christians. God doesn't want me here.* Although so many thoughts were reeling through her mind, she was absolutely certain about one thing. She was done with church. Done with St. Paul the Apostle Church and any other church for that matter. Done.

As soon as they got into Benjamin's beat up Chevy she slammed the door.

"Why did you make me come here today?" she shrieked.

"What do you mean? It's church, Kathryn. I thought it would be nice if we went to church together."

"Just take me home," she ordered.

They drove the five minutes back to Kathryn's house in silence. Benjamin walked her inside, hoping that he could calm her down. "Kathryn, are you all right?"

"No, I'm not all right! Does it look like I'm all right?"

"I don't understand why you're so upset."

"Well, maybe it's because you have totally judged me for wanting a successful career and a good life."

"What? Kathryn, I never—"

"Who do you think you are anyway? Do you think you're so perfect because you have this simple little life and all you do is sit in your shop and make furniture all day long?"

"Kathryn, slow down, you're not making any sense."

"Oh I'm not, am I? I know you don't approve of me representing these criminals. I know you're jealous of all the things I have. You just can't stand the fact that I got out of this God-forsaken place and made something of my life!"

Benjamin knew that anything he said would be pointless, so instead he listened and let her unload what had obviously been building up for months, or maybe even years.

"You think I'm not good enough. Just like Pastor Matt said, like I have taken my eyes off of what's important. Is that why you brought me to church this morning? To make me feel like I'm worthless? Like I'm a bad person and the only person I care about is myself? Is that what this was all about? Some sort of intervention to help Kathryn see how horrible and stuck-up she is?"

"Kathryn, it wasn't that at all. I just wanted—"

"Well, let me tell *you* something," she hissed. "It's not easy trying to get ahead in this world, and if sometimes I have to put myself first, well then that's just too bad. I don't need your self-righteous attitude! I have plenty of friends who like me just the way I am!"

"It's not that I don't like you," Benjamin tried to explain. "I just want to make sure you're happy."

"Of course I'm happy," she answered indignantly. "Why wouldn't I be? Have you seen my life? I have everything I could ever want and then some!"

"Yes, you have a lot, but is it what you want in your heart?"

"What I *want*," she screamed, "is for people to stop constantly judging me and leave me alone!!"

"Who is judging you?" Benjamin asked.

"I don't know, everyone! You, for one. You treat me differently than you used to, like I'm damaged or tainted or something."

"Kathryn, I'm sorry if you feel that way, I never meant to make you feel—"

"You don't know the first thing about how I feel! I know you don't like me anymore, Benjamin. You pretend like you do, but you're so different towards me. It makes me sick!"

"Kathryn, listen to me. I have never treated you differently, and I have never changed. And I still like you just as much as I did that first day I came to your house in the third grade. I just don't like the way we have grown apart."

"Well, I'm sorry," she said sarcastically. "I suppose that fact that we've grown apart is *all* my fault just like everything else is. Right? *RIGHT??* Well, if you don't like it then you can get out! I don't want to be a burden to you anymore. Get out of this house! Get out of my life!" Kathryn took a step closer to Benjamin, and with both hands she shoved him toward the door as hard as she could.

"Please, I just wanted to spend some time with you. That's all. I promise."

"*GET OUT!*" she screamed, trying with all her might to keep the tears at bay that were perilously close to breaking forth. "Don't call me, don't text me, don't visit me. Just leave me alone! I don't ever want to see you again!" Her eyes raged with pure contempt.

Silence. Benjamin never said a word. He just looked at her solemnly, turned, and walked out the door. He knew that Kathryn wasn't *really* angry with him. No, she was angry with herself. Kathryn condemned herself for becoming someone she had never wanted to be. For getting caught up in the ugliness of the world. A world that can easily seduce us into believing its pleasures are fulfilling and necessary. Kathryn couldn't admit it to herself, but she was lost. She had taken her eyes off what was truly important and sold her soul to the devil in the process. And since she couldn't accept the truth of the matter, she desperately needed someone who would shoulder that burden for her. Someone who would take the blame and pay the price, even if that person was completely innocent. A scapegoat. Benjamin.

Kathryn remained frozen in the hallway, speechless. She heard Benjamin's car start and the sound of the muffler gradually disappear down Magnolia Lane. She couldn't move. She couldn't even process what had just happened. She stood there for what seemed like hours, stunned. What had she done?

Over a hundred guests arrived at the exclusive Greenwood restaurant on the crisp spring evening in the most upscale district of the city. Reservations were typically required almost a year in advance, so Griffin made sure to act early and he booked the entire place. He wanted this night to be *her* night, the single most memorable night of her life. The big 3-0. And it was memorable indeed, but not for the reasons he had hoped.

Kathryn managed to arrive late to her very own surprise party, something about a Motion for Severance that had to be filed first thing in the morning that she needed to be sure was signed and ready to deliver to the courthouse. She walked into the foyer a good forty-five minutes later than expected, and she discovered her guests in various states of inebriation more than happy to celebrate her birthday with yet another round. A champagne glass was shoved into her hand, and several toasts were offered—one by Griffin, one by Darian Wallingford, and another by a former law school professor. The accolades flowed, and so did the spirits. For over three hours the party continued with good food, great drinks, a four-tiered designer cake with thirty sparklers on top, and company you could find only among the upper class of the city. Kathryn mingled and hugged and kissed countless well-wishers. She danced with Griffin as the band played, her guests mesmerized by their picture-perfect life. Little did they know it was the closest she had been to Griffin in months. They both acted the part so well that for a minute they even managed to fool themselves that it was real.

Kathryn was wined and dined. She was congratulated by judges, courted by city councilmen, and envied by colleagues. Her smile was forced, and her laugh was fake. She started to feel a little claustrophobic in the process. The more she exchanged pleasantries and the more she drank, the more she really *saw* the people attending her party. The go-getters of the city, the cream of the crop, high school's equivalent to the "in" crowd. Oh, they were the beautiful people with their three-piece suits and designer dresses with stiletto heels and manicures. But they were each a façade of a real person. Toy dolls where you could pull an imaginary string and they would do or say exactly as they had been programmed by their creator. And who was their creator? Why, lust itself. Lust for fame, for fortune, for living a life of grandeur. For the first time in her life, Kathryn wasn't impressed by them, and she didn't want to *be* one of them. On the contrary, she pitied them for their phoniness and shallowness; for reducing the gifts that God had given each of them to a paycheck and a status level. It also dawned on her that none of these people was *actually* her friend. Oh, they called themselves her friends because in some way, whether socially or politically, it was advantageous to them. But would she call any one of them in a personal crisis? Of course not. If she did, they would think she had completely lost her mind. On the other hand, if she had a time share she needed to unload for a week, they would gladly line up for the opportunity. No, these people weren't her friends. Kathryn had only ever had *one* true friend in her entire life, and he was nowhere to be found. She was among a room full of people all there to celebrate her, yet she had never felt more alone in her life.

She managed to pry Griffin away from a conversation with Judge Macklin long enough to ask if Benjamin had been invited. "Absolutely," Griffin answered without hesitation. But he had never heard a word back, so Griffin assumed he was busy and couldn't make it. Kathryn knew it was much more than that. After all why *should* he come? Kathryn had made it painfully clear only four months earlier that she wanted nothing to do with him; that he should walk out of her life and never return. He was just doing what he was told, what *she* wanted him to do. The only problem was, that wasn't what Kathryn wanted at all. As she scanned the room of high society guests and noticed herself becoming the slightest bit dizzy after her fourth glass of wine, it hit her like a ton of bricks that the only person she wanted there that night was the one person she had shut out of her life. She had built a wall between herself and Benjamin that just might be impenetrable, and it scared her to death.

For the rest of the evening Kathryn alternated between sipping wine and checking her phone, all while trying to appear genuinely entertained. Surely he would at least call or text. Ever since she had met Benjamin when she was in the third grade, he had never missed her birthday. In elementary school and middle school he hand-designed cards for her, in high school he wrote her poems, in college he sent her flowers, in law school he gave her gift cards to Starbucks, and more recently when she was usually too busy to give him the time of day, he was always the first to text in the early morning hours to wish her a happy birthday. Many times he even remembered her special day before Griffin did. But this year she received nothing. Nothing but silence. And it wasn't just deafening silence. It was maddening. Kathryn didn't know if she would be able to survive it, but she also knew there was no turning back. She had said far too many things and was much too hateful to repair the damage and undo what had been done. She had chosen this course, and she had to live with it.

The celebration wrapped up close to 2 a.m. when the last of the guests bid them farewell and headed home to their opulent estates or condominiums. One well-meaning law clerk had offered to drive Kathryn's Benz back to their condo, partly because Kathryn was in no shape to drive it herself but more because he wanted the thrill of driving a Benz. Griffin gratefully accepted the offer and took Kathryn home himself. When they arrived at the condo she glanced at her phone one final time, the battery almost dead, to see if she had any messages waiting. Her heart skipped a beat when she noticed that she had three new text messages. But as she clicked the icon, the disappointment flooded her as she read messages from three of the up-and-coming attorneys at her firm expressing what a wonderful time they had at her party and how grateful they were to have been included in such a special evening. *Brown-nosers*, Kathryn thought. That's all they were, just like she had been only a few years ago. It was officially no longer her birthday, and something else was also official. He was really out of her life for good.

She clumsily changed into her satin nightgown without even washing her face and crawled under the covers, wishing that sleep would overtake her emotions. Only a few minutes later Griffin slid in next to her.

"I hope you had a great birthday, babe," he said as he caressed her arm.

"I did," she lied.

"I hope it's one you'll never forget."

"I won't," she said truthfully.

As he drew himself closer to her, he could feel the rigidity invade her body. She didn't give him the opportunity to ask for an invitation.

"Not tonight, Griff, I'm so tired. Can't we just go to bed?"

"Sure we can," he said as he rolled in the opposite direction. It wasn't the first time he had heard those words from her. And it certainly wouldn't be the last.

Kathryn could feel the bedroom spinning until she closed her eyes tightly and fought the nausea within her. She thought about what a miserable thirtieth birthday it had been. Not because of having turned thirty. She couldn't care less about the number of candles on a cake. But because the one thing that ever brought true meaning to her life was gone, and it was all her fault. That night she was sure she had just experienced the lowest of the lows. That things would have to look up. She was wrong. Little did Kathryn know, but she was about to be set adrift at sea in a furious storm that was headed directly for her. And she had just thrown away her only life preserver that could save her from drowning.

CHAPTER 11
I DON'T

"For this reason a man will leave
his father and mother
and be united to his wife,
and the two will become one flesh.
So they are no longer two, but one."
Mark 10:7-8

She should've seen it coming a mile away. All the signs were there. In fact, when she called her mother to tell her what had happened, she was astounded by the response.

"I'm so sorry, sweetheart," her mother said tenderly.

"Can you believe it?"

"Actually, I'm not surprised."

"What???"

Apparently everyone except Kathryn knew it was going to happen. Instead of facing reality and doing something about it while there was still time, she had chosen to live in a dream world she had created for herself where everything was picture perfect and went according to plan. Unfortunately, her dream was about to turn into a nightmare.

———

It was almost seven o'clock. Kathryn got off the elevator and walked into their kitchen, tossing her keys and briefcase on the marble countertop. It had been a long day at the office, and she was looking forward to a drink and an evening out on the town. "Griff! Griff!" she called as she searched the condo for his whereabouts.

"Out here," he yelled from the patio.

She slid the screen door open and joined him on their expansive rooftop patio overlooking the horizon of city lights at dusk. Griffin was seated at the glass table in one of their wicker chairs. As she approached him she noticed something on the tabletop next to his sweating glass of water.

"What's this?" she asked, picking it up and examining it. "An airline ticket?" She fumbled through the papers and pulled out the ticket.

"Are we going somewhere? . . . Florida?"

Griffin didn't say a word.

"What's in Florida?" she wondered aloud.

He took a deep breath and exhaled. "Kathryn," he said pensively, "I love you, but I can't do this anymore."

"What are you talking about?"

"The firm has asked me to head their malpractice department at the Miami office."

Kathryn still wasn't connecting the dots. An expression of relief crossed her face. "Griff, that's fantastic! What an opportunity! So you're going down there to talk to them about it?"

"Not quite," he replied.

"Then what?"

"Kathryn, I accepted the position."

She looked deep into his eyes, and a fear began to invade her. She was sure she must be misinterpreting what he was saying.

"That's great," she replied tentatively, "but don't you think this is something we should've talked about first? I mean, moving to Florida is a big deal. That's thousands of miles away; my job is here, my mother is here. There's a lot we need to consider before we make any decisions."

Then it hit her. In her hand she clutched only *one* ticket. She held it up to him. "Griffin?" she asked desperately.

"I'm sorry, Kathryn." It was all he could say as the emotions threatened to overtake him.

She mindlessly crumpled into the chair across from him, completely dumbfounded. This couldn't be happening. Once again in her life, utter silence.

She cleared her throat, determined not to let her voice crack. "So, you're going?"

"Yes."

"When?"

"They need me for the position in three months, but my last day at the office here is in two weeks. I'm going to take some time to spend with my family before I head to Miami."

"I thought *I* was your family?" she asked sarcastically, able to hold back the tears no longer. They flowed freely down her cheeks. Griffin reached for her hand but she recoiled.

"Don't touch me!" she protested. "Can't we work this out? Why haven't you said anything to me before?"

"I tried, Kathryn," Griffin replied with a shaky voice. "Lord knows, I've tried."

"When?"

"What about all those times I begged you to take a few days off from the firm so that we could get away together? What about the times I told you how I missed the way things used to be? What about when I asked you to slow down a little?"

"Oh, and like you weren't also working sixty-plus hours a week? So what?" she asked, the pitch of her voice raising an octave. "This is all *my* fault?"

"No, it's not all your fault. You're absolutely right. It takes two to make a marriage work, and I definitely could've tried harder. But the point is, I'm tired of pretending. Pretending that we have a real marriage when really we're just two people who happen to live together and sleep in the same bed. Kathryn, that's not a marriage. After all these years I don't think there was really ever an '*us.*' I think it was always just 'you' and 'me.'"

Again, they sat in silence with only the humming of the cars below and an occasional beeping horn to punctuate the tension.

"So then this is it?" Kathryn asked.

"Yes, this is it."

"Where do we go from here?" Kathryn finally asked. "Do we pretend that the last six years never happened?"

"Of course not," Griffin replied. He turned toward her. "Look at me."

Kathryn continued to stare off into the distance.

"Kathryn, look at me!" She hesitantly met his gaze, and as soon as she did she thought she might stop breathing at that very moment. Griffin, too, could barely get the words out.

"Kathryn, I love you. I will *always* love you, and I will cherish the time we spent together. I wouldn't trade it for the world." As she watched him struggle to get the words out, there was no doubt in her mind that this was going to be just as difficult for him as it was for her. "I've gone over this in my head again and again. I tried to figure something out so it wouldn't come to this. You and I had something very special."

"*Had?*" Kathryn asked.

"Yes, had. It was an amazing time in my life, and I will always be grateful to you for that. But I think we have to admit to ourselves and to each other that it has run its course. Kathryn, be honest, we haven't been happy, *genuinely* happy, for years."

"What about kids?" Kathryn interjected, grasping at straws. "We could have kids. You know, refocus our lives on children and start over."

Griffin laughed. "Kathryn, believe me, there is nothing I would've loved more than to have had children with you. Heck, when we first got married I remember talking about us having a whole bunch of them. But having children isn't going to fix what's wrong. If anything it would just drive us farther apart and make us busier than we are now. Besides, are you ready to cut back your hours at the firm once we have a baby to take care of? Every time I ever brought up the idea of children you said it wasn't the right time and we would talk about it later. But 'later' never came." Griffin was absolutely right, and Kathryn couldn't deny it. It was just one more conversation that had fallen by the wayside in their marriage.

"Well, maybe now *is* the time," Kathryn said, desperately clinging to any shred of hope. "I'm thirty-one, I don't have anything to prove in the courtroom anymore. I could take some time off and we could start a family."

"Is that *really* what you want?" Griffin asked.

Kathryn knew at the very least he deserved her honesty. "I don't know. But I *do* know that I don't want this to end."

"Neither do I, babe, neither do I. But I think if we're honest about it, we would realize that this actually ended a long time ago. We've been going through the motions, that's all. And that's not fair to either one of us."

Kathryn took a deep breath and slid further back into the oversized chair. "I can't believe this is actually happening."

"Me neither," Griffin said as he extended his arm to her. "Come here."

"No," she instinctively replied.

"Please, Kathryn." He reached out and pulled her toward him. She sat across his lap, buried her head in his shoulder, and sobbed. So did he.

"I can't imagine my life without you," she mumbled.

"In many ways I can't either," he agreed. "But I think we're both going to be all right."

After what felt like hours when there were finally no more tears to cry, Kathryn withdrew to their bedroom, utterly drained and wanting nothing more than to put an end to this horrendous evening. The sensor activated the lights, and the moment she entered the room two oversized suitcases stared her in the face, packed and ready to go. Griffin came up behind her, but she didn't bother to turn around.

"Were you going to go without even saying goodbye?" she asked.

"Of course not, you know I would never do that. But I thought it best that I leave. I've rented a room at the Marriott downtown and I'll be staying there until I head down to my folks' place."

"And what about all of *this*?" Kathryn looked around the opulent condo at the product of six years of marriage—paintings, ornate furnishings, trinkets, sculptures, *stuff*.

"It's yours," Griffin answered. "You can have it, Kathryn, I'm not looking to take away anything you worked so hard to buy."

"*We* worked so hard to buy," she corrected him.

"Yeah, I guess so."

In legal terms their divorce would be an easy one. When they married they had decided to keep separate bank accounts, so their finances didn't need to be sorted out, and nothing was jointly titled. Even the condominium was in her name only. They figured at the time that it would make things easier, "just in case." She had never thought about it back then, but "just in case" of what? Perhaps somewhere deep down inside both Kathryn and Griffin knew what the end result of their marriage would be long before they ever said "I do." Kathryn had even decided to keep her maiden name, for professional reasons, of course, so even that wasn't an issue. No, it was completely cut and dry. No courtroom battles, no "he said-she said," no duking it out for property or pensions. All they had to do was sign a few papers and go along their merry way. She tried to sell the idea to herself that she would once again be a single woman and no worse for the wear. No one to answer to, and she could come and go as she pleased. Maybe this would actually be freeing for her. Yes, this was only a little speed bump in the road of life, she told herself. But deep down inside she wasn't buying any of it.

That night Griffin slept on the couch and was gone before Kathryn awoke. As the morning sunrise overtook their bedroom in shades of fuchsia and tangerine she rubbed her eyes, wondering if perhaps the whole thing had been a bad dream. Maybe she had imagined everything and Griffin was at the gym per his usual early morning routine. But when she sat up in bed, she immediately noticed that the two suitcases were gone, and as she crept into the kitchen she found his house key on the counter. Next to it was a single white rose. Was it Griffin's way of making a peace offering? A truce? Friendship? Or was Kathryn reading too much into it, and Griffin was simply trying to soften the blow?

She called the office and informed Pam, her legal secretary, that she was ill and would not be coming into work. In her entire seven years at Engel, Wallingford, and Driscoll, it was the first time she had ever called in sick. *Surely this will get the rumor mill going*, she thought. But she couldn't have cared less. Let them talk. She instructed Pam to postpone all of her appointments and reschedule her pretrial conference. She also said she wasn't sure if she would be in the following day, so she would text Pam later to let her know. Pam obediently took copious notes of all of Kathryn's directions and wished her well before they hung up.

Kathryn looked around the condo. Even though nothing had physically changed, since Griffin had taken only his clothes and a few personal belongings, it suddenly seemed completely different. It was empty. She couldn't bear the thought of sleeping there by herself, so the next phone call was to her mother. Kathryn broke the bad news. The conversation was brief. She didn't have the energy to go into the tedious details, so she asked her mother one question.

"Mom, can I come home?"

"Sweetheart, you never have to ask."

She absentmindedly threw a few things into a duffel bag and left as quickly as she could, refusing to look back on the emptiness that seemed to permeate her life these days. The trip to Bakersville was a blur, her mind preoccupied with a collage of memories from days past. The first time she met Griffin while on *Law Review*. The night he proposed to her on the pink beaches of Bermuda. When he carried her over the threshold of their first condo. When she made partner at the firm and he was waiting for her with roses and a night of celebration. She missed his smile. She missed his laugh. She missed his touch. She missed *him*. Then she daydreamed about the memories never to be made. The house in the suburbs with the white picket fence. The two kids, dog, and a few cats. The anniversaries, the milestones with children. Their growing old together. All memories that would never come to fruition, dreams shattered like glass into a million tiny chards on the hard, cold floor.

As soon as Kathryn walked in the kitchen door, the customary sounds and smells of her childhood home overtook her. Funny, she thought to herself, you never realize that your home feels or smells a certain way. That is, until you leave and you return one day so desperate for the familiarity it brings.

"Mom, I really don't want to talk about it just yet," Kathryn told her mother not long after she had arrived. "It's not that I don't want you to know what happened, it's just that I don't think I have it in me right now."

Her mother more than understood and never pressed. "You can share if and when you're ready," she reassured her daughter. "I'm here, and I'm not going anywhere."

Then Kathryn's mother did what came most naturally to her. She cared for her daughter. She gave Kathryn the space to grieve, and she helped her take her mind off of reality, even if only temporarily. With a little encouragement, Kathryn accompanied her mother to the local nursery to pick out spring flowers for her garden. Kathryn, as always, chose the pansies. Pinks, yellows, whites, and purples, all with little faces cheerfully staring back at her. A tribute to another woman who, were she still with them, would have been just as compassionate and sympathetic as her mother had been. They returned home, changed clothes, and both got good and dirty planting flowers. No doubt about it, there's something cathartic about getting down on your hands and knees in the essence of God's creation. To be one with the very substance that God used to bring Adam forth from the dust of the ground. It's healing. It is humbling. Kathryn tended to the fragile plants with great care, meticulously placing them in the tiny holes she had dug, filling the dirt around them and bathing them with droplets from the watering can. If only she had tended to her own life the way she had tended to these little pansies. Things might've turned out so differently.

After dinner they visited a nearby town famous for its "best ice cream in the world," and they each enjoyed an oversized cone while strolling past the local shops. Finally they ended their evening together on the front porch swing. They shared little conversation, at least not in words. But their closeness spoke more than any words could, and Kathryn was so incredibly thankful to have a little bit of normalcy back in her life. Rocking in the cool evening breeze, she half convinced herself that everything just might be all right. She looked forward to a good night's sleep and a release from the constrictions that the last day had delivered upon her.

Dreams are an interesting phenomenon. They seem quite literally to have a mind all their own. Sometimes when we close our eyes and give ourselves over to that other realm of consciousness, we relive things that had been a part of our day. Places we went, people we interacted with, things we did. Sometimes, if we're anticipating something yet to come—an important event or engagement we will visit that in our dreams. Sometimes our dreams are so random that the only thing expected about them is their unexpectedness. Sometimes if we wake in the middle of a dream, we can will ourselves back to sleep so we can pick up where we left off. (That is, only if it's a good dream. I've never heard of someone trying to do that for a nightmare.) Sometimes when we're dreaming we *know* we're dreaming, and we can literally tell our dreaming selves that we're in the middle of a dream. Other times our dream is so real to us that it feels like an extension of our lives rather than an altered state of awareness. At times we are blessed with a gift that our awakened state denies us—the ability to visit things past. People we once knew, long since gone from our lives, things we regrettably did and would love nothing more than to "redo." We can have those redos in dreams. We can visit those people in dreams. We can even visit those people who no longer walk in this world.

There's no telling from one night to the next what it's going to be. It is a grab-bag of sorts, where you reach your hand in, and you never know what you're going to get. But there are also some dreams categorically different from *any* of the others. They aren't of the past, or present, or future. They are something even better. These are the dreams where God allows us the briefest glimpse of a time and a place that offers no comparison to our worldly life. Dreams that our simplistic minds, even in their state of slumber, could never conjure. Dreams of a place more beautiful than we could ever imagine, of an existence as God had intended it to be, of a destination where we hope and pray we will take permanent refuge once our short time in this world has expired. These are the dreams of paradise.

Once Kathryn was alone in her dark room, the weight of the last several hours hit her. She was exhausted. Emotionally, physically, mentally. She couldn't fathom that only twenty-four hours had passed since her conversation with Griffin on their patio. It had seemed like years ago. She slipped into bed and gratefully allowed the covers to swallow her. Curling up into fetal position, she cried herself to sleep.

As consciousness left her, the darkness morphed into a scene. Kathryn found herself wearing an exquisite wedding gown, peering down an endless aisle with euphoric anticipation. Griffin waited at the altar, beaming with pride in his crisp black tuxedo and vest. At first everything but Griffin was a complete blur. But then, when her surroundings came into focus it suddenly dawned on her that she wasn't in St. Mary's Cathedral. For as breathtaking as St. Mary's was, this sanctuary was far more beautiful than anything she had ever seen before. Its gargantuan walls were crafted out of the most precious gemstones of pearls, rubies, emeralds, and amethysts. The pews glistened of pure gold, and the crimson carpet was sewn out of the finest silk. Kathryn looked up in awe. Chandeliers crafted of millions of diamonds floated above her, creating rainbow prisms dancing everywhere the eye could see. The walls of this sanctuary towered so high that they stretched upwards and met the sky as its ceiling. Yet the most magnificent part of the structure wasn't the adornments, but the light which emanated from the sanctuary itself.

It was a light *beyond* light. Not a light that any man-made inventions or even the sun could provide. This light was more brilliant than all of that—it filled not only every corner of the sanctuary but it also filled Kathryn.

As Kathryn refocused her attention on Griffin and eagerly awaited her journey down the aisle, music softly began to play. A chorus of harps and trumpets and voices sang so harmoniously that she imagined only angels could produce so breathtaking a sound. It was a melody unlike any she had ever heard before. She took her first step and felt like she was floating on air. It was then that she noticed her arm interlocked with someone else's. Through the tulle of her veil she saw her father standing next to her, smiling. He was magnificent—handsome and healthy and very much alive. She smiled in return and the pair glided down the aisle, passing friends and loved ones along the way. Brother Washington was there, her mother, Grans, everyone emanating a radiance and pure joy at being gathered for this special occasion.

Kathryn neared the altar and prepared herself for the glorious moment when she would take Griffin's hand, and they would commit themselves to one another in love. She had never been happier in her entire life than she was in that moment. But the nearer she drew, the more the unfolding scene began to change. Details faded out, and new ones appeared. Once she was only a few steps away from the altar, she realized it was no longer Griffin waiting to greet her. It was someone else. Someone in a glowing white suit purer than any snow, a dazzling white that was brighter than the light in the sanctuary itself. He stood at the front of the altar, his eyes sparkling with his hands folded in front of him. It was Benjamin. But it was Benjamin like she had never seen him before. His face was *his* face, yet it wasn't. It had been transformed into the most majestic face, shining luminously like the sun. His usually unkempt appearance was now more perfect than any human being could achieve. She was speechless, completely spellbound. Her father removed her veil, kissed her cheek as if this had all been part of the plan, and took his place next to his wife. Kathryn's eyes were completely transfixed by Benjamin. She couldn't have looked elsewhere even if she had wanted to, yet she didn't want to. She felt as though she would be complete only if she could spend the rest of her life standing right there at that altar staring directly into his eyes. And when he spoke, it was Benjamin's voice but all the same time it wasn't a *human* voice. It was something that defied description. Benjamin took her hands and his touch alone sent a familiar warmth coursing through her body. "Kathryn," he said, "your bridegroom is here." Kathryn smiled, more content than she ever thought she could be and knowing that at that very moment she had finally discovered her life's fulfillment. Then . . .

Kathryn awoke. Back to reality. Oh, did I forget to mention? That's the other thing about dreams. You can be so deeply immersed in a dream you're convinced you will never leave it, but for reasons unknown you are abruptly and without warning transported back to your world of reality. When Kathryn regained her faculties she felt an unexplainable peace that was strangely comforting, yet she couldn't remember any details about her dream. It was all a fog. She lay there for quite some time trying to recapture pieces of the puzzle so she could reassemble the dream, but the fleeting glimpses weren't enough. All she could recall was feeling this glorious light inside of her and wanting the dream to go on forever. And there was also a man. A beautiful man.

After hibernating at her childhood home for three days, Kathryn was ready to face the music. She bid her mother farewell, assured her that she would be all right, and returned to her condo defeated yet determined to pick up the pieces. The moment she stepped foot off the elevator and scanned her surroundings, she decided she needed a change. She couldn't bear to look at the same furniture, the same paintings, and the same scenery that she and Griffin had amassed over their six years together. Her first order of business was in the bedroom. Kathryn pushed and shoved and prodded and pulled with all of her strength until the king-size bed had been relocated to a different wall. She was not about to sleep one more night in the same spot where she and Griffin had been intimate. Her second order of business was to call the office. She matter-of-factly told Pam that she and Griffin had decided to divorce (which, of course, Pam and the rest of the firm had already surmised but never confessed to Kathryn) and she had needed a few days to process things. She told Pam she would be in the office bright and early the next morning and the two would meet to discuss the rescheduling of appointments and anything else Kathryn had missed. Once she hung up with Pam, her third order of business was to call the friend of a friend who was one of the top interior decorators in the city. "I want a complete change," Kathryn told the designer. "New paint, new window treatments, new furniture, a whole new look. And I want it as soon as possible." The interior designer was a bit skeptical at first until Kathryn made two things quite clear. First, time was of the essence. And second, cost was no issue. The designer arrived by late morning with paint swatches, fabric samples, and a thick catalog of the latest furniture. A new home for Kathryn was about to be born. A Griffin-free home. Perhaps if everything *looked* different, she wouldn't be reminded of the other person who had once shared a life with her there.

Kathryn and the designer spent a good two hours brainstorming before the designer left with a pad full of scribbled notes and a fat check in hand. Kathryn was once again alone. She poured herself a vodka and cranberry juice with a twist, mentally noted that she would need to make a liquor store run sooner rather than later, and cautiously approached the patio. She dreaded setting foot out there—the site where their fateful conversation had taken place. But she was determined not to let that nightmare get the best of her. She slid open the door, took a deep breath of fresh air, and intentionally sat in the same wicker chair where Griffin had held her on what was the last night of their marriage. The city below bustled with activity, people going about their daily routines oblivious to Kathryn watching them from above. She sipped the mixed drink and stared blankly into the distance, thinking about the implications of the divorce on her life, her future. The more she thought, the more frightened she became. Not so much frightened of life without Griffin. Although she definitely wasn't looking forward to the loneliness and would miss him, she knew she would manage.

Financially she was more than well off, so she could clearly take care of herself in that regard. And socially she would be one of the most eligible attorneys in the city, so she would never be at a lack for company if and when she wanted it.

But there was something more about Griffin leaving, and it ate away at her soul. It meant she had failed. Kathryn Kirby was officially a failure at something. For as long as she could remember failure was not an option. It was a pressure she had put on herself since her childhood days. She had always expected to succeed in everything she did, and she always *had* succeeded. Her grades were exceptional, she excelled in anything she did, and she was awarded countless accolades in college and law school. She won her court cases and climbed the corporate ladder to partner. She had done it all. Yes, Kathryn had overwhelmingly succeeded in every endeavor she had set her mind to. Until now. Now in her losses column there was one big fat check mark. A permanent stain on her pristine record. She had lost her husband, she had lost her marriage, and she had failed at something. It was more than she could handle. Because after all, if Kathryn had failed at *this*, then it meant she could fail at other things too. And it also meant that perhaps she wasn't as perfect as she had always hoped to be. Perhaps she was only human too, just like everyone else.

Just as the interior designer had promised and after Kathryn had paid a small fortune, within one week her condominium was completely transformed. Other than the fact that the walls hadn't moved (because after all, it's rather difficult to move a wall in a condominium), you would've never known it was the same home she had once shared with Griffin. It was beautiful, of course, for it boasted all of the finest furnishings. Yes, the condo could easily have been featured on one of the myriad television shows about the high life in the city. It was opulent, decadent even. Yet in spite of this, it was also sterile. Kathryn couldn't admit it to herself, but this "new" condo felt less like home to her than the old one. No matter though, because Kathryn had plunged back into her work with a determination like never before. Her once sixty-hour work weeks became more like seventy-five- or eighty-hour work weeks. No sense in going home to an empty condo. She took on extra cases and was more vicious in the courtroom than she had ever been before. The more "wins" in the win column, the less obvious the one huge loss might look to the outside world. Her colleagues were concerned, her mother was concerned, and her acquaintances were concerned (because when it came down to it, Kathryn never had the time for actual *friends* in her life), but Kathryn paid no mind to their warnings. This was *her* life, and she was going to live it the way she wanted to. She may have failed once, but she would never fail again!

About a month into her new life, Kathryn had come to grips with being single again as she settled into a new routine. She kept busy and wouldn't allow herself to think of things in the past, whether that meant Griffin or anyone else who had once been a part of her life. She refused to dwell on the "could've beens." No point in doing that. No, from this point forward she would dream new dreams rather than lament the ones that never came to be.

It was a Tuesday afternoon around 2 p.m. Kathryn was busy working at her desk with three different files spread across the desktop and two computer screens facing her, one with her email inbox and the other a Motion to Suppress she was drafting. Several empty Starbucks cups littered her desk, her nourishment for the day which had started before 5 a.m. Her law clerk interrupted only when absolutely necessary to update her on legal research findings, and as she glanced at her watch she figured she could make it at least three more hours before she would have to stop and get some real food. As she poured over cases and statutes, Pam knocked on the door.

"Come in," Kathryn said while responding to an email.

"Excuse me, Kathryn, but someone is here to see you."

Kathryn stopped typing and looked at Pam. "I don't have any appointments today," she said.

"That's correct, this man did not have an appointment. He has some paperwork to deliver to you that he says needs your immediate attention and your signature."

Pam didn't have to say anything more. Kathryn knew it would be coming sooner or later.

"Let him in, please."

The man was in his mid-forties. He looked to be an off-duty police officer as many of the private process servers often are, his buzz cut and military-like posture giving him away.

"Kathryn Kirby?" he asked. In his hand was an oversized yellow envelope.

"Yes."

Once he received the affirmation, he carefully placed the folder on her desk so as not to knock over the collection of coffee cups. "I'll need you to sign here," he said, pointing to a line on his clipboard. It was all business.

She signed it immediately and he left just as quickly, wishing her a nice day on the way out.

She picked up the envelope and, with her eyes closed, she held it for a few moments before unsealing it. She knew what she had to do. No sense in postponing the inevitable. She opened it and pulled out a small packet of contents. On the top page she read the case caption, "Griffin Robert Harris, III versus Kathryn Ann Kirby." And then her eyes focused on the title: "COMPLAINT FOR DISSOLUTION OF MARRIAGE."

The day had arrived. Her dream was over.

But her biggest nightmare was yet to come.

CHAPTER 12
APRIL SHOWERS

"Why have you made me your target?
Have I become a burden to you?"
Job 7:20

When it rains, it pours. That's what they say, isn't it? Well, whoever *they* are, they clearly know what they're talking about. We've all been there at some point in our lives. When something terrible happens that knocks you flat off your feet. A loss. A diagnosis. That unexpected bad news. Then, *another* loss. Before you even have a chance to get on your knees to try to regain your balance, something else comes along out of nowhere and takes you right back down. It seems like it's one thing after another until you find yourself lying in the bottomless pit, trying with all your might to claw your way out and catch the tiniest glimpse of sunlight through the black storm clouds. You're physically and emotionally exhausted, and you've got no more fight left in you.

Of course you have a few well-meaning Christian friends who, much like Job's friends, should've learned when to keep silent but instead chose the foolish route: "God wouldn't give you more than you can handle," they tell you optimistically. *Okay then*, you think to yourself, *God must feel like I can handle an awful lot, because he sure isn't letting up*. Or, "God works all things together for his good." *What good can possibly come of all this?* you wonder. And what do *they* know, anyway? Have they ever walked in your shoes or been dealt the blows you've been dealt? No! Then you have your not-so-Christian friends who use your suffering as a weapon not only against you, but against God as well. "See, I told you there *is* no God. If God were real why would he ever let these terrible things happen to you? He clearly doesn't care that much about you, or worse, he does but he's powerless to do anything about it. Either way, that's not a God *I* would ever bow down and worship." You listen to all of it while constantly repeating the same theme in your head: *Why me? What did I do, God, to deserve this wrath that has been thrust upon me? WHY ME????* After all you've been through, you know without a doubt that Job had nothing on you. You also know that if one more bad thing happens, you just might not be able to get back up again. Nor would you want to.

In the months following Kathryn's divorce she held herself together well, at least by outward appearances. She remained dedicated to the firm and maintained a social calendar that most would envy. But inwardly was quite a different story. No matter how hard she tried, she still couldn't forgive herself for the fact that she had failed at something. So she withdrew. She continued working grueling hours to keep her mind occupied with anything other than the gaping voids that had become a permanent part of her life. She refused to let herself think of the past. Yet when she looked ahead, she no longer saw that bright future of promise and potential that had once been just on the horizon. Now she saw only bleak days ahead, punctuated by repetition and emptiness. It was slowly eating away at her like a parasite hidden just below the surface yet fighting to worm its way out.

During that time Kathryn also sought solace in the one thing that she had come to count on more than anything. Alcohol. It had become her last and best friend. It brought her the gift of dulling her senses and numbing her mind to the reality of what her life had become. It would never judge her, talk back at her, or try to persuade her in another direction. And best of all, it never let her down. After a few glasses she knew that she could escape into a blur of another world where the pain wasn't so sharp and the shame wasn't so great. It had become Kathryn's kryptonite, and it was controlling her life. In fact, she was so busy immersing herself in a bottle that she never even saw the approaching storm.

Any good downpour usually starts with those first few drops of rain. The drops so big and fat they look like pellets splattering the ground with purposeful fury rather than the gentle rain that trickles down the springtime mist. When those drops douse creation, they warn you of the deluge that isn't far off. For Kathryn, those first pellets of rain fell the winter after her divorce.

"Excuse me, Miranda," Kathryn said coldly, "but do you have my files ready for court yet? I asked you at *least* an hour ago, and I don't see them." Kathryn tapped her foot impatiently as she hovered over her assistant's desk. Miranda had been her fourth assistant in ten months. Apparently the more Kathryn worked, the more demanding she became to the point of absurdity. Her expectations were unreasonable, her tone disrespectful, and because of it she had set a new firm record for the number of assistants any attorney had gone through in less than a year. Yes, word had definitely traveled about Kathryn, and although several eager applicants vied for the job of assistant to one of the most powerful attorneys in the entire state, they usually smartened up within a few months and realized that no amount of money was worth putting themselves through all that misery. So her assistants dropped like flies. Kathryn, however, paid no mind to any of it. After all, there was always another one lined up at the door and ready to go.

"Yes, Ms. Kirby, the files have been sitting on the edge of your desk just like you asked. I brought them into your office some time ago; you must not have heard me come in."

"I suppose not," Kathryn replied without making eye contact.

"Here, let me get them for you," Miranda kindly offered.

"Don't bother, I'll do it." Kathryn turned to her office when Brandy, a relatively new law clerk, approached. Brandy was a second-year law student who was interning at the firm in the hopes of being offered a position after graduation, and Kathryn couldn't stand her. She was bright and cheerful and beautiful and smart. All of the things that Kathryn once saw in herself. It was like looking into a mirror of the past, and Kathryn couldn't stomach it. Brandy was also happy. *Too* happy. She was bubbly and bouncy, she never had a negative thing to say about anyone, and she was *always* in a good mood. It was sickening. Kathryn had a nickname for Brandy that she had more than once almost called the intern to her face. *Twit.*

"So, did you hear the news?" Twit blurted out to Miranda, unintentionally within earshot of Kathryn.

"No, what news?" Miranda asked, hopeful for some juicy gossip.

"It's about Griffin Harris."

"What about Griffin?" Kathryn interjected, not the least bit concerned anymore about retrieving the court files on her desk. "Is he all right?" A sense of panic filled her at the sound of his name. She hadn't heard or spoken his name in months, and everyone at the firm knew that mentioning anything about Griffin Harris was taboo. Everyone, except of course stupid Twit. What if something had happened to him? What if he were sick? What if he were dead? The last she had heard about him was back in the summer. He had settled into Miami but was making frequent trips home to visit his aging parents. Was he back in town for good? Maybe he would even come groveling back, realizing what a terrible mistake he had made in leaving her.

"Oh, he's *more* than all right," Brandy replied cheerfully, not realizing her own insensitivity to Kathryn's circumstances. "He's engaged, *and* his fiancée is expecting twins!"

Kathryn was floored.

"Where did you hear that?" she snapped.

Brandy, now clearly aware that she had managed to put her foot in her mouth, tried to backpedal. "Um, I heard it from my best friend, Curtis, who's interning at the law office where Griffin used to work." Brandy fidgeted nervously with a paperclip holding some files together. "I could be wrong though, you know how rumors start."

Kathryn shot Brandy a venomous stare that would've put her six feet under in a flash if looks could kill. Miranda's eyes widened, and Brandy took the cue to make herself disappear as quickly as humanly possible.

Kathryn stood for a moment in complete silence, stunned. Engaged. He was engaged. He had found someone else. And he had not just one, but *two* children on the way. *"Kathryn, believe me, there is nothing I would've loved more than to have had children with you."* The words echoed in her mind like he had said them only yesterday. Sure, he would've loved to have had children with her, but he didn't love her enough to fight for their marriage. Instead, he bought his airline ticket and left. Just like that. And, to rub salt in the wound, Kathryn had to find out about it from some Twit law clerk. Griffin hadn't even had the decency to call her and tell her himself. He owed her at least that much.

Kathryn refocused her attention. "Miranda, I thought you were getting my files."

"Yes, ma'am," Miranda replied politely as she quickly scurried into the adjoining office for the documents, not mentioning Kathryn had said she would retrieve the files herself. "I will get them right away."

The rest of the afternoon Kathryn did what she did best. She operated on autopilot. She successfully argued two motions in court to the praise of the judge and then returned to her office for several witness interviews, but all she could think of was curling up at home on her couch with a few glasses of Jack and Coke to take the edge off of what had been a lousy day. Jack would take her mind off of Griffin for a while, and she was looking forward to their date.

The first drops of rain had fallen, but it was only the beginning. The storm was about to be unleashed.

The next morning Kathryn arrived at the office well before 7:30 to find Miranda waiting for her with a host of messages.

"Your mother called to confirm your lunch date at Antonelli's this afternoon," Miranda informed her, handing her the yellow slip upon which she had scribbled the information.

"That's right," Kathryn answered while glancing at the paper. She had totally forgotten about it. Her mother had been pestering her for at least a month to get together, and a few weeks ago Kathryn finally relented and told her mother to meet her at Antonelli's for a quick bite to eat. It was the perfect place—an upscale Italian restaurant only two blocks from her office which was frequented by professional guests on a tight schedule, so Kathryn knew she could get in and out in an hour tops. She had avoided any in-person conversations with her mother for the last few months simply because she was in no mood for the concerned look which would undoubtedly creep across her mother's face or the questions that would go with it. *How have you been, sweetheart? Are you taking care of yourself? Is everything all right?* It was the last thing Kathryn needed to deal with. But yet, this morning for some reason she welcomed the time with her mother. She could use a shoulder to cry on, and she needed to unload her latest information about Griffin on someone who would understand. She could use a good hour of venting over a dish of chicken piccata and a glass of Merlot, so perhaps her lunch date wouldn't be such a bad thing after all.

"Please call my mother and let her know I'll meet her at noon."

"Also," Miranda interrupted her train of thought, "Mr. Wallingford asked that you come to his office as soon as you arrive."

"He did. What for?"

"He didn't say, Ms. Kirby."

That was odd. Darian Wallingford never called impromptu meetings unless there was either a problem or a very important case had come up. *That must be it*, she thought, *he has another big case he needs me to handle for him.* Ever Kathryn to the rescue.

She dismissed any uneasiness and walked down the narrow corridor until she came upon Darian's secretary busily typing something on the keyboard.

"You can go in," she said without looking up from her computer screen, "Mr. Wallingford is expecting you."

Kathryn walked past the secretary without so much as acknowledging her presence and simultaneously knocked and entered his office.

"Kathryn, come in. Have a seat."

Kathryn took to one of the plush leather armchairs facing his desk. "You wanted to see me, sir?"

"Yes, I did." He briefly glanced at a newspaper resting atop a pile of papers and then folded it and deposited it in the trash. "I wanted to speak with you before you heard it on the news or the reporters descended upon you."

"About what" she asked, her mind drawing a blank. Was this all about Griffin? Surely his marriage and impending family weren't *that* important that they would make the news. Were they?

"Gerald Lyons was arrested late last night."

Oh God, Kathryn thought. "For what?"

"Assault," he said matter-of-factly.

She could feel the blood draining from her body and her stomach churn.

"Another college student?"

"Not quite," Darian replied. "His daughter's best friend."

"But his daughter is only—"

"Sixteen," Darian answered before Kathryn could finish her sentence.

"Oh, Lord." The weight of it all began to overwhelm her. Only a few years ago she had allowed this man to walk free. A murderer, released back into society. Just another face in the crowd, appearing innocuous enough but a predator nonetheless. A wolf in sheep's clothing.

"He is seeking our firm's representation once again."

"Well, I'm sure Todd Graham would be happy to handle the case, or Marcus Weir, or—"

"Kathryn," Darian interrupted her, "he has specifically asked for you."

"Me? Oh, Darian, I'm not sure I'm the right p—"

"I know you will do your utmost to represent him with zeal and—"

"Or perhaps Meghan McConnell could represent him, I think she would be a wise choice to—"

"Kathryn," Darian commanded.

"Yes?"

"You misunderstand. I am not asking for your input in this matter." The implication was clear. She would once again be representing Gerald Lyons. This was one argument she wasn't going to win.

"Yes, sir," she replied quietly, defeated.

"I have taken the liberty of scheduling your consultation with him tomorrow at noon. If you have anything else on your calendar, please see to it that it is changed."

"Yes, sir."

"Thank you, Kathryn. That will be all." And with that, she was dismissed from his office.

The rest of the morning Kathryn didn't accomplish much of anything other than Googling Gerald Lyons and reading every article she could about his latest arrest. She consulted only two different sources before she thought she might become ill. The victim was, in fact, his daughter's best friend, although the news sources gave her the small reprieve of not mentioning her by name. She was only fifteen years old. The article alleged that she had been drugged. Apparently the only reason it came to light was because she had confessed to her mother she suspected something had happened between the two of them when she spent the night at the Lyons's beach house. She said she had woken up dazed and bruised, and the last thing she remembered was Gerald walking her up the stairs to the guest room. Her mother immediately took her to the hospital, which confirmed their suspicions. Gerald, of course, had denied everything. But once again the evidence was overwhelming.

Kathryn was a mess. It was one thing after another. First the news about Griffin, and then this. How on earth was she supposed to handle it all? Her ex-husband had moved on with someone new. What did she look like? Kathryn wondered. Was she as pretty as Kathryn? Was she as smart? Did she stay home all day cleaning the house and then greet him at the front door when he came home from the office with his slippers and a glass of wine? Then her mind quickly shifted to Gerald Lyons. She detested him, and she loathed the fact that she would have to stand before a judge and defend him. He should've been behind bars years ago, not walking the streets where he could prey on another innocent victim. She thought back to Emily Porter's mother, and Kathryn could almost feel the sting on her cheek all over again. Charlotte Porter had known all along what Kathryn chose to deny. And someone else had suffered because of it.

She glanced at her watch and realized it was almost noon, so she hurried out of her office with a cursory wave to Miranda and found her mother already seated at a table for two at Antonelli's. She sipped a glass of water with a lemon slice and smiled lovingly when she saw her daughter enter the restaurant. Kathryn could feel the warmth emanating from her mother, and it brought her a profound sense of relief to know that she would be able to unburden the events of the past day upon her. After all, mothers always had a way of making things better.

Kathryn joined her at the table and ordered a glass of Merlot as soon as the waiter arrived.

"Sweetheart, how have you been?" her mother asked as Kathryn perused the daily specials on the menu.

"I've been good, Mom," she lied. For some reason Kathryn couldn't bring herself to have the conversation with her mother she really wanted to have. Again, she preferred to bask in the denial of what her life had become. She had thought it would be so easy to open up and she needed so desperately to have someone listen, but when presented with the opportunity, she clammed up. "You know, just the usual work and going out every now and then."

"Oh?" her mother asked. "Anyone special in your life at the moment?"

"No, nothing like that," Kathryn replied wishfully. "I'm not really interested in something serious right now. I'm more focused on my cases." On one case in particular, she thought.

After the waiter took their orders, they spent the next several minutes making small talk. Kathryn's mother told her about the new housing development that was coming to Bakersville within the next year. Kathryn feigned interest as her mother described in detail the protests lodged against the 100-plus home community after one of the farmers had sold his land at a premium. Of course, the locals all wanted their town to remain picturesque and the last thing they needed was a bunch of transplants moving in and overcrowding their roads and schools. Kathryn tried to blot out Griffin and Gerald Lyons and focus on the conversation, yet she couldn't help but notice something off about her mother. Something different. Something distant. She couldn't quite put her finger on it, but whatever it was, it alarmed her.

"Mom," Kathryn interrupted, "is everything okay?"

"What do you mean, sweetheart?"

"I'm not really sure," she confessed, "I just feel like something's bothering you."

Kathryn's mother swallowed her mouthful of food and gently placed the fork on her plate. She took a sip of her ice water and held out her hand. Kathryn instinctively reached out as dread spread throughout her body.

"Kathryn, I asked you to lunch today for a reason."

"What is it?"

Her mother hesitated ever so slightly. "There is no easy way to say this, so I am just going to come out with it."

"What, Mom?" Kathryn asked, the panic evident in her voice.

"I have cancer."

"What???"

"I have stage four lung cancer."

Kathryn felt like she was sinking inside of herself. She was hearing the words, but she wasn't processing them. This couldn't be true. This had to be some nightmare that she was about to wake up from, or some cruel joke. Suddenly the room became hazy and all she could see was her mother's hand holding hers. Without even realizing it, the tears began to stream down her cheeks.

"That's impossible," she said defiantly. "You don't even smoke."

"I know, sweetie," her mother replied reassuringly. "Not all lung cancer patients are smokers."

"But how do you know? I mean, you don't even seem sick. It must be a misdiagnosis," Kathryn rationalized.

Her mother shook her head. "I'm certain of it. I had been fighting a cough for the last few months, and I've also been feeling much more tired than usual. I figured it was just the wintertime bug that's been going around. So many young children visit the library each week, so with all the germs floating around I had just assumed I caught something and was having a hard time shaking it. When I went for my annual physical a few weeks ago I explained how I had been feeling, and my doctor did a series of tests. She sent me to a pulmonary oncologist as a follow up who confirmed everything."

Kathryn pushed the almost full plate of chicken piccata away from her. She had completely lost her appetite. The two remained silent for a moment before Kathryn could muster the courage to ask the one question she feared having answered the most.

"What is your prognosis?"

"It's not good, sweetheart. I'm sorry. The cancer has metastasized. The doctors tell me six months at most, maybe less."

"*Six months?*" Kathryn repeated. It was truly unbelievable.

"Well, then we're just going to have to fight this." Kathryn's voice was shaky but determined. "If the doctors here think your chances aren't good, then we will just have to find specialists somewhere else who *can* help you. We can get you started on chemo right away. I've even heard of people with late stage cancer traveling to Europe for those alternative healing remedies. Mom, cost is no option, I'll pay for all of it. We can start making arrangements now to get you to all the right doctors so you can beat this thing. I'll start researching today, and we can have a flight booked by the end of the week."

Kathryn's mother took her other hand and firmly clasped it over her daughter's.

"Kathryn, stop."

"Stop what?"

"Stop trying to make it go away. This is not something that we can wish away, and there are some things that money can't buy. I'm dying, Kathryn, and no amount of money or specialists can change that."

"So, what? You're just going to give up? You're going to sit back and let it overtake you and give in?" Kathryn was becoming furious at her mother's lack of willpower.

"No, sweetheart, I am not giving up at all."

"But you're not going to do anything about it," she said harshly.

"I *am* doing something about it." Her mother smiled. "I am going to live each and every day the Lord has given me to the fullest. I am going to enjoy life while I can. I don't want to spend my last days in hospitals hooked up to machines with medicines coursing through my body that make me feel a hundred times worse than I do now. I want to be surrounded by loved ones, not by doctors and nurses. If I were twenty years younger, or if the cancer hadn't progressed as far as it has, perhaps I would feel differently. But I want to live what's left of my life on my own terms, giving thanks to God for each day."

"Some God," Kathryn blurted aloud before she could stop herself.

"Kathryn, the Lord will see us through this." As Kathryn studied her mother's face, she saw a peace that defied words.

"Aren't you scared?"

"No, hon, I'm really not. I have lived a good life, and I've been very blessed. I know I am in the Lord's hands, and he will take good care of me. It's you that I'm worried about."

Kathryn was incredulous that after everything her mother would be worried about her.

"*Me?* Why me?"

"Because the next several months are going to be difficult for you, and you're going to need help getting through this." Her mother didn't have to say another word. Here she was, dying of cancer, and yet she had a faith so strong that the only thing she was worried about was how her daughter would cope once she was gone. Kathryn's mother knew her better than she ever let on. Kathryn no longer had a husband to cling to, and although she had many acquaintances she had no true friends. It was all her own doing, a wall she had built around herself to shield her from anything that resembled a real relationship. Before Kathryn could offer any response, her mother took the conversation the one place where Kathryn couldn't bear to go.

"Kathryn, sweetheart, why don't you call Benjamin." Hearing his name took her breath away.

"Mom, I—"

"I know it's been a long time," her mother interrupted, "but I know Benjamin. He misses you, and he would love nothing more than to reconnect. And I also know that he will walk with you through this journey."

Kathryn thought about her mother's suggestion but dismissed it almost immediately. "Mom, we haven't talked for a couple of years now. I don't even know where he is."

"Oh, hon, he's exactly where you left him, and I'm sure he is waiting to hear from you when you're ready."

"I don't know."

"Please just promise me you'll think about it. All right?"

"Okay, Mom, I'll think about it."

"Thank you, sweetheart."

"Is there anything I can do for you? Anything at all?"

"Just pray." Her mother smiled encouragingly. "And try to come home and visit when you can find the time."

"Of course I will," Kathryn said as the tears brimmed in her blue eyes.

Kathryn never did go back to work that day. After their lunch she hugged her mother goodbye and wanted to hold on forever. She promised that she would come home that weekend so they could spend some time together, and she made plans to leave early Friday to make the trip to Bakersville. On her way back to the condo she texted Miranda that she would be off for the rest of the day without offering any explanation why, and the moment she walked in the door she made a beeline for the liquor cabinet. She poured herself a glass of wine, changed into a T-shirt and sweats, and curled up on her couch. She stared blankly across the room, in shock. Griffin Harris and Gerald Lyons were suddenly the furthest things from her mind. They had become only minor irritations in the daily grind of life. What her mother had told her changed everything. How could God take away her mother like this? So quickly, and likely with so much pain and suffering? It was beyond unfair. In Kathryn's mind it bordered on masochistic. Her mother was a much better woman than Kathryn could ever hope to be. She was a woman of faith. She had never done anything but worship God with all her heart and soul and mind and strength, even during times of trial like the death of her beloved husband. Through it all her mother never once doubted, never once complained. Even now, faced with a grim outlook and far too few days ahead, her faith still never wavered. And this was God's reward for her faithfulness? What kind of God would do this, or at the very least allow it to happen? Her sips of wine soon became gulps, and she welcomed the temporary relief as the burgundy liquid took its effect on her body. Meanwhile, her rage only grew stronger. Maybe God was punishing *her* for all the things she had done wrong in her life. She remembered Pastor Matt's sermon from the Sunday she had returned to St. Paul's with Benjamin a few years before. Was all of this because she had taken her eyes off Christ? Was God unleashing his wrath on Kathryn for her poor choices? Vengeance at its best? *Fine*, she thought. *Then take me! Let me be the one to suffer, not her.* All her mother deserved was love and happiness, and instead this was what she got. *Just what kind of God are you?* she thought.

She emptied her glass several times and spent hours on the couch trying to process the storm that was upon her. And then she remembered what she had promised her mother. "Why don't you call Benjamin," her mother had said. Kathryn would need someone to help her get through this. As much as she hated to admit it, her mother was absolutely right. When it came down to it, she had no one. No one who truly cared and would do anything more than superficially pat her on the back with a "there, there," and be on their way. She stared at her cell phone on the coffee table beside her. She picked it up tentatively, wondering if his number was even the same. She so desperately wanted to make that call. It was a conversation she had imagined in her mind a million times over, but for some reason she couldn't bring herself to do it. Not even now, when she was about to lose the one person she loved most in the world. When the walls seemed to be caving in around her. Maybe it was her pride, maybe it was fear, maybe it was shame, maybe it was all three. But no matter how much she knew deep down that she needed Benjamin back in her life, something was stopping her.

As the alcohol overtook her and her anger alternated with waves of exhaustion, she finally reached her boiling point. She cursed God, threw her half empty glass of wine across the room with all of the strength left within her, and watched dizzily as it smashed against the wall, spilling shards of glass, the red wine dripping like blood down the wall.

"So where are you, God?" she screamed at the top of her lungs. "Where are you in all of this? Am I supposed to feel you now? Why have you forsaken me?" She waited a few moments, half anticipating a direct answer to her questions. All she heard was silence, which infuriated her that much more.

"Yeah, that's what I thought," she laughed sarcastically. "You're nowhere to be found, as usual. Just what I expected! Well, you know what, God? Thanks for nothing. You can take your Bible and you can shove it! I don't need you anymore! If you hate me so much, then why don't you just finish me off and leave my mother alone!"

Kathryn lifted her arms up to the heavens in the hopes that maybe she would be snatched off this wretched planet full of pain and disappointment at that very moment. When nothing happened, she collapsed into sobs, hyperventilating and blubbering uncontrollably into the pillows on the couch. She watched the few drops of wine puddle on the hardwood floor, and she laid her head on the pillow as the room began spinning. The floodgates had opened, and the storm was barreling down on her full force. All she could do was close her eyes and pray for it to be over, but she wouldn't give God the satisfaction of praying. He had abandoned Kathryn, or so she thought, and she wasn't about to let him forget it.

Within two months she was gone. Almost eight weeks to the day after their lunch together at Antonelli's, Kathryn's mother died. Kathryn watched it unfold right before her very eyes. True to her mother's wishes, there were no hospitals or treatments. She lived all of her days at home with a full heart and in thanksgiving. Hospice was called in only during the last few weeks to make her transition as painless as possible. It was the very least her mother deserved. Kathryn had put everything else on hold and cared for her mother no matter how much it pained her to see the suffering and agony her mother endured. Thus, Kathryn sat helplessly by and watched the woman who was always so vibrant and full of life wither away to a shell of what she had once been. The disease had taken its hold of her and gripped her tight until it sucked every last ounce of life from her. She aged decades in only a few months' time, and she lost at least twenty pounds if not more. She was frail and pallid, her eyes sunken deep into their lifeless sockets. She was barely recognizable. At the end every movement was a Herculean effort. During the final few days she lay in bed at home unconscious, her breaths shallow and irregular. Even still, it seemed to Kathryn as though there would always be one more breath. Until there wasn't.

Kathryn was there late that Thursday night in mid-April, holding her mother's hand, when she took her last breath. A Bible sat on the nightstand next to the hospice bed that had been brought into the dining room they converted into her bedroom, but Kathryn refused to pick it up or even to touch it. When her mother asked to have scripture read to her in those final days, Kathryn enlisted some of her mother's church friends to comfort her. Kathryn wasn't about to recite words of love and joy and promises of eternal glory that seemed so callously hypocritical to her. False promises and false hope. The bitterness of cancer, now that's reality. She had come face to face with death, and there was nothing beautiful about it. It was horrendous, and it was surely nothing that a truly loving God would allow.

Friday morning Kathryn made all of the requisite phone calls to the funeral home and fed Oreo breakfast after realizing that the young cat, much like herself, was now an orphan. The rain outside was relentless. April showers might bring May flowers, but she could barely handle the dreariness that enveloped the entire area. Everything was gray and hazy, much like Kathryn's life. She thought for a minute about calling Griffin to tell him the news of her mother's passing, but she decided against it once she had time to really think it through. Sure, Griffin would be sympathetic, but then what would they say to one another? *So, how's the new fiancée and little ones on the way?* It hardly made for small talk, so Kathryn thought better of it. She made the trek back to her condo with Oreo in tow, deciding that the very least she could do for her mother would be to give her cat a loving home. Besides, it had been ages since Kathryn had a companion, so she was looking forward to the company. Oreo protested vehemently from the confines of her cat carrier during the car ride back to the city. The meows and yowls sounded like someone experiencing a slow and painful death which distressed Kathryn to no end, but she constantly reassured the petrified cat that everything would be all right. After spending the better part of the day exploring the spacious condo and getting accustomed to the location of her food and litter, Oreo seemed to relax a little. The country cat was now officially the city cat.

The darkness of the last twenty-four hours weighed heavily on Kathryn's shoulders. She needed to get out for a while, even if it meant fighting the torrential rains that had battered the entire area since mid-week. It was just past dusk when she grabbed her oversized umbrella and headed down the elevator and through the revolving doors of her condominium. She immediately found herself quite soaked, the rain pouring down in horizontal sheets. So much for the umbrella, she thought. She might as well have left it home. Kathryn quickly decided on O'Leary's Pub simply because it was the closest bar to provide her shelter, and it was also the least likely place she would encounter any of her colleagues. She opened the door quickly and had to force it shut against the winds howling outside. Tommy, the bartender, stood watching a baseball game on the flat screen television affixed to the wall while drying a beer mug. The sole patron, a retired business executive, relaxed on his usual stool at the end of the bar nursing an amber-colored liquid. Chester was his name, Chester Arthur. The first time he met Kathryn about a year ago he introduced himself and immediately remarked, "Mo, not Chester Arthur as in the twenty-first President of the United States. He was Chester *Alan* Arthur, I'm Chester *Aaron* Arthur. Same initials though," he said with a knee-slapping laugh. Chester enjoyed his perch on the barstool while watching all of the comings and goings of the young professionals in the city. It reminded him so much of back in the day when he was among those go-getters in the financial district feeling the pulse of city life invigorate him. Now a widower in his early seventies with barely a comb-over of hair on top of his head and a beer belly extending well beyond his belt, those days were long behind him. No harm in living vicariously through others, right? Since the day he had met her, Chester developed a certain fondness for Kathryn and he always lit up when their paths crossed. He smiled when he saw her soggy figure cross the room.

"Well, look what the cat dragged in!" he said as he pulled out the adjacent stool as a signal to join him. "How are we doing this evening, Counselor? It's an awfully dreary night for you to be out and about in the city."

"I'm okay," Kathryn replied unconvincingly.

"Hi, Kathryn," Tommy offered as he pried himself away from the TV screen. "What can I get you?"

"I'll have a scotch on the rocks with a twist. Thanks, Tommy."

"Sure thing." Tommy went to retrieve the scotch from behind the bar that sat with the dozens of other multicolored bottles.

Kathryn shook her hair to try to get some of the water out of it and brushed aside the wisps plastered to her face. She sighed heavily as she watched Tommy prepare her drink.

"So what brings you out on a night like this?" Chester inquired. "I figured a good girl like yourself would be in church tonight."

"Church?" Kathryn asked, confused. "Why on earth would I be in church on a Friday night?"

"Well, I hear it's Good Friday. I don't know, but for some reason I had you pegged as one of those faithful churchgoers, that's all."

"Ha!" she laughed sarcastically. Good Friday. The day her Lord and Savior delivered himself willfully to the cross. The day they cruelly spat on him, mocked him, flogged him with glass-embedded whips until he was bleeding and practically unconscious. The day they made him carry his own instrument of execution to the site where they nailed him to the cross and watched him die a slow, excruciating death. In many ways Kathryn had felt like the last few months she had lived through something not too far off from that. She could relate.

"Well, I can tell you one thing, there's nothing *good* about this Good Friday, that's for sure."

"Having a bad day?" Chester inquired sympathetically.

"Bad day? Try a bad year."

"Would you like to share? I'm a very good listener. At least that's what Tommy tells me," he said as he winked at the bartender.

"Well, let's see, where should I begin?" Kathryn replied, gulping the scotch like it was water. "First I find out that my ex-husband, who once claimed to be so madly in love with me, is getting married and expecting twins with some woman in Florida. Then my boss assigns me this case to represent a complete jerk and all I want to do is put him behind bars for the rest of his life, but I can't. Then, to top it all off my mother dies."

"Well, I guess you're right, seems like one heck of a year. I'm so sorry to hear about your mother. When did she die?"

"Yesterday," Kathryn answered impassively as she motioned to Tommy for another drink. "And make it a double this time," she instructed the bartender.

"*Yesterday*?" Chester asked incredulously. "Well, dear child, what on earth are you doing here? You should be with family right now." Clearly he ached for her.

Kathryn took a deep breath. "That's the thing, I don't really *have* any more family. My mom was it." It sounded so pathetic even to Kathryn, but the well was dry. She had no more tears to shed.

Outside they heard the rumblings of thunder in the distance and the television screen flickered briefly.

"Storm headed out this way," Tommy informed his patrons. "Supposed to be a bad one, so you might want to wait it out here for a while."

"Suits me," Kathryn replied, "I've got nowhere to be anyway."

Chester lifted the glass with the remnants of his drink and motioned for Kathryn to do the same. "To your mother," he began, "may she rest in peace where the days are never ending, the storms are never coming, and the drinks are never better!"

"Amen to that," Kathryn agreed as they clinked glasses, and she downed her second drink. She set the glass on the bar with a thud as the lightning flashed and the thunder roared louder. The storm was approaching quickly.

"Hey, Tommy," Kathryn said, "how about a shot this time around?"

"Sure, what'll it be?"

"Let's make it a couple of fireballs, one for me and one for Mr. President here." Kathryn smiled for the first time in days. The warmth of the alcohol was beginning to take effect. *Thank God*, she thought. Relief was finally on its way.

"Well, that's awfully kind of you, Counselor, but please let me do the honors," he said as he placed a twenty on the bar.

"Thank you kindly, sir."

"You sure you're up for it? Little girl like yourself needs to watch how much she puts down."

"Oh, don't you worry about me," Kathryn said reassuringly, "I can handle my liquor. I might not be able to handle much else right now, but *that* I can definitely take." She had had lots of experience.

The two clinked shot glasses, and Kathryn opened her mouth wide to allow the peppery concoction to glide smoothly down her throat into every crevice of her aching body. She started to lose the feeling in her fingertips. Ah, the numbness she craved. It was the best medicine she could ask for.

As the three made small talk at the bar, the storm overtook the skies outside. The lights flickered more than once, and the booms of the thunder grew so loud that it drowned out their conversations. The rain pelted the front door like a thousand soldiers marching in unison. One more shot of fireball and the storm grew closer still. Two more shots and it was right on top of them. By then Kathryn was too numb to care. She processed her words slowly and slurred her speech. Her eyes felt dry, and Chester and Tommy looked like two silhouettes that drifted back and forth. For as much as Kathryn could handle her liquor, this time she had misjudged her limits. She didn't care though. Her mother had just died, for crying out loud. She was entitled to go a little overboard. One more drink and Kathryn could feel the waves of nausea coming, erupting in her stomach and sliding up toward her throat. The last thing she wanted to do was vomit in front of these two men.

"Well, gentlemen," she slurred, "I think it's time for me to head home." She rose from the barstool and grabbed her purse, steadying herself in the process.

"Whoa, wait a second there, Counselor," Chester said as he gently took hold of her arm. "You see what it's doing out there? You don't want to leave now. Why don't you give it another ten or fifteen minutes, and I'm sure the storm'll pass by then."

"How about a nice tall glass of ice water?" Tommy offered.

"Thanks, guys, but I'm good, really." She took two steps toward the door and her heel turned awkwardly under her, sending a searing pain from her ankle all the way up to her hip as she cursed.

"Really, Kathryn." The tone in Chester's voice was dead serious. "I really think you should wait it out. You're in no shape to go out. Or at least let me walk you to your building."

Although both men meant well, Kathryn defensively interpreted their concern as a suggestion that she couldn't take care of herself.

"I'm *fine*," she replied harshly, slowly enunciating the word "fine" as best as her drunken state would permit. "My building is only two blocks away. I'll be home in less than five minutes."

Before any additional protests could be raised, she swung open the door and slammed it shut, leaving her umbrella behind in the far corner of the bar.

Outside, the rain furiously pounded the city streets. Kathryn was completely soaked within seconds. But rather than shield herself from the showers, she lifted her face toward the sky and welcomed the wetness that covered every inch of her until her clothes stuck to her body and she shivered from the dampness. She stumbled more than once, but on the desolate streets no one was there to notice or care. The lightning flashed overhead and the thunder clapped so loudly it made her jump. She could barely see two feet in front of her through all the rain and mist that was rising off of the warm city streets.

She had almost made it to her apartment building when she fumbled through her purse and pulled out her car keys. She stared at the Benz key in the blackness of the night and realized how all she wanted to do was to go home. Not home to her condo, but *home*. Home to where her mother had raised her and loved her and sheltered her. Home to where she might be able to feel her mother still with her, not to some sterile condominium in the city where she had never really once felt like she belonged. In her drunkenness she never once thought about the fact that she was in no shape to drive. Or the fact that anyone would be downright stupid to make the trip in a thunderstorm so fierce. Or the fact that Bakersville was an hour away. All she thought about was *HOME*. The place she needed to be.

She grasped her keys tightly and walked one block beyond her condo to her reserved spot in the garage complex. How she even managed to navigate the hairpin turns of the winding garage was in itself a feat, but soon she exited onto Tenth Avenue and the rain pounded her windshield like percussion drums. She clicked her windshield wipers on full force, but even that didn't help. She turned onto Eastern Avenue only to hydroplane across three lanes and practically strike a parking meter on the curb, but she regained control, determined to make the trip to Bakersville. After navigating a few more turns less than accurately she found herself on the interstate, four lanes of traffic in each direction connecting the city to the dozens of suburban towns surrounding it. There was hardly any traffic except for the occasional red blur of what Kathryn surmised were tail lights, so she leaned heavily on the accelerator, eager to be warm and dry again. Eager to be *HOME*. The lightning lit up the pitch-black sky, and the thunder shook the car as she widened her eyes thinking it would bring clarity to her vision. Another set of red lights in the distance. She pressed harder on the accelerator. Her foot was to the floor. She could hear the engine working strenuously beneath her and the fast clicks of the wipers like a metronome steadily lulling her to sleep. She purposefully blinked several times to try to keep awake, and she opened the driver's side window for some fresh air only to recoil at the rain stinging her face. Another blur of red. A blur of white. An overhead sign for an exit. This could be her exit, she thought, but she couldn't read any of the words. It was all so hazy and unfocused. She braked hard to try to focus on the sign when suddenly the car began to skid. She braked harder and steered away from the direction of the skid as much as she could, but it only made matters worse. She began to slide. The car spun wildly, and it became evident to her that she was losing control. A whir of images circled in flashes around her until she felt like she was going to be sick—different-colored lights, blinding white flashes, reflections of the rain illuminated in the sky. The car pulled to the left no matter how hard she tried to turn the steering wheel in the opposite direction. And then, in spite of the fact that it happened in only seconds, everything changed to slow motion. Out of the corner of her eye she first caught a glimpse of the enormous tree off the exit ramp and the guardrail that she was heading directly toward. The tires skidded, the brakes locked under her feet. She instinctively removed her hands from the wheel and shielded her face with them. She heard the crunching and twisting of metal as the car collided with first the guardrail, and then, as it flipped into midair, the tree. She felt the violent sting of the airbag enveloping her and forcing her backward into the seat. She struggled for breath as her seatbelt locked across her chest and held her firmly in place. In that split second she thought about the fact that it was Good Friday and how she desperately needed a resurrection of her own. She also knew she wasn't going to make it home.

In her last moments of lucidity, Kathryn felt something drawing her attention to the passenger seat. She glanced over and did a double take. How could it be? Was she dreaming? Was she hallucinating? Was she seeing a ghost? Was she dead? He sat there calmly, completely focused on her, unaffected by the chaos or the horrific scene unfolding around them. "It's all right. I'm here. You're safe with me, Kathryn," he kept repeating softly. And as long as she looked into his eyes, she found peace amidst the storm. Benjamin.

Everything went black.

CHAPTER 13
HUMBLE PIE

"Humble yourselves before the Lord,
and he will lift you up."
James 4:10

Kathryn squinted and tried to process her surroundings as she spied a dim light coming from across the room. She shifted slightly in bed and immediately regretted her decision. She had the worst headache imaginable. It pounded furiously as though someone had split her skull clear open. And when she tried to sit up to gain some bearings, a torrid pain shot through her chest and took her breath away. She immediately decided against moving again any time soon.

"Well, look who's decided to join us," an unfamiliar voice said.

"Wh . . . where am I?" Kathryn asked groggily.

"You're in the hospital, sweetheart."

"The hospital?"

"You had quite an accident," the voice said.

"What day is it?" she whispered.

"Why, it's Easter Sunday," the voice replied in a joyous tone, "the day our Lord and Savior arose from the grave! Hallelujah!"

Kathryn wearily scanned the room with her eyes, careful to remain completely still in the process. Standing next to her bed was a very plump African-American woman dressed in a white nurse's uniform like the ones they used to wear in the old days before scrubs became the attire of choice. She had a delicate silver cross dangling from her neck. The woman noticed Kathryn studying her features.

"I'm Nurse Delilah," she offered kindly. "I've been taking care of you since you joined us late the other night."

"What happened?" Kathryn asked. The last thing she could recall was hours before the accident when she was driving back to the city from Bakersville with a very unhappy Oreo protesting in the cat carrier. Then it dawned on her.

"Oreo!" she said as she instinctively tried to shift her weight and winced in pain.

"*Oreos?*" Nurse Delilah asked curiously. "Honey, I think you'd better work on a glass of water before you try to eat any Oreos." She chuckled at the thought of it. Here this young woman wakes up from one nasty accident and the first thing she asks for is a cookie! "Now I think I've heard it all," she murmured under her breath.

"No, Oreo is a cat. My cat. She needs food." Kathryn began to panic at the thought that she may have already failed at the one thing she wanted to do for her mother.

"Don't worry, sweetie, I'm sure the cat is fine. Anyway, you have a visitor who I think would be more than happy to look after your cat until you can go home."

A visitor? Who would be coming to visit Kathryn? Was it Griffin?

"Who is it?"

"He says he's a friend of yours. Mr. Arthur."

The name wasn't ringing a bell. "Mr. Arthur? I don't think I know a Mr. Arthur."

"Well, he definitely seems to know you."

Before Kathryn could make any further inquiries, she heard a soft knock at the door, and a man entered the room. He was clearly worried.

"I thought I heard voices in here," he said, carrying a bouquet of carnations which looked as though they had been purchased at the hospital gift shop.

"Chester, what are you doing here?" Kathryn asked in complete surprise.

"I heard about the accident Saturday morning. I remember you saying you didn't have any family, so I figured you'd need someone here when you woke up. So . . ."

"So, Mr. Arthur has been here ever since Saturday afternoon, sittin' with you and talkin' to you," Nurse Delilah interrupted.

Kathryn managed a faint smile and felt her heart warm. She had never made the slightest effort to find out the first thing about Chester Arthur, except that his favorite drink was a gin and tonic, yet he had been at her bedside non-stop for over twenty-four hours.

"Thank you, Chester," she said, genuinely meaning it.

"I'm happy to do anything I can to help."

"Well, there is one more thing," Kathryn shared hesitantly.

"You name it. Anything at all."

"On Friday I brought my mother's cat home with me. Her name is Oreo. And she needs someone to go over and feed her. It's been over a day now and she's—"

"Don't you worry your pretty little head one bit." Chester smiled. "I'd be happy to take care of her for you."

Kathryn asked Nurse Delilah to retrieve the house key from her purse, which had been securely placed in a locked cabinet along with the remnants of the clothes she was wearing Friday night. Chester lightly kissed Kathryn on the forehead and immediately set out for his cat sitting duty, eager to be of assistance in any way he could.

Kathryn's eyelids became heavy, and she fought to stay awake. Nurse Delilah clearly picked up on it.

"You need to get some rest, sweetheart. You've got a lot of healing to do." Nurse Delilah was more right than she could possibly know. Yes, Kathryn might need physical healing, but it went far beyond that.

"Can you just tell me," Kathryn asked as she fought the exhaustion that was quickly triumphing over her determination to stay awake, "what happened? I can't seem to remember anything."

"From what I was told when they brought you in, it was a single car accident in that nasty storm we had Friday night. You totaled your car. Wrapped it around a guardrail and then a tree. Sweetie, you're lucky to be alive. Paramedics said your car was clear flipped over and they had to use the Jaws of Life to cut you out. It's a miracle you survived, and not even one broken bone. You've got a good concussion, two black eyes, and several bruised ribs, but after a few days of R&R, you should be as good as new." Kathryn remembered bits and pieces from O'Leary's. She had been drunk when it happened, but Nurse Delilah had spared her the humiliation of mentioning it.

"Oh my," was all Kathryn could say in response.

"Yep, oh my is right," Nurse Delilah agreed. "You must've had one fine guardian angel sittin' next to you the whole time."

Something triggered in Kathryn's mind. Was there someone next to her in the car? She could see the outline of a face in the passenger seat. But that was impossible. No one else had been with her. She tried to put herself back in the car those final moments before impact, but her mind unwillingly surrendered to the pain medications coursing throughout her body, and her eyes closed heavily as she drifted off.

Kathryn slept soundly for another twelve hours straight. It was a deep and dreamless sleep which provided her body a much needed restoration. When she awoke she was still in a great deal of pain, but an energy coursed through her that she hadn't felt in months or maybe even years. She felt as though she had been given a second chance. A rebirth. And she was famished.

Nurse Delilah intently studied the various machines surrounding her bed and recorded notes on her clipboard.

"Everything's looking good, Miss Kathryn. You keep it up, and within a few days you'll be home."

"I'm starving, Delilah, could I please have something to eat?"

"Now that's a good sign," Nurse Delilah said with a smile. "You sure can, honey. In fact, you can have whatever you want. Just don't try nothin' too heavy just yet. You're still on a good bit of medication, and you don't want to upset your stomach."

Kathryn thought for a minute. "How about some chicken soup and a grilled cheese?"

"I think we just might be able to make that happen. Let me call down to the cafeteria and I'll have it for you in no time. Oh, and Chester called a little while ago and said Oreo is doing great and not to worry. I think your friend has really taken to the little cat, and vice versa." Kathryn smiled. Who knew she had such a faithful friend in Chester Arthur, her drinking buddy whom she never thought twice about? Maybe there *were* genuine people out there after all.

Nurse Delilah was about to leave when someone else entered. Someone in a three-piece suit appearing stiff and hurried. He was sorely out of place in this hospital, and by his uncomfortable expression he knew it.

"Excuse me?" Nurse Delilah said as more of a question than a statement. "This is a private room."

"It's all right, Delilah," Kathryn replied as she scooted herself up in bed as best as she could without allowing the pain to overwhelm her. "I know him, he can come in."

He walked over to her bedside and hovered over her, not bothering to take the chair adjacent to the portable tray table.

"Kathryn." He said her name with a mixture of pity and disdain.

"Hello, Darian."

"We at the firm were very sorry to hear about your accident." His words sounded rehearsed and disingenuous. Kathryn sat in silence, not the least bit interested in making small talk or justifying her actions over the past few days. There *was* no justification, she knew that. But she also knew she wasn't the same person she had been only two days ago. She would never in a million years expect for Darian to believe or understand that, but it was the truth. That accident had changed her, and it had all been a blessing.

He cleared his throat awkwardly as if waiting for Kathryn to participate in the conversation, but when it became clear to him that she had no intention of doing so, he continued.

"Kathryn, I know you've been through a tremendous amount in these last few months. We sympathize with your circumstances." *Funny,* Kathryn thought, *he doesn't sound the least bit sympathetic.*

"And we are concerned about you. We're concerned about your physical and emotional health." He paused. "And we are also concerned about your ability to fulfill your obligations as a partner at the firm."

There it was. He finally said the one thing he had come to say all along. He didn't care about her health or well-being or any of the crap that he had just fed her. They were just hollow words meant to break the ice so he could get to his *real* concern. His precious law firm. But Kathryn didn't care about the firm anymore. She didn't care about Darian or the other partners or Gerald Lyons or any of the cases sitting on her desk at that very moment waiting for her undivided attention. None of it was important. Life was so much bigger than that.

"I see," she replied coolly.

"And well, let's face it, you were *drunk*." His pompous demeanor was full of self-righteousness. He looked down upon her just like he had condescendingly looked upon countless clients over the years.

"Yes, I know," Kathryn agreed, much to Darian's surprise.

"There will be criminal charges to follow from your little *incident*, and given our unblemished reputation at Engel, Wallingford, and Driscoll, we just don't think it would fare well to have you return to your duties without some sort of repercussions."

"I understand, Darian. What is it that you are suggesting?"

"Kathryn, we are asking you to take a leave of absence from the firm. Take some time, get yourself the help you need and get through the legal ramifications of your actions. Then, perhaps, we can discuss the possibility of your return on a limited basis. Your cases will all be reassigned forthwith."

Kathryn couldn't help but laugh at the irony of the situation. She had spent the last eight years of her life slaving for this law firm. She had brought them countless clients and publicity. She had been the Golden Child since she walked through the doors. Darian had told her on countless occasions that she was truly the gem of the firm. "I don't know what we would ever do without you," he flattered her.

"You're irreplaceable, a gift to the legal profession." All empty words meant to inflate her ego and sense of self-worth in the process. And for many years, those words worked. Darian had molded her into this little protégé, his puppet on a string. But no more. Kathryn could see through the pretense. One mistake and they were ready to throw her to the curb, discard her like some useless has-been rather than show her any real compassion or offer her help. She looked good and hard at Darian, his fluffy white hair and designer suit with gold cuff links and silk handkerchief tucked neatly in his pocket. He didn't look like half the man that Chester Arthur was. Chester was a true friend, and one she had least expected.

It was obvious that Darian was expecting Kathryn to argue with him. He looked ready to do battle with more rehearsed words, anticipating her protests. But much to his surprise, Kathryn's response was quite the opposite.

"I agree, Darian."

"You ag—you agree?" he stuttered.

"Yes, I agree. You're absolutely right. It has been a very difficult few months, and I need some time off. In fact, I may need quite a while."

Darian stood befuddled.

"I so appreciate how understanding the firm has been about my situation. I mean, to put my well-being first is just heartwarming to me." The edge of sarcasm in her voice wasn't lost on Darian. "And well, I do need some time to regroup and get my life in order before I make any decisions as to where to go from here. So Darian, thank you so much for your visit this morning. And please, thank the others for their genuine concern. You have done your duty," Kathryn informed him as she glanced at the door, giving him a not-so-subtle hint. "You may go."

Darian stared at Kathryn blankly and turned to leave.

"And Darian?" she said before he was able to open the door.

"Yes, Kathryn?"

"I'll be in touch."

The door shut quietly behind him. Darian was gone. Out of her room. Out of her life. Kathryn sat silently processing what had just happened. If it had been only a few years ago, she would've been mortified at the thought of losing bragging rights as the top attorney at Engel, Wallingford, and Driscoll. But strangely enough, she didn't feel that way anymore. Instead she felt free. Like Darian possessed the golden key and he had just unlocked the door of the prison cell she had been wallowing in for nearly a decade. She could finally breathe fresh air again and see the sunshine instead of nothing but suffocating concrete walls from the confines of a high rise.

Nurse Delilah entered the room with a lunch tray, and the aroma of the hospital food smelled better than anything she could remember, except Grans's apple pie, of course.

"What are you smiling about?" Nurse Delilah asked as she carefully set the tray on the table next to her.

"Oh, nothing much. Just an old friend who stopped by to chat for a few minutes."

"Well, I know it ain't none of my business, but if you ask me he didn't look too friendly."

"Yep, I guess looks can be deceiving," Kathryn replied. After all, Darian had done one heck of a job deceiving her for many years. No more though. Kathryn ate heartily and enjoyed her chicken soup and grilled cheese more than any of the gourmet meals ever once prepared by her personal chef.

Two days later Kathryn was discharged from the hospital. She still had a long way to go before she would be completely healed, but her head didn't hurt nearly as much and she could finally walk without assistance. Chester was ready and waiting to chauffeur her home with all kinds of stories about his adventures with Oreo while she was recuperating in the hospital. Nurse Delilah hugged Kathryn and told her to take good care of herself and to stay out of trouble. Kathryn promised she would, and she meant it. Kathryn thanked

Delilah profusely for her kindness and told the portly woman she hoped their paths would cross again someday. And she meant that, too.

After Chester had exhausted all of his stories about Oreo, the remainder of the drive home was mostly silent. Kathryn peered up at the tall buildings as if she had never seen them before. When she first came to the city years ago for law school she was in awe of the towering skyscrapers, as if they were personally challenging her to conquer them. But now she felt only a distance and a sense of longing for something much different. The city had somehow changed. Or perhaps she was the one who had changed.

She also thought of her mother. She missed her so much. Kathryn pictured her mother's smiling face, not the one ravaged by cancer but the familiar face that had loved her unconditionally for so many years. It sent an aching through her body far deeper than any concussion or bruised ribs could create. Had it only been a week since she had passed away? So much had happened in that one week. It felt like years, but then it also felt like her mother was right there with her. Maybe *she* was that guardian angel that Nurse Delilah had talked about. Maybe.

They passed the city park, and she thought back to the conversation that afternoon in Antonelli's. "Why don't you call Benjamin," her mother had pleaded. But Kathryn's stubborn pride wouldn't let her. She had promised her mother she would think about it. Maybe it was time. It was something she needed to seriously consider.

As Chester pulled alongside her condominium building and waved off one of the valets, Kathryn knew there was a lot she had to consider about her life. Or perhaps the more appropriate word would be *re*consider. She needed a fresh start. She needed to reevaluate. She needed to own up to her mistakes and move forward. Finally her future didn't look so bleak anymore.

"I'm going to be all right, Mom," Kathryn said with a smile.

"I'm sorry, did you say something?" Chester asked as he gingerly helped her out of his car.

"Just talking to myself," Kathryn answered.

"No harm in that," Chester said with a grin. "I do it all the time. In fact, I happen to be one of my very favorite people to talk to. I have some very interesting conversations with myself."

Kathryn full out laughed and grabbed her side to ease her aching ribs.

"I'm so sorry, I didn't mean to make you laugh. I know it hurts."

"Not at all." Kathryn patted him on the hand fondly. "It felt good. It's about time I laughed. It's about time."

Kathryn sat anxiously in the parking lot for at least fifteen minutes, staring at the immense brownstone building through the windshield of her Honda. The whir of the hybrid engine and the blowing of the A/C comforted her on the steamy summer evening. As much as she *wanted* to, and as much as she knew she *had* to, she wasn't sure if she could get out of the car. Tonight was the culmination of it all. The night when she would have to swallow her pride and start over. She remembered a C.S. Lewis quote she had once heard. "A proud man is always looking down on things and people; and, of course, as long as you are looking down, you cannot see something that is above you." It was time for Kathryn to stop looking down on everyone and to meet them eye to eye so perhaps she could once again see the things above that mattered most. It had been such a long time though, and old habits die hard. As she sat in the parking lot absentmindedly twirling a strand of her long blonde hair, she felt frozen in her spot.

It had been two months since Kathryn was released from the hospital, and she was well on her way to turning her life around. She was charged with drunk driving and other minor traffic infractions, but since she had a clean record she received only a slap on the wrist. She had anticipated as much. Judge Macklin, the very same judge who had celebrated her thirtieth birthday with her at the lavish surprise party, sentenced Kathryn to a PBJ and imposed various stipulations on that sentence, one of which resulted in her sitting in the parking lot that evening. "A peanut butter and jelly, huh?" Chester joked cheerily when she told him. "No, not a sandwich," Kathryn played along. "A probation before judgment, meaning if I fulfill all of my requirements and don't get into trouble again then no criminal conviction ever results. In effect I am being put on probation *before* any guilty decision is entered." It was an expected and reasonable outcome. She was required to perform a handful of community service hours comprised of meeting with recent law school graduates and advising them on the perils of alcohol to the young, overworked, and impressionable attorney. She was more than happy to contribute in that regard, only wishing she had received a similar lecture when she was fresh out of school. And she was also required to come *here*. This would be the hard part. Yet regardless of any decision a judge could make or stipulations placed upon her, Kathryn had more than learned her lesson.

She glanced at her watch. It was 6:55. It started in five minutes. She didn't want to be late. She had always prided herself on her punctuality, so she would have to find some way to pry herself out of the vehicle and enter the building. Luckily she didn't have to go through the front doors. That would've been more than she could handle. The burgundy double doors arced at least two stories high, with wrought iron handles shaped into twists and turns. On either side of the doors were two circular stained glass windows, one side with a cross and the other a crown.

6:57. It was now or never.

She hurriedly exited the silver Honda and activated the alarm with her remote. After all, this definitely wasn't the best part of the city. Sad though, she thought. This beautiful church, which she surmised had been built around the turn of the century, was probably once part of a bustling community of city dwellers. But as more people moved out to the suburbs for better homes and more property, neighborhoods like this one fell by the wayside. Residents moved out, and crime moved in. Now it was a lower middle class area at best where the row homes had iron bars on the ground floor windows, and the pit bull or Rottweiler was the watchdog of choice. Kathryn had pulled into a space on the far side of the parking lot closest to the nearest street light, so she quickly crossed the lot past the sanctuary doors. She headed for the basement entrance which was to the side of the building. She spied the concrete steps and felt a foreboding as if they were leading to a dungeon. She was told the meeting would take place there. At least it might not *feel* so much like a church in the basement, she reassured herself. And for as far as she'd come in the last few months, she just wasn't sure if she was ready for this. But ready or not, here she came.

She entered the oversized room and could smell the mustiness that came from years of poor ventilation. The linoleum floor was polished but had several scuff marks and stains. At the far end of the room there was a large stage which had faded purple curtains pulled halfway, betraying an upright piano and perhaps a set of drums behind it. The pale yellow paint on the cinderblock walls flaked in several places, and half a dozen small rectangular windows were covered with cotton print curtains on a tension rod to mask their unsightliness. The curtains were probably the handiwork of one of the church's women's groups, she thought. It was certainly plain, but there was also something comforting about this room, although Kathryn couldn't quite put her finger on why she felt that way. Several tables had been pushed to one corner, and a little over a dozen folding chairs had been arranged in a large circle in the center of the room.

Kathryn watched as the people milled around, some talking pleasantly to one another like they were old buddies, others keeping to themselves off to the side. More than one helped themselves to the coffee carafe on a small table near the revolving kitchen doors. A sign written on an index card next to the coffee read, "PLEASE CLEAN UP AFTER YOURSELF. YOU ARE IN GOD'S HOUSE, NOT YOUR OWN. THANK YOU." All of the people looked very much like she did in terms of their appearance. Some in jeans, others in more professional attire. One young woman smiled warmly at her, and Kathryn returned the smile. She looked so young, Kathryn thought. She couldn't be more than eighteen. Before she could ask who was in charge, a slender man wearing jeans and a light blue polo shirt spoke.

"All right, everyone, it's seven p.m. Let's all take our seats so we can get started."

Kathryn took a deep breath and exhaled slowly, but it didn't calm her nerves in the least. Show time.

Kathryn hesitated a few seconds to let most of the others settle in before taking a seat. After all, she didn't want to start off her very first night by encroaching upon someone else's claimed space. But much to Kathryn's surprise, no one seemed to have any assigned seats. Each person randomly took a chair, obviously used to the logistics of the evening. The slender man, who soon after introduced himself only as Adam, took a chair in the circle and encouraged anyone who felt comfortable to begin the discussion.

She studied each person carefully, but she couldn't bring herself to make eye contact with any of them. Though not in reality, they were in essence the same people Kathryn had represented at one time or another in her career. The ones she would look down upon and had concluded were worthless and weak because they didn't have enough willpower to resist temptation. These were the people whom she sent to counseling and meetings just like this one without ever giving them a second thought. She never had an ounce of sympathy for any of them. She never once asked what drove them to the point in their lives where they felt there was no other alternative. She never once asked if there was anything she could do to help them. No, they were all just case numbers in the pile on her desk, another check mark in the victory column when she ensured that they were spared any jail time. And she couldn't have cared less what happened to them after that, as long as they paid the firm's bills and put in a good word for her on the streets among the others just like them.

Yet here she sat among them. It's ironic how fate works sometimes, isn't it? As they introduced themselves one by one she heard the stories that easily could've been *her* story as well, and it dawned on her that really they were no different than she was. One a banker who got caught up in the fast-paced city life and resorted to the bottle as an outlet. Another a Realtor of million-dollar properties who, despite her socially demanding job, wasn't a people person and used the alcohol as a way to relax and let her guard down. A father of five who craved an escape from a chaotic household so his evening beers turned into an evening six-pack, and then more. A schoolteacher. A stay-at-home mother. A city councilman. A postal carrier. All of them baring their souls and publicly admitting their sins in the hopes they would find the one thing they needed to pick up the pieces and move on. Redemption. Each person sat intently listening to the next, not preoccupied with checking cell phones or staring blankly at the floor, but genuinely listening and caring for one another. It reminded Kathryn of a story from the Gospel of John she had heard so many times before. A woman had been caught in the act of adultery, and before the crowds could stone her to death as the law required, Jesus rebuked them. He said to the masses, "If any one of you is without sin, let him be the first to throw a stone at her." One by one, each person dropped their stone to the ground and left, leaving the woman alone with the Lord. There wasn't a single person in that room without sin. No stones would be cast here. Instead, they fulfilled the greatest commandment of loving one another as they loved themselves. It was humbling, and it was beautiful.

Kathryn fidgeted slightly in her chair once the person beside her began speaking. She was next. She wasn't sure if she could get the words out and she hung her head in shame, still reluctant to bring her eyes to meet anyone else's in the room. But as Adam motioned for Kathryn to begin, she took a deep breath and looked up. When she did, something caught her eye. Not the other eyes that were all on her, but something else. Hanging on the wall directly across from her chair was a cross. A simple wooden cross, no more than a foot high, smooth and plain. And in that moment the cross spoke to Kathryn. It reminded her of her Savior and the sins that he took upon himself for her and for everyone else in that room; for everyone in the world. It told her that she would be forgiven for her transgressions, and they would be removed from her as far as the east was from the west. And it comforted her with a love that she hadn't felt in as long as she could remember. An everlasting, perfect, unconditional love. It was a cross of salvation, and it was all for *her*. Tears welled in her eyes, but not tears of sadness of shame. No, these were tears of joy. Pure joy. She knew what she had to do, and, focused on the cross in front of her, she finally knew she could do it. After all, he was right there with her, giving her the strength she needed.

"My name is Kathryn," she began confidently, "and I am an alcoholic."

As soon as she managed to get that first sentence out the rest flowed effortlessly. It was liberating, and she was amazed at how easily she shared some of the most personal details of her life and her most humiliating moments with a group of complete strangers. Yet they weren't strangers. After about ten minutes of quickly summarizing her life history and what led her to this meeting, she was finished. Everyone smiled and clapped, and the schoolteacher sitting next to her even briefly took her hand and squeezed it for reassurance. Kathryn felt a relief that no bottle had ever brought her.

The meeting lasted about an hour, and as they collected their belongings and placed their chairs back on the cart, Adam instructed them regarding their agenda for the next meeting. "Same time, same place next week. Good job everyone," he encouraged them.

Kathryn made small talk with a few others before gathering her purse and checking her cell phone for any messages. Dusk had draped itself over the city, and when she reached the top step from the basement she was greeted by a lavender sky mixed with navy blue. The street lights had already come on, and the lantern at the main entrance to the sanctuary glowed against the cherry trees planted strategically on either side of the sanctuary doors. A cool breeze blew her golden hair off of her shoulders.

She had just stepped off the curb to cross the parking lot when she saw the figure of someone leaning up against her car. She crinkled her nose, thinking perhaps it was one of the meeting attendees who wanted to chat further or needed a ride. But then as she drew closer, she recognized him. He was unmistakable. It was

Benjamin. She blinked once, wondering if it was only wishful thinking or her imagination playing tricks on her, but there he stood, plain as day. She felt a rush of emotions that would've been impossible to sort out if she had even tried. Instead of fighting to maintain her cool as she had done for so many years, she let herself be led by the moment. She approached him and took in every last feature of his face, savoring the moment. His crooked smile, his worn jeans and stained T-shirt. His hands in his pockets and his hair, which as usual looked like it needed a good cutting, pushed carelessly to one side. She couldn't help but smile. She hadn't seen him in years, and yet he hadn't changed a bit. There were so many things she wanted to say to him, so many questions she wanted to ask that she didn't know where to begin. But before she could, he did.

"How did it go?" he asked casually, as if they had last spoken only yesterday.

"How did you know I was here?" she asked incredulously.

"It doesn't matter."

Kathryn agreed. It didn't matter. All that mattered was he was there.

"It went well, actually. It's a start anyway, right?"

"I'm real proud of you."

"Ya know what?" Kathryn said as she drew nearer to him. "For the first time in a really long time, I'm proud of me too."

She looked deep into his eyes and could feel the tears coming again. It seemed like she cried a lot these days, but not in a bad way.

"I can't even believe you came," she said. "After everything I said to you that day. After the way I shut you out." Her eyes searched his, silently pleading for forgiveness even though she couldn't find the right words. "After the way I treated you for so many years, here you are."

"I've always been here for you, and I always will be. I promised you that, and I never break my promises, Kathryn."

She gazed at him lovingly and took his hand in hers, looking down at their intertwined fingers. Just like when she was a little girl, she was completely enveloped by his presence. It was as if nothing in the world existed but the two of them.

"You know something?"

"What's that?" he asked.

"I don't want to be Kathryn anymore. I think I'm done with her. How 'bout just plain old 'Kate'?"

"Come here," Benjamin said, engulfing her. As he wrapped his sturdy arms around her she felt protected and loved and complete all at the same time. It was overwhelming. A dam broke that had been holding back a sea of emotions, regrets, and self-loathing for years. He pulled her closer still, and she could literally feel the transformation taking place within her. She was no longer Kathryn Ann Kirby, Esquire, attorney extraordinaire. She was the same little girl who sat under the swaying branches of the willow tree next to her very best friend. And here she was years later, cradled in the arms of the one person who she knew without a doubt loved her more than anyone else in the entire world. And in that single, precious moment she realized just how much she loved him too.

"Let's go home, Kate," he said with a smile.

Part III
Ben

"If anyone is in Christ, he is a new creation;
the old has gone, the new has come!"
2 Corinthians. 5:17

CHAPTER 14
MAY FLOWERS

"See! The winter is past; the rains are over and gone.
Flowers appear on the earth; the season of singing
has come . . ."
Song of Solomon 2:11-12

Let's go home.

She replayed the words over and over in her head. It was nearly two in the morning yet Kate lay in bed wide awake, Oreo sprawled out next to her in a deep slumber that rivaled unconsciousness. Kate marveled at how the relatively small creature could stretch herself out appearing six feet long, like a piece of taffy that you just keep pulling and watching it grow. And, of course, Oreo *had* to sleep smack up against Kate each night, leaving a full three quarters of the bed completely untouched. Well sure, Kate could've scooted the feline over or even altogether banished her from the bedroom, but how could she be so cruel when Oreo looked perfectly adorable lying next to her? Kate would just have to sacrifice a little bit of her own comfort for the sake of Oreo's contentment. The story of a cat owner's life.

Unfortunately, Oreo's sleeping position didn't do much to aid Kate in attempting to go back to sleep. At a little past midnight something unknowable had stirred her awake, and just as she rolled over to continue her night's rest, it happened. Her mind started processing. Like a switch abruptly flipped on, she was full-on in prime thinking mode. She thought of this and that, her mind wandering from one subject to the next, and before she knew it she was staring at the alarm clock every fifteen minutes willing herself to go back to sleep. But it was too late. Her brain had won the battle, and no matter how badly her body may have needed the rest, it wasn't going to happen. Kate glanced jealously over at Oreo breathing lightly with the occasional twitch of a paw, deep in the middle of what must've been a dream. Admitting defeat, Kate slowly rose from her bed (taking great care not to disturb Oreo's ever-so-peaceful repose), shrugged on her robe and slippers, and headed to the kitchen to brew herself a cup of coffee.

Let's go home.

Kate absentmindedly reached for the K-cup of her favorite Colombian dark blend, and after the push of a few buttons she was comforted by the hot, black liquid gliding smoothly down her throat. She instinctively headed for the patio where the glow of the lights never quite let the darkness completely invade the city. It was so different from Bakersville, where the blackness of a night devoid of stars was like a thick blanket draped over the entire town. Here in the city there was always someone awake, whether being shuttled in a taxi at all hours of the night, working late in their sixteenth-floor office, or opening up shop early for the local deliveries. And there were always lights to prove it. Kate settled into the oversized loveseat that had replaced the chair where Griffin had once told her that their marriage was over. She breathed the air deeply into her lungs and stared at the halo the lights created over the cityscape.

Let's go home.

Ben had said it only hours ago in what was quite unpredictably shaping up to be the best night she had had in a long time. Maybe even the best night *ever*. The irony of it all almost made her choke on her coffee. Never in a billion years would she have thought that the *best* night of her life would come in the form of an AA meeting at some obscure church in the dilapidated outskirts of the city. But it had nonetheless. God showers blessings upon us in all shapes and sizes, sometimes *when* and *where* we least expect them. That's why they're called blessings.

Let's go home.

The words Ben lovingly uttered in the parking lot carried a much deeper meaning to Kate than just the place where she would lay her head each night, and Kate was pretty sure that Ben had intended it that way. But that was just the problem. Where *was* home? Even though Kate had several places to claim as her own, she wasn't so sure any of them felt like home. In fact, what was so unsettling about it all was that, at the moment, Kate was feeling almost home*less*.

Sure, there was the condo where she had lived for almost a decade and built a life for herself and, at one time, Griffin. But with all of their comings and goings in their high-society lives, she had to be honest with herself that it had never once really felt like home. A dwelling, an occupancy, a residence, a domicile, a showplace. Yes, all of those things. But never really a *home*. Then there was her childhood home in Bakersville which sat painfully empty after her mother's death only a few months prior. Every last piece of furniture was still in place, and Kate could easily return to the town where she had been raised and settle into her very same bedroom with lemon yellow walls and dormers overlooking the happenings of Magnolia Lane. But could she really go back to all that? And if she could, did she even *want* to? Something inside of Kate told her that she needed to move ahead and stop looking back. That no matter how much she loved the house on Magnolia Lane and cherished the memories she had created there, it was no longer her home.

So then, where exactly *was* her home? The question simultaneously disturbed and exhilarated her. After all, if she *had* no home currently, then she would just have to create a home for herself. She could relocate somewhere else in the city. She could find a new home in Bakersville. She could even move across the country if she wanted to. The sky was the limit. Ideas raced through her mind like a giant invisible map of the country with imaginary push pins inserted in random locations. But before she got too carried away she stopped herself. Kate had spent the last decade of her life making decisions on the spur of the moment without a thought of consequences or long-term plans, and she had paid dearly for that outlook. So no more. The decision on this next chapter of her life wasn't going to come over a cup of coffee during a sleepless night at three o'clock in the morning. It would come when the time was right, no matter how much time it took.

Let's go home.

"Yes, let's," Kate said aloud to the nothingness of the city. "Oh, Lord, you just need to show me where that is. Tell me, God, where *is* my home?"

Staring into her empty mug, Kate realized that, in spite of the caffeine, she was ready to rejoin Oreo for what was left of the night. What she didn't realize, however, was that for the first time in what felt like an eternity, Kate had talked to God.

Three days later Kate arose early, full of energy and resolve. The past few days had brought some major changes in her life, *good* changes, and now there were only a couple of loose ends to tie up before she would be ready. On today's agenda: the final two people she needed to see. She had called ahead so they were both anticipating a conversation with Kate, although about what they had no clue.

She ascended the steps of the modest duplex in what had obviously once been an upscale community on the north side of the city. Although the row homes were aging and the cobblestone streets were uneven, she could tell the neighborhood was still a source of pride for its residents. The homes were well cared for with manicured lawns and crape myrtles lining the sidewalk, so she couldn't help but feel welcomed as she rang the doorbell of the red brick home occupying the corner of First and Thurmont Streets. Within only a few moments Kate was warmly greeted by someone who was turning out to be a much closer friend than she had ever anticipated.

"Counselor, so nice to see you. Please, come in." Chester gestured into the modest living room, and Kate happily accepted the invitation, scanning the small yet comfortable quarters in the process. The room betrayed many signs of the woman who once lived there with her loving husband—the needlepoint pillows on either end of the sofa, the doilies on each end table underneath the lamps, the floral print drapes pulled to the side with sheers underneath, the pine rocking chair in the corner of the room with a multicolored afghan draped over one arm. If Kate had to guess, she would say that Chester hadn't changed a thing since his wife had passed away several years before. It brought Kate a warmth and a sadness for her dear friend.

"It's not much, but it's home," Chester offered as he noticed Kate surveying the room.

"It's absolutely lovely," she said in return, meaning every word of it.

"Yes, Mina and I had a lot of happy years here," he said wistfully. "I still think about her every day." His melancholy eyes looked past Kate's into a time and a place only he could visit.

"I don't plan on going anywhere any time soon, mind you. But in some ways it will be nice to rejoin her one day. You know what I mean?"

"Yes," Kate answered genuinely. "I do know what you mean."

Chester shook his head as if to break the trance to which he had momentarily succumbed and redirected focus to his friend. "I'm sorry, I'm being so rude. Can I offer you something to drink? A cup of coffee, or tea maybe? Or some water?"

"No thanks, I've already had my morning coffee so I'm good."

Kate took a seat on the velvety pink couch while Chester settled into one of the armchairs near the fireplace. He glanced over at the rocker.

"That was her chair, you know." He smiled, but it was a sad smile. "She could sit in that chair for hours on end. Sometimes watching television, sometimes doing crossword puzzles or reading a book, other times talking on the phone with friends or our children. But that was always *her* spot." As Kate listened to Chester speak so fondly of his wife, she was quite sure that Mina was the only person to have ever sat in that rocker.

The two remained silent for a few moments, but it was a comfortable silence.

"It gets kind of lonely around here," Chester admitted while absentmindedly fiddling with the fringe on one of the lampshades.

"Well actually, Chester, it's funny you say that, because that's why I asked to see you today."

"Oh?" he asked curiously.

"Yes. You see, ever since the car accident I've been doing a lot of thinking. *A LOT.* And I think I'm at the point where I need to figure out where my life is headed. Obviously I wasn't in a very good place for a long time, and I don't want to live like that anymore. And, well," Kate hesitated, "I kind of need to regroup. I need to figure out what God's plan is for my life and where I belong." She looked around the room again. "Chester, you have such a beautiful home. And that's just it. At the moment I'm not quite sure where 'home' *is* for me. So that's where you come in."

"Me?" Chester asked. "You know I'd do anything to help you Kate, but I'm not so sure what it is you want me to do."

Kate took a deep breath, anxious to share the plan that God had put on her heart. "I'm going away for a while. I need to take some time to get to know myself, if that makes any sense. I need to put some space between myself and this place so I can regroup and find out exactly where it is I'm supposed to be."

Chester was finally beginning to catch on, although the details remained fuzzy.

"Where are you going?" he asked.

"Honestly, I'm not sure."

"How long will you be gone?"

"Again," Kate replied, "I'm not sure. I don't want to put a time limit on it. I guess I'll be gone as long as it takes."

"What about your job? And your condo?"

Kate smiled. "As for my job, yesterday I officially tendered my resignation to the firm." The look of surprise on Chester's face was inescapable. "Believe me, they will do just fine without me." She thought back to when Darian visited Kate in the hospital and the condemnation he exuded. She knew she wouldn't miss him or the firm in the least.

"As for the condo," she continued, "I met with a real estate agent a few days ago, and it is currently on the market. I'm selling it fully furnished. If there's one thing I've learned these past few months, it's that the *stuff* in life really doesn't matter one bit. It will be nice to simplify and get rid of all the clutter."

"Wow," Chester remarked admiringly. "It sure looks like you've got your mind made up about this."

"I do," she answered firmly.

"But I still don't understand. What does all of this have to do with me?"

"Well," Kate began as she moved closer to him and took his hands. "You said that sometimes you get lonely. And I'm going to be traveling for quite some time. I don't know where I'll be staying or even how long I'll be gone. Oreo is such a sweet little thing who doesn't deserve to have her life upset because of my—"

Kate wasn't able to finish her sentence before Chester cut in. "You want *me* to take Oreo?"

"You don't have to give me an answer right away," Kate interjected. "If you would just think about it, I would be so grateful. I know how much Oreo came to love you when you took care of her while I was in the hospital. And well, *she* needs a home. It wouldn't be fair to uproot her just because I'm leaving, and I couldn't bear to take her back to the shelter. She's already been through so much in the last few months."

"So you want me to keep her until you come back?" It was obvious from Chester's question what he was implying.

"No, Chester, I want you to keep her for good. I couldn't leave her with you for what could be months only to come back and disrupt her life all over again. If you would take her, she would be yours forever."

Chester tried unsuccessfully to suppress a grin. "I would be honored," he answered, his voice cracking ever so slightly.

"Thank you so much, my dear friend," she said as she embraced him.

"Think nothing of it," he replied. "It will be good to have some company in the house. I think Mina would approve."

"I think she would too," Kate suggested in return.

Chester arranged to collect Oreo at the end of the week once he had had a chance to shop for all of the critical kitty supplies—litter, food, toys, and, of course, a bed and a scratching post. Kate offered to reimburse him for the expenses, but Chester wouldn't hear of it. Kate laughed at the thought that Oreo was about to become the most spoiled cat on the planet. She knew her mother was smiling down on her.

Kate bid Chester farewell and returned to her condo, where the second person she was due to meet would arrive at any moment. As soon as she set foot in the foyer of the condominium complex, she saw him leaning up against the wall waiting for her. People hurried by without even noticing him, all having someplace to go in a hurry, but Kate saw him immediately. She went over and hugged him.

"Thank you so much for coming on such short notice," she said as she took his hand and led him to the elevators.

"So what's this all about anyway?" he asked.

"You'll see." Kate eyed him mysteriously as they entered the elevator, and she pushed the corresponding button for the penthouse suite. For a moment Ben flashed back to their grade school days when she would get this mischievous sparkle in her eye, and he immediately knew she was up to something. Yes, her wheels were definitely turning.

The second they entered her condo she couldn't hold it in any longer. Her thoughts spilled out so quickly that Ben could hardly keep up. She explained how she had spent the last several days contemplating three simple words he had said to her outside the church—*Let's go home*. She told him how she wasn't sure where her home was, but yet she knew it wasn't a decision to be made quickly. Then she shared how the revelation came to her as the sunrise peeked in through the bedroom blinds after a long night of soul searching. She needed to leave. Not permanently, but at least for a little while. She needed to step back, take an inventory of her life, and figure out where she was headed from here. Ben listened intently, never once interrupting (it wouldn't have done any good anyway, Kate was on a roll), and overjoyed at the passion bubbling over in her voice that had been absent for so long. She told Ben how she had put the condo on the market, resigned from her position at Engel, Wallingford, and Driscoll, and enlisted her dear friend Chester to adopt Oreo. She even explained that she had reached out to Adam, her AA coach, and made arrangements to call in each week so that she could maintain her sobriety while traveling since she wouldn't have the opportunity to attend weekly meetings. Finally, after talking non-stop for over half an hour and barely taking a breath, she looked at Ben expectantly.

"Well?"

"Well what?" Ben played along.

"What do you think?"

"I think you have certainly thought of everything. And if this is what you feel you need to do, then I support you one hundred percent."

Kate sighed deeply and allowed herself to relax as soon as she felt Ben's approval.

"I know it probably sounds crazy," Kate admitted, "but this is just something I need to do."

"Actually, I don't think it sounds crazy at all. If anything, I give you credit for not rushing into any decisions before you settle down. When are you leaving?"

"I'd like to leave one day next week if I can get everything in order by then. But there *is* one thing I really want to do with you before I go." A sneaky grin spread across her face.

"What's that?" Ben asked.

"Don't laugh, but I would really love to go back to our willow tree."

"Kate—" Ben started, but he didn't get very far.

"I know it sounds silly, and we haven't been there in years. But I feel like we should visit it again, just once more. For old times' sake. We can sit under the branches and contemplate life just like we did when we were kids." Kate hesitated when she saw the expression on Ben's face. "What's wrong?"

"I guess your mom never told you. They cut down that old tree a few years ago. Sold the land to build some new housing development with over two hundred homes."

Kate's memory immediately revisited the conversation in Antonelli's months ago when her mother had told her about a new development in Bakersville that was causing quite the stir. At that time Kate had been too self-immersed to give it a second thought. Never once had it occurred to her that the development could have been on the site of their tree. After all, there was lots of farmland in Bakersville.

"She did tell me about it," Kate replied sorrowfully. "I just didn't know it was the same land where our tree was."

"Yeah, it was. They even named the development *Whispering Willow*. Funny, it's called Whispering Willow, and there isn't a single willow tree on the property anymore. I'm sorry, Kate."

"Oh, that's okay," she answered, trying to hide her disappointment. She reminisced about the countless trips the pair had made to the tree over their childhood years. Their own God-created sanctuary of peace and solitude they could call upon whenever they wanted. Kate had laughed under that tree, cried under it, and hidden within its delicate branches she and Ben had shared some of the deepest and most complex conversations of her entire life. That single willow had been entrusted with a treasure trove of confidential conversations between two grade-schoolers trying to understand the world around them. Kate could hardly believe it, but even though she hadn't visited the tree in years, she was actually going to miss it now that she knew she could never return. "It was a good tree to us for all those years," she shared stoically as if she had just lost a dear friend.

"Yes, it was," Ben agreed.

"I guess everything does change over time. Even in Bakersville. Who would've thought?" They both laughed at the premise.

"Hey, there is one thing I need to ask you," Ben said, changing the subject.

"What's that?"

"Do you want me to go with you on your trip? I mean, I'm working on a few pieces of furniture at the studio, but I could finish them up quickly and come with you."

Kate smiled and took his hand. "Actually, I was hoping you would ask me that. And to be totally honest, in a way, yes, I would like for you to come with me. But I've spent way too many years running from myself and not liking the person I had become. So I think this is something I really need to do on my own. I hope you're not offended."

"Not in the least, I totally understand."

"And besides," Kate added, "even though you won't be *with* me, I know you'll still be with me." She winked at him knowingly.

"Now you're finally getting it." Ben smiled. "Just promise me a couple of things."

"What's that?"

"Promise me you'll be careful, and promise you'll stay in touch."

"I absolutely will," Kate agreed. "I will write you each week no matter where I am. And don't worry, I won't be gone too long."

"Well, whenever you do come back, I'll be right here waiting."

Kate and Ben spent the next several hours envisioning the journey upon which Kate was about to embark. They discussed the places she might decide to go, the logistics of what she would need to bring with her, and how they would get hold of each other in case of emergency. All the while Kate felt utterly exhilarated at the thought of venturing into the world on her own. She couldn't wait to see what was out there waiting for her, and she couldn't wait to rediscover Kate.

After lunch on the patio and one of those conversations with an old friend that you wish could go on forever, Ben told Kate he had to be back in Bakersville before dusk for an appointment, and she escorted him to the elevators. They said their goodbyes, unsure of when they would see each other again but knowing the reunion would be a glorious one. Ben turned to leave.

"Ben, thank you."

"For what?"

"For giving me another chance. For forgiving all of the terrible things I did and said. And most of all, thank you for not judging me for all of my mistakes. I really can't even begin to tell you how much I missed you, or how glad I am to have you back in my life."

"I'm glad too. That part is behind us now, there's no use dwelling on the past. And Kate, there is nothing you could ever do that would change how I feel about you."

As soon as he stepped onto the elevator Kate held the doors open.

"Ben, I have a favor to ask of you."

"Anything," he answered.

She looked deep into his warm brown eyes and felt the magnetic connection that only he could create.

"When I get back, I want you to teach me everything that your father taught you about the Bible. I think it's about time I reconnect with God. And I don't know why, but I just have this feeling inside that you're the one who has to help me do it."

Ben nodded his head, half grinned, and silently thanked his father for the blessing of that very moment.

"You got it."

The elevator doors mechanically slid together until Ben was gone from her sight.

On the first of August, with little more than a medium-sized suitcase and all of the proper documentation in tow, Kate set off for her journey. After much thought and prayer, Kate decided that her first destination would be Williamsport, a quaint seaside town on the opposite side of the country where her father had been raised from the time he was a young boy until the family moved cross country immediately after high school. If Kate were going to figure out what lay ahead for her, she also wanted to know where she came from, so she decided to spend a little time tracing her roots. While in Williamsport she learned that a few very distant relatives from the Kirby side of the family still lived there, so Kate was blessed with the hospitality that a small handful of her second and third cousins provided while she visited.

From Williamsport, however, Kate let the Lord take the lead, and her travels quickly became global. For ten months she explored the world. She visited famous landmarks and wonders of the world. She traveled to ancient historical sites that, as you pondered the thousands of years of civilization which had come and gone since their erection, made you realize just how fleeting your brief time in this world really is. Kate walked barefoot on beaches so breathtaking she was sure they were replicated after paradise. She stood before mountains so grandiose they looked as if their peaks touched heaven. She navigated through the dense forests of jungles and knelt down upon the sands of a desert so vast it appeared as though it went on to the end of the earth. Kate discovered creatures that she never knew existed. She met people of all different races, ethnicities, and walks of life. She did her best to communicate in the various languages she encountered and immersed herself in the myriad beautiful cultures she experienced. She crossed paths with some of the wealthiest people in the world and also some of the poorest. She visited villages which had no running water, and she witnessed poverty that was inhumane. Kate saw disease and illness and also the miracle of healing. Through each encounter two things happened. Kate could clearly see the hand of God at work in the world far beyond the confines of her comfort zone, and she came to know herself a little better. Just as she had hoped, she gained a deeper understanding of who, exactly, Kate Kirby was and what it was she was meant to do in this world.

Faithful to her promise, Kate regularly kept in touch with Ben by sending him postcards from all over the world. Sometimes a more detailed letter would follow, and other times she scribbled only a few words on the back of the cardboard square with a photo of her latest destination just to let him know that she was safe. She also frequently included Chester in her correspondence to ensure that he felt a part of her journeys as well.

The weeks quickly turned into months. Although part of Kate wished her voyage could last forever, she also grew restless of the nomadic life and longed to put down roots of her own. She had experienced so much since she had set out, but she knew it was time to begin a new season in life. Almost ten months after her journey began, Kate pasted the stamp on the last postcard she would send Ben. She stared at the photograph on the front of the never-ending fields of poppies. She flipped it over, considered for quite some time what she should write, and then scrawled the brief message on the back.

It's time to come home.

See you soon. Love, K

Ben received the cryptic text just as he was closing up shop and preparing to head to St. Paul's for their May Day covered dish supper. He glanced at his cell phone and did a double take.

> Meet me tomorrow morning 9 a.m., 704 Front St., Riverton. Don't be late!

It had been almost a month since Ben had received Kate's last postcard, so he was expecting to hear from her any day. But he anticipated it would likely be a phone call or even a visit to his shop, not some odd message about a rendezvous in another small town only a stone's throw from Bakersville. What was in Riverton? And why did he need to meet Kate there? Once again, she was up to something.

Riverton was a historic town steeped in tradition with a population of less than a thousand, most of whom were locals who could trace their roots back to the immediate area for several generations. Situated at the juncture of two rivers which were once major sources of both travel and trade, Riverton's claim to fame was that a record nine presidents of the United States had at various times lodged at one of the inns peppered throughout the cozy town as they traveled across the country. The town itself was divided into equal quadrants by two main thoroughfares: Commerce Street, where all of the businesses were located, and Front Street, which was graced by Victorian residences of all shapes and sizes. Hanging baskets overflowing with red and white petunias dangled from the lanterns lining the streets. At Christmastime the baskets were replaced by twinkling snowflake lights creating a picturesque winter wonderland.

Ben was familiar with Front Street since he had often delivered his unique carpentry pieces to its residents. He drove slowly down the street, enjoying the feel of having momentarily stepped back in time as he passed the Victorian-era homes, no two of which were alike. He spotted the enormous mansion which over a century ago had been owned by the wealthiest man in the state, but several decades back was converted into a series of apartments. Next he drove by Judge Greene's home, then the county commissioner's, then the Bailey family's, who had owned the local hardware store since as far back as anyone could remember. As he continued along the asphalt road toward its intersection with Commerce Street, the homes, although still ornate and adorned with gingerbread woodwork, became noticeably smaller; some had unfortunately been let go quite a bit. That was when he spotted the *For Sale* sign on the overgrown lawn of a three-story blue shake shingle home. Kate was already there, standing next to the sign looking up at the home and beaming with delight. Ben exited his car and joined her.

"Isn't it beautiful?" she gushed.

Kate couldn't take her eyes off of it. You would've thought she had been standing before a masterpiece, something that only Michelangelo could conjure on canvas. When Ben looked at Kate it was obvious; clearly what she was seeing wasn't the house as it currently existed, but rather the home that it *could* be.

Ben considered her statement as he carefully examined the narrow one-room-deep structure. The wooden steps leading to the front porch were rotted, and the left hand rail was missing. The storm door hung crooked on the front, and the white trim on the porch was peeling in such large flakes it looked like skin after a bad sunburn. Cobwebs claimed every corner of the porch. Several panes of glass on the large bay window next to the door were either cracked or completely missing. As his gaze took him upward, he noticed a missing shutter from the second-story window and a bird's nest tucked into one of the sills. The fishtail shingles on the gabled top floor were painted two hideous shades of pink in what looked like a miserable attempt to brighten up the place in contrast to the faded baby blue of the rest of the home. Perhaps the previous owners were colorblind, thought Ben. Or perhaps they were going for a cotton candy look. Several of the slate shingles on the roof were missing, and the brick fireplace partially hidden around the side looked as though it might crumble to the ground at any moment. And that was just the house itself. The yard hadn't seen the likes of a lawnmower in years. Who could tell what creatures might have taken up residence in the towering weeds?

"Well," Ben finally answered as Kate stood mesmerized by the picture in her mind, "if you say so. I guess there's a reason they say beauty is in the eye of the beholder." He tilted his head as if changing his orientation might present the house in a better light.

Kate nudged him playfully. "Oh, come on. You of *all* people should be able to see the potential in this home. All it needs is a little TLC."

"How long has it been on the market?"

"Well, it *had* been on the market for a little over three years. Apparently a sweet elderly couple lived here all their lives and raised six children in this home. Can you imagine? Six children and only *one* bathroom in the entire house! Good grief! Well, when the husband passed away about five years ago, it was just too much for the wife to take care of, but she refused to leave. So she lived here until she died. Since that time the children have been trying to sell it, but it was in such bad shape they weren't having any luck. Until now, that is."

"And what exactly do you mean, 'until now'?"

"It's mine, Ben. I bought it three days ago."

"Why am I not surprised?"

"I know it's been a little neglected over the last few years."

"A *little*?"

"Okay," Kate admitted, "a lot. But it has a good foundation, and with some love and elbow grease just think of what it could be! I know it might sound ridiculous, but in many ways this house reminds me of myself."

"How so?" Ben asked.

"Well, for many years I feel like I let go of myself. This last year has proven to me that I needed a rebirth. A fresh start. That's why I decided on Riverton. I thought about going back to the city, but there are just too many bad memories there. That was where *Kathryn* lived, and that's not who I am anymore. Then I thought about going back to Bakersville to the house on Magnolia Lane, but part of me felt like I would be trying to hold onto the past, and I need to move forward. I've always loved Riverton, so when I saw the house for sale I knew in my heart that this is the place God intended for me to call my home. Much like me, all this house needs is to be given a second chance. It needs loving hands to help bring it back to life. A rebirth."

Ben tentatively set his foot on the front step before putting any weight on it for fear he might fall through. "Well then, it looks as though you've found your home after all."

"So, will you help me?"

"Help you what?" He feigned ignorance.

Kate rolled her eyes. "You know. Will you help me bring this place back to life?"

Ben looked her straight in the eye quite seriously, although he found it difficult to suppress the joy he was feeling. "Do I have a choice?"

"Not really," Kate giggled.

"Then I guess you can count me in." Kate squeezed him so hard he thought she just might suffocate him.

"You do realize this is no small undertaking?"

"I know." Kate wasn't the least bit fazed by his warning.

"I mean, the outside alone needs quite a bit of work. I can only imagine what the inside looks like."

"Yep, it's pretty much just as bad on the inside. Everything needs updating, and we'll definitely have to add another bathroom."

"It's going to take time."

"We have all the time in the world," Kate countered.

"It's going to be expensive."

"No problem there, I still have all the money from the sale of the condo."

"It's going to be a lot of work."

"Then what are we waiting for?"

Kate grabbed Ben by the arm as she had done so many times in her youth and trudged up the front porch steps in a zigzag path to avoid the holes in the wooden planks. That was when Ben first entered 704 Front Street, Kate's blank canvas. They spent the next hour touring the home room by room, mercifully overlooking the eyesores of peeling wallpaper or crumbling plaster. Instead, they marveled at the glorious oak banisters (that desperately needed refinishing), the crown molding in each room (that needed repainting), or the antique claw-foot tub in her bathroom (that needed a good, old-fashioned scrubbing). Potential indeed.

Once Kate was finished giving Ben the grand tour, they sat together on the front porch step and enjoyed the crisp spring breeze.

"There is one thing I'm kind of confused about," Ben admitted.

"What's that?"

"Well, Riverton is an awfully long commute from the city."

"Oh, I guess I forgot to tell you." Kate's face lit up. "I won't be working in the city anymore."

"Is that right? So where *will* you be working?"

"The whole time I was away I had been praying about that too. Not just where my home would be, but also what I should do with the rest of my life. I really feel that God has given me a gift as a lawyer, and I feel like I'm good at it, but before I only used it for my own benefit. The only thing I cared about was my reputation and making money. But now I want to use that gift for someone who really needs it."

"I think that sounds amazing. So what are you going to do?"

"Well, last week when I got back into town I visited Hope's House."

"You mean the domestic violence center in Clark County?" Ben inquired.

"Yes, that's the one. It's less than twenty minutes from here. Did you know each year they help hundreds of women and children in the tri-county area who are victims of abuse?"

"I heard it was something like that."

"It's amazing all of the resources they put in place for these women. Some of them have nowhere to go. They leave in the middle of the night, scared to death with literally nothing more than the clothes on their back. They need help, Ben. And they need attorneys to stand up for them in court and make sure they are protected. It made me think back to Maddie Taylor in middle school. Maybe if Maddie's mother had sought help from Hope's House things wouldn't have gotten as ugly as they did. And then it also made me think about Gerald Lyons and how I've spent far too many years protecting the wrong people in the system. So I met with their director and found out they were desperately in need of attorneys."

"How come they're so desperate?" wondered Ben.

"Sadly, because they can't pay very much, at least not in comparison to salaries that most attorneys are accustomed to. And honestly at one time I would've thought the exact same thing. But it's not about the money, Ben. I want to help these women get back on track and find their own path in life. A paycheck isn't important to me anymore. And besides, I have enough in savings to sustain me for quite some time."

"So when do you start?"

"They need to finish processing my paperwork, which should take a few weeks at most, and then I'll be cleared to begin any time. And do you know what the best part is?"

"What's that?"

"I told them about my DUI and the circumstances of the accident that night last spring. Do you know what the director said to me?"

"What?"

"She said, 'Everyone makes mistakes.' Isn't that beautiful?"

Ben put his arm around Kate, and they sat together on the front porch for quite some time, enjoying the glorious spring day that God had gifted them. The time passed much quicker than they had anticipated when Ben realized he was due back in Bakersville, so Kate walked him to the curb and kissed him on the cheek.

Kate suddenly remembered something. "Oh, before you go. Look down the street over there. Can you see the tip of the steeple?" She pointed past the other homes lining Front Street as Ben strained his eyes as far as he could see.

"You mean the one down the road a little ways at the intersection? Yeah, I see it. Why?"

"That is Amazing Grace Chapel. My new church."

"Really?" Ben asked.

"Yep, I've worshipped there the last two Sundays. The people are so warm and welcoming. I immediately felt the Holy Spirit's presence there."

"Well, you'll just have to take me with you sometime."

"I'd love to," Kate agreed.

"Say, do you want to head into town with me and get a quick bite to eat before I have to head back?"

"Thanks for the offer, but I think I'm gonna hang out here for a while. There are a few things I need to do."

"Suit yourself," Ben responded as he got into his car and rolled down the window. "Just don't go fixin' everything all in one day now. You need to leave me a little something to do."

"Ha, ha, very funny," Kate retorted at his sarcasm. "Don't you worry one bit, there will be plenty for you to do!"

"That's exactly what I'm afraid of," Ben replied with a dramatic sigh. "Welcome home, Kate. I'm glad you're back."

"Me too," she agreed as he slowly pulled away from the curb.

As soon as Ben was out of sight Kate turned back to the house and meticulously considered every last inch of her new home. She couldn't wait to make it her own. But there was something she needed to do first. Kate weaved her way through the tall weeds that had long since overtaken the footpath leading to the backyard. Adjacent to the screened porch was a beat-up wooden picnic table. On that table were two flats of pansies that she had bought at a local nursery the day before along with a few flower boxes, some top soil, a pair of gloves, a watering can, and all of the proper gardening tools. Kate rolled up her sleeves, and for the next hour she carefully planted the hardy flowers in the boxes. She hummed softly and thought back to the day when she and her mother had planted pansies after Grans's funeral, and she remembered how excited she was that Thanksgiving morning to see the tiny stems peeping up through the soil. She thought of how much she missed her mother and her grandmother, and then it dawned on her. This perfect May day with a cloudless blue sky and sparkling sun was Grans's birthday. Kate smiled. God always does have perfect timing.

Once the boxes were finished, she carefully transported them one at a time onto the railing of the front porch. "There," she said as she rested the final box on the rail farthest from the front door. She stood back to survey the scene and couldn't help but be pleased at the way the pansies livened up the dilapidated house.

And the flowers were only the beginning.

Springtime had finally dawned. A new season was upon her.

CHAPTER 15
HIDE AND SEEK

"You will seek me and find me
when you seek me with all your heart."
Jeremiah 29:13

"Once upon a time there was a man who worked in the fields, plowing and harvesting the crops. Well, one day he was doing his job just like any other ordinary day. But as he was digging in the dirt with his pick, all of a sudden he struck something in the ground. So the man became very curious. *What could it possibly be?* he thought to himself."

"What was it?" Five-year-old Cassidy Parker interrupted.

Pastor Connie smiled at Cassidy's typical youthful impatience. As the pastor shared her weekly "Children's Church" message prior to the sermon, the cluster of children focused as best they could from their front row seat on the step leading to the altar. Seven-year-old Caroline Crawford sat perfectly still with her hands folded across her lap in a red velvet dress, her parents beaming from their pew at what a well-behaved child they had raised. Caroline's classmate Bobby Whitaker was next to her, fiddling uncomfortably with the clip-on tie his mother had forced him to wear. Next to Bobby sat four-year-old T.J. Evans. Well, perhaps "sat" is too strong a word. Because, after all, "sat" implies a stillness of sorts, and believe me T.J. was anything *but* still. He fidgeted and kept fastening and unfastening the Velcro on his brand new pair of light-up tennis shoes, wriggling and squirming around on the step like a snake. On the step below Caroline sat little Amanda Dryer, who vigorously waved at her mortified parents and screamed, "Hi, Mommy! Hi, Daddy!" at the top of her lungs. And next to her were the two-year-old Morganson twins, Michael and Matthew, who were more interested in wrestling with one another than in anything the pastor might have to say. Their brief time at the front of the sanctuary quickly became a rolling-on-the-ground wrestling match until their father hurriedly retrieved them and carried them back to their pew, one tucked under each arm like two oversized footballs. From her pew about midway down the center aisle at Amazing Grace Chapel, Kate chuckled under her breath at the gaggle of children. Yes, Pastor Connie had better make her point quickly.

"That's an excellent question, Cassidy. Hang on one minute and we'll find out." Pastor Connie didn't give any opportunity for further participation and instead hurried to her next point. That was one thing Pastor Connie had learned the hard way. Pauses during Children's Church were extremely dangerous.

"So," she stalled in order to recollect her thoughts, "the worker carefully retrieved his shovel and began digging all around the spot where the object was. And the more he dug, the more this object in the ground started to appear. He got down on his hands and knees and brushed away what was left of the dirt, revealing a treasure chest." With that Pastor Connie leaned over and pulled out of an oversized bag a plastic toy treasure chest. The children all collectively "ooohed" and "aaahed," while the adults laughed at the youngsters' complete enrapture at the prop.

"And inside the chest," Pastor Connie continued as she unlocked the chest and opened the lid, "he found *this*." She grabbed a handful of plastic gold coins and rubbed them together in her fingers.

"Wowwwww!" T.J. said enthusiastically. "Is that *real* gold?"

The congregation roared. "No, T.J., it's not real gold. But I wish it were!"

After a quick survey of her young audience, Pastor Connie knew she had to make her point and call it a day. She was quickly losing them.

"So you see, the man was so excited he had found this priceless treasure that he bought the field just so he could keep it. He knew how valuable it was and what a difference it would make in his life. And that is what we're going to be talking about today, boys and girls. Jesus told a very similar story to his disciples in the Gospel of

Matthew. And he was telling them this story to show them how important God is in our lives. God is the best treasure we could ever find! You might think of a treasure as gold or diamonds or things like that, but the real treasure in our lives is our relationship with the Lord. So make sure that you know just how much of a treasure God is in your lives, and don't ever let go of that treasure! Okay?"

A collective "okay" erupted from the group of youngsters as they began to disperse before being directed to do so. "Okay, boys and girls, you can return to your seats with your parents." Pastor Connie sighed in relief as the choir director prepared for the anthem. Who would've thought that the most difficult part of her weekly morning service would be the five minutes she had to deliver a message to the children? Mercy!

Following the service Kate greeted Pastor Connie warmly and thanked her for such a meaningful sermon. Once again in her life, Kate had felt as though the message had been written specifically for her, although, unlike the last time that had happened to her, this time it was a very *good* thing. Kate was invigorated and couldn't wait to tell Ben all about it. She bid goodbye to several of her church friends, buttoned her coat, wrapped her scarf tightly around her neck, and braved the bitter cold winter afternoon. She and Ben had a standing lunch date after their respective church services, and they would alternate between Riverton and Bakersville just to make it fair. This week it was her turn to travel. Whenever they met they brought their Bibles and discussed the Word of God. They had no set agenda, and they let the conversation go where the Lord led them. Much like the days under their majestic willow tree, Kate had some of the most profound conversations of her life with Ben on those Sunday afternoons. And she couldn't get enough. She deeply drank of Ben's wisdom and always hungered for more.

As she backtracked along Front Street, she came upon her home; after checking her rearview mirror to ensure no cars were behind her, she couldn't help but stop for a minute to gaze upon her masterpiece. In the six months since Kate had bought the home, she and Ben had literally transformed it into a new creation. In fact, it was barely recognizable from the pitiful home she had first introduced Ben to in May. The lawn was well kept with a new front walkway and stone steps winding around back. The porch had been completely redone, new shingles, new roof, the chimney repaired, the shutters sanded and painted. You name it, they fixed it. And no more of that hideous pink-and-blue-bubblegum look. Kate had decided on painting the home a pale seafoam green with the shutters and fishtail shingles on the top floor a deep teal. The trim and the front porch were crisp white, and artificial candles adorned every window. It was truly a vision of elegance, and the inside was just as nice. True to form, Kate had made the home her mission as soon as she had set eyes on it. She had taken up temporary residence at her childhood home in Bakersville until her new home was move-in ready, and by early fall she had made the transition. It was everything she had hoped it would be and more.

For as much as Kate would've liked to sit and stare at her new home all day long, she didn't want to be late for her lunch date. She had so much to tell him! She made the trip to Bakersville in less than ten minutes and found Ben waiting at their usual table at Marty's, a causal yet eclectic restaurant four doors down from Ben's shop that had opened less than a year before. Apparently the mass influx of transplants into the Whispering Woods community had created a small boom in the Bakersville economy, and several new trendy shops and restaurants had sprung up in an effort to revitalize the small town.

Ben ordered his usual BLT with extra mayo and fries while Kate tried the daily special, Asian salad with dressing on the side.

"I can't wait to tell you all about Pastor Connie's sermon this morning! Oh, Ben, it was like she was sharing my life story!"

"Oh yeah? Tell me about it."

"So, she preached from Matthew 13, the Parable of the Hidden Treasure." Kate opened her Bible and quickly flipped about three quarters of the way through until she found the first book of the New Testament. She located the parable in no time and read it aloud. That, in and of itself, was a major accomplishment for Kate. A few years ago Kate would've had no clue where to locate the Gospel of Matthew in the Bible. Much had changed in a short time.

"Oh, and she had the most adorable Children's Church message about it," Kate digressed. "Remind me, I have to tell you about that too. So anyway," she continued excitedly without giving Ben the opportunity to get a word in edgewise, "she talked about how the kingdom of heaven is like the treasure the man in the field found. That sometimes it's hidden from us and we don't even know it's there. But once it's revealed to us, it is more valuable than anything we could ever imagine and we need to do anything to hold onto it."

Ben listened intently and nodded his head in agreement.

"And the man wasn't actually seeking the treasure, he was just blessed to have found it." Kate paused, waiting for some recognition from Ben. "So?"

"So, what?" Ben asked.

"Don't you see? Pastor Connie was describing my life to a tee! For so many years I wasn't doing anything to try to find God in my life. I was just like that man, going along and minding my own business. God's presence in my life was completely hidden by all of the *stuff* that had become so important to me, like the treasure hidden in the ground. The money, the power, the recognition, the homes and fancy things—like Paul describes it, the things of this world. But then, when I finally hit rock bottom I found the treasure! I found God! And as soon as I did, I realized that nothing else in this world is as important as my relationship with the Lord. Ben, *I* am that man! I am the man in the parable that Jesus is talking about!"

"That's pretty deep," Ben replied, taking it all in.

"But it's so true. I spent far too many years hiding from God. I knew I didn't like the person I had become, so I thought if I distanced myself from God that I could hide from Him what was in my heart. But of course, you can't—"

"—hide from God," Ben finished her sentence for her.

"Exactly! And I don't want to anymore. Oh, Ben, I want to know God like you do! I want him to be a part of every aspect of my life. What does that scripture say? Seek and you shall find."

"Yes," Ben answered. "Ask and it will be given to you; seek and you will find; knock and the door will be opened to you. For everyone who asks receives; he who seeks finds; and to him who knocks, the door will be opened." He quoted the scripture perfectly without even needing to open his Bible.

Kate looked at him in awe. "See, that is exactly what I'm talking about. I want to be able to quote scripture like you do. To know the Bible like the back of my hand, and to make sure that I never hide from the Lord again. That in everything I do, I am seeking him with all my heart!"

Ben took a large bite out of the sandwich the waitress had brought over while Kate was immersed in her story. As he swallowed, Kate motioned for him to wipe the mayo lingering in the corner of his mouth. Kate, on the other hand, was too excited to eat, so she barely nibbled at her salad and asked for a second glass of ice water. After backtracking and filling him in about Pastor Connie's Children's Church message with the "real" gold coins and giving him a good hearty laugh, she then broached the next subject she had planned to discuss during their time together.

"So, a few of us at church are talking about starting an early morning Bible study. It wouldn't be anything too time consuming. We would meet each Wednesday morning for about an hour before work at 7:30. We decided to meet in the back room at the Coffee House in Riverton. We're going to start with the Gospel of John. Pastor Connie always says that if you want to learn who Jesus Christ is then a great place to start is with the Gospel of John."

Ben finished off the remaining crust of his sandwich and squirted more ketchup onto his fries. "I think that sounds fantastic, Kate, what a great idea."

"Well"—Kate looked at him and batted her eyes dramatically— "I was hoping you'd think that."

Ben raised his eyebrows.

"I was thinking maybe you could join the study with me. I know it would be a little farther for you to drive, but it's only one day a week and maybe you could open your shop a little later on Wednesdays. Please? Pretty please? You know *everything* about the Bible, Ben, and, well, I love it when we get together on Sundays. I just think it would be so great if we could get even deeper into God's Word together." Kate's pleading was persuasive to say the least, but unbeknownst to her it was wholly unnecessary.

Ben acted as if he were seriously considering the invitation before speaking. "I would love to join."

"Really? Great!" Kate was ecstatic. "There are four of us so far, including me, so you'll make five."

"Would you mind if I brought someone?"

"Not at all!" Kate quickly replied. "The more the merrier! Do you have anyone in particular in mind?"

"Just an old friend who I think would enjoy the fellowship."

"Wonderful! Our first meeting is this Wednesday. Read chapters one through three of John. I'll let the others know you're joining us. It's going to be amazing, Ben, just you wait!"

"I'll be looking forward to it."

"Me too!"

And she *was*. All Kate wanted was for Wednesday to arrive. What was normally considered "hump" day for the working class was shaping up to be the best day of the week for Kate. She spoke with the director at Hope's House and agreed to put in an extra hour Tuesday afternoons and work through her lunch break on Wednesdays so she could come in a few hours late each Wednesday morning. Kate was blessed to have a supervisor who was so understanding and accommodating, but she didn't mind the extra work. She loved her position at Hope's House, and in spite of the sometimes unexpected hours and sad circumstances of her clients, she truly felt as though she was making a difference. And one thing about Kate that hadn't changed a bit was her tireless work ethic. Once again she represented her clients passionately, fully committed to their cause and utterly determined to help them. The annual salary more than sustained her, and now that the house renovations were complete she had very few expenses. In fact, she had enough left over each month that a large portion of it went right to various charities supporting abuse victims. Kate viewed her job as a gift—her own second chance at life.

Wednesday morning finally arrived, and Kate arose before dawn. She dressed quickly and took her routine morning walk through the neighborhood while silently praying. Then she fixed herself a cup of coffee, read her morning devotionals, and reread the first three chapters of John for about the tenth time so she would be prepared for their Bible study discussion. Kate's mornings these days were overflowing with her own personal spiritual time with the Lord. It had been like an explosion in her life, and she couldn't get enough. The more she read the Bible and learned from it, the more she craved it. She read commentaries, biographies of biblical characters, devotionals, biblical fiction, and she studied the history of the world during biblical times. Like any good attorney who is worth his or her weight, Kate *loved* to research. But these days she didn't research cases or statutes (at least not as much, she still had to do some of that kind of research for her job), she researched scriptures. She cross-referenced what she learned in different translations of the Bible, and she sought out people who were steeped in the holy book and could explain things to her when she hit a stumbling block. For every question she answered, two more popped up. So she only dug deeper. It was a never-ending cycle, but Kate loved every minute of it. She quickly became prolific in the Bible, and she found her faith being challenged and growing in the process. All the while she grew closer to Ben. Their conversations took a whole new direction as they pondered some of the most difficult questions in life. She sponged off of his limitless understanding and was always amazed at how he could interpret scripture with a knowledge and authority unparalleled to anyone she had ever met. If at one time she had hidden her life from the Lord, she was certainly doing her best to completely change course.

She hurriedly drank her cup of coffee, bundled up in her winter coat, and rushed out the door for the four-block walk to the Coffee House. She entered the quaint shop, and her presence was announced by the jingle bells hanging from the door knob. Laurie, the owner, was in the process of changing the front door sign from "Closed" to "Open." Kate breathed in the delicious aroma of brewing coffee and cinnamon buns that were already baking in the oven.

"Morning, Laurie," Kate greeted her warmly as she helped herself to a cup of coffee from the side counter. "It smells fantastic in here! You know I can't resist your cinnamon buns. They're like a little bite of heaven!"

"Hi, Kate! Well, I knew you were all coming in this morning so I even made extra. You all set for your first Bible study?"

"Yep," Kate answered cheerily. "I can't wait! Anyone else here yet?"

"No, you're the first. I've got the back room all ready for you, so you can head on back; I'll take your orders once everyone arrives."

"Sounds great, thanks!"

Kate took a seat at the round table in the small room overlooking the park situated alongside the river. On a frigid day like today in the depths of December, the park was expectedly desolate save for one brave soul who was walking a Labrador puppy, although Kate couldn't help but laugh when she noticed it looked more like the puppy was walking the man. As she spread her Bible and notebook on the table, careful not to take up too much room, the other participants of the study entered and took seats. The three additional members of Amazing Grace had come together, and just as they were getting situated Ben arrived. Kate was just about to greet him when she caught sight of the friend he had brought with him. Of course, he was easy to notice, considering he stood a good head taller than everyone else. He took off his woolen overcoat and fedora and placed them on the coat rack in the corner of the meeting room. He made eye contact with Kate and immediately smiled.

"Brother Washington!" Kate exclaimed. "How lovely to see you!"

Brother Washington nodded appreciatively and took Kate's hand in his. "The pleasure is all mine. Thank you for allowing me to join your study."

"Not at all," Kate replied, "I'm so happy you have come."

Kate couldn't help but notice the hush that fell over everyone the moment Brother Washington entered the room. His presence was a bit imposing, because, of course, it's rather difficult for a six-foot-five African-American man *not* to be imposing. But rather than draw attention to himself, he quietly took a seat and pulled from his inner coat pocket a Bible so worn it looked as if the pages might fall out.

Kate leaned over to Ben and whispered in his ear. "You didn't tell me the friend you wanted to bring was Brother Washington!"

"Well, you never asked. Why? Is there a problem?"

"No, not at all. I think it's wonderful. I always admired his spirituality and closeness with God. He will be a wonderful addition to our study!"

Once all six seats were filled and everyone had placed their orders and received their hot tea or coffee, a small woman in her mid-fifties with curly brown hair sitting to Kate's right commandeered the conversation.

"Good morning everyone," she said

"Good morning," the group echoed in return.

"I think the first thing we need to do is introduce ourselves. I'll start. I am Evelyn Foster, but everyone calls me Evie. And this is my younger sister Eleanor." She then gestured to the woman seated beside her sipping coffee. Eleanor peered up timidly from her mug. Apparently her introduction had already been taken care of by her sister.

"Yes," Eleanor said, not sure of why she needed to speak up at all by that point, "I'm Eleanor."

"But her friends call her Ellie," Evie inserted.

Ellie just smiled politely. She looked like she was more than used to her sister speaking for her.

Next to Ellie sat Tom, an attractive bachelor in his late twenties new to Riverton. He lived next door to the Foster sisters, so they persuaded him to join the study after he told them one Sunday at church that he had hoped to get to know more people in the area. Tom shared that he had just received his doctoral degree in history and was teaching full time at the local college. His Wednesday classes didn't begin until noon, so it was the perfect opportunity for him.

Next to Tom sat Brother Washington. "I am Isaiah Washington. I am a seventy-one-year-old widower, a father, a grandfather, a former marine, and I love the Lord. I am happy to be here." The warmth in his voice quickly put aside any uneasy notions from the rest of the group. Kate had learned more about Brother Washington in that one introductory sentence than she had ever learned during all of her childhood days at St. Paul the Apostle Church. And she had a sneaking suspicion that there was a lot more about Brother Washington still to learn.

Next came Ben, who modestly shared that he made furniture and was a life-long resident of Bakersville.

And finally the introductions circled back around to Kate. Where should she start? She wanted to tell everyone about the path that had led her to that very Bible study on Wednesday mornings. The years growing up with Ben sitting on the pew next to one another sharing stories about the adults in the church; the tumultuous years where she lost sight of the Lord and selfishly thought only about herself; and her revelation after the car accident and alcoholism that blessed her with a whole new perspective on life and love of the Lord. She had so much to tell, but she knew that this was neither the time nor the place. Instead, she kept it simple.

"My name is Kate Kirby, I grew up in Bakersville, lived in the city for a while, and moved to Riverton about six months ago. I work at Hope's House, and I can't wait to learn more about the Lord through our time together."

And with that the introductions were complete. The group engaged in a brief bit of small talk while enjoying their breakfasts. Usually there were a few conversations about different topics at the same time, until Evie decided it was time to move on to the purpose of the gathering. She took it upon herself to clear the used dishes from the table and used a napkin to wipe it clean. "Okay, everyone, I think it's time we begin our discussion. We were supposed to read the first three chapters of John. Tom, why don't you start us off with your thoughts?"

Although Evie asked it as a question, it was obvious that he had no choice in the matter. With a what-did-I-get-myself-into expression on his face, Tom tentatively shared how the first chapter challenged him as to what his perceptions of "the Word" were. How it tested his own vocabulary and knowledge that the Word, in the biblical sense, carried a much greater meaning than something used for communicative purposes. Everyone could tell that Tom was well educated; he spoke articulately and his thoughts were well organized, just like a teacher. Kate was very impressed with his opening volley, which sent their conversation deep into the Gospel of John. They stayed on the disciple's introductory words in the first chapter for a while, then moved on to the water-into-wine miracle that occupied chapter two. Evie was the first one of the group to go out on a limb. "What was so necessary about this miracle?" Evie remarked. "Didn't Jesus have bigger and better miracles to perform besides making a few wedding guests happy? Shouldn't he use his miracles for something more important like healing lepers or raising people from the dead? Who cares about some silly wine?" That was when Brother Washington, who sat characteristically silent, spoke up.

"The wine wasn't significant in and of itself. It was what the wine represented that matters."

"And what did it represent?" Evie challenged politely.

"Us." Brother Washington answered plainly.

"What?" several of them asked in unison.

"The wine represents us."

Brother Washington turned to his right. "Ben, with your authority surely you can enlighten us further." All eyes were immediately on Ben.

"Well," he began, "the miracle shows that the Lord has the power to transform something ordinary, the water, into something extraordinary, the wine. And he can do the exact same thing within each one of us. If we give our lives over to the Lord, he will transform us into something more wonderful than we could ever imagine. Not only that, but we will have *more* than we ever need—just like the banquet had more wine than they needed. And just like it was the very best wine, so it will be for us. The best we could ever imagine. The wedding banquet is a spiritual banquet for us. It should be a celebration because of the transformation within us."

As Ben spoke, Ellie rested her head on her hands and sat completely still, listening intently to every last word like she had never heard anything so illuminating. Kate knew exactly how Ellie felt; she was long since used to Ben's powerful exegesis of the Word. Evie continued to wipe a few crumbs from the table that she had missed on her first go-round, scolding herself for having overlooked them.

Once they left the miracle, they spent the remainder of their discussion in chapter three, dissecting the curious character of Nicodemus. The group was quite divided about the mysterious religious leader who seemingly wanted to believe in Jesus but was held back by his years of teachings and traditions. Half of them felt as though Nicodemus genuinely wanted to understand what Jesus was trying to tell him, while the other half believed he was too pompous to care. The difference of opinion made for an interesting debate. As they further pondered the question of Nicodemus's intentions, the conversation took a very interesting turn. Tom was the one who first brought it up.

"When was each of you born again?"

The question was simple enough. But simple questions don't always have simple answers. The group became unusually quiet as they all contemplated.

"First, let's clarify something," Brother Washington requested. "What exactly do you mean when you say 'born again'?"

Tom nodded, appreciating Brother Washington's point and wanting to avoid any confusion.

"When was the moment you actually came to know Jesus as your Lord and Savior? When did you have that spiritual rebirth and dedicate your life to Christ?"

As usual, Evie spoke first. "For me, it was the moment of my confirmation in middle school. I'll never forget it. I stood at the altar of Amazing Grace Chapel, and as I said the words that I would live my life for Christ, I saw this glow in the church that I had never seen before. I knew without a doubt that it was the Spirit coming down upon me. That was when I was born again." Everyone smiled at her in affirmation. "What about you, Brother Washington?"

"I was nine. My grandma took me down to the river for the Sunday gathering. There were dozens of us on that sweltering hot summer day. All dressed in our finest, singing spirituals and raising our hands to the heavens. Brother Walker led me straight into the water, told me to hold my nose, and before I knew it he dipped me straight back into the river three times. When I came up the third time I was a sopping wet changed man. I can't explain how, but I just knew the Lord was with me."

Kate sat completely enthralled by their testimonies, yet at the same time she felt an uneasiness and reluctance to share.

"Tom?" Brother Washington prompted the young scholar.

Tom chuckled a bit. "Mine was a little different from both of yours. It wasn't in a church or during a religious ceremony, and it was when I least expected it. It was actually on an airplane. I was traveling to Seattle on the redeye. I was all but asleep when suddenly some nasty turbulence struck the plane. The captain came over the intercom trying to calm everyone, but the turbulence just grew worse. Now keep in mind, at that time religion wasn't much of a priority in my life. I mean I went to church every now and then and I called myself a Christian, but I don't think I really *knew* what that meant. As the plane started shaking harder, the oxygen masks dropped from overhead and all I could think about is that we're all gonna die. So I immediately began to pray. I closed my eyes tight and talked to God about everything. I owned up to my sins, I asked him to bless my family, and, of course, I prayed that he would help our plane safely reach its destination. And as I prayed I heard a voice. I know it wasn't either person sitting next to me. And the voice said, *'Do not fear. I am with you.'* I opened my eyes to look for the voice but as quickly as I heard it, it was gone. In that instant the turbulence completely stopped. From that moment on I committed my life to the Lord and knew that I had been born again."

"What a beautiful story," Ellie said genuinely.

"Let's see." Evie surveyed the group. "Who's left? Ben? Kate? Ellie?" She glanced at all three of them, waiting for one of them to take the lead. Kate sunk in her chair ever so slightly.

Ben spoke up. "I was born again through my father. My father taught me everything. The things I say don't come from me but from him, and I would know nothing were it not for him." Tom looked at Ben, a bit puzzled by his brief explanation, but Brother Washington just smiled as if he had anticipated every last word of it.

"Come on, Ellie," Evie prodded her sister. "Share your story, or would you care for me to share it for you?"

Ellie smiled warmly at her sister. "Thank you, Ev, but I don't mind. I was at church camp one summer as a teenager. After closing worship one night they had an altar call. I'm not sure why, but something was coaxing me to go forward. So I did, and I felt a hand upon my shoulder. But no one was touching me."

"Kind of like when I heard the voice yet no one was talking," offered Tom.

"Yes, just like that." Ellie seemed happy that their stories shared a common thread. "And I knew it was the hand of God. From that moment on I knew I had been reborn."

Kate looked down at her Bible, hoping that she might be able to avoid the inevitable by finding a quick escape. She glanced at her watch and discovered exactly what she was looking for. Before anyone could ask her to share her story, she held up her wrist and began gathering her books from the table.

"Wow, would you look at the time?" Kate said abruptly. "We've been talking almost an hour and a half. If I don't get going now I'm going to be incredibly late for work!"

"But what about your story?" Evie demanded.

"I'll tell you what," Kate stalled, "I'll share it first thing next week. Sound like a plan?" It was obvious that for whatever reason Kate didn't feel comfortable sharing, and they didn't want to push. They reassured her that they would look forward to hearing her story the following week.

They collected their coats and winter apparel from the coat rack as Evie pushed in the chairs, cleaned the table once more, and reminded them all (for the fourth time) next week they were to read chapters four through seven. As they bid each other goodbye, Kate took Ben by the arm and pulled him aside. "Call me tonight?" she asked.

"Sure thing. Everything all right?"

"Yeah, I think so. I just need to talk."

Kate spent the rest of the day waiting impatiently for evening to come.

―――――――――――――――

It was a little past seven when the phone finally rang. Kate was curled up on her couch listening to the crackling of the fireplace and watching her annual Christmastime favorite, *It's a Wonderful Life*. Her oversized cable-knit sweater hugged her slender frame, and her fuzzy socks completed the ensemble of leggings and a pullover shirt.

Her blonde hair was pulled back in a loose ponytail except for a few wisps which had escaped. A live tree with clear twinkle lights adorned the front bay window, and Kate had pulled back the sheers so everyone could enjoy the tree as they traveled down Front Street. The fir tree was a massive eight feet tall and almost as wide. Kate had to convince Ben that she needed such a huge tree since the high ceilings of the historic home commanded as much. A smaller tree would look too puny and Charlie Brownish, she rationalized. So Ben hauled it into the house, and it took them over an hour to set it just right so it didn't lean in one direction or the other. Then they spent the better part of an evening sipping hot chocolate and decorating the tree, mostly with ornaments Kate had retrieved from the attic of her childhood home on Magnolia Lane. Each ornament seemed to bring back another memory, which gave her a nostalgic feeling that her family was celebrating the holiday with her. In the distance she could hear a group of carolers from the Catholic church across town going door to door. Christmas was less than a week away, and it felt every bit of the holiday season.

Kate checked the screen of the phone on the second ring hoping it was Ben and answered immediately.

"Hey there," she said as she muted the volume on the television.

"Hey! What are you up to?"

"Oh, nothing much," Kate answered casually. "Just watching *It's a Wonderful Life*. I'm almost to the part where the gymnasium floor opens and they all fall into the swimming pool. I love that part!"

Ben laughed. "How many times have you seen that movie now? About a thousand?"

"Something like that," Kate admitted. "So how was your day?"

Ben could tell that Kate was stalling. "It was good. Just trying to finish up a few pieces before Christmas, so I've been putting in some extra hours at the shop."

"Oh, Ben, the holidays are so hard for some of the women at Hope's House. It's unfair how Christmas is a time to be joyous and celebrate the birth of our Savior, yet for so many people it brings only sadness."

"Is that why you asked me to call you? Is something bothering you at work?"

"Oh no, not at all. I love my job. Everything's great."

"Then what is it?"

Silence.

"Come on, Kate. I know you well enough by now to know that something was clearly bothering you at the end of our study this morning. What is it?"

"I don't know," she balked.

"Yes, you do. And you also know that eventually you're going to tell me what it is. So just let me have it. You know you can tell me anything."

"I know I can," Kate admitted. "And I am so grateful for that, Ben. You're the only person I could share this with. In fact, I feel a little bit silly even telling you."

"So then, let's have it."

"Well, you know this morning when we were talking about Nicodemus and his conversation with Jesus about being born again?"

"Yes."

"And you know how Tom asked everyone to share their stories about the moment they were born again?"

"Yes."

"Well, that's just it."

"Kate, I'm not sure I'm following you. What's *it*?"

"Everyone in the group could pinpoint the exact moment in their lives when they came to accept Jesus as their Savior. They all remembered every last detail. Tom talked about the airplane flight. Evie shared about confirmation and Ellie talked about summer camp. For Brother Washington it was his baptism in the river. Even you talked about being reborn through your father's teachings. And some of them could actually hear or feel God's presence when it happened."

"Yep, they were all really beautiful testimonies. But what's that got to do with you?"

"That's the problem. It *doesn't* have anything to do with me. I don't have a story like they do."

"What do you mean?" Ben asked, a hint of concern in his voice.

"I can't pinpoint one moment or one event when God revealed himself to me and I was born again. I never had that a-ha moment like they did when all of a sudden I realized I had given my life to the Lord. And well, what if I'm *supposed* to have that moment but haven't yet? What if I *haven't* been born of the spirit like Jesus says because I never had an experience like the rest of you did?"

Ben could hear Kate's self-doubt, and he wished more than anything that he could take her into his arms and comfort her. But when you're on the telephone, that is a little difficult to do.

"Kate, whatever would make you think that?"

"I don't know," she questioned. "I just feel like as Christians we are all *supposed* to have that moment. Kind of like an initiation into Christianity."

"Let me ask you something," Ben began. "Do you love the Lord?"

"Yes, absolutely."

"And do you believe the Spirit works through you?"

"Yes, I do."

"And are you willing to share with others the Lord's gift of salvation to you?"

"Yes, actually I already do that. I often talk to the women in the shelter about Jesus and encourage them to visit church."

"Then Kate, you've *already* been born of the Spirit."

"But I don't have a story to share like everyone else does."

"None of us has the same story, but we *all* have one. God works differently in each and every one of us. Some people need to get hit over the head, so to speak, to wake them up to the Lord. Some people need that single encounter. But other people are quite different."

"How so?" Kate asked.

"Just like you. When did you start truly feeling the Lord's presence in your life?"

"Well, I guess it was right after the car accident. I really felt like Jesus must've been there with me that night, otherwise I never would've survived. Then when I woke up in the hospital I knew I had changed. My priorities changed. My outlook on life changed. I knew that God was with me, and he would help me regain my bearings."

"Go on," Ben encouraged his friend.

"Well, then after things started to fall into place and I saw you that night outside of the AA meeting you said, 'Let's go home.' That got me started praying and asking God where he wanted me to call 'home.' On my trip I prayed all the time and even started a journal to God. And then once I came to Riverton and joined Amazing Grace Chapel, I wanted to get as close to God as I could. I started attending every Sunday morning, I began volunteering in their food pantry, and eventually I joined our Bible study. I don't know, feeling God's presence was such a process for me. It just grew stronger each and every day."

"Kate."

"What?"

"I think you just described your rebirth."

"Really?"

"Really. You had that moment just like the rest of us did. It's just that your moment wasn't a finite moment in time. Instead yours was a series of smaller moments all put together into one big moment."

Kate smiled at the realization that Ben was onto something. "Ya know what? I think you might be right."

"I think I am too," Ben agreed.

"Like during that year or so of my life God gradually revealed himself to me more and more until I knew I had fully committed my life to him."

"Exactly. Like I said, Kate, God has a plan for each and every one of us. He made us all in his image, but he also made us all unique. So no two of us are ever going to have the exact same experiences in life or be reborn in the same way. That's the beauty of it. We can all share our testimonies and lift each other up, but we've received that gift from God in our own special way. A way that will never be duplicated by someone else. And Kate, I would say your rebirth in Christ was extra special. Their experiences were over quickly, but yours lasted months. So God must know you're pretty special."

"Yeah," Kate laughed, "or he thought I was extra stubborn and needed to work on me that much longer!"

The two chuckled on the phone together as Kate caught the scene on the television of the old condemned mansion that Mary Bailey decided would be their home. It reminded Kate an awful lot of the story of 704 Front Street.

"Do *you* think Nicodemus was ever born again?" Kate asked her friend.

"Oh, he definitely was."

"What makes you so sure?" she challenged.

"Oh, I don't know," Ben quickly backtracked, "call it a feeling."

"Ben, thank you."

"For what?"

"For helping me see what is sometimes right in front of me yet beyond my understanding, if that makes any sense. You always seem to know right where my thoughts are headed and how to make sense of them, even when *I* can't make sense of them myself. How do you do that?"

"Let's just say I know you pretty well and leave it at that."

"Well, I'm glad you know me better than I know myself!" Kate shifted position so she could reach far enough to poke the fire. "So, what did you think of our Bible study group?"

"I thought everyone was great. Definitely an interesting bunch, but I think we'll all have different perspectives to bring to the table which always makes for a more fruitful discussion."

"Yeah, I was thinking the same thing. Tom seems really nice, and bright too."

"I agree. And the Foster sisters are quite an experience to say the least!"

Kate laughed. "I know, right? Everyone at church calls them 'The Antithesisters of Riverton.'"

"The antithe-what?"

"Antithesisters. It's a name one of their friends made up for them years ago. It's a combination of antithesis and sisters. As in they are complete opposites."

"That's an understatement," Ben concurred. "Ellie just sits quietly taking it all in and enjoying the moment."

"Yep," Kate chimed in. "And Evie constantly has to be in control and doing something. She can never sit still, and she *always* has something to say."

"Agreed. I like them both, but sometimes I wish Evie would take a lesson from her sister and slow down a little. She always seems to be worrying about everything going on around her. If she just focused on the Lord it would all fall into place."

"You're right about that. But one thing I have to say is that they both love the Lord. They are such generous people. Either one of them would do anything for you. I actually enjoy them quite a bit. And of course there's Brother Washington. How did you ever get him to come to the study?"

"Actually it wasn't difficult at all. He told me he was interested in joining a Bible study a few months back, so when I suggested your study he jumped right on it."

"Well, I'm glad. I would love to get to know him better."

Kate glanced at the clock on the mantel. They had been on the phone almost an hour.

"Well, friend, I guess I should be going."

"Yeah me too, I've still got some work to do in the shop before I call it a night. Sleep tight, Kate."

"Thanks. I think I will now."

The following week passed swiftly in a blur of holiday festivities. Their Wednesday morning Bible study met promptly at 7:30 a.m. as scheduled; after the opening prayer led by Brother Washington, Kate offered to pick up where they left off and share the story of her rebirth. At first she was quiet, and her wavering voice betrayed her nervousness. But when she glanced Ben's way every so often, he nodded in reassurance. By the time she had finished her story, Tom looked at her in utter amazement, Brother Washington said an "Amen" loud enough for the other patrons of the coffee shop to hear, and Ellie had tears in her eyes. "That is the most beautiful testimony I've ever heard," Ellie complimented her. The validation Kate felt brought her a whole new confidence in herself and her relationship with God.

The next day Kate traveled to the north side of the city for a much anticipated holiday lunch date with Chester. Not wanting to arrive empty-handed, she came loaded with Christmas gifts and freshly baked chocolate chip cookies thanks to Grans's prize-winning recipe. She gave Chester a book wrapped in shiny red paper with a gold bow; a biography of the twenty-first president Chester Allan Arthur, his name-twin. (Well, *almost* his name twin, he once again reminded her. They shared the same middle initial but not the same middle name). Chester was delighted with the thoughtful gesture and wondered aloud whether he could find any other commonalities between himself and a man who had lived over a century ago. And, of course, Kate couldn't forget Oreo. In a small Christmas stocking she had tucked a number of treats and toys for the spoiled cat, although from the looks of things Oreo could have done without the treats. It was immediately obvious that Oreo had gained a pound or two (or more!) since she had been in Chester's care. Regardless, the cat looked healthy and happier than ever. Kate was so thankful that her friend had found a companion in the little feline, and vice versa.

Christmas Eve arrived on the heels of a bitter cold wind that would chill you to the very bone. Kate attended the candlelit service at Amazing Grace Chapel, where Pastor Connie preached an inspiring message from the second chapter of Luke, before making the brisk walk home on the desolate streets a little past midnight. The busyness of the week had finally caught up with Kate, and she slept soundly as soon as her head hit the pillow.

The next morning Ben arrived promptly at nine for their gift exchange and the Christmas morning feast Kate had prepared. That was another change in the new Kate; she had become quite the amateur chef. After taking a beginners' cooking class at the local community college for fun, Kate discovered a whole new world of culinary cuisine, and she had quite a gift for it. She had already made plans come springtime to plant a small vegetable garden in her backyard so she could enjoy the freshness of her own herbs and produce.

Kate blessed the food and they both ate heartily, but just like a little kid Kate could hardly wait for the gift exchange.

"Come on, let's go into the living room," she persuaded Ben, stacking the plates in the kitchen sink.

Ben followed and situated himself on the loveseat facing the Christmas tree. Kate knelt and pulled out a rectangular gift from under the tree, about the size of a cigar box.

"Merry Christmas, Ben." She handed him the package.

"Hmm, what could it be?" Ben harassed her as he shook it and held it next to his ear as if it might make some telltale sound.

"Oh, would you just open it?" Kate demanded impatiently. "If you don't, then I will!"

"All right, all right!" he chuckled. "Hold your horses, I'll open it."

He tore into the wrapping paper to reveal a designer set of carving knives. Ben had never owned anything so valuable before.

"I don't know much about your trade," Kate admitted, "but the woman at the store said these are some of the best you can buy. Since you do such beautiful work, I figured you deserved the best."

"Kate, you shouldn't have."

"Oh, yes I should have. Do you like them?"

"I love them, thank you so much." He paused briefly and could see the anticipation on Kate's face. It was almost too much for him to handle. "Now it's your turn."

Kate looked around and, not seeing any signs of a gift, she became curious as to where Ben had hidden it. Perhaps he had left in the car.

"Go upstairs into your study."

"What?" Kate was completely perplexed.

"You heard me. Go upstairs into your study."

"If you say so." Kate quickly climbed the stairs and rounded the corner to the back room that had become her home office. Floor-length lace curtains hung from the windows, and a multicolored Oriental rug she had bought for next to nothing at a nearby flea market covered most of the hardwood floor. In the center of the room facing the door was the exquisite mahogany desk Ben had given her when she graduated from law school. It was the one and only thing she cared about salvaging from the firm when she submitted her resignation. As she quickly scanned the room she noticed a petite bookshelf between the two windows overlooking her backyard that hadn't been there the night before. It was a rich mahogany to match her desk, standing about as tall as Kate with three shelves, and it couldn't have been more than two feet wide. At the very top a plank of wood had been cut in swirling patterns, and in the center had been carved the most lifelike butterfly she had ever seen.

Kate was practically speechless. "Ben, this is gorgeous!"

"Well, with all of the reading you've been doing lately, I figured you were gonna need somewhere to put all of your books."

"How did you get this in here?" she asked in complete disbelief.

"Oh, I have my ways," Ben replied slyly.

"Seriously, when did you put this here? Did you come yesterday when I wasn't home? But wouldn't I have noticed it?" she questioned herself.

"Don't worry about that. The point is, it's here."

"Did you make it?"

"Well, no, not exactly. Actually, it has a kind of interesting story behind it. Have you ever heard about the origins of Amazing Grace Chapel?"

Kate thought for a minute. "Well, I know the chapel was first built almost two hundred years ago when Riverton was a prosperous trading town. But about fifty years later it burned down during the horrible fire in town. I don't think much was left of it, so they rebuilt it completely. I'm pretty sure that's the chapel that still stands today, with lots of updates, of course."

"Yep, that's the story. But there's a little more to it. You see, when the church members came to salvage anything they could after the fire, they found that only two things had survived. The brass cross that sat on the altar, and this bookshelf."

Kate was astounded. "Do you mean to tell me that this bookshelf is almost two hundred years old?"

"Sure is," Ben answered. "It was in the pastor's office at the time. It was in pretty bad shape, so I refinished it and did a few other things to reinforce the shelves."

"Ben, how on earth did you find it?"

"Oh, just looking around some of the antique auctions."

Kate walked over to the piece and ran her fingers along the butterfly. "And was this part of the original piece?"

"Actually no, I added that. I got to thinking about what you shared with me the other day. You know, about being reborn. And I thought the butterfly might remind you of that. How you transformed from the cocoon into a beautiful butterfly through the Spirit in your life."

As always, Kate was completely overwhelmed at the thoughtfulness and care he had put into his gift. The tears of joy welled in her eyes, but before she could thank him, she noticed a book lying on its side on the top shelf. She looked closer.

"Go ahead," Ben encouraged. "Take it."

She picked it up carefully and examined the binding. It appeared to be made of some sort of animal hide, a dark color crossed between maroon and brown. She opened the front cover; Ben had written an inscription on the first page.

To Kate –

John 14:6

Yours always—Ben

"I know that scripture!" Kate said proudly. "I am the way and the truth and the life; no one comes to the Father except through me."

Ben smiled at her feeling of accomplishment.

"Ben, it's a Bible."

She began to leaf through the pages. They were so delicate and thin they were almost transparent, and it was obvious they weren't made of any ordinary paper. But when she expected to open to the book of Genesis, she found something very odd instead. The words weren't English. In fact, she couldn't tell what they were. They were more like a series of symbols—some looked like boxes or the symbol for pi, another looked like a house with a flat roof, and yet others slightly resembled musical notes. Then she flipped through the Bible further and the language appeared to change, although she still couldn't begin to decipher any of it. This language had symbols that were more rounded and looked to have accent marks above or below the letters. Kate was fascinated by it but yet thoroughly confused.

"Ben, what are these languages?"

"Well, the first language you saw was Biblical Hebrew, or what is sometimes called Aramaic. That is what the Old Testament was originally written in. And then the second language begins with the Gospel of Matthew. That is Biblical Greek, the language of the New Testament.

"Wow." It was all Kate could manage to convey the awe she was feeling. "But Ben, I can't read it."

"I know you can't. But you can *feel* it."

Kate turned to the beginning of the Bible and began to trace her index finger from left to right along the symbols in the first row, staring at the beautiful script that was the original source of words for the Biblical authors.

"Actually, it's like this." Ben took her hand and gently changed the direction of her finger. "Hebrew was actually read from right to left, not from left to right like we do now."

"I never knew that," she confessed. "But where are the chapter and verse numbers?"

"Ah, that's another thing," Ben explained. "When the books of the Bible were first written, there were no chapter or verse numbers. It was all one big jumble—not even paragraph breaks. All of that was added later."

"Ben, where on earth did you get this?"

"My father gave it to me once they had completed it."

"What do you mean once *they* had completed it?" She crinkled her nose. "Once *who* completed it? And anyway, this Bible looks like it's about a thousand years old. How could your father have *possibly* given it to you then?"

"What I meant was, my Father gave it to me when *he* was finished with it. It's been in the family for a while."

"Oh, I see." Kate eyed him suspiciously. "Ben, I really can't accept this. It must be so valuable, and it's been in your family for generations. What would your father say?"

"Don't worry about that. My father is happy to share. I want you to have it. Look!" Ben gently turned the pages until the symbols changed, signifying to Kate that he was now in the New Testament. "Here is the scripture from the Gospel of John about Nicodemus." Ben pointed to a word near the center of the page: Νικόδημος. Kate stared at in in amazement, able to see the resemblance to the English translation of the word. Here it was right before her, written in the ancient language of the disciples, the apostle Paul, and others who walked the earth when Jesus did. It was too much for her finite mind to process.

"Ben, this is so incredible."

She closed the book and rested her hand on top of the soft cover, and she felt a closeness to God that no earthly book could ever bring. No, this was something much greater. It was almost magical, but it was even better than that. It was *spiritual*. It was a connection she had never experienced before in her life. And it affirmed in her mind that the Bible isn't just some other book. It is the living, breathing Word of God.

"Merry Christmas, Kate."

"Merry Christmas, Ben."

Kate took his hand in hers and looked at him so seriously that for a moment he thought something was wrong.

"The bookshelf and the Bible, they are amazing. Thank you so much. But can I tell you something?"

"What?" Ben asked.

"*You*, Ben, are the best Christmas gift I could ever ask for."

If she only knew.

CHAPTER 16
CALLER ID

"Each one should use whatever gifts he has received
to serve others, faithfully administering
God's grace in its various forms."
1 Peter 4:10

The following year barreled through like the express train Kate had watched from her penthouse patio so many times before, full of city commuters wrapping up last-minute work, reading the paper, or sending a final email before they signed off for the evening and headed home to the suburbs. They were all oblivious to the train speeding down the tracks, whizzing by town after town until it reached their respective destinations. That was precisely what the last year had been like for Kate. She could barely believe it when *another* Christmas had passed and she found herself in the kitchen fixing hors d'oeuvres for a New Year's Eve party that she was both very excited and very nervous about.

Perhaps the year had flown by because it had been such a good one for Kate. For starters, she continued to flourish as one of the staff attorneys at Hope's House. She had represented a number of women in the wake of abusive marriages, and she returned home each night feeling fulfilled and blessed to be able to make a difference in someone else's life. In fact, Kate's director said she had a "calling" (a word that would soon creep up again in her life) and offered her the position of supervisory attorney. The step up would include a modest pay raise and the opportunity to oversee six staff attorneys who worked in shifts at Clark County's non-profit organization. Kate had seriously considered taking the position, but when she learned that it involved much *more* managerial oversight and much *less* interaction with the clients, she declined. Kate's heart and soul were invested in helping these women secure a future for themselves, and she wasn't willing to give that up. "I thought that's what you were going to say," her director conceded, "but I had to try." The days of Kate wanting to get ahead or make an extra dollar had long since passed.

Also during the past year Kate had tried her hand at dating, something she had sworn off for quite a long time after the divorce. She had been so afraid of failure she reasoned she would rather be alone than admit she couldn't make a relationship work. But that was before she met Caleb, a social worker who regularly counseled the women at Hope's House. His persistence finally led her to accept a dinner invitation, and the pair ended up seeing each other for quite a few months. The relationship remained casual until it was prematurely cut short when Caleb accepted a job opportunity halfway across the country. The two said their goodbyes and promised they would stay in touch. Although it was short-lived, Kate felt a renewed sense of hope that maybe there *was* someone out there just for her. She knew the Lord would lead her to that person if and when the time was right.

By far, however, the best part of Kate's year was the Wednesday morning Bible study that had just marked its one-year anniversary. Over the course of the last twelve months, the six of them had grown so close that everyone became like family. Not a single one of them ever missed a gathering—even when Tom had to rearrange his teaching schedule to avoid Wednesday morning classes, when Ellie came three weeks in a row with a painful case of shingles and never once complained, or when Brother Washington had to drive overnight straight to the Coffee House after visiting his brother who had been hospitalized unexpectedly. Their time together had been far too important to let anything else interfere. It had become sacred.

During the year they had studied most of the New Testament and had just completed a new study called, *"Why, God? The Tough Questions in Life."* Kate in particular had found the study cathartic. Chapter Two, "Why did they leave me, God?" brought forth a rush of emotions in losing her father, grandmother, and then mother all when she had been so young. Chapter Five, "Why can't I stop, God?" addressed addictions of all varieties and brought her back to the days when she had drowned her problems in a liquor bottle. And Chapter Six, "Why can't I fix it, God?" transported her back to her marriage with Griffin. It was definitely a tough study to get through at times, but for Kate it was also necessary because she was finally able to reflect on the demons in her past and learn from them. She no longer needed to pretend they hadn't in some way shaped her into who she had become, and instead of regret Kate felt acceptance. Each experience in her past, whether good or bad, had in some way led her to this very moment in time, and for that she was eternally grateful. It was a study where they laughed together, they cried together, they got angry, and they supported one another. And in the process Kate learned that not only was *she* very human and had made mistakes, but apparently so had everyone else. Tom confessed that as a teenager he had become addicted to painkillers after a shoulder injury while playing soccer. It got so bad he ultimately tried to take his own life because he thought it was the only way he would ever be able to stop. Brother Washington shared the effects of PTSD after serving two tours of duty and seeing things that no man should ever have to witness. He said that for the longest time he questioned the good of humanity and a God who would allow such things to take place. Evie and Ellie told of a tragedy that had forever changed their family. When they were ten and eight respectively, their mother had told them to watch their four-year-old brother, Lawrence, while she hung laundry out to dry. The older sisters became preoccupied in a typical sibling spat; after about ten minutes when they finally resolved their differences, they looked for Lawrence, but he was nowhere to be found. Soon the search involved the entire community, and less than two hours later Lawrence was discovered in the river. He had wandered into the water and drowned. Evie and Ellie had never forgiven themselves and had carried a heavy burden ever since that day.

Of everyone in the group, Ben was the only one who remained completely silent. When asked if he ever questioned God or why something had happened to him, his response was illusive at best. "There was only one time I thought my father had deserted me. But it was during a very painful, difficult moment in my life, and I soon realized I was wrong. He would never abandon me." Although they each desperately wanted Ben to fill in the gaps about the mysterious circumstances of his so-called *abandonment,* none of them felt comfortable asking.

They all looked very puzzled. That is, except for Brother Washington.

"Of course he would never abandon you," he said matter-of-factly. "Just like he would never abandon us."

"How would Ben's father have anything to do with *us*?" Evie curiously asked, but Brother Washington just kept on talking.

Although it was painful for each of them to own up to their past mistakes, for Kate it was a beautiful thing to witness. They trusted one another with the deepest, most intimate moments of their lives. Kate soon realized that she wasn't the only one who had messed up before. "We are *all* sinners saved by grace." Brother Washington repeated the Apostle Paul's words, and he was absolutely right.

The six of them had become the best of friends. They celebrated one another's birthdays with cupcakes Evie always lovingly prepared, and they delivered home-cooked meals when one of them was feeling under the weather. After a year that had brought them closer than ever, Kate decided to host a New Year's Eve party. She promised them delicious food, fun games, and an unlimited supply of sparkling cider for the night's festivities.

Evie and Ellie were the first to arrive promptly at seven o'clock. Tom followed a few minutes later, so excited he could hardly contain himself since he would finally be able to introduce the group to Michelle, his fiancée as of Christmas Eve. Michelle was a professor in another department at the college, and they met while serving on a college-wide committee. They immediately clicked. Tom didn't see the point of waiting around, so about nine months after they began dating he proposed. Ben graciously accepted a ride from Brother Washington and his "lady companion" (in Brother Washington's words) Judith, and the three of them arrived just shy of 7:30.

After introductions Kate unloaded a small feast of appetizers onto the dining room table, and they visited with one another while Christmas music played softly in the background. Kate had decided to leave her decorations up until after the party so her home would be extra cozy and festive. Next came a series of games including charades and Bible trivia, where the group separated into two teams with Kate serving as the moderator. The high point of the evening arrived when they played "Scripture Pictionary," as Kate had called it. The teams switched up for a boys-against-girls match to see who could draw the scenes from the scriptures fast enough to gain points. Over three dozen scriptures were written on paper, neatly folded and placed in a basket, and they each took turns drawing as many as they could before the timer buzzed. The women's team had no trouble racking up points drawing Moses parting the Red Sea and Jonah being swallowed by the huge fish, but when Tom tried to tackle Paul being lowered from the city wall in a basket, his stick figures were so rudimentary that the whole room erupted at the hieroglyphics on the poster board. Everyone laughed so hard they cried; even Brother Washington had to wipe his eyes with his handkerchief.

As the midnight hour approached, Kate turned the television on so they could watch the official countdown and they all settled comfortably into her living room—Tom in the armchair in the corner of the room with Michelle on his lap, Edie and Evie on the loveseat, and Judith perched on the couch sipping her hot apple cider. Kate collected a few of the empty cups to return to the kitchen when she passed the dining room and noticed Ben and Brother Washington standing in the far corner of the room by the windows deep in conversation. Their voices were hushed and their tones serious. She stopped briefly, not wanting to interrupt, and she couldn't help but overhear.

"Are you going to tell her?"

"Now is not the time, Isaiah."

"But she has come so far in her faith. Don't you think she ought to know the truth about you?"

"That is for my father to decide, not me. He will reveal it to her when the time is right."

Brother Washington shook his head in disagreement. "How are those of us supposed to prepare the way for you if you always insist on keeping it a secret?"

Ben looked at him resolutely. "Now is not the time."

"Now is not the time for what?" Kate couldn't help but interject. The conversation had piqued her curiosity. Ben stared at Brother Washington and no words were necessary. The warning was in his eyes.

"And exactly *who* did you want to tell *what*?"

Ben, unable and unwilling to deceive Kate, allowed the responsibility to fall on Brother Washington to respond.

"Not a thing," he replied. "Just a few matters that began in Bakersville many years ago that for some reason I brought up this evening. I apologize for my rudeness in appearing secretive. Would you please forgive me?"

Kate, touched by Brother Washington's genuine show of emotion yet still suspicious, quickly decided it wasn't worth pressing the matter when she heard the countdown cheers from the direction of the living room. "Ten! . . . Nine! . . . Eight! . . . Seven!"

"Come on, you two. You can have your private conversation later. Now is the time to celebrate!" She grabbed them each by an arm where they joined the others in the New Year's countdown. The second the television flashed the new year on the screen, everyone hugged and toasted their sparkling cider glasses. Out on the street Kate detected fireworks exploding in the distance and the clangs of pots and pans banging together. A new year. A new beginning.

Once the commotion subsided, Brother Washington positioned himself in the center of Kate's living room adjacent to the twinkling Christmas tree.

"Kate, would you mind if I offered a New Year's blessing?" he asked as all attention was drawn his way.

"Not at all, I would be honored," Kate replied.

Everyone stood and joined hands. Brother Washington's baritone voice reverberated like a beautiful stringed bass.

"Let us pray," he said. All heads bowed.

"Oh, Jesus. Most holy and precious Jesus. You have taught us that when two or three gather together in your name, you are with them. Tonight we have humbly gathered together in your name, and we acknowledge your presence among us. Not just your spiritual presence, Lord God, but your *physical* presence. I ask you now, Jesus, to reveal your presence to each and every one of us, so that we may see you for who you are, we might feel the comfort of your touch, and we might know your unfailing presence in our lives. Come, Lord Jesus! Amen."

"Amen!" everyone shouted.

Brother Washington kept his head bowed a second longer than the rest, and when he finally lifted it, his eyes met Ben's in a fleeting moment pregnant with meaning. It had escaped everyone's notice. Everyone's except Kate's. There was something between these two men. Something that had started years ago when Kate was still "Katie" sitting in the pew in St. Paul the Apostle Church. But for the life of her, she couldn't quite put her finger on what it was.

The following morning Ben arrived as promised bright and early for clean-up duty. He found Kate already at work in the kitchen, stacking the floral blue dishes that had belonged to her mother in the cupboard.

"I thought you were gonna wait for me," Ben said as he unloaded the dishwasher and handed her a stack of bowls.

"Oh, I was, but I woke up super early and figured I might as well get started."

"It was a great party last night, Kate."

"Yeah I thought so too. Everyone seemed to enjoy themselves."

"They sure did," Ben agreed. "Even Evie seemed to relax a little."

Kate laughed. "I noticed that too, who would've thought?"

As soon as they finished putting dishes away, they next tackled condensing the leftovers haphazardly shoved into the refrigerator the night before. Ben was opening a Tupperware container of shrimp cocktail when his cell phone rang. He retrieved it from his pocket and looked at the number on the screen. He frowned.

"No idea who would be calling so early in the morning on New Year's Day," he told Kate.

"Hello?"

Kate listened to Ben's end of the conversation as she filled a ziplock bag with raw vegetables.

"No, this isn't David. I'm sorry but I think you must have the wrong number . . . No problem at all. You have a Happy New Year too." Ben ended the call and replaced the phone in his back pocket.

"It's odd," Ben said, "that's the third wrong number I've had in the last week."

Kate continued to work among the dozen containers spread across the kitchen counter and replied without making eye contact.

"Really? It's funny you say that," Kate said nonchalantly, "because I think I've been experiencing the same thing lately."

"You mean you keep getting calls from the wrong number too?"

"Kind of," Kate replied ambivalently as she continued organizing the refrigerator. Ben stopped what he was doing and focused on his friend. Something wasn't adding up.

"Okay, Kate, something's going on. What is it?"

"What do you mean?" Kate's innocent look wasn't fooling Ben one bit.

"You said you've been getting calls from the wrong number. But something tells me there's more to it than that. What gives?"

Kate finally made eye contact and couldn't help but smile. Ben knew her inside out, and he could always tell when something was on her heart. She wiped her hands with the checkered dishtowel tucked in the refrigerator handle and sat at the small table still littered with plastic cups and soda cans from the prior evening's festivities.

Kate took a deep breath. "I'm not sure where to start," she confessed.

"How about at the beginning," Ben offered.

"Okay, the beginning." Another deep breath and a slow, purposeful exhale. "Several months ago I got this idea. You see, there's this woman in my church named Stephanie. She's in her early twenties and she just finished college. She's going to grad school to be an architect, and she just got an internship with one of the big architecture firms in the city. She and I had become friendly and started chatting each Sunday after church."

"Okay," Ben answered as he listened intently, wondering where the conversation was headed.

"Oh, Ben, I can see myself in Stephanie about ten years ago. She's bright and energetic, but what scares me is that she's falling into the *exact* same trap I fell into once I started law school. She used to come to church with her family all the time, and now she comes maybe once a month at best. I asked her where she's been, and she said she's too busy for church on Sunday mornings. She used to talk about her boyfriend and friends, and now all she ever talks about is how this prestigious firm might hire her, and she will make a small fortune. It's like déjà vu. I see her going down the same path I went down, and it literally makes me sick to my stomach. But I don't feel like I know her well enough to warn her about it. I mean, for one thing it's really none of my business. And for another, I'm afraid if I tried to talk to her I would just push her even deeper into that world. I know I probably would've felt that way if someone had tried to tell me I was losing control ten years ago."

"I'm kind of lost," Ben said compassionately. "What does your friend Stephanie have to do with a wrong number?"

"Right." Kate quickly got her thoughts back on track. "It got me to thinking about *all* of the Stephanies out there. You know, young women who are fresh out of college and so excited for the next chapter of their lives but so naïve as to the snares that can trap them. I thought if they had something to help keep them grounded in the church and in God's Word maybe they wouldn't be led astray like I was. You know, something to keep their focus and priorities where they should be."

"And?"

"And you might think I'm crazy but I had this idea about starting a Bible study at Amazing Grace Chapel for women in their early to mid-twenties who are at that point in their lives when they can easily get swept up in the temptations of the world. I know that if I had had something like that in my life when I was their age, it might have saved me from making a lot of mistakes later on down the road."

Ben was intrigued. "Tell me more."

Kate's eyes sparkled and her words came faster as she shared what had been on her heart for some time. Ben could tell she was completely exhilarated by the idea.

"Well, I thought we could center our study on women of the Bible who stayed true to God even when the world was pulling them in a different direction. I mean, look at Ruth. She and her mother-in-law faced hardships when they returned to Jerusalem from Moab. They didn't know how they would survive from one day to the next, and plus Ruth had willingly left her family and homeland to be with Naomi and worship the Lord. But Ruth never once complained, and she stayed true to God every step of the way. And look at Rahab. She made some pretty big mistakes by giving herself over to a life of prostitution; but when the Israelite spies went to Jericho to overtake it, she risked her life to help them. All she wanted was to worship their God and go with them. And oh my, look at Mary, the mother of our Lord. Can you even imagine the ridicule and contempt she must've experienced when people realized she wasn't yet married to Joseph yet she was pregnant? I'm sure most people thought she had flat out lost her mind when she said she was carrying a child given to her by God himself. But Mary was faithful, and she humbly accepted God's gift no matter how the world might have perceived it. Then there's Esther, and Jochebed, and Hannah. The list goes on and on. There are just *so* many of them, Ben, and I thought we could lift these women up as examples for how we should be living our lives." The passion practically seeped from her pores.

Kate shifted her focus somewhat. "I talked to Pastor Connie about it, and she said we could have one of the Sunday school classrooms as a regular meeting place. And I was also thinking we could invite some of the other local churches to participate if they want." True to form for Kate, she had thought of every last detail. She paused.

"I don't know, Ben."

Here came the doubt.

"I think if I could just reach Stephanie or someone else like her, it might save them from having to go through what I went through. I was blessed, and the Lord rescued me before it got too bad; the next girl might not be so fortunate."

Ben sat silently for a moment, carefully contemplating his words. Kate stared at him in anxious anticipation. She could only stand the silence for so long.

"You think I'm totally crazy, don't you?"

"Why would I think that?" Ben's eyes penetrated into Kate's very soul until she could physically feel the warmth coming from him. "I think it's a wonderful idea. I just don't understand what's holding you back."

"Because, Ben, how do I know this is God calling me to do it?"

"What do you mean?"

"People at church always talk about being *called* to do something. Called to prayer ministry. Called to outreach. Called to assist in worship. How am I supposed to know if God is actually calling me to do this or if it's just me? The more I study the Bible the more it seems like when God is calling someone to do something, he has a way of making it very obvious. Look at Moses. He saw the burning bush when God told him he was supposed to return to Egypt to set the Israelites free from slavery. Or look at Paul. He had his road to Damascus experience where he saw the risen Lord and was blinded for three days. After that he had no doubt that his calling was to preach about the Lord to anyone who would listen. Even young Samuel—God literally woke him in the middle of the night speaking to him. All of these people got some sign from God that this is what they were called to do. But Ben, I haven't gotten any *signs* like they did." The frustration was slowly creeping into Kate's voice.

"I mean, is that too much to ask? People talk about hearing the voice of God or having this out-of-body experience, and I don't understand why he can't do that for me just so I can be sure it's God who's really calling me to lead this Bible study. I don't need a burning bush or anything like that, but maybe something small. I don't know, a scorched twig would be nice."

Ben couldn't help but laugh at Kate's request. And once she realized just how ridiculous it sounded, she joined him.

"I know it all sounds so silly, but I want to make sure I'm being obedient to God and not just doing this because *Kate* wants to. Besides," Kate continued before Ben could offer any counsel, "what if I'm getting myself in over my head? I've been studying the Bible only for a couple of years now. What if I'm not experienced enough to actually *lead* a Bible study? What if these women ask me questions that I don't have the answers to? It's not like I'm a minister. What if they expect too much from me or worse, what if somehow I mess up and don't do justice to God?" Kate began to twirl a strand of her long, flaxen hair around her finger, a clear sign she was preoccupied. "I almost feel that if God really *is* calling me, maybe he has the wrong person. Like you've been getting those wrong number calls, maybe God has the wrong number on this one."

The excitement in her voice had steadily transformed into an anxiousness. The idea had been more than just on Kate's heart. It had been *weighing* on her. She looked to her friend pleadingly, knowing that he was the only one who could help her navigate through her thoughts.

"Wow," Ben said calmly as he poured her a cup of coffee and set it on the table in front of her, "that was a lot to take in."

"I know, and I'm so sorry about that," Kate interjected.

"It's okay, but let's take it one thing at a time."

"Okay." Kate took a deep breath. "What's first?"

"First, let's talk about whether or not this is really a calling from God."

"Well, I *think* it is, but I'm just not sure. Sometimes people in the church use the word 'calling' so casually. Like if they feel like doing something on a particular day, they label it a *calling* and that way no one will challenge them. Because after all, if you are called by God to do something, then that's nobody's business but yours and the Lord's. I don't want to be one of those people Ben. This is a big deal to me if God is actually calling me to do it."

"It *should* be a big deal, and I think it's great that you've been taking the whole thing so seriously."

"I have, Ben. You have no idea. I've been praying about it non-stop for months now."

"Well, if it's been on your mind for that long, why are you doubting it?"

"Because like I said, I haven't gotten that *sign* yet. No burning bush."

"Kate, you need to remember that God speaks to each of us in different ways. Moses and Paul were stubborn men, so God probably felt as though He had to get their attention in a big way. But that doesn't mean your experience should be the same. Remember last year when you talked to me about being born again in Christ?"

"Sure, that was after our first Wednesday morning Bible study."

"Right, and you were upset because everyone had a story to share about an exact moment when they were born again."

"Yes?"

"And you never had that one moment like the rest of them. Instead, your rebirth came over time in many small ways until you knew in your heart that you had given your life over to Christ."

"Yes, but I'm not sure how it relates to whether God is calling me to do this."

"Kate, I think that's precisely how God works through you. Rather than giving you that one 'a-ha' moment, he silently and methodically works on your heart until you know the path you're supposed to take." Kate sipped at her coffee, tentatively considering what he was trying to tell her.

"Let me ask you this," Ben continued, "how long has this been on your mind?"

"Oh, I don't know." Kate thought for a minute. "At least four or five months."

"And has it been constant?"

"Yes, for the most part. I mean some days I become preoccupied with work or other things, but then my mind goes right back to it. And like I said, I pray about it every day."

"Well, then I think you already have your answer."

"You do?"

"Sure I do. God is calling you to lead this Bible study, Kate. This is exactly how he works in your life. A little bit at a time, but you keep coming back to it. And I think deep down you probably already know that. That's part of how we grow in our faith. Not just learning *to* listen to God, but also learning *how* to listen to God. We need to become close enough in our relationship with God to understand how he talks to us. And I think God is speaking to you right now through his Spirit that keeps nudging you to do this."

"Maybe you're right." For the first time Kate felt a confidence in herself that she hadn't before. "But I don't know the Bible like you do, Ben. What if these women ask me questions that I don't know the answers to?"

Ben smiled. "Of course they're going to ask you questions you don't know the answers to."

"Thanks for the boost of confidence," she joked.

"Kate, the Bible is the living, breathing word of God. Not only that, but it's an enormous book. No one except God himself can answer every question about it."

"You sure seem like you can," Kate interjected, but Ben continued on.

"Think of it this way. When you're getting a case ready for trial, what do you do?"

"I don't know." Kate shrugged. "I interview my client and witnesses, research the law, file pleadings or motions with the court, make sure I have all of my information straight."

"You prepare. And that is exactly what you'll do with this Bible study. If I know you at all, one thing I know for sure is that you'll research the scripture and any other materials you can get your hands on. You will be *more* than prepared. And when that occasional question comes your way that you don't know the answer to, you will write it down and tell them you'll get back to them the next time. That's the beauty of this study, Kate, because not only will these women be learning more about God's Word from you, but you'll learn from them in the process."

"I guess you're right," Kate replied. "I will make sure I'm prepared each week."

"And as for your comment that you're not a minister . . ."

Kate laughed and practically spit out her coffee. "Well, that's a no-brainer. I'm nowhere close to that."

"You're wrong, Kate."

"What?" She crinkled her nose at Ben. "Now I think *you're* the one who's lost your mind!"

"We're *all* ministers. What did Jesus say in the Great Commission? He told us to 'go out and make disciples of all nations.' Kate, that applies to each and every one of us. We are all ministers for his kingdom, and we *all* have the responsibility to make disciples in his name. Or in Paul's words, we are the ambassadors for Christ. It just looks different for each of us. We might not all be ministers in the sense that we have a seminary degree and preach from a pulpit each Sunday, but that doesn't make us any less ministers to God's Word."

"You know, I never looked at it that way before," she admitted.

"Kate, you minster to the women at Hope's House each and every day. They *need* you. They need to see that love of Christ from someone who wants to help them and show them the good in this world. You also have so many gifts. You have the gift of compassion for young women going through exactly what you went through. You have the gift of being able to teach others through your own research and preparation. God gives each of us gifts for a reason, Kate. He wants us to use those gifts to glorify his Kingdom. You're doing exactly what you are supposed to be doing. You're being obedient and using your gifts to benefit these women. I couldn't imagine a more perfect person to lead this study. I have no doubt you will bless so many other people by sharing your time and your gifts. And I also have no doubt that God has placed this call on your life. Remember, God's timing is perfect. Even when we feel like we don't know what we're doing, we can always trust that God knows exactly what *he* is doing."

"You're right, Ben, I do know that. It's just sometimes it can be difficult to believe in yourself."

"Well then you need to make sure you remember something a good friend once told me."

"What's that?" Kate inquired.

"God doesn't call the equipped. He equips those he calls." Ben stopped to let his words sink in. "I promise you, Kate, God will provide you with absolutely everything you need to get this study off the ground. And if there's anything at all I can do to help, I'm always here. Just say the word."

"Actually . . ."

"Actually what?"

Kate didn't waste a second. What was supposed to be a clean-up day abruptly changed course and instead turned into a planning day. Kate hurriedly cleared the kitchen table and retrieved her laptop from the upstairs study. For most of the day she and Ben hammered out an outline for her new Bible study, including the Biblical women she would profile, discussion topics, and reflective devotionals. Kate's fingers tapped the keyboard so fast as the ideas flowed from her mind that Ben became dizzy watching her. Although Kate had first hesitated about her calling, Ben couldn't help but notice that she was the one who did most of the talking. Sure, Ben was her rock and her strength. She needed him for that. But the Spirit had lit a spark deep inside of her that would ignite solely through Kate's zeal for serving her God. And what a flame it would become!

Springtime arrived late that year, mid-April to be exact and right around the time when Kate celebrated her thirty-fifth birthday. In honor of her special day, she was blessed with cupcakes twice in one week. Once, of course, at her Wednesday morning Bible study when Evie had baked Kate her very favorite carrot cake cupcakes. Kate was indeed grateful to Evie but not the least bit surprised. Somehow Evie always managed to find out what everyone's favorite cupcakes were, and they magically appeared on each one's birthday. They sang "Happy Birthday" and laid hands on her to bless her for the upcoming year of her life.

The second time she received cupcakes that week was completely unexpected. Kate arrived at Amazing Grace Chapel early as usual, ready to set up the cheese, crackers, and fruit she brought to the women's study each week. As she unloaded the grocery bags from her car, her heart overflowed with joy. What had started with a group of six women when the study began only two short months ago soon turned into ten, then twelve, and now sixteen young women all eager to stay on the path the Lord had set for them. Word had spread on social media and among the local churches what an uplifting study it was, and after a few of the women told some of their friends, Kate quickly found she had new faces joining them every day. Dear, sweet Stephanie hadn't missed a class. It seemed like each week Kate had to buy more food to keep up with the growing numbers, but she didn't care in the least. If she had to hire a catering company she would gladly do so!

Kate arrived at the Sunday school room barely able to handle her purse and tote slung over one shoulder, and the four plastic bags she juggled, two in each hand. She managed to find one free finger to switch on the lights in the room, and as soon as she did she was greeted with a loud "Surprise!" and practically dropped everything on the spot.

The small powder blue room with a free-standing chalkboard and posters of the twelve disciples on the walls was filled with balloons, streamers, and a poster board with "Happy Birthday" written in block letters and signed by each of her sixteen new friends. On the table where Kate normally arranged snacks were at least two dozen red velvet cupcakes.

Stephanie took the lead.

"Happy Birthday, Kate! After all you've done for us in these last few months, we just *had* to do something to show you how much we appreciate you!"

Kate was speechless.

"So," Stephanie prompted her, "are you surprised?"

Kate could barely get the words out. "I am more than surprised," she said as she surveyed the room. "I am truly blessed. How did you even know it was my birthday?"

"Oh, we have our ways," Stephanie responded coyly.

Kate hugged each one as they celebrated together, devouring the cupcakes in no time. Then they settled in to their study routine. This week's profile: Deborah, from the book of Judges. They explored the young woman's courage in leading the Israelites as the only female judge mentioned in the Bible and faithfully serving God in everything she did. Per the usual, Kate had read and reread the scriptures countless times, and she had consulted every resource she could find. She knew Deborah backwards and forwards, just like she had done with Rahab before Deborah, and for Tamar before Rahab, and for Rebekah before Tamar, and for Sarah before Rebekah. True to her training as an attorney, Kate reasoned that if you researched something long enough and looked hard enough, you would eventually cover every last detail and find answers to all of your questions. And so far at least, Kate had led with confidence and wisdom.

What Kate didn't realize, however, was that she had barely scratched the surface not just of the depths of their faith, but of her own as well. And what she was about to find out was that in spite of our own wishes, sometimes when it comes to God the questions we ask don't have answers that come wrapped up in nice, neat packages with bows on top. On the contrary, sometimes the answers can be quite messy.

That's why it's called *FAITH*.

CHAPTER 17
SIMPLY COMPLICATED

"Faith is being sure of what we hope for
and certain of what we do not see."
Hebrews 11:1

Oxymorons. By their very nature they can't be true. They are a contradiction in terms; polar opposites. For instance, how exactly can something be "old news"? Is it really possible to have an "unbiased opinion"? Have you ever found yourself scratching your head when you extend an invitation to a friend and they reply that they are a "definite maybe"? Well, in many ways *faith* is its very own oxymoron, all packed into one short, sweet, little word. On the one hand faith is something so simple for us. It doesn't take a college education, a genius IQ, or an impressive resume to have faith. It just takes belief. Some of the world's most uneducated, unpretentious people have had the most extraordinary faith. And that's exactly how we tend to treat faith; as if it were simple. Have you ever been faced with a challenge in your life, maybe some obstacle or something unforeseen comes up, and your friend lovingly says to you, *"Oh, just have faith."* The "just" in that sentence implies having faith is such a simple thing to do—a mundane task even the most hardheaded person should have no problem mastering. Thus, when properly translated your friend is more or less saying, *"What's wrong with you? All you need to do is stop your fretting and give everything over to God who is in total control of the situation. It's easy, silly!"* Jesus teaches us that if we have faith as small as a mustard seed (and that's small!) we can move mountains. All we need is that minuscule amount of faith, and we can accomplish the impossible. It's simple.

But is it?

Yes, it is. But no, it's not. On the other hand, faith in all of its glorious simplicity is hugely complicated, more so than any quantum physics equation or rocket science algorithm ever could be.

Faith leads us away from our comfort zones to believe things that defy any rational explanation. Faith challenges us, it confounds us, and while faith can be inexplicably comforting, it is also uncomfortable all the same. Faith forces us to acknowledge our humanity with all of its limitations. Faith is the end result when our human minds can no longer use reason or logic to carry us from Point A to Point B. To have faith is to admit we can't explain everything, we don't have all of the answers, and there are many things in this world bigger than we are.

Make no mistake about it, to have faith is dangerous indeed. It will lead us to those moments of frustration when we realize we are finite creatures in an infinite world created by our God. Faith will ever push us to understand the mystery of this world even though we know that, in this lifetime at least, we will never fully do so. It will always leave us wanting more and perhaps always feeling as though our convictions could be just a little more secure.

But not to have faith? That is downright lethal. If we never ask those questions or explore the unfathomable, what would our lives be? At best we would be arrogant beings so self-consumed we truly believe the world revolves around our every move. (Which, I'm sure we all know a few people like that.) At worst it leaves us completely devoid of hope in anything greater than this brief hiccup in time that we call our earthly lives. So yes, we *have* to ask those tough questions; we have to be constantly challenged; we have to embrace the struggles that faith brings; and we have to admit that we neither have all of the answers nor ever will. So when someone tells you to "have faith," it is both one of the simplest and one of the most complex things that will ever be requested of you. Faith is, without question, *simply complicated*.

As for Kate, she was learning this more with each passing day. Three different sets of circumstances, three separate conversations, but one common thread: All explorations in faith.

The gentle summer breeze wafted into the kitchen through the opened windows and the checkered curtains billowed in response, infusing the air with a crisp freshness after the previous night's rain. Kate busily removed several containers from the refrigerator and handed them to Chester, who had been tasked with setting them on the porch table. After retrieving the mint tea and a few extra napkins, the two friends settled into the spacious screened-in porch that overlooked a small vegetable garden in her backyard. Birds visited a nearby feeder and sang a melody for their lunchtime entertainment.

For the last several years Kate had made a point to visit with Chester in June. It was always a particularly difficult time for him, since it was the month in which he lost his beloved Mina and also the month in which they had celebrated forty-eight anniversaries together until she had passed away. Ever since he lost her, Chester struggled with an emptiness following him like a dark shadow he couldn't escape. Sure he had children and grandchildren who stopped in when they could and kept in regular contact, but it wasn't the same. Chester had lost his life partner, his soul mate, and nothing would ever replace that. The month of June brought all of those memories flooding back, and while they comforted him they also served as a painful reminder that she was no longer by his side. Kate, ever grateful for Chester's friendship during some of her darkest hours, vowed to help him in any way she could, even if it was something as simple as a lunch date to take his mind off his burden of grief.

"So, how is my four-legged friend doing these days?" Kate scooped a generous portion of chicken salad onto Chester's plate and offered him a bowl of freshly cut fruit. If there was one thing that lit up Chester's world these days it was Oreo, and Kate knew it. Chester would share stories about the cat until he talked so long that he actually came full circle and started telling the same stories all over again.

"Oh, she's a crafty little thing," Chester replied as he put his chicken salad onto a cracker. "And boy, can she get into the darndest places sometimes! Do you know the other day I lost her? I looked everywhere—under the sofa, behind the curtains, even in the bathtub. But no matter where I looked, no Oreo. I was beginning to think maybe she got past me and ran out the front door. And just as I was really starting to panic, I heard this faint little *meow*. At first I couldn't tell where it was coming from, so I kept calling her and she kept meowing, until lo and behold I found her curled up on one of the towels in the linen closet. She must've gone in there to take a catnap, and I accidentally shut the door. I was so relieved to find her, and she just looked at me like I should've known all along where she was. That little stinker!"

Kate couldn't help but laugh. She had spent plenty a day searching for supposedly *lost* cats only to find them in some unique napping place.

"Yep, that sounds about right for a cat!" Kate agreed. "I'm glad she's doing so well, Chester. And I have to thank you. She couldn't have found a more wonderful home."

"Think nothing of it." Chester began to blush. "I think I probably need her more than she needs me. But enough about me, what's been going on in your life?"

"Well, let's see." Kate thought for a minute. "I still love my job at Hope's House, and of course Ben and I spend lots of time together. Oh, and about four months ago I started a Bible study for women in their twenties. It helps keep them focused on God's plan for their lives during a time when the world is pulling them in so many different directions. You know," Kate looked at Chester with a smile, "kind of like what I went through at one time. The study has been wonderful, and I now have about sixteen women who come each week."

"Wow, that's really great," Chester offered encouragingly. "What do you all talk about?"

"It's all based on women from the Bible," Kate shared excitedly. "We use these women as examples of how to live our lives for God no matter the circumstances. This week we're in the Gospel of Luke studying Elizabeth and Anna."

Chester stared blankly at Kate. Although he seemed genuinely interested, Kate could immediately tell that Chester had no clue who either Elizabeth or Anna was. And then it dawned on her. Perhaps the one person with whom she very much needed to have a conversation about the Lord was sitting right in front of her. Kate said a quick prayer to herself for God to give her the right words, and she didn't waste the opportunity she had been given.

"Chester, do you know Jesus?" Kate didn't know much at all about Chester's religious background except he once told her that he was raised in one Protestant denomination, switched to another when he got married, was never really a devout follower, and then kind of fizzled out from church entirely when Mina died.

"Sure," Chester replied, "I know who Jesus is."

"That's great," Kate answered, "but that's not exactly what I meant. I know you know *who* he is, but do you know him personally?"

Chester fumbled with his napkin and tried unsuccessfully to look relaxed.

"I'm sorry, Kate, I guess I'm not sure what you mean."

The wind chimes added to the birds' melodic hymn as the breeze provided a refreshing coolness. Kate's tone was gentle and caring.

"That's okay, Chester. What I mean is, do you know Jesus as your Lord and Savior? Do you know that God sent him into this world to die for our sins and to live forevermore so that we can have eternal life through him?"

Chester stared at his fork as if very carefully considering his words.

"Well, let me put it this way. I know there was a man named Jesus who lived a long time ago. And I know he did lots of great things while he was alive. He was a great teacher, and he also healed a lot of people from what I understand. But to be honest with you, there's a lot about Jesus that I don't think I can buy into."

"Like what?" Kate asked curiously.

"Well, for starters, I have a hard time believing that he was born from some woman who had never, well, you know." Chester's voice trailed off but his implication was clear. He struggled with the virgin birth. "And for another thing, I have a hard time wrapping my mind around the fact that he told some man to rise from the dead, and it happened just like that! And I guess even more I have a hard time believing that Jesus rose from the dead himself after three whole days and he's *still* alive to this day." That Chester was being so forthcoming about his doubts made Kate want to share the Good News with him all the more.

"I mean, don't get me wrong. I'm sure Jesus was a really great guy, but the Son of God? That I'm not so sure about."

Kate listened intently, not wanting to interrupt her friend sharing some of his deepest and most personal thoughts. "But I don't really worry about all of that, because I figure I'm covered if you know what I mean."

Kate's nose crinkled. "Actually I'm not sure I *do* know what you mean. Could you explain it to me?"

"Well, even if I don't believe in Jesus as this Son of God guy, I do believe in God. I like to think I'm a relatively bright man, and I know there's no way that this world and everything in it got here just by chance. There has to be *some* higher being that made it all happen. Course I don't know what he looks like or how he works, but I know there is some God out there."

"Okay." Kate delicately continued the conversation with the hopes of planting a seed inside Chester's heart but not pushing too hard. "So if you believe in God, then who do you think Jesus is?"

"Like I said," Chester reiterated, "I think he was a good man who was trying to get people to love each other in a very chaotic world, but he lived and died just like the rest of us do. As far as I'm concerned, as long as I believe in God I'm covered for heaven. Even though I may not believe in Jesus, I do believe in God, and I'm pretty sure that's enough."

Kate sipped her iced tea while trying not to let the heartache she felt for her friend get the best of her emotions. She couldn't believe that for as many years as they had known each other, she had never had this conversation with him before. Chester had taken a wrong turn to which so many others had fallen victim, and Kate felt compelled to help point him in the right direction.

"I can see where you're coming from," Kate replied, not wanting to make him feel uncomfortable. "But have you ever considered that Jesus and God are one and the same?"

"Yeah, I've heard about that. In fact, I know all about that trinity stuff with the Father, Son, and Holy Spirit. But good lands! How can three be one, but yet still be three? Doesn't make a whole lot of sense if you ask me."

That was one point Kate couldn't argue with; she had struggled with the trinity herself at times. "I totally agree it's tough for us to wrap our minds around," Kate acknowledged. "But Chester, Jesus himself said that he and God are one and the same. In fact, Jesus told his disciples, '*Anyone who has seen me has seen the Father.*' And even more than that, Jesus tells us that the only way to God is through him. In other words, it's not enough *just* to believe in God. In order to have eternal life we need to go through Jesus first. It's almost like Jesus is the mediator between us and God. God wants a personal relationship with each one of us, and he accomplished that by sending his Son into the world as a human being."

"So now you're saying Jesus was human?"

"Yes, he was completely human. But he was also God."

"How can that be, Kate? First you're telling me that Jesus is both Jesus and God. And now you're telling me that Jesus is a human but also a god?"

"Not *a* god," Kate corrected him. "God. Chester, in order to truly believe in God, you have to believe in his Son."

"I'd like to believe it all, I really would. But how am I supposed to understand all of that? That this God-man was born to a virgin and lived and died and was raised from the dead and is still alive some two thousand years later? It just seems like an awful lot to swallow about some poor carpenter from an insignificant town in an ancient culture."

"I know, it's not easy," Kate said sympathetically. "And you *can't* understand it all. No one can. I don't think we're *supposed* to understand it. But we are supposed to *believe* it. We won't always have those rational explanations, Chester, and we won't always be able to see it with our own eyes. That's where the belief in our hearts comes in. We are supposed to live by faith and not by sight."

"What do you mean live by faith and not by sight?"

"Look at Jesus' disciple Thomas. He's a perfect example. Thomas struggled with Jesus' resurrection just like you struggle with it now, except he was actually *there*. When the other disciples came to Thomas and told him they had seen the resurrected Jesus, Thomas refused to believe it. He told them he would never believe it unless he could actually see the nail marks in Jesus' hands and put his hands in Jesus' side. And do you know what? Jesus came to Thomas and allowed Thomas to touch him and see for himself. Jesus told him not to doubt but to believe, and he said that those of us who believe without seeing are truly blessed. In other words, that's what faith is all about. Even though we can't see it or even explain it, we know in our hearts it's true."

Chester took Kate's hand in his, and the urgency in his eyes seared deep into Kate's heart. "Mina believed all of it. She loved Jesus just like she loved each of our children. In fact, she loved him *more*. And I want to believe it all too. More than anything I want to see her again one day, and I'm afraid if I don't believe in Jesus the way you do that I never will. But it's just so hard. I mean, I'm a good person. At least I *think* I am. I know I've made my fair share of mistakes, but I do plenty to help others, and I think God knows that."

"Yes, you *are* a good person," Kate emphatically agreed. "You are *such* a good person. Chester, you were there for me when no one else was, and I could never repay you for that kindness. But when it comes to salvation, being a good person isn't enough. You need to know Christ as your personal Savior."

"I don't know, Kate." Chester shook his head in confusion. "My mind wants to rationalize everything, and when I do it all seems so impossible."

"I know it does, I know it does." Kate squeezed his hand. "That's why we have faith. Because we don't *have* to be able to explain or rationalize everything. We just have to trust in God that it's the truth. He loves us, Chester, more than we could ever imagine, and he would never deceive us. Please, for me, take some time to pray about this. I want you to really get to know Jesus. Not Jesus the man, teacher, preacher, or healer, even though he was all of those things. But Jesus the Son of God and God himself. I know it's not easy, but I promise it will change not only your life but your eternity as well."

And then Chester asked her an impossibly straightforward question, yet one she wasn't quite sure how to answer.

"So then tell me, Kate, how can I get some of this *faith* you keep talking about?"

Kate stopped in her tracks. How could she help spark a faith in someone who had struggled with his beliefs for so long? How could she make something so complicated seem so simple? How could she persuade him to allow faith to bridge the gap between the explainable and the unexplainable when she often wrestled with those very same questions herself? How indeed?

———————————

Less than two weeks later the crispness of the June breeze turned into a sweltering summertime heat when air conditioners were cranked down a few degrees, curtains were tightly shut to keep the boiling sun out, and newscasters warned people to stay indoors as much as they could. Kate spread her papers out on the plastic tabletop in the Sunday school room, glancing out the window through the partially opened blinds as the first few cars pulled alongside the curb at Amazing Grace Chapel. Today's case study: the woman at the well. Kate had always particularly related to this story of the nameless woman from the Gospel of John. Well no, Kate hadn't had five husbands, but she had felt a deep shame during many years or her life just like this woman had. Even though she may have lived thousands of years ago, Kate shared an unspoken bond with her.

Attendance was on the light side due to the vacation season, but Kate didn't mind. She only asked of God that he might bring to her class whoever needed to hear the particular message each week, so Kate knew that whoever was supposed to be there would be there. As the women filtered into the small room, they fixed themselves a plate of snacks and took their usual seats around the table, chatting initially about the stifling heat and their summer plans. Before long, though, they gravitated to the discussion topic for the evening. Kate always loved watching this part of the class unfold. The church bells hadn't even chimed, yet these women were so hungry for God's Word that they eagerly began the discussion even without Kate's official prompt to start class.

This week the opening prayer fell to Olivia, a stunning Asian-American woman with shiny black hair who was studying to be an orthodontist. "Dear God," she began as the room fell silent, "thank you for this time together. Thank you for teaching us how to live righteous lives through the lives of these women. Help us to follow their examples and be the best we can be, and help us always to seek your will in our lives. Amen." The prayer was short and simple yet perfect. Kate had encouraged each woman to take turns praying aloud. Although they hesitated at first, most of them had at one point or another volunteered to pray. "It doesn't have to be anything fancy," Kate encouraged them, "just speak from your heart." And so they did.

Kate opened her Bible to the fourth chapter of John. "Who would like to summarize our reading for this week?"

"I will," offered Rachel, a graduate student who also happened to be Olivia's best friend.

"Great, thanks," Kate responded.

Rachel flipped opened her Bible to the page she had earmarked and took a few seconds to collect her thoughts before responding. "Jesus was traveling with his disciples, and he went through Samaria. He came to a small town and sat by a well because he was tired and needed to rest. While he was sitting there, this woman came to the well to draw some water. Jesus asked her for a drink, and the woman was very surprised. I wasn't quite sure about this part but it seemed to me like the Samarians and the Jews didn't get along, so the woman thought Jesus wouldn't want anything to do with her."

"You're absolutely correct," Kate encouraged her with a smile. "What happened next?"

"Well, Jesus and the woman had a conversation about a few things. First about the water in the well, and Jesus promised the woman he could give her not just any old water, but *living* water."

"Great, Rachel," Kate replied, "and what was the other conversation about?"

"It was actually about the woman. Jesus basically told the woman he knew everything about her. That she had had five husbands, and she was currently living with a man who wasn't her husband."

"And what impact did these conversations have on the woman at the well?" Kate prompted.

Julia, another young woman in the study, spoke up. "She came to believe that Jesus was the promised Messiah."

"Exactly, Julia, and why was that?"

"Well, for one thing Jesus knew all these things about the woman's past. I think she must've been a little freaked out by everything he knew because right away she said, '*I can see that you are a prophet.*' But for another, Jesus told her he was the promised Messiah and that if she drank of the water he gave her, she would never thirst again."

Kate smiled as the women all sat totally enlightened by the conversation. "And what exactly did Jesus mean when he told the woman she would never thirst again?" Kate was trying to lead these women deeper into the discussion without giving away too much.

"I think Jesus was speaking metaphorically," Olivia answered. "Jesus didn't mean that the woman literally would never need water again. The water Jesus had was a spiritual drink, not an earthly drink. I think Jesus meant that if the woman believed in him she would never need for anything more."

"Right," Rachel added, "she would be full spiritually."

Kate was pleased at how well the women had grasped the meaning of the story, but they weren't quite finished yet. "So then once the woman realized who Jesus was, what did she do about it? Julia, can you tell us?"

"Sure. The woman left Jesus and went back to the town to tell everyone who Jesus was. And the Bible said that many people in Samaria believed in Jesus because of her."

"Exactly, so let's look at some of our discussion questions based on this story." Scanning her notes, Kate led them to the first question on the page. "How did Jesus use the woman at the well to serve him, and what can we learn from her today?"

"I'd like to share," Olivia offered.

"Go right ahead," Kate replied.

"As for the first part of the question, Jesus used the woman at the well to become one of his disciples. She went out and told others about him, so in a way she was kind of the first female evangelist. She believed in Jesus as the Messiah, and she shared that belief with other people. She fulfilled the Great Commission before Jesus ever even said it!"

"That's an excellent point." Kate's eyes sparkled with excitement.

Olivia continued. "As for the second part of the question, what can we learn from her today, I think Jesus is trying to teach us that he wants to use everyone to spread the word about his kingdom, no matter who that person is or what their past may have been. Obviously this woman was shunned because of her history with men, not to mention the fact that she was a Samaritan *and* a woman in a very paternalistic culture. But that didn't matter to Jesus. He saw her for who she was, so he used her gifts just like he would anyone else. He didn't judge her or think she wasn't good enough."

Kate surveyed the room as several of the young women scribbled notes on their pads. All of them appeared completely fascinated by the conversation.

"Olivia, I think you've summarized the meaning of this story beautifully. So I have one last question. What can the woman at the well teach us about ourselves today? I think we have several life lessons we can take from this story."

"One lesson," Rachel began, "is that we will all make mistakes in our lives, but we still have worth and value in the eyes of Jesus. Our mistakes won't change his love for us."

Allison, a shy young woman who up until that point had remained completely silent, finally spoke in a soft voice. "Another lesson is that only Jesus can fill us spiritually. Nothing in this world can do it, only our belief in Christ."

"Amazing point, Allison," Kate responded in the hopes of encouraging the young woman to participate more often.

Julia replied next. "I think the story teaches us that we *all* have a duty to spread the word about Jesus, no matter who we are or where we may be in our lives. Other people need to hear about Jesus, and the responsibility falls on us to do it. And I think it also teaches us that if you are sincere in your testimony about him, people will listen. It doesn't matter who you are, because the people in the town believed her and in turn came to know Jesus through her."

Kate was beaming with pride. What at first was a group of sometimes self-involved young women had turned into a class of budding theologians, dissecting God's Word and teaching one another in the process. The class had come such a long way in such a short time, and Kate could see the transformation taking place within these women. With each week's discussion they gained a deeper understanding not only of scripture but of themselves. And that was Kate's biggest hope; that through all of the worldly challenges and temptations they would never lose sight of themselves in the process. Kate had been down that road before, and it was a long, difficult journey back.

Kate led the closing prayer and most of the women said their goodbyes to Kate, invigorated to tackle the week ahead with the Lord firmly leading the way. Kate began to collect her belongings and straighten up the room while Olivia and Rachel hung back to help.

"Kate, can I ask you something?" Rachel inquired as she collected a stack of Bibles from the table and replaced them on the bookshelf in the corner of the room.

"Sure, what's up?"

"Well, when I was studying about the Samaritan woman, it got me to thinking about something."

"And what was that?" Kate responded.

"One of the things we talked about this evening was how she was faithful to Jesus by telling other people about him."

"Right," Kate agreed.

"I was also reading the Bible, and I forget exactly where it is but I remember reading somewhere that in order to be saved we have to do two things. First, we have to believe in our hearts that God raised Jesus from the dead, and second we have to proclaim that Jesus is Lord."

"That is exactly right, Rachel. I believe Paul wrote that in the book of Romans."

A concerned expression spread across Rachel's face. "Well, if it was so important for the Samaritan woman to tell others about Jesus so they could believe, and if the Bible says that one of the things we must do to be saved is to believe in our hearts that Jesus is Lord, then what happens to all of those people who never hear about Jesus or have the chance to believe? Or what about those people who for one reason or another wouldn't understand about Jesus even if they did hear about him? What happens to them?"

The full meaning behind Rachel's question slowly sunk in for Kate. She flashed back to the conversation with Ben on New Year's Day when she had been so nervous about leading the Bible study for fear she would be asked a question she couldn't answer. "*Of course they're going to ask you questions you don't know the answers to . . . when the occasional question comes your way that you don't know the answer to,*

you will write it down and tell them you'll get back to them the next time."
The only problem was, this *wasn't* a question Kate could simply write down and research as she did with everything else. This was a question of *faith*. Kate hesitated to respond for fear of misleading her younger friend.

"That's a very good question," Kate answered honestly. "Can I ask what got you to thinking about that?"

As Rachel explained, Olivia stopped what she was doing and joined the conversation, apparently just as concerned as her best friend.

"Well, right now I'm in graduate school studying special education. After I get my degree I was hoping to work with special needs children in the public school system, and eventually I'd like to open my own private school for these children. I have always loved working with special needs kids. They are such a gift from God. They are so beautiful on the inside, even though most of them have significant disabilities by all outward appearances. When I think about the Samaritan woman and Paul's words that we need to believe in Jesus in order to be saved, I immediately think of these kids. Kate, some of them have the mental capacity of only a toddler, if that. They can't understand basic arithmetic or grammar let alone something as complex as Jesus Christ. So does that mean because they never actually *believe* in Jesus and can confess him as their Savior, that none of these children will ever be saved?"

Kate was both fascinated and terrified by the conversation. Before she could respond, Olivia shared her perspective on the issue, unintentionally complicating matters even further.

"And what about my great-grandparents? They were from China where the government wouldn't *let* Christians spread the word about Jesus. In fact, a group of missionaries from Europe who tried to visit their village was killed. My great-grandparents had never heard of a Bible before let alone Jesus, but it wasn't their fault. So does that mean they weren't saved because they never even got the chance to know about Jesus? Or what about babies who die in infancy and are never old enough to understand who Jesus Christ is?"

Both young women looked pleadingly at Kate, hoping she could supply answers to their burning questions. Kate suddenly felt herself very much sympathizing with their thoughts but also wholly unqualified to provide them the wisdom they sought. She put her things down, took a seat, and motioned for them to do the same.

"And not to throw a wrench in things," Olivia continued, "but as I was reading the Bible the other day I came across this passage from Ephesians. It says that God chose us and predestined us to be adopted as sons of Jesus Christ. So does that mean that God chose only *some* of us and not others? That maybe my great-grandparents were purposefully *not* chosen and were intentionally left out?"

Kate took a deep breath as her head swirled. "Those are all really good questions, but I'm afraid they don't have simple answers. I will try to answer you as best I can from my heart, but I can only share with you how I feel. You are going to have to pray that God might reveal His divine answers to you. Yes, you're right the Bible teaches us that in order to be saved we must believe in Jesus and confess him as our Savior. And yes, all of the people you mentioned for whatever reason either never had the opportunity or the ability to know of Jesus and confess him as their Lord. But one thing I know without a doubt from studying the Bible is that our God is a God of love. He loves us more than we could ever possibly imagine. He created each one of us in His own image, he cares for us, and he gives us a hope and a future. And since God is love, I can't imagine that God would ever intentionally exclude anyone from the saving grace of his Son."

"But how does that work?" Olivia asked. "I mean, how does God work through people like my great-grandparents or the special needs kids that Rachel will be working with?"

Kate hesitated for a moment. All she could do was be completely honest. "I'm not exactly sure. I think there are some questions we just can't answer. You have to remember scripture teaches us that God's ways and thoughts are higher than our ways. In other words, there are some things we as humans aren't *meant* to understand. That's when we need to trust in God and have faith. I have faith that God gives everyone the opportunity to know about his Son, even if that opportunity might not be in the traditional way like the woman at the well who told the townspeople about Jesus. I have no doubt that through God's love he reaches out to those people who have never heard of his Son. And I think God wants every last person to belong to his Kingdom. If he excluded anyone on purpose, then he wouldn't be a God of love at all, and that contradicts the very heart of scripture about God."

"I understand what you're saying," Rachel admitted as she mindlessly clicked a pen she grasped in her hand, "but how can we be sure?"

"You just need to trust in the Lord and have faith," Kate replied. "Even if we don't have all of the answers, we have to trust that God does. And God's answers are far better than anything we could conceive with our own minds. We need to let our faith deepen so we can give it over to God when we don't have all of the answers."

"I do have faith," Olivia said, "but sometimes it's still so hard to understand it all. How can I have such a deep faith so things like this won't bother me anymore?"

Her question had spoken volumes to Kate, and she meditated upon Olivia's words long after the three women had parted ways. How could anyone in this lifetime ever achieve such a secure faith that the mysteries of our world didn't bewilder them? How could faith adequately fill in the gaps where the spiritual and the worldly were at odds? And how could Kate justifiably convince others that their faith needed to grow when she still had so much growing to do of her own? How indeed?

Kate's mind was still reeling from the conversations she had had over the last several weeks when she opted to join Ben for a two-hour car ride into the country while he delivered a piece of furniture to a loyal client. Ben had invited Kate along because he was eager for some company, promising her a scenic ride alongside of winding streams and across ivy-covered bridges. But it was Kate who actually needed the company much more than Ben. The last few weeks she had been preoccupied with the state of her *own* faith after engaging in some weighty conversations. She thought of Chester with a sense of sadness at his complete misunderstanding of Jesus, yet at the same time she was filled with hope. She prayed daily that the small seed she had planted during their lunch together would take root and blossom, and she asked the Lord to help Chester come to know Jesus the same way she did. Then she thought of Olivia and Rachel. At first Kate had scolded herself for answering their questions so inadequately, or at least so she thought. But then after time and prayer Kate realized that perhaps there *were* no concrete answers to their questions, so Kate did the best she could by sharing her own beliefs with them. Through it all Kate was slowly starting to realize that not only did she *not* have all of the answers, but she still had some very pressing questions of her own.

The air conditioner in Ben's pickup had died several weeks before, and since Ben never felt the need to get it fixed, they made their journey with the windows down and the fresh country air invigorating them. Kate kept her hair pulled back in a high ponytail and she hung her arm out the window, feeling the warmth of the sun as the force of the wind naturally carried her arm up and down like waves along an ocean beach. She had already updated Ben regarding her lunch with Chester and the women's Bible study. She had secretly hoped that Ben might give her all the answers she so desperately sought, but to her disappointment he remained mostly silent except to offer a few words of encouragement.

"You did beautifully, Kate. No one except the Father holds the answers to all of our questions. He will work on their hearts to help their faith grow through the answers they seek."

"Well, I thought Jesus had all of the answers too." It was an assumption Kate had always made without ever stopping to think it through.

"Kate, there are some things the Father knows that not even the Son is privy to."

"Really? Like what?" Kate's nose crinkled.

"Like the return of Jesus to reclaim his kingdom. Only the Father knows the day and the hour."

"But if Jesus and God are one and the same, how could Jesus *not* know?"

Ben smiled while never taking focus off the two-lane road meandering ahead as far as the eye could see. "As you said, Kate, there are some things that weren't meant for human understanding. And while yes, God and his Son are both wholly distinct yet wholly a part of one another, God has chosen to reveal that information to the Son only when the time is at hand. God is completely in control and will work all things out for good according to His plan. That's why God has given us the gift of faith. It helps us know in our hearts what our minds cannot explain."

Kate was immediately struck how just listening to Ben talk about faith made her feel foolish for doubting herself in the first place.

"When you talk about faith you make it sound so simple," Kate replied.

"Oh, don't think that for one second. There isn't anything simple about faith. In fact it's probably one of the most intricately mind-blowing conceptions of the Father. But all the same, it's a gift. We don't manufacture faith on our own like you grow tomatoes in your garden or I carved the furniture in the back of this truck. It's not like that. Faith is something given to us freely by God out of God's love for us so that we can trust in him when we *can't* answer all of life's questions. God gives us faith so we can have the promise of peace we wouldn't otherwise be able to have."

"Okay," Kate continued on his train of thought, "so then how do you help someone have faith who doesn't have it? Like Chester. How can I help him have faith that Jesus Christ is Lord? Or how can I help Rachel have faith that her great-grandparents are in heaven with God even though they never heard of Jesus during their lifetimes?"

"Kate, God gives *everyone* the gift of faith. It's not something that some of us have and some of us don't have. By God's grace he gives us *all* faith, it's just that some people don't know how to *use* that gift. That's why you need to pray for your friends, Kate. Ask God to help them discover the faith that's already inside of them so they might come to understand."

Kate pondered what Ben had said. Never once in her life had she thought of faith as a gift from God. It had simply never occurred to her to look at it that way. Kate has always assumed that faith was something *she* had instilled within herself as she grew closer to the Lord. Yet now that she saw it from Ben's perspective, she realized how arrogant her thinking had been all along. Her faith really *was* a gift, and since all gifts come from God, her faith had to come from God as well.

Ben slowed the truck as he turned from one highway onto the next. The scenery looked identical on the remote countryside, and Kate felt as though they could drive for days without ever passing a hint of civilization. Her thoughts continued to process what Ben was saying and went deeper still.

"Ben, why did Jesus have to die?"

Despite the fact that Kate had asked a question the entire human race has grappled with since the resurrection itself, Ben didn't seem the least bit fazed. In fact, he almost appeared as if he had been expecting it.

"Why do *you* think he had to die?"

"That's just it," Kate admitted, "I'm not sure I really know. When I was a kid in Sunday school I remember being taught that Jesus died for me because he loves me so much. That sounded good enough to me, so I never really thought about it much more than that. But then in the past few years the more I studied the Bible and learned how we are all no-good, hopeless sinners, I came to think that Jesus died for me to save me from eternal damnation because of my sins. But even *that* doesn't add up if you ask me."

"Why not?" Ben inquired curiously.

"Well, I understand *why* he died, but I guess what I don't understand is why he *had* to die. In other words, how did his death on the cross reconcile all of humanity to God?" Kate paused. "Think about it this way. God is God, right?"

"Right," Ben agreed.

"Well, if God is omnipotent and can do anything he wants to do at any time, then why couldn't God have just forgiven us for our sins without having to send his Son to die for us on the cross? And I guess what I struggle with even more is *why* would God have ever allowed that to happen? I hate to say it, but that doesn't seem like something a very good father would do, sacrifice their own son in such a brutal and horrific way."

Ben listened intently as Kate tried to make some sense of the jumble of thoughts running through her mind. He pulled out his atlas and checked to see how long until the next turn. Ben wasn't one for GPS or phone apps—he was quite happy with a good old-fashioned map plotting his course. Kate smiled and wondered if Ben even needed the atlas at all. He seemed as if the destination were somehow programmed in his mind.

"Have you shared your questions with anyone else?"

"Well, I haven't actually talked to anyone else about it, but I did do some research on it."

Ben smiled. Ever the attorney at heart. A question you don't know the answer to? Research it, of course.

"And what did you learn from your research?"

"I learned that sometimes research can just confuse you more." Kate tucked a strand of hair back into her ponytail that had escaped in the breeze.

"How so?"

"Apparently there are a lot of different theories out there as to why Jesus had to die on the cross. *A lot*. One theory says there was this cosmic battle between God and Satan. So God sent Jesus into the world to die, thus making it appear that Satan has won the battle. But when Jesus is resurrected God shows everyone he has the upper hand and Satan is defeated once and for all. Under this theory people say Jesus' death was necessary as a way for God to have the ultimate victory over the forces of evil in this world."

"Okay," Ben asked, thoroughly enjoying the conversation, "so do you agree with that theory?"

"Actually, no, not at all. I mean, for one thing this whole idea of a 'cosmic battle' seems a little too far-fetched for me to believe. It almost sounds like a bad sci-fi movie if you ask me. But even aside from that I still have problems with it."

"Such as?"

"Such as, this whole theory seems to give way too much credit to Satan. I mean don't get me wrong, I know that Satan is real and spreads lots of evil in this world, but to say that Satan exercised *that* much control over the world so that God had no other choice but to send his Son to die on the cross just doesn't add up to me. In a way it almost puts God second to Satan in terms of control over the universe. And also, if people who believe this think that the forces of evil have been defeated once and for all, I'm wondering if they are living in the same world I'm living in. All you have to do is turn on the evening news; unfortunately, it still seems like there's a whole lot of evil and hatred all over the world. So in that respect I would have to say that Jesus' death on the cross didn't accomplish what it was supposed to."

They approached a green road sign. "Only twenty more miles to Clarksburg," Ben said. Kate, however, was so engrossed in the conversation that she didn't hear a word of it.

"Then I read about another theory which basically says that Jesus died to pay the price for our sins when we couldn't do it ourselves."

"Okay, that makes some sense. Tell me more."

"Well, under this theory, humans can't help but sin. They also can't rectify themselves and stop sinning. So Jesus, as the only sinless human, is substituted on the cross for everyone else and pays the ultimate price for our sins in order to satisfy God's need for divine justice and restore the broken relationship between God and humanity. Basically, satisfaction with God can't be achieved unless someone can pay for the sin of humanity. And the only *someone* who fit the bill was Jesus. So Jesus voluntarily took the punishment that was really meant for each of us."

Ben didn't have to ask what Kate's thoughts were about this second theory; the expression on her face said it all. "Obviously you don't like this theory either."

"Well, when I first started reading about it I thought I'd like it a lot. As a lawyer I'm used to dealing with concepts of punishment and justice. So I thought *hey, finally an explanation I can make sense of.* But the more I read the more I disagreed with it."

"Okay, so what are the problems you have with it?"

"For one thing, in the justice system it's completely unheard of to let one person take the punishment for another. Just look at Gerald Lyons. What would a judge have done if his wife said she wanted to go to prison for him so he could remain free? I'll tell you what a judge would have done—laughed in her face and then probably sent her to a psychiatrist to see if she had lost her mind. Gerald was the one who had committed the crime, he was the danger to society, and he was the one who would have to pay the price for his crime. So to let one person pay such an incredible price for another's sin just seems completely unrealistic to me. But even more important than that, this theory makes it seem like the number one priority for God is justice. Like God cares about getting even with humanity more than anything else."

"Okay." Ben spoke carefully so not to put words in her mouth. "So if you don't agree with the whole cosmic battle thing or that Jesus was strictly a substitute for us, then where are you with it all?"

Kate crinkled her nose. "I guess I'm back to square one. I think both of the theories make some very good points, and you can definitely find scripture to support them. I *do* think Jesus' death impacted all of creation and not just humanity. And I do think that Jesus died on the cross as a substitute for my sins. But I still think something is missing."

"And have you figured out what that might be?"

"Well, I'm not positive, but the thing I keep coming back to is love."

"Love," Ben echoed and smiled.

"Yes, love. From everything I have ever learned or know about God, God is a God of love. Plain and simple. God wouldn't send his Son to die just to one-up Satan, and he also wouldn't send his Son to the cross just to satisfy some need for justice or retribution. So in my mind, the *only* reason God would send his Son to the cross is out of love."

"Love for?" Ben began the question.

"Love for all of us. Love for humanity and love for the world. First, because God knew that if Jesus took on our sins as his own we would once and for all be cleansed of those sins. Second, because in order to defeat death Jesus himself had to die and be resurrected. Death *had* to be a part of the equation for us to have the promise of eternal life. If Jesus hadn't died for us, then maybe our sins still could've been forgiven, but death would have been final. I think Jesus *had* to die because it was the only way we could ever have *both* forgiveness of our sins and eternal life. God wanted us to experience eternity just like his Son has. And I think God allowed Jesus to die, although obviously he didn't want to, because he loves us that much."

Ben merged onto a gravel road that narrowed considerably. Their destination was only a few miles down the road. Kate reached over to the steering wheel and rested her hand atop Ben's.

"Ben, do you think I'm right? Do you think the reason Jesus *had* to die for us is because of God's love for the world?"

"Do *you* think you're right?"

"Hey, no fair," Kate snickered, "you're not allowed to answer a question with a question!"

"Well, I just did," Ben chuckled. "But seriously, do you think that's why Jesus died for you?"

"In my heart I do, yes. I still can't explain it all as well as I'd like to be able to, but yes. I believe that Jesus died for me out of God's love."

"If you believe that in your heart, Kate, then I think what might be right or wrong by the world's standards is irrelevant. What's inside of you is all that matters."

As they neared the end of the lane the old farmhouse came into view, a beautiful quilt hanging over the front porch railing and chickens running aimlessly in the yard. Ben smiled at the tranquil scene, but as he glanced over at Kate, he noticed the slightest hint of a frown on her face.

"What's wrong? It sounds to me like you've done a very good job of working this all out on your own."

"But I haven't, not at all." Her blue eyes glistened in the sun as she blinked several times trying to hide the tears that were beginning to form.

"What is it?" Ben asked lovingly.

"How can I be sure that I'm not getting it all wrong?"

"Kate, that's where your faith comes in."

"I do have faith, but if love is really the reason why Jesus died for me, then how can I ever repay him? How can I make amends for all of the mistakes I've made and the sins I've committed? How can I live my life every day giving thanks for what he did? How can I be worthy of such a blessing? And how could God love me *that* much to do something so wonderful for me?"

How indeed?

Faith, simply put, is complicated.

CHAPTER 18
THE ROAD NOT TAKEN

"And having been warned in a dream
not to go back to Herod,
they returned to their country
by another route."
Matthew 2:12

"Excuse me. Kate? I don't mean to bother you, but line three is for you." The young receptionist at Hope's House peeked around the corner through Kate's partially opened office door. Kate was busy preparing documentation for a protective order. She looked up and smiled.

"No problem at all, Jessica. Thanks so much. Do you happen to know who's calling?"

"No, I'm sorry, I didn't get a name. It's a man though." Jessica paused for a moment. "And one thing was a little odd to me."

"What was that?" Kate asked.

"Well, whoever it is, he called you Kathryn."

Kathryn. It was a name she hadn't heard in years; the name of a person who no longer existed. There were only a small handful of people who would've asked for Kathryn. But why on earth would any of them be calling her here?

"Thanks again, Jessica," Kate replied, staring tentatively at the blinking red light on the dial pad. She tapped the button and picked up the handset.

"Hello? This is Kate Kirby."

"Kathryn." It was all he said, but he didn't have to say more. She would've known his voice anywhere.

"Griffin?"

"Yeah, hey, stranger. It's been a long time."

Kate was at a complete loss for words, yet she tried desperately to avoid the awkward silence when you're on the telephone with someone and don't know what to say.

"Griffin, how did you know I worked here?"

"Oh, I have my ways. A few phone calls here and there. How've you been?"

Boy, if that weren't a loaded question. Where should she start? Should she give him the long, tortuous version of what the break-up of their marriage had done to her; about the many nights drinking, the accident, the AA meetings, and the redemption she finally found? Or should she give him the condensed version where she focused only on the last few years? Kate quickly decided on the latter.

"I'm really good. I moved out of the city, and I've been working at Hope's House for almost five years. How about you?"

"Things are great. Still heading up the malpractice division at the firm."

Kate wanted to ask about his wife and children, but for some reason she just couldn't bring herself to do it.

"I'm sure you do an amazing job. You always did succeed at anything you put your mind to," she replied.

"Actually the firm is moving me back to the city again, right down the road from you. I'm due back in a little over a month."

"Well, that's great," she replied, not entirely sure if she meant it or not.

Another awkward pause. For two people who had been married for six years, they had surprisingly little to talk about anymore.

"Kathryn, I've been doing a lot of thinking."

Without realizing it, Kate found herself clutching the handset so hard that her knuckles turned white.

"About what?"

"About us."

The word *us* hung in the air like a mammoth gong reverberating long after the instrument has been struck.

"*Us?*" Kate asked incredulously.

"Yes, us."

"What about us, Griffin?"

"That maybe we ended things too prematurely. That maybe we should've given it more time or gone to marriage counseling. Or like you had suggested, maybe we should've tried having children. I just can't help but have this feeling that we made a big mistake. Kathryn, I think about you quite frequently."

"I think about you too." She wasn't lying.

"I think if we gave it a second chance, we might be able to make it work this time. I mean, we know all the things we did wrong the first time around so we won't make the same mistakes. I just feel like if we could go back and start over again we could get it right."

Kate was quite certain that her heart had stopped beating. She looked around her office and suddenly felt dizzy. Everything was a blur the papers spread across her desk, the ficus tree in the corner of her office, the pamphlets for various counseling services atop a credenza against the back wall. She couldn't see any of it through the blinding bomb that had just gone off in her life. A few moments ago she had been in the middle of another ordinary workday, and now this. How could this be happening? And so completely out of the blue?

"Griffin, I don't know. What about your family? You have a wife and children now."

"Kathryn, I am meant to be with you and no one else." That was apparently all the detail Griffin was willing to share about his life since he and Kate had parted ways. Yet Kate knew there was much more to the story Griffin wasn't sharing. "What do you say? Do you think we could give it another try?"

"I just don't know." It was all Kate could say. "So much time has passed, so much has happened since then. I'm not the same person I was when we broke up."

"Neither am I, Kathryn, and that's the beauty of it. I've learned what's important in life. Believe me, I have my priorities straight. And I know that right now what's most important is you."

His words melted her heart, but at the same time they also infuriated her. Why hadn't he said that six years ago on the balcony of their penthouse suite instead of presenting her with a plane ticket to Miami and saying he was on his way? Why couldn't he have cared *then* like he did *now*? It wasn't fair.

"Griffin, I don't know what to say—"

"Then don't say anything," he cut her off. "Promise me you'll at least think about it. I'll be back in town next weekend to take care of some preliminary matters at the firm before I officially return. We could have dinner one night and talk about it more. And besides, it would be so great to see you again and spend some—"

Suddenly, Kate heard a ringing. An incessant, obnoxious ringing. It startled her to the point where she no longer focused on what Griffin was saying. Instead, she frantically tried to determine where the annoying sound was coming from. And then it dawned on her. It was the phone ringing. But how could that be? She was *talking* on the phone. She removed the handset from her ear and stared at it. She pushed buttons on the dial pad but nothing worked. It just kept ringing. Frustrated, she put her ear back to the handset.

"Griffin? Griffin? Can you hear me? Are you still there? *Griffin????*"

Ringing. Ringing. Ringing. Ringing.

Ringing.

Not ringing. *BUZZING.*

Kate bolted upright in bed and immediately saw the flickering electric candles in her windowsills, barely illuminating her bedroom as the sun greeted the earth at the start of a new day. She glanced over at her alarm clock. 6:20 a.m. She had overslept. It must've been going off for the last twenty minutes. And then it dawned on her. There *was* no phone conversation. There never had been.

Kate exhaled loudly and sunk back into her pillow, replaying the conversation a thousand times over in her mind. It took her a few minutes to regain her composure, but then she immediately reached for her cell phone and clicked the conversation icon on her home screen. She then did her best to text with what little daylight she had.

Morning. Ok if I stop by the shop after work today?

Ben was an early riser and replied within seconds.

Ben: Sure thing.

Kate: Thanks.

Ben: Was it another dream?

Kate: How'd you guess?

Ben: Come any time.

Kate: ☺

Kate replaced the cell phone on her nightstand. More than anything else she craved a glass of Merlot, or maybe perhaps a shot of whiskey. Just a little something to take the edge off. But as quickly as the thought entered her mind, she forced it out. *"Lead me not to temptation . . ."* she repeatedly murmured as she shut her eyes. Maybe if she closed them tight enough she could erase all the thoughts running through her head. But she couldn't.

The day passed slowly, and Kate felt as though she were in a haze. As she sat behind her desk trying to finish some last-minute paperwork, she eventually gave up all hope of accomplishing anything of substance. She caught herself more than once staring at the line three button on her phone and expecting to see the blinking red light. Shortly after lunchtime Jessica poked her head around the corner into Kate's office.

"Excuse me. Kate? I don't mean to bother you, but—"

Kate froze. It was happening all over again, except this time it wasn't a dream. It was *real*. Kate stared at Jessica with such penetrating eyes that Jessica literally took a step backward.

"What is it?" Kate said in a rush. "Is there a phone call for me?"

"No," Jessica replied, quite confused. "I was just going to ask if you had received a hearing date yet for the Miller case. Ms. Miller stopped in a while ago and was wondering."

Kate regrouped and felt foolish.

"Yes," she said as she flipped through her calendar, "it's on the twenty-first of this month."

"Great, thank you." Jessica lingered in the doorway.

"Did you need something else?" Kate asked, noticing the receptionist's hesitation to leave.

"Is everything okay?"

"Sure it is," Kate replied unconvincingly, "why do you ask?"

"I don't know, you've seemed very preoccupied lately. And when I came in just now, you looked at me like you had seen a ghost."

"Thanks for asking, but I'm fine. I really do appreciate the concern." Kate's smile was genuine and apparently enough confirmation that Jessica left and thought nothing more about it. Little did she know.

By the time early evening arrived Kate was already on her way to Bakersville, stopping briefly at a local convenience store to pick up a cheese and crackers "to-go" container in place of her dinner. Although she had been encouraged to eat healthily, she simply didn't have an appetite at the moment. She made the drive down Main Street, and even though the heater was cranked up, she could feel the bitter cold of the winter air penetrating the car. It was one of those nights where your bones ached from the frigid temperatures, and as soon as you stepped foot outside your teeth chattered uncontrollably. Kate parked quickly and rang the doorbell to Ben's shop. He buzzed her in, and she flew up the steps and into his studio apartment without knocking. She huddled her shoulders and shivered, but somehow she knew it wasn't only from the cold. Ben was waiting for her with two mugs and a box of Swiss Miss on the counter.

"How about something to warm you up?" Ben offered as Kate removed her coat.

"I'm good, but thanks."

"Oh, come on, it'll feel good going down on a night like this. Temperatures are supposed to drop below freezing. And hey, I even splurged and bought mini marshmallows."

Kate couldn't help but smile, so she relented and accepted his invitation. After he fixed their steaming drinks and added a generous heap of marshmallows, he handed Kate the mug. She sipped it and let the liquid glide down her throat. She couldn't help but feel warmed inside.

"Come," Ben said as he found a place on the couch. Kate joined him. For a few moments they just sat there together, sipping their hot chocolates and gazing out the windows at the streetlights punctuating the otherwise black night.

"Do you want to talk about it?" Ben finally asked.

"I really don't," Kate replied honestly. "I just needed to be with you."

"Then that's exactly what we will do."

Ben sat back onto the mismatched cushions and Kate joined him, leaning into his chest and resting her head on his shoulder. She curled her legs underneath her and held the mug in her lap with both hands. That was what Kate loved so much about Ben. He never pushed. If she needed to talk, he was ever ready to listen. If she was frustrated, he helped her through it. If she was sad, she could cry to him. But if all she needed was his company, he was more than content for the two of them just to *be*. No words were needed. Kate had learned this many years ago about Ben. What was unspoken between them was just as powerful, perhaps even more so, than what was spoken.

As Kate rested her head on Ben, she could actually feel the heaviness of her day being lifted off of her. She closed her eyes and sighed in relief. It was almost as if the weight of physically leaning on Ben was transferring her burdens upon his shoulders. She thought back to the conversation in the pickup truck that summer afternoon when she joined Ben for a trip into the country. A conversation about faith, and most of all about God's love for her. That had been over a year and a half ago, yet she still had so many unanswered questions. In some ways the conversation seemed like it was only yesterday, but so much had changed since then. Kate's faith had been tested like never before and in ways she never would've expected at only thirty-six. And in the midst of it all, for some reason her past had decided to unexpectedly visit in her dreams, trying to muddle her present with a very uncertain future. The lines between what was, what is, and what will be, seemed dangerously blurred to Kate. Why was that happening? Usually her dreams were about Griffin, but occasionally she dreamed about her mother, the firm, and once she had even dreamed about Gerald Lyons. In each dream she had a choice to make; an opportunity to go back and do something differently. Was this God's way of telling her she should've made different choices in life? That the paths she had chosen weren't really the ones meant for her? It was unnerving to say the least.

The only thing that brought her comfort through it all was Ben's presence. As they sat silently together on his couch, Kate couldn't help but be overcome with joy at how blessed she was. To have Ben in her life was more than she had ever deserved. Someone who loved her for who she was, who never held a grudge, who was faithful, who was forgiving, and who was there through good and bad. She caught herself pitying the people in the world who didn't have a Ben to share their lives with; how did they manage on their own? And even if they could manage, why would they want to? Yes, life without Ben would be scary indeed. She needed him more than she ever had before.

That evening Kate never did share her most recent dream with Ben. Not because she didn't want to, but because she didn't need to. For some reason Kate felt as though Ben already knew all about it. The silence was more comforting than any words could be. When she lay there with her head on his shoulder she feared nothing, for he was with her.

Kate's third annual New Year's Eve party was in full swing, and nothing would dampen her spirits and ruin such a festive evening. After all, it had become quite the anticipated event among her group of friends, and each year the guest list grew just a little larger. Of course the entire Wednesday morning Bible study gang wouldn't miss it. Brother Washington brought Judith each year, and Tom came with Michelle, who now had the slightest hint of a baby bump—the kind just barely detectable and would make you do a double take, but if you didn't know she was pregnant you would never dare ask for fear of being wrong and feeling quite foolish. Michelle beamed; she certainly had the pregnancy glow, and Tom doted on her every move. Kate watched the two interact and was so happy for them, just starting their lives together with so much to look forward to; although amidst the happiness, Kate felt the slightest twinge of sadness. In addition to the Bible study group, several of Kate's friends from the women's study also attended. Stephanie, Rachel, and Olivia all arrived with an appetizer in hand ready to usher in the New Year. Even sweet, shy Allison was there and managed to come out of her shell enough to make small talk with Ben and a few of the others. Kate's cozy house was bustling with friends who had all become so dear to her over the last several years. She glanced around her home and watched everyone, almost as if she were a distant observer rather than the host of the party herself. Ellie and Judith were deep in conversation about local politics; Ben and Brother Washington helped themselves to the sweet and sour meatballs (which, of course, Ben managed to drop one leaving a meatball-sized stain trailing down his shirt); Tom lovingly rubbed Michelle's abdomen while sharing details with Rachel and Olivia about plans for a nursery and potential baby names. Evie collected empty plates from the coffee table and straightened the napkins and silverware on the dining room table while Allison trailed behind to help. Kate just smiled. So many different people from so many walks of life, but they all shared one very important thing in common—their love for the Lord. If this were to be the last New Year's Eve Kate welcomed in this world, she couldn't think of anyone she would rather spend it with or anything she would rather be doing. The countdown to midnight began, and as the ball dropped and friends hugged one another Brother Washington led a spontaneous chorus of "Old Lang Syne," and soon everyone joined in. Tears brimmed in Kate's eyes. She took in every last second and tried to savor the beautiful moment she had been given. *Thank you, Jesus,* she said to herself. And just as she did, Ben caught her attention from across the room and smiled.

A little over a week later Kate felt a renewed sense of calm as she awoke eager for their Wednesday morning Bible study. The last few nights had brought her a sound, dreamless sleep, and she thanked the Lord for an answer to prayer. She arrived at the Coffee House a few minutes before seven, and as usual Laurie was already behind the counter arranging pastries on a tray. Multicolored Christmas lights still hung in the oversized bay windows of the small shop, and a Christmas tree adorned the corner with empty boxes underneath wrapped in festive metallic paper. They exchanged pleasantries, and Kate headed to the back room where Evie and Ellie were sipping coffee, already deep in conversation. No sooner did Kate take her seat than Tom arrived, followed immediately by Ben and Brother Washington, who always drove together.

The group placed their orders with Laurie and opened their time together in prayer. Before they could even begin to discuss their latest study on the Book of Acts, the conversation took an abrupt turn to the sermon Pastor Connie had preached the previous Sunday about the visit of the Wise Men.

Evie, per the usual, initiated the dialogue. "In all my years as a member of Amazing Grace Chapel, I don't think I've ever heard a more captivating sermon."

"I couldn't agree more," Tom chimed in. "The way she tied the poem into the scripture was really enlightening."

Kate glanced over at Ben and Brother Washington. Since of course they both attended St. Paul the Apostle Church in Bakersville, they hadn't had the privilege of hearing Pastor Connie's message. The rest of the group quickly caught on.

"I'm so sorry," Tom offered. "I didn't mean to be rude, I forgot for a moment that you weren't there."

Brother Washington nodded his head graciously. "Why don't you share with us?"

"Absolutely," Tom agreed. "Pastor Connie preached from the Gospel of Matthew, the story where the Wise Men followed the star to meet Jesus and bring him gifts. She talked about how after the Wise Men worshipped Jesus, they had two choices to make. On the one hand they could've returned to King Herod to tell him where Jesus was. And of course, even though Herod said he wanted to go and worship Jesus too, they knew he had ulterior motives."

"He really wanted to kill Jesus because he feared Jesus was a threat to his crown," Evie interjected.

"Right." Tom continued on. "But on the other hand, the Wise Men were warned in a dream not to go back to Herod, so they could've taken another route instead. What was so neat about her interpretation of the scripture was how she took the Robert Frost poem, 'The Road Not Taken,' and integrated it into the message."

Brother Washington's baritone voice recited the first two stanzas of the poem flawlessly. "'Two roads diverged in a yellow wood, and sorry I could not travel both, and being one traveler long I stood and looked down one as far as I could, to where it bent in the undergrowth. Then took the other, as just as fair, and having perhaps the better claim, because it was grassy and wanted wear; though as for that the passing there had worn them really about the same.'"

Everyone sat in awe at his recitation.

"How did you know that?" Kate asked.

"My high school English teacher was a Robert Frost fan, and as part of our final exam we had to choose one of his poems and memorize it. I chose 'The Road Not Taken,' and I've remembered it ever since."

"That was amazing," Ellie said. "Can you tell us the rest?"

"Let's see," Brother Washington thought for a second. "Where did I leave off? Ah, yes. 'And both that morning equally lay in leaves no step had trodden black. Oh, I kept the first for another day! Yet knowing how way leads on to way, I doubted if I should ever come back. I shall be telling this with a sigh somewhere ages and ages hence; two roads diverged in a wood, and I—I took the one less traveled by, and that has made all the difference.'"

"How beautiful," Ellie offered.

"Yes," Tom agreed. "Like Pastor Connie said, the man in the poem had a choice of two roads to take when he came to the fork in the path. After he thought it through and made his choice, he realized that the path he took made all the difference in his life. Just like the Wise Men. Certainly the easier and probably safer path would've been to return to Herod and tell him where to find Jesus."

"Why do you think that path would have been safer?" asked Kate.

"Well, because Herod was the king, and when the king tells you to do something, you follow orders. Besides that, Herod wasn't exactly a very nice king either."

"That's an understatement," added Brother Washington.

"You're exactly right. He murdered his own family members because he was so paranoid of losing his crown. So you can imagine how mad he would've been at the Wise Men if they disobeyed him." Tom sat silently for a minute before continuing. "But that didn't matter to the Wise Men. They were warned in a dream not to return to Herod, so they took the other road, so to speak, the one leading away from Herod. Can you imagine what would've happened if they had gone back to Herod? Herod probably would've hunted Jesus down and had him killed. The world as we know it wouldn't exist."

Evie could keep quiet no longer. "Then Pastor Connie said that just like both the man in the poem and the Wise Men had a choice between two paths, we also have a choice between two paths in our lives. We can take the path that leads us to a life with Christ, which in her interpretation is the one 'less traveled by,' or we can take the path of the world, which most people take."

Ben, who had remained silent during the entire conversation, finally spoke. "Narrow the road that leads to life."

"What?" Evie asked.

"The two paths," Ben explained. "Enter through the narrow gate. For wide is the gate and broad is the road that leads to destruction, and many enter through it. But small is the gate and narrow the road that leads to life, and only a few find it. Perhaps Mr. Frost had this in mind when writing his poem."

"Maybe he did," said Tom. "You never know."

"I don't mean to complicate things," Ellie said in an apologetic tone, "but do you think the Wise Men really *did* have a choice?"

"What on earth do you mean?" challenged her sister.

Ellie took a deep breath and shared what was on her heart. "Perhaps they didn't have a choice at all. Perhaps God had planned all along that they wouldn't return to Herod. So even though the Wise Men *thought* they were making their own choice, it was actually preordained by God."

"You mean like they were just puppets and God was pulling the strings?" Tom asked.

"I don't know about puppets," Ellie admitted, "but I do struggle with it. After all, God is all-knowing and all-powerful. And God knew in advance that if the Wise Men had returned to Herod to report the location of Jesus, that Jesus would have been killed immediately. So maybe the choice had already been made for them even though they never knew it."

"I think I understand what you mean," said Tom. "I often think about that same thing when it comes to Judas. I wonder if Judas ever really had any other choice but to betray Jesus. After all, someone had to do it. So maybe God set Judas up from the beginning as the ultimate traitor or fall guy. Maybe Judas was destined to be the one who gave Jesus over to the authorities and there was nothing he could do about it."

The group paused in silence as the conversation drew them further out of their comfort zones.

Kate crinkled her nose. "Okay, but if the Wise Men and Judas didn't really have any choice, then how are we any different today?

If you follow the logic that God predestined the Wise Men to protect Jesus and Judas to betray him, then does God have everything planned out for us too? Do we have any real choices in life, or are we just going through the motions because God is dictating it all to us whether we know it or not?"

"That's a good question," Tom replied.

"And not an easy one to answer," said Ellie.

Kate analyzed it a step further. "If that's the case and we never really have choices, then to me that is saying I was destined to become an alcoholic no matter what I did, or Griffin and I were destined to divorce no matter how hard we may have tried to salvage our marriage."

"I don't think it works like that," Tom replied. "If God were controlling everything in our lives, then he wouldn't really be a God who loved us. He would just be a God who manipulated us like pawns."

Brother Washington, who had been listening intently ever since he recited the poem, spoke. "Think of it like an ice cream cone."

"What?" several of them asked in unison. Brother Washington faintly smiled at the bit of confusion he had fully intended to generate.

"I am simplifying things a bit, but I hope you might be able to follow my train of thought. Let me explain."

"Please do," encouraged Evie.

"First, you need to think about how well God knows each of us. The Bible tells us that he created us in his image and knows everything about us. He created our inmost beings, knit us together in our mothers' wombs, and he saw our unformed bodies before we ever came to exist. Correct?"

"Correct," they all replied.

"Second, think of the one person who knows you better than anyone else. Ellie, who would that person be for you?"

"Why I'd have to say Evie, without question." Evie smiled in approval.

"So Ellie, if I were to ask you whether you would like a chocolate or vanilla ice cream cone, would Evie be able to correctly guess which you would choose?"

"Oh, that's easy," Evie blurted out before Ellie could answer. "She would choose vanilla."

Ellie blushed and looked down at her coffee mug. "Yes, she's right, I would choose vanilla. Unlike most people, I never have been one for chocolate."

Brother Washington kept his focus on Ellie. "So does that mean because your sister knew ahead of time which flavor you would choose that you didn't really have a choice?"

"No, not at all. It was still my choice, it's just that Evie knows me well enough to know which choice I was going to make before I even made it."

"Exactly," replied Brother Washington as he folded his hands on the table.

"So let me get this straight," Tom said as his mind worked through the implications of Brother Washington's analogy. "You're saying that God knows each of us so well that even though we have choices we can make, God knows which choices we *will* make."

"Yes, something like that," answered Brother Washington.

"But that doesn't negate the fact that it was our choice in the first place," Tom added.

"Precisely. Just because God knows us well enough to know what our choice will be, it doesn't mean we never had the choice in the first place. It's called free will."

"Not only that," Tom replied, "but if we never had free will, as you call it, and if we could never make our own choices in life, then I don't think it would be possible for any of us to be truly saved by Christ."

"How do you mean?" asked Ellie.

"Think of it this way," Tom explained. "God wants us to choose his Son as our Lord and Savior, right? Well, if God were in reality doing nothing more than dictating the choice for us to claim Jesus as our Savior, then it wouldn't really be *our* choice at all. And if we weren't actually choosing Christ as our Savior, we wouldn't be saved."

"Excellent point," said Brother Washington.

Kate finally felt as though she were beginning to grasp it all. "Besides," Kate continued, "if God were simply dictating the outcomes of the choices in our lives, we would never make mistakes and learn from them. When I look back on my life and think about those times I could've taken a different path, I definitely could have saved myself some heartache. Like the choice to move to the city, or the choice to drown my problems in a bottle, or even the choice to focus on my job more than my marriage. It makes me think of that line from the poem about going back to a path you meant to take but didn't. If I could go back in time and take the *other* path, so to speak, things might've been so different for me. But all the same, I learned from those mistakes and I don't regret them, because if I had never made those choices in the first place I wouldn't be where I am today. And in many ways, I know they were the right choices for me even though they may have caused me pain."

"I'm not sure I understand what you mean," admitted Ellie.

"Well, I'm certainly not proud of the fact that I'm an alcoholic, and to this day I still sometimes yearn for a drink, but I can see the blessings God gave me through that difficult time in my life."

"And what was that?" asked Tom.

"God taught me through my alcoholism that I am a sinner saved by God's grace and mercy. I was always such a perfectionist, and in some ways the alcoholism made me realize I'm no better than anyone else. It was all quite humbling to say the least. And do you know, the weird part is, it was a relief for me. I didn't have to set such a high standard for myself that I would never be able to live up to. And then there was Griffin." Kate's mind flashed back to the dream from the other night.

"You never really talk much about Griffin," said Tom. "If you don't mind my asking, what happened?"

"I don't mind at all," Kate answered. The six of them had come to share some of their deepest thoughts and feelings, so Kate was totally comfortable bearing her soul. "I guess I should start by saying that Griffin is really a wonderful person. He loved me, and we had a good life together. But somewhere along the line I became so focused on being *Ms. Kirby*, attorney at law, that I never really gave myself the chance to be *Mrs. Harris*. Over time we just drifted apart. It was nothing scandalous, no affairs or abuse or anything like that, we just kind of fell out of love with each other. Or, I don't know, maybe we were never really *in* love in the first place." Kate thought back to the evening on the patio, and for a moment she felt as though she were sitting there next to Griffin feeling the same sense of failure and loss that had been so poignant that night.

"Do you ever talk to him?" Evie inquired.

Sure, in my dreams all the time, Kate wanted to say. "No. We haven't talked since he moved to Miami six years ago. I got a Christmas card from him about a year after the divorce. He sent it to the firm, although by that time I had already left. One of the law clerks tracked me down and forwarded it to me."

"What did it say?" Ellie blurted out but then quickly clasped her hand over her mouth, ashamed of having pried.

"It's okay," Kate reassured her. "The card didn't say much. Just that he wanted to wish me well, and he hoped I had found happiness in my life. I do know that he is still living in Miami. He has three children, the twins and another daughter, and his wife is a pediatrician."

"How did you find all of that out?"

"Oh," Kate smiled, "I read his bio on the firm's website, and the rest I found out through the magic of Google. It's kind of funny. When he told me he wanted a divorce, I was so desperate I actually asked him if he wanted to have children."

"I don't understand, why is that funny?" Ellie asked.

"Because I was so self-absorbed that I never would've been a good mother. I could barely take care of myself let alone someone else. But just like we've been talking about, that was a choice I made, and I think it all worked out the way it was supposed to. Motherhood was not the path for me."

Tom, excited about the new life he was about to bring into the world, felt compassion for Kate. "Well, that's not to say marriage and kids are out of the picture for you. I mean you're what, thirty-five, right? You could meet someone and start a family whenever you want. You still have plenty of time for all that."

"I'm thirty-six," Kate responded, her mood becoming more serious. "And I really don't have plenty of time."

"Sure you do," said Tom.

"Actually, I don't."

A hush fell over the room as they all watched Kate in anticipation.

"What do you mean?" Ellie asked quietly. They could sense that there was something Kate hadn't yet shared, and they could also sense that whatever it was, it wasn't good.

Kate looked over to Ben knowingly. He instinctively took her hand and squeezed it, as if to say it was all right to share what she had been keeping to herself for almost a year.

"Let's see, how can I best explain it?" Kate began. "Have you ever heard the song by Jim Croce, 'Time in a Bottle'?"

"Of course," answered Evie, "it has always been one of my favorites."

"Mine too." Kate took a deep breath and smiled. "Well, there's this one line in the song, *there never seems to be enough time to do the things you want to do once you find them.*"

Everyone stared at Kate, hoping against hope they were misunderstanding what she was trying to tell them. For a few moments no one spoke, but then Tom felt he had to know for sure.

"What are you saying, Kate?"

She looked to Ben. He nodded.

"What I'm saying is that apparently I'm running out of time."

CHAPTER 19
LOOSE ENDS

"Peace I leave with you; my peace I give you.
I do not give to you as the world gives.
Do not let your hearts be troubled
and do not be afraid."
John 14:27

The next morning. Kate sat at the kitchen table sipping her coffee and staring at the pill box in front of her. She had just finished her devotionals and prayer time. She used to say her prayers while briskly walking through the neighborhood, but it didn't quite work that way anymore. It was starting to become an effort for Kate to make it up or down a flight of steps, so a walk of any distance was unfortunately out of the question. No matter though, on this freezing cold January day, with her robe wrapped tightly around her small frame, she rationalized it was better to be indoors where it was nice and warm. She couldn't help but laugh at the mammoth pill box that had become a part of her daily ritual. It contained compartments for each of the seven days of the week, and then it was further divided into morning, noon, and evening. Kate had seen pill boxes like this before, but usually only when she had visited elderly church members. Pill boxes this size belonged to someone in their eighties or nineties, not a woman going on thirty-seven. But so it was. No sense in fretting about it, because fretting wouldn't change a thing. She emptied the *Thursday Morning* compartment onto the table and stared at the array of medications and vitamins. There were more than a half a dozen pills, and they would only get her a third of the way through her day.

After finishing her coffee, she fixed herself some cereal and a whole grain bagel with orange juice while she pondered the Bible study from the day before. She really hadn't meant to drop such a bomb on her friends, but for months now she had been praying for the Lord to let her know when she should share her news. When the conversation led to a future husband and children, Kate knew that God was giving her the signal that the time had finally come. Thank the dear Lord she had Ben. His hand in hers brought her a strength that she couldn't articulate in words. Just knowing he was there next to her, supporting her, loving her, gave her the courage to be honest with her friends.

She had anticipated where the discussion would lead and was surprisingly prepared for the conversation that followed. *How long have you known?* Almost a year, Kate told them. *What about treatments?* Medicine can help manage the symptoms for a while, but unfortunately there is no cure, Kate explained. Also, due to a preexisting genetic condition she never knew she had until recently, the illness would be accelerated. *Did you get a second opinion?* Yes, a second opinion, third, and fourth. In fact she spent the first six months doing nothing but visiting doctors and specialists, getting referral after referral, undergoing every medical test imaginable, and filling out about a phone book's worth of insurance papers and forms. The doctors themselves were even shocked; they had never seen it in someone so young before. But no matter how many specialists she saw or tests she took, they all came to the same conclusion. *How are you feeling?* A little more tired than usual, she told them, and sometimes she had trouble catching her breath, but right now that's about it. *Are you in any pain?* None at all. *Do you need anything?* The answer was simple: Prayer. The one question that everyone *wanted* to ask was the one question no one *would* ask—How long? And, of course, no one really knows the answer to that question except the Good Lord himself. Doctors can tell someone six months and yet they have the resilience to last for years. Doctors can tell someone years, and it can be only months. Or sometimes the doctors can be right on target. But it's really God's timetable we're all on, not our own. We so often forget that, but Kate was now reminded of it every single day. When she woke up each morning, she gave thanks to the Lord that she could greet another sunrise. Besides, if anyone had asked, what could she possibly say? *I don't know exactly, but I do know it's not long.* It was a sad reality Kate had come to accept many months ago.

Amidst some tears and moments of silence, the conversation then turned to faith. *Are you mad at God that this is happening to you? Has your faith been shaken?* No, was her emphatic answer to all of it. Sure, after learning of the diagnosis she had gone through a range of emotions to say the least. First came the denial. *This can't possibly be true,* she justified. After all, she took good care of herself, ate well, exercised, kept up with her annual physicals, and lived a relatively stress-free life. The doctors had it all wrong. But they didn't. Then she went through a time of anger; the "How could you?" stage as Kate liked to call it. She shook her fist at God like Job had and demanded to know how God could possibly allow this to happen to her. She was finally doing so much good in the world between her work at Hope's House, the women's Bible study, and any other opportunity she had to give back. *How could you take me away from all of this?* she challenged God. *Don't you want me here in this world to serve you?* But the angrier she became, the more she realized her illness was winning. It was building a wall between her and God; a God she loved so much, and a God whom she knew infinitely loved her. Anger didn't do one bit of good except to give the devil a foothold he so desperately wanted. She would not let her illness win. Then, of course, came the self-pity. *Why me? Why do the people who abuse their bodies and don't care one iota about serving the Lord live to be in their eighties when I will never see forty?* But Kate had rarely been one for self-pity, so that stage was short-lived. And finally she experienced the regret of things left undone or decisions made she would never have the opportunity to rectify. Perhaps that was the reason for all the dreams. She had let her subconscious get the best of her to the point where her dreams haunted her at night, teasing her by giving her the choices she would never be able to make.

So yes, Kate told her friends, she had experienced all of those feelings. Yet she did so quietly, privately, and with the one person standing beside her every step of the way who she knew would be her rock and her strength. He listened to her shouts of rage, he collected her tears of sorrow, and he eased her fear of regret. Through it all she had come to a peace in her life. She made the choices she had, chose the path to take, and she had learned to live her life for the Lord. And Kate would continue to do exactly that; whether it was for one more day or month or year, she would spend her days on this earth living for her Savior. And when those days were over, she told them as they choked back the tears, she would meet her maker in glorious eternity. Not only that but she had a lot of catching up to do with loved ones who had joined the Lord before her—Grans, her mother, and especially her father. How could she be mad at God when in reality she had so much to look forward to?

What was typically a one-hour Bible study had turned into a morning-long time of prayer and ministry. Kate left the Coffee House feeling a hope beyond anything she had ever anticipated. Not only did she have one person to support her through whatever the future might bring, she had six. How blessed she was not to have to travel this journey alone.

She buttered the bagel, poured the milk in her cereal, and swallowed each pill, one at a time. Then she took a small pad of paper she had set on the table and began her list. A to-do list of sorts. A checklist. She wrote slowly and with intention as she considered what bore enough importance to be included on the list. This was no time for triviality. It was a time to set things right. When she was finished she stared at the paper. Five items. Five things she had to do before she . . . Well, just *before*.

March. Kate left Amazing Grace Chapel in a hurry after greeting Pastor Connie and a few others. The service had run longer than scheduled, and she didn't want to keep Ben waiting for their standing lunch date each Sunday morning after church. Wouldn't it figure that thanks to the unpredictability of early March weather, the usual ten-minute trip from Riverton to Bakersville took her almost twice as long? The precipitation varied between slashes of freezing rain and a blustery snow, and it was just enough to create a mess on the roads and bring cars to a crawl. She pulled into Marty's, their usual spot, and while she was lucky enough to get the last available parking space, she wasn't so lucky in that it was also the farthest one from the restaurant entrance. A few months ago her doctor had given her a handicapped hang tag, but to this point Kate couldn't seem to bring herself to use it. She was *not* handicapped, she told herself. So the hang tag remained tucked away in her glove compartment amidst the registration, tissues, and hand sanitizer. She navigated the parking lot clumsily, losing her balance on the slippery blacktop and practically falling face first on more than one occasion, so by the time she made it into the restaurant she was more than a little damp and painfully out of breath. Ben was already seated at their table.

"I'm . . . so . . . sorry . . . I'm . . . late," she huffed.

"Kate, are you okay?"

She nodded her head and held her finger up, signaling for him to give her just a minute. Eventually the gasping turned to wheezing, and gradually her chest didn't heave quite as much as her breathing returned to normal. Kate closed her eyes, took one deep, purposeful breath, and exhaled.

"There," she finally said. "Sorry about that. I think between the dampness of the weather and my rushing in here, it got the best of me for a second."

"That's all right. I'm just glad you're okay. And I told you, Kate, we don't have to keep meeting on Sunday mornings, or I could come to Riverton each week. It's really no trouble at all, and I—"

Kate cut him off before he could finish his sentence. "Now we've already been through this. We are going to keep doing what we're doing for as long as we can. I'm fine, I promise. When it gets too much for me I will let you know. Deal?"

"Deal," Ben reluctantly agreed.

The two placed their orders and spent over an hour discussing the sermons from their respective churches. Both pastors were in the middle of a Lenten sermon series with Easter arriving in about a month's time. The conversation blissfully took Kate away from her own physical ailments as they discussed the cross. When Kate thought of the suffering her Savior voluntarily took upon himself even though he deserved none of it, she felt foolish for being frustrated that her body wasn't working the way it was supposed to. Sure, Kate had a cross to bear, but how could it even begin to compare to the cross of Christ? It couldn't. That alone helped Kate put everything in perspective, especially in her darker moments.

As they finished their meals Kate thought about the first item on her to-do list.

"Ben, there's something I want to share with you."

"Oh yeah, what's that?" he asked while mopping up every last sign of ketchup from his plate with a few remaining French fries.

"I drafted my will the other day, and I'd like for you to have a copy."

Ben just looked at her.

"I decided to do something, and I hope you'll understand my decision."

Ben stopped eating and gave her his full attention. "Kate, you know I'll support you in whatever you decide to do."

"I hope so." Kate took out a blank legal envelope and handed it to him. "Here, put this away someplace safe so you'll know where it is when the time is right."

Ben took the envelope without looking at it and put it on the table. "So what was this decision you made?"

"Well, I've been thinking a lot about how I want to leave things when I'm gone. I mean, I don't have any family left, and I thought about giving everything to you, but I also know you wouldn't take it."

"You're right about that," Ben answered matter-of-factly.

"And then I got to thinking about all the women I've met over the years at Hope's House. I have been so blessed to represent them, but all I have been able to do is make them legally free from their abusers. They need so much more than just a piece of paper saying they are divorced to get a fresh start in life. A lot of these women have no income, no family, and no financial means to survive on their own. And to top it off, many of the women also have children. It's a bit of a catch twenty-two. They are so desperate to be free of the abusive relationships and of course rightfully so, but then when they finally are free they don't have a leg to stand on in terms of the economic security they need to be self-sufficient."

"Okay," Ben replied as he tried to guess where the conversation was headed.

"So, I have decided to donate my home and everything in it to Hope's House. It could be sort of a halfway house, if you know what I mean."

"I think I know what you mean, but tell me more."

"Well, a woman could live there for an extended period of time, completely cost free, while she gets a job and then saves enough money for a place of her own. It would be fully furnished so she wouldn't need to worry about buying anything for it. I also created a trust to help them with things like groceries and other bills until they are back on their feet. You know how much I love that home," Kate said as she stared off into the distance. "I feel like in many ways it was my second chance at life, and I also feel like it could do the exact same thing for these women who probably need it more than I did."

Ben watched Kate intently and smiled.

"So," she asked, "what do you think?"

"Kate, I think it's the most selfless gift you could give. I think you are blessing someone with a chance they may not otherwise have had, and I think it's beautiful. But are you sure you want to give everything to them?"

"Yes, I actually feel really good about it. It makes me happy to know that someone might be able to start her life over with my help, even though I won't be there to see it."

"Have you told anyone at Hope's House about it yet?"

"Yes," Kate said as she sipped her hot tea. "I told my director. After she got over the initial shock, she was overwhelmed. She said she wanted to write an article for the local paper, but I asked her not to. It's not about the recognition, it's just about helping someone in need."

"'Bear one another's burdens, and so fulfill the law of Christ.'"

"Galatians." Kate immediately recognized the scripture Ben had quoted.

Ben chuckled. "Not bad. You're becoming quite the Biblical scholar, I must say."

"Well, I don't know about *that*, but I do know in my heart it's the right thing to do."

"Then of course I understand," Ben answered. "Why wouldn't I?"

"Well, there is one small thing I need your help with." Kate's nose crinkled. Oh, how Ben loved it when her nose crinkled! That always meant she was up to something.

"And what makes you think I would want to help you?" he asked jokingly.

"Because you're too nice to say no to me, especially now that I'm sick."

"Oh, no," he protested, "you can't use the sick card on me!"

"Well, I just did," she laughed.

Oh, how good it always felt to be with Ben. Everything seemed so *normal* around him, even when life was anything *but* normal. Here she was, joking with him about her terminal illness that would claim her life before very long as if she had nothing more than a common cold. But all the same it felt so good to laugh about it. She had cried her fair share of tears, and they had gotten her nowhere. And besides, what is life without laughter?

"All right," he conceded, "let me have it."

"Well, like I said, someone might move into my house who has a child or children. And right now on the second floor it's my bedroom, bathroom, and my office. But if a woman moved in with children, the kids would definitely need a bedroom on the same floor as their mother. So we need to move the office to the third floor and then make the extra room on the second floor a children's bedroom. I was thinking maybe we could make a set of bunk beds and decorate it in a neutral way so that it could be for a girl, a boy, or even both."

"Wait a minute," Ben said as his eyes narrowed. "Something is terribly wrong here."

"What?" Kate asked.

"I might have heard you wrong, but I'm pretty sure you just said *we* could build some bunk beds."

"Cut it out!" Kate said, pinching his arm. "Okay, smarty pants, *you* will build the bunk beds. What do you think?"

"Kate, I think it sounds perfect, and I would be honored to help you."

With that, Kate began her final renovation project at 704 Front Street. Within three weeks' time Ben had enlisted the help of several youth from St. Paul the Apostle Church to move the office furniture up to the third floor; he worked round the clock to construct a set of bunk beds; and he even managed to finish a matching chest of drawers and small bookshelf so the room would have everything a child might need. Kate, for her part, picked out a daffodil-colored paint for the room along with blue-and-white checkered curtains and bedspreads. She filled the bookshelf with some of her favorite childhood books, including C.S. Lewis's *Chronicles of Narnia*, some Dr. Seuss books, and various Bibles for children of all ages. But her very favorite part of the room was a pastel painting she had found at a local thrift shop. It depicted a group of young children holding hands in a circle, almost as if they were playing ring around the rosie. Under the picture was the scripture, *"Let the little children come to me and do not hinder them, for the kingdom of heaven belongs to such as these."* Kate hung it above the dresser where the lamp would illuminate the words of her Lord. Perhaps Kate had never been blessed with children of her own, but in some small way she could help mother the children who would come after her in this home.

The day after Ben helped her put the finishing touches on the bedroom, Kate sipped her usual morning coffee and pulled out the checklist from her kitchen drawer. She reread Item Number One. Kate retrieved a thick black Sharpie from the drawer and put a check next to it. One down.

April. Easter season always brought Kate a renewed hope. After all, Easter marked the day her Savior had risen from the grave and also the day she inherited the promise of eternal life through him. Now more than ever, Kate relied on that promise.

Kate had specifically chosen Mary Magdalene for her women's study the week after Easter Sunday. Mary was one of Jesus' faithful followers right up to the cross, and she had the distinction of being the first person to see the risen Lord. Oh, how we could all learn from Mary's faithful discipleship through times of trial and tribulation! As much as Kate had cherished her time with the women in the study over the past several years, it had recently become a struggle. A struggle to find the energy to prepare the lessons each week, and a struggle to lead the class for over an hour without becoming exhausted. Of course, everyone knew of Kate's circumstances. She had been on every prayer chain since word got out in January, and the women in the group were willing to do anything they could to lighten her burden. But Kate had to acknowledge that her season of leading the study had ended. Much like Paul had done with his faithful protégé Timothy, Kate discerned it was time to let someone else take the lead. Paul knew his earthly days were limited, and he wanted to ensure his ministry was left to someone who would continue to carry the torch of Christ burning bright. Kate was ready to do the same.

That evening Kate made it through almost an hour of the study, but then she hit a wall. The discussion was fruitful, and even though Kate sat in a chair the entire time, she couldn't seem to catch her breath. At one point in the middle of the study Rachel interrupted and suggested they all pray for Kate, which they did while surrounding her and laying hands on her. Kate was eternally grateful for their outreach, but the air would just not fill her lungs. It's a debilitating thing when your mind is telling your body to do one thing, but your body is being totally uncooperative.

They closed their time together with prayer requests, and the young women filed out of the room wishing Kate well as they went on their way. Kate asked Stephanie to stay behind a few minutes. She still hadn't gotten up from the table, and she pulled a chair out for Stephanie to join her.

"Stephanie, there is something I want you to pray about."

The young woman, who had come to consider Kate a role model, had a confused expression on her face.

"Sure, Kate, what's that?"

"I don't think it's any big secret that I'm not going to be able to continue leading our study. I can barely keep up with all of you, and for as much as I love it, I'm just not well enough. You are all such an amazing group of women that it's not fair to all of you if I were to keep trying to do this when I know in my heart that it's time to bow out."

Stephanie's eyes were wide with grief. "That's not true at all, Kate. You don't understand, we can't imagine anyone leading this study *but* you! Ever since the first day we met, you have cared so much about each and every one of us. You have taught us so much about the Bible and what it means to live by faith. Kate, you just can't give up on us now." Stephanie's eyes pleaded with Kate to reconsider her decision.

"Oh, I'm not giving up on you at all. Actually it's quite the opposite."

"What do you mean?" Stephanie asked.

Kate took Stephanie's hand and smiled. "I never told you this, but you were the whole reason I started this Bible study in the first place."

"Me?" Stephanie asked incredulously. "Why me?"

"Because when I first met you, you were so excited about the Lord and about life. Then as you got a little older, you got so wrapped up in your ideas of success that I saw you changing. You hardly ever came to church anymore, and when you did, all you could talk about was the high-profile job you were going to have and how much money you were going to make."

"Yeah," Stephanie admitted ashamedly, "I guess I was a little misguided."

"Don't feel bad about that," Kate interjected, "because believe me, I lived that way too for a very long time. I went down more than one wrong path, and I paid the price for it. That's why I wanted to begin this women's study. I saw what you were going through, and I didn't want you to lose your love of the Lord through the temptations of life. I also figured if you were feeling that pressure, then there were probably a lot of other women your age feeling the exact same way."

"Wow, I never knew any of this."

"So in many ways I have *you* to thank for this study. If it hadn't been for you, Stephanie, I don't know that it ever would've gotten off the ground in the first place." Kate's eyes sparkled with gratitude. "And I have watched you grow so much during the four years since we've been meeting. You have become a beautiful young woman both inside and out, and your faith has grown immensely." Kate paused to take a deep breath. "And that's why I need you to lead the study in my place."

"Kate, I can't!"

"Yes, you can," Kate reassured her.

Panic overtook Stephanie. "I could *never* take your place. Kate, you are irreplaceable!"

Kate looked deeply into Stephanie's eyes. "First of all, we are *all* expendable. Yes, sometimes it might be difficult or challenging, but the only person in this entire world who is truly irreplaceable is Jesus Christ himself. And second," Kate continued, "yes, you can take my place. Stephanie, I wouldn't ask you to do this if I didn't believe in my heart that you're ready. You have the maturity, the love of the Lord, and the passion to lead these women. You will do an amazing job. For my own peace of mind, I need to know that this study will continue with as much love and compassion as when it began."

"Oh, Kate, I just don't know," Stephanie balked. "I don't know the Bible that well. What if someone asks me a question I don't know the answer to? What if I say something wrong?"

Kate laughed aloud and took Stephanie quite off guard.

"That's not funny!" Stephanie protested.

"I'm sorry, I wasn't laughing at you. You're right, it's not funny. But what *is* funny is that's the *exact* same thing I said when I was contemplating whether to start the study. Just like you, I didn't feel like I was good enough or that I knew enough about the Bible to undertake this."

"So what did you do?"

"Well, I did two things. The first thing I did was pray about it. Then I sought the advice of a very dear friend, and he told me something that I'll never forget."

"What was it?" Stephanie asked.

"He told me that God doesn't call the equipped, he equips those whom he calls. Stephanie, if God has called you to do this, then you can be confident that he will give you every tool you need to succeed. Sure, you might be nervous at first and, yes, there may be times when you don't know all of the answers. After all, who *does* know all the answers? But God will see you through it and bless you richly. Just pray about it."

Stephanie sighed and looked down to the floor. "Okay, Kate, but I can't make you any promises."

"That's all I'm asking, just pray about it. God will take care of the rest."

Kate went home that evening feeling confident the Lord would make Stephanie's path straight. Three days later she received her confirmation. It was a text from Stephanie:

Been praying about what you asked. Then I got to thinking more about Mary Magdalene. She wasn't afraid to tell others about the risen Lord. I figured if she had the courage to do it, so should I. It would be an honor to take over the study. Just please say lots of prayers I can make you proud and I don't mess up!

Kate put her phone on the dining room table and went immediately to her kitchen drawer. Item Number Two: Check. Two down; three to go.

June. The doctors told her it would happen. In spite of the wonders of modern medicine, there would come a day when the medications would stop working. And when that day came, there was nothing more anyone could do. Her decline was sure to be rapid, and the end wouldn't be far off. Of course the specialists didn't say it exactly in those words, but she could read between the lines.

Kate rested in the living room armchair bundled in a sweater, even though it was in the mid-eighties outside. Her small frame sunk into the cushions, and the oxygen tank clicked beside her while dutifully delivering the very breath of life to her lungs through the clear plastic tubes running to her nose, her chest rising and falling with the pattern of the clicks. She reached over to the end table that separated the chair from the hospital bed which had been delivered about two weeks' prior. Yes, Kate's days of navigating stairs were over. Thank goodness she had added a second bathroom on the main level when she first moved into the home, although she never dreamed she would be needing it for this. Kate took hold of the devotional and once again began reading. She was almost finished the book, and she had only started it a week ago. These days there wasn't much else she could do besides read or sleep.

Ben, who had moved into Kate's upstairs bedroom the same day the hospital bed had been delivered, made sure she had everything she needed. He did the cooking, the cleaning, the laundry, and he spent practically every moment with her other than the few occasions he would run to the shop to finish up a project or two. He had stopped taking on new projects for the time being; when he did have to leave, he made sure that Ellie or Evie had some free time keep watch over Kate. Kate, of course, felt like it was completely unnecessary. "*I'm fine,*" she would protest to Ben, "*you don't have to babysit me. Go do your thing. I'll be fine on my own.*" But Ben knew, and so did Kate, that she *wasn't* fine.

Ben had just finished washing the lunch dishes and had taken a seat in a matching armchair by the fireplace. That was when his cell phone rang.

"Hello? Okay. Sure, okay. You ready? Now? Sounds good. See you in a few."

Kate looked at him suspiciously.

"Well, that was awfully Sherlock Holmes of you. If you don't mind my asking, what was that all about?"

"I don't mind your asking at all. In fact, I was just about to share with you."

"Oh yeah? And what, exactly, do you have to share?"

"Well, in order to find out, you're going to have to come with me. A little excursion, if you will."

"Where are we going?"

"I can't tell you. You'll have to wait and see, but I promise it won't be far."

Kate was exhilarated at the prospect of venturing outside. For the last month she hadn't made it much farther than one of the rockers on her front porch.

Ben walked over to where Kate was sitting and extended his hand, helping her up. It took her more than a few moments to rise and steady herself. She flung the oxygen tube over her shoulder, and Ben proceeded to switch over to the portable oxygen tank. Kate took only a few steps toward the front door when she began wobbling.

"I'm sorry," she said, clearly embarrassed. "I guess I just don't have the strength like I used to. Ben, I'm not sure if I can do this."

"Not to worry, I've got just the solution." Before she knew what was happening Ben scooped her up in his arms and carried her to his pickup parked out front. He then managed to open the passenger side door and set her ever so gently in the front seat of his truck.

"Are you comfortable?" he asked as he helped her fasten the seatbelt.

"I'm perfect. But what on earth is this all about?"

"You'll see," he said with a wink. Oh, how the tables had turned. Ben could remember so many times when his childhood friend Katie, her mind brewing with *something*, simply told him *"you'll see"* and left him wondering.

Ben drove slowly down Front Street, turned at the corner by Amazing Grace Chapel, and then proceeded two blocks on Commerce Street until he reached the sign: Riverton Park. He pulled in.

"What are we doing at the park?"

"Didn't I tell you? You'll see. Boy, do you ask a lot of questions!"

Kate laughed, making her cough.

Ben meandered through the lane heading toward the riverbank. That was when Kate saw them standing there in a semicircle, all eagerly awaiting Kate's arrival. First she saw Brother Washington, then Evie, then Ellie, and on the far side was Tom. Ben pulled over, got out, and walked over to the passenger side.

"Hi, guys, I think it's best we let Kate stay in the truck for this. She's feeling a little tired."

"No problem at all," Ellie remarked.

"What is this?" Kate asked as she took Ellie's hand through the open window.

Evie began. "You see, Kate, we wanted to do something special for you. And the other morning when we were at Bible study, Ben told us about how when you were kids you had this willow tree you liked to visit."

"Yes, it was my very favorite," Kate shared as she smiled widely, her mind returning to childhood days filled with sunshine and swaying branches of the mammoth tree. "Oh, it was so beautiful, it was our secret spot. We spent so much time under that willow, passing the time or solving life's greatest mysteries." She glanced over at Ben with love.

"And Ben also told us how the tree was cut down several years ago to make room for the new housing development in Bakersville," Evie continued.

"Yes, it was," Kate said wistfully. "Such a shame."

"Well, in honor of your time under that tree, we got permission from the county to plant this on your behalf."

In that moment the five of them parted straight down the middle like Moses had parted the Red Sea, revealing the most precious willow tree she had ever laid eyes on. It was no taller than she was, and she could probably count how many branches were on the sapling. It might have been miniature in size, but it was gigantic in other ways. Tears welled in Kate's eyes.

"I know it's small now," Ellie explained, "but someday it will be just as big and beautiful as the tree you and Ben knew. And we hope that children will come to this tree and find joy just like you did."

Tears flowed freely down Kate's cheeks, but they weren't tears of sadness. On the contrary, they were tears of hope. Hope that this tiny creation of God's would grow into something magnificent, providing shelter for the birds, beauty for passersby, and a place where perhaps one day another little Katie could learn the lessons of life with a cherished friend.

"You all, I don't know what to say."

"No need to say anything at all," Brother Washington said stoically. "It was our pleasure."

At that point Tom, who had remained quiet and stood further back than the rest, approached the window of the pickup.

"Kate, there's someone I'd like you to meet." Tucked in Tom's arm was a pink blanket in which slept the most beloved baby she had ever seen, completely oblivious to the world around her.

"Tom!" Kate exclaimed.

"I would like to introduce you to Amelia. Amelia Kathryn. She's one month old today."

"Tom, she's absolutely precious. Look how content she is in her daddy's arms." Kate's heart overflowed.

"Well, don't let her fool you too much," Tom chuckled. "She's got one good set of lungs on her, and she is quite the night owl!"

"Oh, Tom," Kate replied, delicately touching the infant's cheek, "I would love to see how you are going to handle this! You are truly blessed."

"Yes, I am," Tom agreed.

Kate slunk back into seat, astounded at how such a small amount of activity could exhaust her so much. Ben took the cue immediately.

"All right, friends, I think it's time I got our girl back to the house."

And so they bid their goodbyes. Before they pulled away Kate took hold of Brother Washington's arm.

"Could you stop by this evening for a few minutes?" she asked.

"Of course," he said.

Kate watched through the side mirror as Ben circled around and headed back toward Commerce Street, the tiny willow tree blowing in the summer breeze. What a glorious tree it would grow to become one day. A place of peace.

That evening after dinner Brother Washington came to visit just as Ben was putting a load of laundry in the dryer and folding clothes. Kate, who was already settled into her hospital bed for the night, was thankful Ben was occupied with other things.

Brother Washington sat in the armchair next to her bed. He wasted no time getting to the point.

"I must admit you've got my curiosity. Why is it you asked me to come?"

Kate, who no longer had the stamina for prolonged conversations, appreciated his directness.

"Isaiah, I need to ask a favor of you." She had never called him by his first name before.

"Anything."

"I'm sure you know Ben and I have been friends ever since grade school. And well, I'm not saying this to be boastful so please don't think that, but in many ways I feel like I have been the center of his whole life."

"I can see why you'd think that," Brother Washington answered knowingly.

"And when I'm gone, well, I just want to make sure he's okay. I would appreciate it greatly if you would look after him for me."

Brother Washington watched Kate intently. He could see the conviction in her eyes and knew more than anything she needed the peace of knowing that Ben would be fine without her.

"I assure you, Kate, I will take good care of Ben. You needn't worry."

Kate could tell that he meant every last word of it.

"Thank you." Kate fought back a yawn. "There is one more thing I wanted to ask you."

"And what would that be?"

"Many years ago when Ben and I were kids, we were in the narthex after church one day. You probably don't remember this, but you were with a group of men having a conversation and Ben joined in."

"Yes, I think I vaguely recollect what you're talking about."

"Well, after the conversation was over, you walked over to Ben and you said something to him I'll never forget."

"And what did I say?" he asked, even though he didn't need to.

"You said, '*I know who you are.*' Brother Washington, what did you mean by that?"

"My goodness, Kate, that was years ago. I'm surprised you even remembered."

"Yes, well, it has always stuck with me. Almost as if you knew something about Ben that the rest of us didn't."

Brother Washington sat in silence, contemplating his response. He was not about to lie to a dying woman. No, in his mind that would be one of the most un-Christianlike things a man could do. But by the same token, he could not answer that question for Kate. Not that he couldn't *tell* her, but that he truly couldn't *answer* it for her. What Brother Washington had come to learn over the years was that Ben was an extraordinarily complicated man, even though he appeared to live the most simplistic life. Brother Washington thought back to a conversation with Ben one New Year's Eve a few years past. He became frustrated with Ben for not revealing himself to Kate, and Brother Washington considered stepping in and telling her the truth. But what he learned through it all was that no one, *no one,* except Kate herself could answer that question as to who Ben was. If Brother Washington tried to explain it to her she would probably think him crazy. She would hear his words but not comprehend them. She would question Brother Washington's faith and probably hers in the process. *Who is Ben?* That was a question only she could answer in her heart when the Lord was ready to reveal it to her. The answer wasn't Brother Washington's to give. It was Kate's to learn. The only problem was, Kate stared at him eager with anticipation, expecting and deserving some kind of response.

"Kate, when I told Ben, *I know who you are,* I meant simply this. Ben is someone who offers friendship and comfort without expectation. He is honest. He doesn't judge. He knows no prejudice. He forgives. And most importantly, he loves. That is what I meant."

After more than twenty years of being seared in Kate's memory, she finally received an answer that had satisfied her.

"You're absolutely right, Ben *is* all of those things and more."

"Much, much more," Brother Washington answered.

Kate could barely keep her eyes opened, so Brother Washington touched her lightly on the shoulder and bid her farewell. On his way out he caught a glimpse of Ben from the hallway holding a laundry basket.

"Thank you," Ben mouthed.

Brother Washington nodded and left.

Kate settled back into her pillow, unable to escape the weariness that plagued her. But before she would allow herself to give in to the illness that had invaded her body, she leaned over to the end table and opened the drawer. She reached for the pad and the pen and put a thick black check mark next to Item Number Three. Only two left.

Mid-September. God has a way of blessing us in the most unexpected ways when we need it most. In Kate's last days she was blessed when her path crossed yet again with an old friend, who would now become a new friend. What a small world it really is.

Kate had fought the idea of hospice care for as long as possible, but when she could no longer muster the strength to get out of bed and she realized she was helpless to take care of her own needs, she knew there was no other choice. That was precisely when God sent an angel to watch over her. Delilah walked into the living room and at first didn't recognize Kate. Why should she? Kate was a thin shadow of the woman Delilah had treated at University Hospital some five years ago. Although she probably looked quite different on the outside, what was more important was that Kate was completely different on the *inside*. She was a changed woman. A *saved* woman. Once the recognition finally set in, Delilah was flabbergasted.

"Sweet Jesus!" she said as she took Kate's hand in hers. "I knew our paths would cross again someday. The Lord told me as much."

"How come you're not working in the ER anymore?" Kate asked.

"Oh, the shift work and long hours got to be too much for me. Besides, I wanted to be closer to my grandkids, so I've been a visiting nurse at County Hospice now almost three years." Delilah surveyed Kate as she sadly thought about the file she had just read before her first visit. Kate didn't have very long at all.

"Dear child," Delilah said, "I'm so sorry our paths crossed in this way."

"Nothing to be sorry about," Kate said with a faint grin. "I'm firmly in God's hands and He is taking very good care of me."

"Praise the Lord," Delilah replied cheerfully. "Praise the Almighty!"

Delilah cared for Kate as if she were her own daughter. She tended to Kate's every need, made sure she was comfortable, and helped her shift positions often enough to avoid the danger of bedsores. She tended to the IV in which the medications swiftly entered her bloodstream since Kate could no longer swallow the myriad of prescribed pills. This medication wasn't for healing, it was only to make her comfortable for as long as possible. Delilah bathed Kate and fixed her hair in the most beautiful French braid. But most of all, she miraculously did it all without once infringing upon Kate's privacy or sacrificing her dignity. An angel indeed.

It was a crisp September afternoon, and Delilah had opened the windows in the living room so Kate could breathe in the fresh air. Ben was in Bakersville until early evening to work on a few things at the shop, so Delilah sat in the chair next to Kate while she napped. The doorbell rang. Delilah greeted a man at the door who looked strangely familiar.

"May I help you?" she asked politely.

"Yes, I'm here to see Kate." Delilah looked the man over, unsure of how much he knew about Kate's condition and unwilling to share anything.

"Ms. Kirby is not up for visitors, perhaps you could call again later?"

"Wait," Delilah heard a faint voice call from the living room, "it's okay, Delilah, that's Chester. I asked him to come."

Delilah showed him into the living room and encouraged him to take a seat next to Kate.

"She tires easily," Delilah informed him. "Please make your visit brief." She was cordial yet firm.

"Absolutely," Chester replied.

Chester hadn't seen Kate since the previous winter when she was still her old self with golden blonde hair and sparkling blue eyes. Sure, he knew about her illness, but it almost seemed as if it were only a bad dream. Kate had looked so healthy and full of life the last time they met. But this was a totally different Kate. Death had its grips on her and was pulling hard. He fought to maintain his composure. He would not allow himself to be overtaken by grief. At least not in Kate's presence.

"It's so good to see you," Chester said as he leaned over and kissed Kate on the cheek. "How are you feeling?"

"Very tired, and like no matter how hard I try I can't catch my breath," Kate answered truthfully. Chester glanced at the oxygen tank on the floor next to her bed and the IV coursing through her veins.

"Are you in any pain?"

"No, I'm really not. Just very tired."

"Are you scared?"

"Scared?" Kate asked in surprise.

"Yes, scared about what's to come."

"No, not at all." For as ill as she was, Kate knew that Chester was the one who desperately needed reassuring.

"Seeing you like this just takes me right back to Mina all over again." Chester was dangerously close to losing control.

"Chester, I know God has a beautiful plan for me. And if this is part of his plan then I will gladly take what little suffering I must endure and give all honor and glory to him. He will never leave or forsake me."

Chester smiled, not knowing what to say next. He was in awe of her faith, although in many ways she spoke a language totally foreign to him. But, oh, how he longed to learn the language she spoke.

Chester considered telling her some stories about the latest mischief that Oreo had gotten into, but for some reason it all seemed so pointless and trivial.

"Chester, I asked you to come today for a reason."

"Sure, Kate, what can I do for you?"

"You see that end table? Please open the top drawer." Kate pointed to the table next to her bed. Chester obliged.

"In that drawer you should see an envelope."

"Yep, I've got it." He read the unsteady print on the front. "Griffin Harris, Esquire, Doyle, Bendermann, Richards and Schwartz, 2300 Sunset Towers East, Suite 110, Miami Florida." Chester didn't have to ask who Griffin was.

"Yes, that's the one," Kate said as she closed her eyes and tried to take a deep breath. "Chester, I need you to mail that letter for me."

"No problem, Kate, I'll send it out right away." He stuffed the letter in his coat pocket.

Kate shook her head. "No," she said as a sadness swept across her face. "Not yet." She paused. "Chester, you will know when the time is right." She didn't have to say more. "Just a few loose ends I needed to tie up, if you know what I mean."

Chester knew.

"Kate, are you sure you wouldn't rather have this conversation with him in person? I'm sure if he knew you—" His voice cracked and he stopped for a moment to fight the aching inside of him. "If he knew you were ill, he would come."

"I'm sure," Kate answered. "It's better this way, believe me. Just please promise me you will get it to him."

"You got it, Counselor."

Delilah poked her head around the corner and gave Chester a look, signaling that it was nearing his time to depart.

"Um, I know I haven't been one for religion, but I've been thinking about going back to church."

"Chester, that's wonderful," Kate said as she sat up ever so slightly.

"I don't know though, I've got a lot of years on me. Do you think God would still be interested in and old geezer like me?"

"I *know* God would be thrilled."

"The other thing about it is that I'm not even sure what kind of church to go to. There's a nice Methodist church right around the corner from my house. Or maybe it's Presbyterian. And then Mina was raised Episcopalian so I was thinking maybe I should go to that kind of church. Heck, it's been so long I don't even know *what* I am anymore. What do you think?"

"I think you should go wherever you feel the Spirit leading you to go. Don't worry about what denomination it is. Just go where you feel led to go."

"Yes, I think I might do that. Kate, you are such an inspiration to me."

"Me? How so?"

Chester gulped and fiddled with his keys. "I don't know, I just look at everything you're going though, and you are at such peace with it all. I don't know how you do it."

"Chester, I do it because I have Jesus. And when you have Jesus in your life, that's all you need."

Chester rose from his chair and rested his hand atop the blanket on her bed. "Well, I think I'll have to visit one of those churches this Sunday. And I'll be sure to say a prayer for you."

"That would be lovely, Chester," Kate replied. "Thank you."

"No, Kate, thank *you*. Thank you for everything." Chester did the best he could to smile as Delilah stood watch by the stairs.

"I'll see you again soon, Counselor," he said as his vision blurred and his voice trailed off.

"I will look forward to that day," Kate answered.

And then he left.

Kate, too, was having a hard time controlling her emotions.

"You all right?" Delilah asked, adjusting the blanket.

"Delilah, I'm more than all right. I'm ecstatic."

Delilah looked at her with a puzzled expression. "And what's got you so giddy? You got too much medication in you?"

"No, it's not that at all. I'm happy because several years ago I planted a seed. And I think it just took root."

"Well then let's just hope and pray that the seed grows."

"Yes, let's." Kate smiled. "Delilah, in the drawer over there is a list. Could you please get it out and check off Item Number Four for me?"

Delilah honored Kate's request and tucked the items back in the drawer. "You've only got one item left on your list."

Kate, drifting off, responded. "Yes. Ben."

"Yes, sweetheart. Number five on your list just says *Ben*."

Early October. There was only one thing left to do. One item to take care of on her checklist, and then she would truly be at peace. The only problem was, she had no clue how she would ever find the courage to do it.

Kate listened to the sermon Pastor Connie had taped for her while Ben flipped through the Sunday morning paper. She looked over at Ben, who was apparently engrossed in the sports section. She prayed silently that the Spirit would give her the right words.

"Ben, I owe you an apology." Her tone was serious.

He looked up from the paper. "Apology? For what?"

"For all of those years when I thought I was better than you. For the times I pushed you aside and seemed like I didn't care. For the time when I shut you out of my life and said those horrible things to you. For not being a better friend, and for wasting all of that time we could've spent together. Ben, I—"

"Kate, that was all years ago. It has long since been forgotten."

"Maybe by you it has, but not by me." It's funny how when one comes face to face with the end of their time on earth, things that happened in years past suddenly take on such great importance in the present. When amends need to be made the time is always at hand, no matter how long ago the wrong was committed. "Ben, I was horrible to you. I was self-centered and judgmental, and I never once stopped to think about how you felt."

"It's okay, Kate, really."

"But it's not okay," she emphatically replied, her voice cracking. "I just need you to know how sorry I am. And I need to know that you forgive me."

"Kate, I forgave you a long time ago."

Kate hesitated.

"What?" asked Ben. "Come on, Kate, I can tell there's more."

She wiped a tear from her cheek. "During all those years without you in my life, I was so alone. I don't think I realized it at the time, but there was this huge void and no one could possibly fill that void but you."

"And?" Ben prompted her.

"And, I know that when I die I'm going to heaven. I know heaven is going to be more wonderful than I could ever imagine. But Ben, I can't ever imagine being anywhere again without you."

Kate gave up trying to contain her emotions. "I know that probably sounds terrible, like I don't trust God. I believe in my heart that eternity is going to be the best thing that's ever happened to me. I just can't help but feel that if you're not there with me, then it can't really be that beautiful. I don't know, Ben," she continued as she moved the oxygen tube to the side and wiped her nose with a tissue, "I just feel like I'm losing you all over again. And I don't know if I could say goodbye a second time."

Ben put the newspaper on the coffee table and approached Kate's bed. He bent over and took her face in his hands.

"Kate, I need you to listen to me."

She looked at him expectantly.

"You will never have to say goodbye to me. I will be with you until the end of time."

"But how?" she asked.

"Remember, sometimes we can't explain it all, and sometimes we don't have all of the answers. We just have to have faith. Have faith, Kate, to know that I will always be with you and will never leave you. Have faith to know that I forgive anything you ask forgiveness for. And have faith to know that God has a glorious eternity in store for you where you will inherit that crown of righteousness he promises to all who believe in his Son. Have faith. I promise you, Kate, if you do have that faith, you won't be disappointed."

Kate smiled through the tears, so thankful she had found the words and had managed to see to everything on her list before the Lord took her. But there was one thing yet she hadn't told him.

"I love you, Ben. More than you'll ever know."

Mid-October. The vigil began on a Tuesday morning. Delilah and the other hospice nurses said it would be a couple of days at most. They had training with these things. They knew the telltale signs when a body begins to shut down, and they could predict with an uncanny accuracy what would come next and how long it would be. But the one thing neither Delilah nor the rest of them counted on was God's timetable. The vigil that was supposed to be no more than forty-eight hours lasted nine days.

The first few days Kate was alert and grateful for the constant company. Pastor Connie visited regularly as did the hospice chaplain; several of the employees from Hope's House came; her many friends from the women's study dropped by after work; and just about everyone from Amazing Grace Chapel stopped over at one point or another. The visits weren't really goodbyes, per se. Instead, they were meant to remind Kate that she was very much on everyone's minds and in their prayers.

On the third day Kate requested the Bible that Ben had given her a few Christmases ago. He brought it down and set it in her lap. She folded both hands on top of the Bible, and they never moved. Shortly after that Kate stopped eating. Her bread of life was no longer food.

The following day Kate stopped drinking. Delilah moistened Kate's lips with a sponge-like utensil and tried to squeeze a few drops of water into her mouth, but Kate would rarely swallow. Her breathing had become labored; guttural groans, uneven and forced. She drifted in and out of consciousness. Pastor Connie arrived and anointed Kate's head with oil while she recited the Twenty-Third Psalm. Kate's eyelids twitched, but otherwise she remained motionless.

On the fifth day Kate barely opened her eyes. She scanned the room and looked panicked when she couldn't find what she was looking for. Ellie, who was there humming "How Great Thou Art," spoke softly to Kate.

"What do you need, honey?"

Kate mouthed the word: *Ben.*

"He'll be right back, sweetheart. He said he had something important to do, but that he'd only be gone for a few minutes."

Kate nodded but refused to close her eyes. Ben returned a few moments later.

"Where did you go?" Kate whispered faintly.

"Shhh," Ben replied, "save your strength. I had to do something real quick."

Kate crinkled her nose.

"I just had to go and get someplace ready for you, that's all."

"I'm going somewhere?" Kate asked, barely audible.

"Yes."

"Now?"

"Soon."

She closed her eyes again.

On the sixth day her faithful Bible study took the lead. With Ben by her side holding her hand, they took shifts standing watch over Kate while reading scriptures and singing her favorite hymns. Brother Washington hummed the melody of "In the Garden" while Ellie sang the words. Evie chose 1 Corinthians 13 to remind Kate of the love that would never fail her. Tom read the story of creation from the first chapter of Genesis, and Ben recited from memory the fourteenth chapter from the Gospel of John. Through it all Kate's chest slowly rose and fell from underneath the blankets. She lay completely still, eyes closed, giving them no indication she was aware of their presence.

The seventh day arrived and Delilah shared with the group that she had never seen such spiritual strength before. "I thought the Lord would have taken her days ago," Delilah remarked, "but I suppose it's just not her time yet." Kate's breathing had become so shallow that oftentimes they weren't sure if she was breathing or not. The house grew eerily quiet as they stared at the blanket, waiting for it to rise. Sometimes the breathing would occur regularly; other times it would be seconds or even a few minutes before the blanket moved ever so slightly. She hadn't had anything to eat or drink for over a week. It was only God sustaining her now.

By the time the eighth day arrived, everyone knew the end was near. Tom took off work, Brother Washington told his men's group he wouldn't be able to meet with them, and Evie rescheduled a doctor's appointment so that she and her sister could both come. The four of them joined hands, surrounded Kate's bed, and took turns praying while Ben kept watch at Kate's side. The blankets were pulled up to her chest, her face like a statue and her hands resting firmly on the Bible. But then, just as Brother Washington began the Lord's Prayer, Kate smiled. Then she giggled. Brother Washington stopped. They each held their breath. Her smile grew so wide that her ashen face glowed brightly and a hint of pink colored her cheeks. She mouthed a few words that none of them could quite make out, and then she laughed yet again. A lighthearted laugh. Before anyone could say a word Kate opened her eyes wide, looking more awake and alert than she had in weeks. She turned her head and looked directly at him.

"Ben," she said.

He came closer to her. "Yes, Kate?"

"I'm ready."

As soon as she said it, her eyes closed. Kate's beautiful smile lingered for several moments, and then it eventually faded back into a void of expressionlessness. Her friends glanced at one another in awe. They weren't sure what had just happened, but there was one thing they knew without a doubt; they had just witnessed a miracle. Ben smiled and squeezed her hand.

The sun had just peered over the horizon in the early morning hours of the ninth day. It was Wednesday, a day that would have been their usual morning Bible study at the Coffee House. Kate's friends had all stayed through the night, taking turns stealing catnaps while others stood watch. As the golden light filtered in through the living room curtains, Brother Washington began to sing "Amazing Grace" in his rich baritone voice. Evie, who had been asleep in the armchair, awakened and joined him. Tom, who had retreated to the kitchen to fix himself a cup of coffee, came too. Ellie harmonized with her sister. Ben kept his hand firmly over Kate's as she held her beloved Bible. Verse after verse they sang, and when they finished the last verse, rather than stopping they started all over again. They watched Kate, lying there so peacefully as if she were an angel herself. And on that glorious morning they sang their hearts out, " . . . *I once was lost but now I'm found, was blind but now I see.*"

Although Kate had no way of telling them, she had heard everything during those last few days. Every word of the scriptures they read, and every note of the hymns they sang. She felt Ben's hand in hers, and she drew strength from the living Word of God resting on her lap. And when they sang "Amazing Grace," she could feel the warmth of the sunshine on her face and the presence of those who loved her most. But the more she listened, the farther the singing became, as if they were slowly moving away from her. The melody gradually faded into the background.

And just like that, the singing stopped.

CHAPTER 20
THE LIGHT AT THE END OF THE TUNNEL

"We will not all sleep, but we will all be changed –
in a flash, in the twinkling of an eye . . ."
1 Corinthians 15:51-52

Death can be a beautiful thing. Dying, no; but death, yes. You see, dying brings with it the ugliness of the finality of life. The goodbyes we are either forced to say, or the lamentations of goodbyes we were never given the opportunity to say. The despair as we helplessly watch our physical bodies fail us. Like a clock in which the cogs cooperate together in an intricate harmony to continually point forward to the next second, then the next, and then the next, perpetually looking ahead to an unknown future. When the cogs fail to cooperate, the clock ceases to work; and time, for that particular instrument anyway, forevermore stands still. So it is with our earthly bodies. When the various components of our physical bodies stop working in cooperation with one another, or when they begin working against each other, the seconds and minutes cease to come. Our earthly time stands still. And that process can be slow, painful, and downright brutal. Yes, dying is messy. Whether it comes quickly and leaves us feeling shell-shocked and deprived of the opportunity of knowing that death was upon us, or whether it comes slowly with all of the suffering and agony it inevitably entails. Rarely, if ever, do you hear of someone who *enjoys* dying. Yet the ironic thing about it is that each day we are living, we are also dying. The only difference is that some of us are aware of the dying part. Others of us are blissfully ignorant of it. And still others of us are so obsessed with its coming that we focus more on the dying than we do the living.

But make no mistake about it, death is an entirely different animal from dying. Humans tend to intertwine them to make them inseparable, but in reality that isn't the case at all. The fact of the matter is, dying is quite repugnant, whereas death is absolutely exquisite. So while we can mourn for someone who is dying, we should never mourn death. In fact, we should celebrate it. We think of death as coffins in the cold ground or the cessation of our existence as we know it. But in reality, for those of us who die in the Lord, death is warm and wonderful. It is only the beginning of an existence more perfect than our earthly minds would ever allow us to comprehend. Kate, quite understandably, never realized just how beautiful death actually was. Until she experienced it.

Kate stood facing Ben, oblivious to her surroundings and completely unaware that she was no longer ill or that she had transformed into something quite different. She was still very much Kate, but she was now a perfect, heavenly Kate, not an imperfect, earthly Kate. In fact, she hadn't even noticed the dramatic change in his appearance. To her, at least for one last moment, he was still just *Ben.*

She was the first to speak.

"Have you ever had a friend who you go so far back with that you can't remember actually meeting them in the first place? A friend who it seems has always been a part of your life from Day One?"

Ben nodded and smiled.

"*You* are that friend, Ben. I know there must've been a time in my life when I didn't know you, but I can't remember it. It feels like you have always been a part of me."

"I have," was all he said.

"But how can you be here?" she wondered aloud. "Did you die too?"

Ben paused. "I did once," he replied.

I DID ONCE.

It was all he needed to say. Instantaneously, the scales fell from her eyes. What Kate had been unable to see for thirty-seven years was now clear. Was blind, but now I see. She stared in complete wonder as she realized it wasn't really Ben at all. It was HIM.

"It's you," she said, her voice full of reverence.

"Yes," he answered.

"It's been you all along."

"Yes."

"But how did I not know? There were so many signs. I can't believe I never saw it." She wasn't chastising herself, she was simply stating a fact.

"We live by faith, Kate, not by sight."

And then, as if a blurry picture had slowly come into focus, she became aware of everything around her. She stood under a tree unlike any she had ever seen during her lifetime. It was more immense than the largest skyscraper, and it was overflowing with succulent fruit. Its branches billowed in a gentle breeze, and as the leaves brushed against her form, they left her feeling refreshed and invigorated, as if the leaves themselves had healing powers. Next to the tree wandered a crystal river which sparkled more brilliantly than diamonds. Everywhere she looked there was light. There was no darkness at all. Her eyes followed the river to what appeared to be a temple, but yet it wasn't an earthly structure. Kate knew immediately; this was something sacred. It was something otherworldly. It was *HIS* dwelling place. Kate instinctively fell to her knees and bowed to the ground in adoration and worship.

Ben rested his hand on her shoulder, and she looked up at him, deep into his eyes. The eyes of her friend. The eyes of her Savior. *I know who you are*, she thought to herself. *I finally know.*

"Kate, there are many here who wait to greet you." He offered her his hand, and all the while she couldn't take her eyes off of him. He was so beautiful. So perfect. And as he reached for her, he said one simple word.

"Come."

EPILOGUE

*"The Word became flesh and
made his dwelling among us."
John 1:14*

Patricia pulled to the curb in her station wagon. The moment she laid eyes on the house her eyes grew wide with anticipation. The pale green siding with crisp white trim; the welcoming front porch on which two rockers sat ready for use; the flowerboxes of purple and white pansies on the railing just beginning to pop up for the season; the meandering footpath of stepping stones leading to the backyard. She couldn't believe this was going to be *her* home. A new beginning.

"It's perfect," Patricia said to her young daughter.

"It looks like a house from a fairy tale!"

"Yes, it does sweetheart, yes, it does."

Patricia barely had time to remove the key from the ignition and her daughter was already out the door, inspecting every last inch of the house with glee. Her bright pumpkin curls bounced in the breeze, and her emerald eyes sparkled in the sun against her porcelain skin. First she ran up the front porch, then she momentarily disappeared around the side of the house, only to come rushing back to her mother with a huge toothless grin that made the seven-year-old that much more endearing.

"Mama, there's a picnic table around back!"

"There is?" her mother asked with an exaggerated tone of surprise.

"Yes! We can have milk and cookies out there tomorrow!"

"I think that'd be lovely," her mother responded.

Patricia, too, was eager to explore her new home. She wandered from room to room, feeling a renewed sense of hope and an overwhelming gratitude that this was truly a gift from God. After touring the main level and then the bedrooms on the second floor, she wound her way up the staircase to the third and final floor. The stairs ended by opening into a single room with slanted ceilings and dormers on all sides filtering light into every nook and crevice. It was a den, and in the center was the most exquisite desk she had ever seen. Patricia immediately noticed a large book resting on the desk. At first she hesitated to touch it for it looked ancient, but she couldn't resist. She carefully opened the binding and stared in awe at what she could only surmise were words in some foreign language. And even though she had no idea what any of it said, merely touching the book filled her with a profound sense of love.

Patricia momentarily lost track of time when she realized she hadn't seen her daughter in quite a while. She headed back outside, and as she peered down Front Street, she couldn't miss those bright curls about three houses down. Her daughter had apparently found a friend; a young boy who looked to be about the same age.

"Hi," the boy said.

"Hi," the young girl replied. "Do you live here?"

"Yep."

"I live here now too. What are you doing?"

"I was watching a robin make a nest in the tree," he answered.

"Cool."

"Want to watch with me?"

"Sure." The girl instantly liked him.

They stood together at the edge of the sidewalk and observed the robin busily gather straw and various small twigs to construct the nest where she would eventually lay her eggs. Patricia watched from a distance, her heart overflowing at the sight of her precious daughter assimilating so well into her new environment.

Although she hated to ruin the moment, it had been a very long day and it was time for some dinner and then unpacking.

"Sweetheart," she called to her daughter. "We've got to get going. You'll have plenty of time to play tomorrow, but we have to run out for some supper."

"Okay, Mama," the girl replied without hesitation. "I'll be right there."

She looked intently at the boy.

"Do you want to play with me tomorrow?" she asked hopefully.

"Sure," he said.

"Okay." Then she pursed her lips together like she had always done when deep in thought. "I think we should be friends," she said to him, as if announcing some monumental proclamation.

"I think so too," he replied.

"Yes, we will be the best of friends," the girl declared with a satisfied smile before leaving him to rejoin her mother.

But then, as if she had caught herself forgetting something of the utmost importance, she turned toward the boy.

"My name is Erin," she said. "What's your name?"

With a flicker of light in his amber eyes, he met her gaze in a way that warmed her very soul.

"I'm Benji."

Benjamin.

Hebrew, meaning "son of my right hand."
~

"But from now on, the Son of Man will be seated
at the right hand of the mighty God."
Luke 22:69

ADDITIONAL SCRIPTURES TO CONSULT

A note to the reader: The scriptures listed below are not meant to be exhaustive. These are merely some of the scriptures that came to the author's mind while writing each chapter. You are encouraged not only to research the scriptures listed below but also to consider whether the Lord led you to additional scriptures when reading.

PART I - BENJI

Chapter 1 – Starry Skies and Fireflies

Psalm 144:4; Psalm 148; Matt. 5:8; 2 Cor. 5:7; Heb. 11:1; John 20:24-29; Gen. 1:1-8, 14-19; Psalm 48:14.

Chapter 2- Inside Out

1 Sam. 16:7; Prov. 16:2; Jer. 17:10; Prov. 20:19; 1 Sam. 16:1-13

Chapter 3 – A Different School of Thought

2 Tim. 1:7-8; Matt. 5:10; 1 Pet. 4:12-14; 2 Tim. 1:9-12; Josh. 1:9; Matt. 28:20; Mark 3:1-6; Matt. 12:1-8.

Chapter 4 – Is There a Doctor in the House?

Luke 5:31; Matt. 8:16-17; Matt. 9:10-13; Luke 8:40-48; Luke 11:9-10; John 8:32: Deut. 31:6.

Chapter 5 – Weeping Willow

Rev. 21:4; Rom. 12:15; Gal. 6:2; Matt. 5:4; Rev. 21:1-27; 1 Cor. 15:35-44; 2 Cor. 5:1-5; 1 Cor. 13:8; John 13:34-35; Psalm 90:4; 2 Pet. 3:8.

Chapter 6 – Sticks and Stones

Matt. 5:44; Luke 6:27-36; Matt. 5:38-48; Matt. 6:14-15; James 3:3-12; Prov. 15:2; Psalm 34:13; Eph. 4:31-32; Rom. 12:17-21; 1 Pet. 3:9-12; Matt. 8:15; 1 Thes. 5:17; Rom. 8:26

Chapter 7 – Ticket to Ride

Ecc. 3:1; 1 Cor. 13:4-8; Psalm 139:1-4, 13-16; Matt. 6:8; John 1:14; Heb. 13:8; Malachi 3:6; Josh. 1:9.

PART II – BENJAMIN

Chapter 8 – The Fast Lane

Matt. 6:27; Phil. 4:6-7; 1 Pet. 5:7; Ex. 16:1-36; Matt. 11:28-30; Matt. 6:25-34; Prov. 16:9

Chapter 9 – Prized Possessions

1 John 2:16; Matt. 6:19-21; Heb. 13:5; 1 Tim. 6:6-10 & 17-19; Prov. 23:4-5; Ecc. 5:10; Mark 10:17-25

Chapter 10 – The Sound of Silence

Eph. 4:26-27; Matt. 14:22-32; Prov. 3:5-6; 2 Cor. 4:18; James 1:17; Phil. 2:3; Rom. 12:16

Chapter 11 – I Don't

Mark 10:7-8; Matt. 17:1-13; Gen. 2:22-24; Gen. 2:7; John 3:29; Is. 61:10; 1 John 1:5

Chapter 12 – April Showers

Job 7:20; Pa. 107:28-31; Ps. 9:9-10; Matt. 27:46; Rom. 5:3-5; Ps. 27:1-3; 2 Cor. 4:8-9; Ps. 22:1-2

Chapter 13 – Humble Pie

James 4:10; John 8:1-11; 2 Chron. 7:14; John 13:34-35; Matt. 7:1; Ps. 103:11-12; 1 Pet. 5:6

PART III - BEN

Chapter 14 – May Flowers

Song of Sol. 2:11-12; 2 Tim. 3:16-17; 2 Cor. 5:17; Ecc. 3:2-3

Chapter 15 – Hide and Seek

Jer. 29:13; Matt. 13:44; Luke 11:9-10; Luke 10:38-42; John 2:1-11; John 3:1-21

Chapter 16 – Caller I.D.

1 Pet. 4:10; Matt. 27:46; Eph. 2:8; Rom. 3:10; Matt. 18:20; Ex. 3:1-10; Acts 9:1-9; 1 Sam. 3:1-14; Matt. 28:19-20; 2 Cor. 5:20

Chapter 17 – Simply Complicated

Heb. 11:1; 2 Cor. 5:7; Matt. 17:20-21; John 14:6; John 14:9-11; John 20:24-29; John 4:1-42; Rom. 10:9-10; Eph. 1:4-7; 1 John 4:7-8; Is. 55:8-9; Matt. 24:36

Chapter 18 – The Road Not Taken

Matt. 2:12; Matt. 11:28-30; Matt. 2:1-12; Matt. 7:13-14; Ps. 139:13-16

Chapter 19 – Loose Ends

John 14:27; Ps. 23:4; Ps. 56:8; Ps. 46:1-2; Gal. 6:2; Matt. 28:20; 1 Tim. 4:8; John 14:1-3

Chapter 20 – The Light at the End of Tunnel

1 Cor. 15:51-52; John 11:25-26; 2 Cor. 5:1-5; Rev. 22:1-5; 1 John 1:5; Ps. 119:105

QUESTIONS FOR DISCUSSION
AND/OR REFLECTION
PART I - BENJI

1. Why do think Brother Washington knew what he knew about Benji?

2. What hints are you given in Part I as to Benji's true identity? List as many as possible.

3. What do you think the willow tree represents to Katie?

4. Considering that Katie is a very smart child, why do you think Benji's true identity eludes her?

5. How would you explain heaven to a grieving child who had just lost a loved one?

6. What role did Katie's mother play in Katie's relationship with Benji?

7. What important lessons did Katie learn throughout Part I that she could carry with her through life?

PART II – BENJAMIN

1. Have you ever experienced a time in your life when the world presented a barrier between yourself and Christ? How did you handle it?

2. Why do you think Kathryn shut Benjamin out of her life?

3. What life lessons did Kathryn learn in Part II?

4. Other than Benjamin, who were some people the Lord put in Kathryn's path to try to get her back on the right track? Why weren't they successful?

5. What does Kathryn learn about the nature of who Benjamin is in this part?

6. What were your feelings towards Kathryn in Part II?

PART III - BEN

1. Have you ever felt as though you needed a rebirth or a fresh start like Kate did? How did it come about in your life? What was the end result?

2. Can you recall the moment when you were born again in Christ? What is your story?

3. Have you ever questioned whether God was calling you to do something or whether it was merely you own wish? How were you able to discern the difference?

4. What are some questions of faith that you have struggled with and why?

5. Do you feel as though you make your own choices in life or that God has already predetermined what those choices will be?

6. What do you think Kate wrote in her letter to Griffin?

7. If you had to summarize the overall message of this book in one sentence, what would it be?

Made in the USA
Columbia, SC
05 January 2018